# Dr. Moratrayas, Mad Scientist

By

Arthur Daigle

Publication Information

This novel is entirely a work of fiction. The names, characters and places portrayed in it are the work of the author's imagination or are used fictitiously. Any resemblance to actual people living or dead, events or locations is entirely coincidental.

**Dr. Moratrayas, Mad Scientist**
**by**

**Arthur Daigle**



Cover illustrated by Jon Hrubesch



ISBN: 978-1986827065

This book is dedicated to my friends who have offered their support in so many ways.

## About the Author

Arthur Daigle was born and raised in the suburbs of Chicago, Illinois. He received a biology degree from the University of Illinois Urbana Champaign, and has worked in such diverse fields as zoo intern, research assistant, fisheries intern and grading essay tests. In addition to his writing, Arthur is an avid gardener and amateur artist. This book was almost inevitable since the author has been a fan of science fiction and fantasy since he was old enough to walk. Dr. Moratrayas, Mad Scientist is his sixth novel, with more on the way.

## Acknowledgements

There are many people who deserve credit for helping with this novel. As with my first book, my inspiration came from the works of the filmmaker and puppeteer Jim Henson and the British artist Brian Froud. I hold these men in the highest esteem for their creativity and humor. I owe a debt to the Millennium Writers' Group, which I belonged to for many years prior to the group folding in 2009. I received helpful feedback from them, and I greatly miss their company. I must also give credit to my family, who helped me improve my book and provided constant support.

# Dr. Moratrayas,

# Mad Scientist

by

Arthur Daigle

# Chapter 1

In the Milky Way Galaxy is a strange world called Earth that has won the 'Most Confusing Civilization' award every year for the last twenty. Every year on Earth, buildings get taller, computers get smaller and lawyers are produced in record numbers (despite numerous intergalactic laws against the practice). These things are considered progress. Earth is home to over seven billion people, most of who don't get along with each other. Nations are judged great only if they can completely destroy at least one neighboring country. Bonus points are awarded if they can reduce entire cities to radioactive dust.

Civilized beings avoid Earth.

There are equally strange worlds in the Milky Way. Not far from Earth is the world of Other Place, a land of magic and mystery. Many intelligent races on Other Place are found nowhere else, for which most people are grateful. Earth and Other Place share the dubious distinction of having lots of people who hate one another. In place of the tanks and nuclear weapons Earth favors, Other Place natives employ magic wands, terrible beasts, golems of frightening strength and an astounding number of lawyers (more proof that anti-lawyer laws are not being sufficiently enforced).

Other Place contains countless powerful individuals. Ruthless kings command armies in the thousands and pious holy men call upon their God for aid. Cunning wizards bend and twist energy to their needs, while mighty heroes battle hordes of enemies single handedly and win. Merchant princes fight just as fiercely using gold instead of swords and spells, and mad scientists perform experiments too insane to be imagined. Every so often a person is born destined to do great deeds. This sounds exciting, but usually consists of the poor fool trying desperately not to be killed. For better or for worse, these are the people who control the fate of nations.

But for every one of these great people who are the stuff of legends, there are thousands more with no power at all. Commoners, peasants, the little people, call them what you will, but when mighty deeds are being performed, they're the ones most likely to get crushed underfoot. They long to be left alone, for kings to be content with wine and tournaments, for holy men to lead prayers and not crusades, and for wizards to build their stone towers and stay in them. Let merchant princes count their vast fortunes and mad scientists stay far away. Commoners want nothing to do with them. For these people a boring life is a beautiful one, and they understand more than most the meaning of the Chinese curse, 'may you live in interesting times.'

Needless to say, few get their wish. This includes Sandra Sower.

"Keep walking," Sandra told herself. "Almost there."

Sandra trudged in the dark through ankle deep snow, trying very hard not to slip as she worked her way around a boulder on the trail. She'd been walking for a long time, and the boulders, pitfalls and fallen trees blocking the trail made her journey that much longer. Luckily she was young and in good health. This trip would have killed the older women in her town.

Sandra was twenty years old, tall and slender, her muscles strong from years of hard work. Her brown hair was bundled under a fur hat and wool scarf, and her brown eyes barely showed at all. She wore a long skirt and blouse, both gray, coat, mittens, felt boots, and wool wrappings tightly wound around both legs. A gray cloak covered her back and head.

She had little besides these clothes. Sandra carried an empty wicker basket and an equally empty purse. She considered dumping them to lighten her load, but her peasant upbringing wouldn't allow such waste. Of more use, she had a bundle of dry sticks for kindling tied to her back, a steel knife strapped to her leg and a lit torch in her right hand.

The land around her was bleak and cold. The Raushtad Mountains were not a healthy place to travel through during summer and infinitely worse in winter. Such high mountains blocked out the sun for most of the day, providing even fewer sunlit hours than normal. The few trails going through the mountains were narrow and poorly maintained, crowded on both sides by tall evergreen trees. Cold wind whipped between the mountains and could blow snow into drifts as high as a wagon.

Sandra was currently traveling toward two nameless peaks and the valley between them. She was tempted to stop for the night and avoid the chance she might trip on a rock or branch buried under the snow, but continued in spite of the risk. She'd already lost eight days to detours around closed trails and digging her way through deep snow. Every delay put her people in peril.

"Just a bit farther."

There was another reason she kept moving. People in the last inhabited valley she'd traveled through had told her she was close to her destination. If they were right, the man she needed to find was only a few miles away. With luck she could reach him by morning and beg for help...and for food.

Sandra stumbled in the snow. Cursing her bad luck, she struggled to her feet and brushed off her skirt. She pulled the scarf off her mouth and ate some of the snow. Despite the cold, she was overheating in her warm clothes and from the heat generated by walking. The snow cooled her down.

Exhausted, Sandra stopped marching and caught her breath. She was in the shadow cast by a tall and foreboding granite peak. The trail was bracketed by pine trees as tall as church steeples and without branches for the first forty feet. That was unfortunate, since she could have broken off low branches for firewood. The sky overhead was clear and stars twinkled around a full moon. Moonlight reflected off the snow and provided enough light to travel by. She could probably get by without her torch, but fire was good for warding off hungry animals.

"Hi there!" a rough voice said behind her. Sandra spun around and came face to face with a werewolf. Taller than her and bulging with muscles, the werewolf had a luxurious coat of gold fur that almost sparkled under the light of her torch. The monster stepped out of a grove of trees behind her and had both clawed hands outstretched, its mouth open revealing long teeth dripping with drool.

Sandra screamed. She stumbled away from it and swung her torch in front of her. The werewolf backed away and lowered its arms, its eyes opening wide in surprise.

"Hey, wait a minute!" the werewolf protested. It looked confused for a moment before slapping itself across the muzzle. "Ah man, I did it again! I'm sorry. I keep forgetting what I look like this time of the month."

Sandra stopped screaming. "What?"

The werewolf backed up and raised both hands in a gesture of surrender. "I'm really sorry. This has been going on for so long you'd think I'd have learned my lesson by now. Smiling doesn't look friendly when you've got teeth like these!"

Sandra kept her distance but stopped threatening the werewolf with her torch. Storytellers told many tales about young women meeting werewolves at night, and none of those stories ended well for the women involved. But the monster was talking, and that was a good sign. Once she managed to stop staring at those terrible jaws, she noticed something odd about it.

"You're wearing pants?" she asked. Sure enough, the werewolf was wearing leather pants with an opening for its tail.

"Yeah, I kind of have to," the werewolf said sheepishly. "One time I changed back before I got home in the morning. Let me tell you, really embarrassing! I made these pants so there wouldn't be more mistakes like that. I overheat in them, but it beats streaking the whole town again."

Some werewolves were ravenous monsters, but Sandra had heard that not all were dangerous. Cautiously, she asked, "You weren't born a werewolf, were you?"

The werewolf shook its head. "I got bit a year ago, and the next full moon this happened. It's been a big adjustment, but my family's been real supportive. Oh hey, where are my manners? The name's Keith Sunter. Pleased to meet you."

Sandra gingerly shook the werewolf's hand while keeping her torch at the ready. Silver was what really hurt werewolves, but she hoped fire would hold it back if it got aggressive. She didn't bother drawing her knife.

Keith the werewolf didn't seem to notice the suspicious looks she gave him. "Surprised to see anyone out this late. I come out here so I can be alone.

Can't scare anyone if there's no one around. Hey, I don't think I've seen you in these parts before."

"I'm passing through."

"Tough time to be traveling," Keith said. "My family would love to help if you need a place to spend the night. Lots of things going on at home you might like. Say, we're having a tent revival this week if you're interested."

"Uh, it's really not a good time for that."

"Never a bad time to have the Good Lord in your life," Keith countered.

Sandra stammered, trying to find a way to end this conversation. "I appreciate the offer, it's just I'm in a real hurry. I need to find a man named Doctor Alberto Moratrayas."

Keith smiled, baring teeth that could rip a man in half. His ears perked up and his tail wagged. "That's easy! The doc lives in my town."

"He does? Where's the town?" she demanded.

Keith pointed a clawed finger up the trail. "Follow the trail for the next two miles until it comes to a valley. There's a town there called Refuge and a castle called Fortress X. The doc lives up there."

"Thank you! You don't know how much you've helped me," Sandra cried. She shook the werewolf's hand again and headed up the road.

"Safe trip!" Keith called after her. His tail wagged as he watched her trudge through the snow. "What a sweet girl."

Keith continued down the road in the direction Sandra had come from. Whistling cheerfully to himself, he set out for another night of exploring the forest around his hometown. Minutes later his keen hearing picked up the sound of men coming up the road. Smiling, he introduced himself.

"Hi there! My name's—" Wham! A steel mace came down on Keith's head and knocked him out. He hit the ground in front of his attacker.

"Is it alive?" a man asked.

"Of course it is," another replied. "Mace isn't silver, and that's what kills werewolves. We just stunned it. Anybody got silver on them?"

There was a pause as the men went through their pockets. One of them offered, "I got a lead fishing weight."

The group's leader bit back a harsh and well-deserved stream of insults, instead saying, "It's not the same thing. We'll have to leave the werewolf. It ain't who we're after, anyway."

Not far ahead, Sandra hurried through the snow. She climbed up a rise in the trail and came onto the top of a hill. She could see light ahead of her. The air was heavy with the scent of wood smoke and cooking food. Food! Sandra's stomach grumbled at the smell, but she pushed on. She forced her way through a cluster of pine trees growing around a wide river, and then stopped to take in the sight before her.

Filling the valley ahead of her was a prosperous town of perhaps two thousand people, far larger than Sun Valley. The houses were made of granite and were well built. Smoke poured from chimneys and light issued from glass windows. Outside the town were empty fields and orchards harvested long ago, and beyond those were brick lined terraces cut into the mountains and filled with more barren cropland. Sandra saw people walking through cobblestone streets, all of them well fed and happy like she used to be.

Scattered around the town were stranger things that showed all too clearly that this town was the possession of Doctor Moratrayas. An ornate clock tower thirty feet tall dominated the center of town, its four faces showing the time as 7:19. Most cities didn't have such an extravagance, much less a town this size. At each street corner stood a steel post with a street sign and a black orb on top. Sandra saw five black boxes scattered across the town, big enough to fit a man inside and attached to the ground by thick cables. The boxes hummed and occasionally sparked. Something flew over her head, buzzing as it headed for a castle dug into the side of a mountain.

Sandra walked into the town. People saw her and waved. Some wished her a good day. They laughed and smiled at each other. She'd been away from home and a normal life for so long that this felt alien.

"You look lost, young lady," a plump, prosperous man said to her. He looked like he was in his fifties and wore warm fur clothing.

"Actually, I think I'm right where I need to be. Does a man named Doctor Alberto Moratrayas live here? I was told he might be in the castle."

The man nodded. "He lives here, all right. I'll take you to him."

The man smiled and led her through the streets. Seeing so many warm homes with cooking fires burning in them made her want to ask (correction, beg) for something to eat. Sandra had abandoned her pride a month ago and no longer minded asking for help. But any delay was too much when she was this close to her goal. Food could wait.

Sandra pointed at a six-inch diameter black tube running through the snow and connecting to a house. "What's that for?"

"Those tubes pump hot water to our homes," the man explained.

Still staring at it, she asked, "But how?"

The man shrugged. "I don't know how it works. None of us do. The doctor put them in and fixes them when they break. He keeps saying it's not magic, but if there's a difference, I don't know what it is."

They approached one of the large black boxes, and to Sandra's amazement the box turned to face her as she walked by. "I'm almost afraid to ask what that does."

"No idea, but my dog got a nasty shock when he peed on it. I'd keep my distance if I were you."

"Do you know the doctor? I mean, have you met him, talked with him?" she asked. She didn't know much about Moratrayas and needed all the advice she could get.

"I've spoken to him, but no one truly knows the doctor," the man said. "What goes on in his mind is a mystery. We live well and he's a better ruler than any of us had before coming here, so we ignore the little things."

"Little things like what?" she asked.

On cue, the highest tower on the castle roared like a dragon. Something as big as a wine barrel flew from the tower so fast Sandra didn't get a good look at it except that it was shiny. It slammed into the opposite mountain and created a deafening boom that echoed through the valley.

"That would be a good example," the man said, unperturbed by the display. No one else on the street seemed to care, either. "We find it best not to ask what he's doing. When we do ask, if we're lucky he won't say."

Sandra hesitated before asking, "And if you're not lucky?"

"He spends hours trying to explain it to us, and nobody understands him."

"I guess that happens a lot with mad scientists."

The man stopped in his tracks. "Don't call him that. Ever."

"I...I'm sorry, I didn't mean to be rude to him or you or oh God, is that an insult with him?"

"Something like that. Call him doctor or sir."

The man led her to a set of granite steps leading up to the castle. There had to be a thousand steps, wide enough for ten men to go up at once and swept clean of snow. At the top of the stairs was a castle.

Sandra had only seen castles in books before now. They were tall and bright and pretty, with soaring towers and pointy rooftops flying pennants. This castle was dark and ugly. It seemed to have grown out of the mountain, a squat thing with dirty walls and narrow windows. Its towers were thick and short. Its gate was closed and made of wood bound with iron bands. What little light came from the dark castle was tinged green.

"Here we are," the man said. "You're lucky he's in. Sometimes he's gone for weeks at a time doing God only knows what. He'll see you if you can get up the stairs."

"*If* I can get up the stairs? What's that mean?" Sandra asked.

"You'll see for yourself."

That didn't sound good. "I know you've already helped me, but could you introduce me? It would look better if I show up with someone he knows than if I come alone."

"Not a chance," the man said firmly. "We don't go to the castle unless we're invited. The doctor doesn't have many rules, but he was clear on that point. He said it's not always safe up there with his experiments, and we believe him."

"But—"

The man sighed. "I can tell this is important to you, but I can't help. For your good and mine, you'll have to do on your own."

The man tipped his hat to her and headed back to the town, leaving Sandra alone at the foot of the stairs. She looked up at the gate high above her and shuddered. Something about the way the man had spoke made her think going up those stairs would be a lot harder than it looked.

Sandra hesitated. Up in that castle was Doctor Moratrayas. He was a mad scientist, regardless of what he liked to be called, and stories about him circulated even in places as isolated as Sun Valley. Rumor was he built life from metal and stone, fearsome things small as a cat or as big as an ox.

Moratrayas was said to be far more frightening than his creations. Ill-mannered, vicious, possibly insane, the doctor had a reputation as a man who seldom started fights but always ended them, usually in the most violent way possible. Sandra should be doing everything in her power to avoid him, and that's what she wanted most of all. But there was a chance, be it however so slim, that his power could save her people, so she went on.

"Great. I'm heading to a big scary castle with a mad scientist to ask for help," Sandra said as she started up the stairs. She talked to herself a lot, more so since she began her long trip alone through the mountains. "Jennet Foster gets to go ask the great hero Julius Craton for help, the little minx. I'm probably going to get dropped into a vat of acid while she's looking for a genuine hero...who's tall and handsome and single and brave and courteous and loyal and single and I'm stuck here!"

Sandra waved her arms toward the castle. "I'm heading toward a mad scientist's castle! There are lots of stories about what happens to young girls that meet mad scientists. They don't end well for the girls. Come to think of it, just about all the girls in stories end up in trouble. I bet that wouldn't happen if there were more women storytellers."

She grumbled and kept climbing the staircase. "This is mother's fault. 'We need help', she says. 'I'm sending you because I trust you', she says. Who does she send her oldest daughter to get? Doctor Alberto 'the mad tailor' Moratrayas. I'm going after a super scary mad scientist who beats up ogres for a hobby. Thanks a lot, mom!"

Still fuming over the injustice of it all, Sandra climbed the stairs in silence for the next few seconds. Tired, hungry and upset, it took her longer than normal to notice she wasn't getting any closer to the castle.

"What the...hey!" Sandra looked down and saw the stairs she was climbing moving down toward the town. The stairs moved so smoothly and silently she barely noticed she was actually going backwards. She ran up the stairs, but they sped up so she still wasn't making any progress. Sandra collapsed in exhaustion and was carried smoothly back to the bottom.

"That's a lousy trick!" she shouted at the castle. If anyone heard her, they didn't reply. It didn't take long to figure out what was going on. Wizards used tamed griffins or unicorns to guard their estates from intruders. But Moratrayas was a mad scientist. He'd build some crazy thing made of steel and bottled lightning to keep people away. Angry, she shouted, "Maybe that keeps salesmen out, but you need way better than that for me!"

Sandra studied the moving stairs. They sank into the ground at the base of the staircase. The stairs were motionless when she wasn't on them, but if she climbed higher than the third stair they went backwards. The moving stairs were a different color than the ones farther up the staircase. It looked like she'd have to get past fifty feet of moving stairs before she could go on.

The sides of the staircase were polished smooth, leaving nothing to grip if she tried to climb around the stairs. To either side of the staircase was a huge drop off. Sandra was a good climber, her getting through the mountains proved that, but a climb this difficult required tools and rope she didn't have.

"Can't go around, can't go under, can't climb up," she mused. "So, what does that leave?" Sandra snapped her fingers. "Got it!"

She pulled out the knife strapped to her leg and poked around the edge of the moving stairs. There was a slight gap at the base of the steps, which she would have seen earlier if there was better lighting. The thin knife fit in the gap, but no matter how far she pushed, the knife didn't press against anything. It went in up to the hilt and she still didn't feel any resistance.

"Come on, there's got to be something here I can cut." She pressed the knife in as hard as she could, but it didn't budge. Suddenly an idea came to her. Sandra left the knife in place and climbed the stairs. One step, two steps, three steps, and like magic the stairs began their descent, but this time there was a thud followed by a whirring noise. The stairs lurched and stopped. Sandra climbed higher. Four steps, five steps, six steps. The stairs made a grinding sound, but with the knife jammed in they couldn't go down.

"Got you!" she said with a smile. Defeating the moving stairs meant leaving her knife behind to keep them jammed. Being close to poverty her whole life made Sandra hate waste in any form, but if losing her knife was the price she paid to save her town then she could live with it.

"That wasn't so bad," she said as she continued onwards. Once she was past the moving stairs she heard the grinding and whirring stop. Apparently the good doctor wasn't going to waste time on a trap that was already defeated. "Yeah, that *wasn't* so bad. If Moratrayas fights ogres and wins then he's got to have a lot meaner tricks up his sleeve than that."

Sandra continued up more cautiously. She didn't see anyone by the castle, but if the moving stairs had turned off then someone was watching her, probably Moratrayas. With his first trap disabled he'd likely spring another. That trap was at the bottom of the stairs. If she were placing these obstacles, Sandra would put the next one near the middle.

"Maybe he doesn't want to be bothered," she said aloud. "Maybe he's doing something dangerous, and if I break his concentration he'll screw it up. Or he might be with a lady lab 'assistant'. I've heard about them. Yeah, that'd be great. I break in his house, asking for help, and he's alone with a pretty girl whose chest measurements are bigger than her IQ. That's a *great* way to make a good first impression."

The next trap announced its presence with a whirring noise and a clank-clank. Huge pincers two feet across lifted up from the left of the staircase to menace Sandra. She backed away and the pincers came closer. The contraption was made of brass and what looked like polished obsidian, and contained glass panels with some strange glowing green fluid moving inside. The pincers hung off an arm made of the same mismatched materials. The pincers snapped open and closed, clank-clank.

Sandra was much closer to the castle now. She shouted, "Doctor Moratrayas! I need to talk to you! It's very important! Please turn this thing off!"

Clank-clank. The pincers snapped again. The arm extended and carried the whirring menace closer. If Moratrayas heard her he wasn't answering. "Fine," she said. "We do this the hard way."

Sandra didn't approach the pincers, fearful of how much damage it could do if it grabbed her. The arm carrying it was long enough to reach the entire width of the stairs and a height of at least twenty steps above her. That was a lot of space to cover for just one weapon, and it moved slowly.

Sandra walked casually to the left edge of the stairs. The pincers and arm followed. Once she and it were as far over as they both could get, she ran to the right end of the stairs as fast as she could and climbed up.

The whirring noise sped up until it sounded like a swarm of angry bees. Moving as fast as a running deer, the arm swung after her. The pincers opened wide, and before she could dodge they closed around her waist. Sandra struggled to pull them apart, but they wouldn't budge. The arm and pincers lifted her effortlessly and set her back down where she'd started. The pincers opened and freed her, then waved in front of her face like a mother scolding a naughty child.

"That's just rude!" she told it. The arm and pincers hung there and whirred away. Clank-clank. "I already heard that line tonight."

Sandra tapped her hand against her wicker basket. "Too fast to go around, too strong to force back, so what does that leave?"

If she jammed the moving stairs, she might be able to do the same with this trap. But with what? The basket was too flimsy. The pincers would crush it and go after her again. She had a bundle of kindling. Unlike her knife it was replaceable, so losing it didn't bother her. The bundle was tied together with a strip of leather. She remembered a fable that mentioned sticks together being stronger than if they were alone. Would that be strong enough so the pincers couldn't break it?

Sandra pulled the bundle off her back and held it in front of her. The pincers waited patiently for her next attempt to get around them. Clank-clank. This time she headed straight for them. The whirring noise sped up again and the pincers opened wide. She jammed the bundle into the pincers and ran around it.

The pincers tried to close on the bundle and crush it. As Sandra ran by she heard the kindling snap and break, but there were so many sticks that when one broke there were others holding the pincers open. The arm swung left to right, then up and down. It slammed against the stairs and dislodged the broken bundle of kindling.

Sandra kept running. The arm swung around and grabbed for her again. She was up another fifteen steps when the pincers grabbed her by the ankles. She tripped and fell, dropping her torch. The pincers were built to grab a person around the waist or chest. Faced with something as small as Sandra's feet, they couldn't close tightly enough to get a good grip. She slipped through the pincers and scrambled up the stairs out of its reach.

Clank-clank. The arm retracted off the stairs, lowering it and the pincers from view, and the whirring noise died away. Her torch was still burning but had rolled down next to where the pincers had been. Retrieving it risked another attack, so she left it behind.

"I'm two for two!" Sandra shouted at the castle. "Can we stop this and talk?"

Again there was no answer. Sandra had met people who assumed she was as dumb as a stump because she was a woman. Could that be the reason she was getting so much trouble? After all, mad scientists had a reputation for being stubborn and proud. Frowning, Sandra asked, "Is this because I'm a girl? You're supposed to be a genius. Aren't you above that kind of thinking?"

There was a crackling noise from the castle, followed by a man's booming voice. "Gender bias has nothing to do with your situation. You face the same tests as those before you. Should I show you favor because you are of the fairer sex?"

"You should hear me out! I don't have time for this!" She stopped shouting and rubbed her eyes. Arguing with him might make him angry enough to refuse her. "I just, can we talk this over like adults?"

"Of course. I am nothing if not reasonable. You simply have to reach the castle and you will have my full attention. You've dealt with the first two obstacles. The third should prove no harder. To turn it off now would cheapen your achievement, and I have no desire to insult you in that fashion."

Sandra stared at the castle and its unseen owner. "Oh yeah, putting me through all this is a *real* honor."

She headed up again. The voice had said there was a third trap. It would probably be right in front of the door. Sandra wondered what else he would throw at her.

"Julius Craton wouldn't test me," she said bitterly. "Tibolt Broadbeard wouldn't test me. Ask them for help and they say, 'sure, we'd love to.' I get sent to a man who sets lethal traps for visitors."

The booming voice said, "None of my traps are lethal."

"Not for you they're not," she muttered, and rubbed her side where the pincers had grabbed her.

Ten steps from the top of the stairs, Sandra heard a whirring noise. She dropped to her knees and prepared for the worst. A cylinder two feet wide and three feet tall rose up from the stair in front of her. Startled, she stepped back. The cylinder was made of brass and obsidian, just like the arm and pincers. Glass panels lit up with the now familiar green glow. A panel opened on the side of the cylinder, displaying row after row of white tipped darts.

"Hey!" Sandra ran back down the stairs while the trap fired darts at her. The cylinder shot them out faster than any man could throw. Most missed her or hit her basket. Two darts stuck in her cloak, damaging the material but nothing else. "You said nothing here was lethal!"

"The poison is merely paralytic," the booming voice said.

Sandra pulled a dart from her cloak. "Poison? That's not fair!"

The cylinder stopped firing once Sandra was fifteen steps away. Breathing hard, she studied the devise. It had fired at least twenty darts, but as she watched more darts slid into place in the panel. How many more were there? Maybe she could trick it into firing all its darts. But it only needed to hit her once to poison her and win. She didn't like those odds.

Sandra plucked the darts out of her basket. They were stuck in good and it took some effort to pull them out. The darts didn't hit with enough force to punch all the way through. It didn't take much to stop them. She looked at the tiny holes in her cloak.

"I'm going to regret this." Sandra took off her cloak and held it in front of her. Cautiously, she advanced on the cylinder. It began firing again once she was close enough. Darts flew out three a second and hit her thick cloak. Dozens of darts stuck halfway through the material. The cylinder ran out of darts, reloaded from some inner reserve and fired again. Sandra advanced steadily, keeping her entire body behind her cloak. She finally reached the cylinder and jammed her tattered cloak into the dart panel. The cylinder whirred in protest, but couldn't fire or even sink back into the staircase.

"That's three," she said. "You owe me a cloak."

Sandra climbed up the last few steps and approached the castle's huge doors. She grabbed an enormous iron ring hanging from the doors and swung it hard. The boom it made echoed throughout the valley. She waited a moment, and when the doors remained closed she swung the ring again.

A small door opened to the left of the ring, and a man poked his head out. He was nothing to look at, with beady eyes, a pronounced chin and a nose like a hawk. The man wore a billowing cloak with a hood. He eyed her suspiciously before speaking.

"We're not buying cookies." He didn't sound like the booming voice Sandra had heard earlier.

Puzzled, she said, "I'm not selling cookies."

"We're not buying candy, either."

"Aren't you supposed to open the door?" she asked.

The man shrugged. "I don't have to. Seriously, we don't want cookies, candy, tins of popcorn or peanut brittle. Mind you, a nice sponge cake would hit the spot right about now."

Exasperated, Sandra demanded, "Why do you think I'd come all this way to sell you treats?"

"In the last four months only one other person has gotten this far, and she was a Girl Scout."

Sandra pointed at the brass cylinder. "A Girl Scout got through that?"

"Surprised us, too. Apparently there was a quota she had to meet, and she wasn't taking no for an answer. Doc was very upset by the whole thing."

"I'm a little old to be a Girl Scout."

The man shrugged. "Some folks advance slower than most."

Sandra put her hands on her hips and scowled. "Listen to me very closely. I spent three weeks getting here, and let me tell you, it wasn't fun. I got through your master's traps, and it cost me a perfectly good knife and my only cloak. I really need to see him, because if I don't a lot of people I care for are going to die. Please open the door."

The man twisted his lips and looked to his left like he was considering her position. "Hmm, well, okay."

The man closed the little door and slowly swung the larger one open. Light and warm air spilled out from inside the castle. Sandra saw the rest of the man she'd been speaking to. He was a foot shorter than she was and his right shoulder had a pronounced hunch. Smiling, he shook her hand and beckoned for her to come inside.

"I'm Igor, professional lab assistant. Come on, the doc is waiting for you in the main hall. I can't promise you'll get what you want, but the doc will listen to you. He's impressed. You beat the Girl Scout's time by four minutes."

# Chapter 2

Igor led Sandra into Moratrayas' castle. The hunchback filled the air with endless trivialities, making it hard for Sandra to focus on her surroundings. That wasn't good. Her father had taught her when she was a child to always be aware of what was around her in case trouble came. It was a valuable lesson for someone living in mountains, where rockslides, avalanches and monsters were a constant threat.

"Of course we didn't build the place," Igor rambled on. "It was empty when we arrived. So was the whole valley. The old owner was still here, but in the shape he was in you'd only recognize him if you were a big fan of jigsaw puzzles. Either a catapult boulder hit him or a dragon sat on him. My money's on the dragon."

"I guess that happens to some people," she replied.

Igor led her down a long hallway lined with arrow slits on the walls and murder holes on the ceiling. Most signs of invasion and war had been removed from the hallway, but there were scratches and dark stains on the walls that suggested someone once tried to force their way in and failed badly.

Doctor Moratrayas had clearly made changes to the castle since taking up residence. Glowing green spheres hung from the walls and provided light. The arrow slits and murder holes were sealed with brass and obsidian panels that hummed. Sandra was willing to bet that those panels could open to release attacks a lot nastier than arrows if someone tried to invade the castle today.

"The problem we've run into is space," Igor said. "The doc needs a lot of room for his experiments. Sure, the troop barrack and dungeon are plenty big enough, but the rest of the castle was cut up into little rooms. We had to knock out a few walls for the third lab. That happens when you don't build the place yourself."

"So who else works here besides you and the doctor?"

"That's it, I'm afraid. There are a few goblins running around the place, but they just watch the fun. The doc can't find good help. That was the reason for those messages he left."

Puzzled, she asked, "What messages?"

Igor leaned in close to her. "You don't know? This is a first, we get a walk in and without advertising."

"I'm sorry, I didn't follow that."

Igor brought her to a set of iron doors. He pulled a lever hidden in the left door, and was rewarded with a series of clanking and whirring noises. The door hummed and opened up to the castle's main hall.

The main hall was bigger than Sandra's home back in Sun Valley, and that included the barn and chicken coop. There was a huge open space with chairs and couches along the walls, and an oak table with chairs in the center of the room. A broad staircase led up to a second floor landing and hallway. Brass chandeliers holding glowing green orbs lit the room. There were two doors on the first floor and three more on the landing. The room was bare of paintings, tapestries, statues or any other decoration.

Igor hurried up the stairs. "Wait here. The doc will be around once he's shut down some equipment. If you see anything move, don't panic."

"The last thing I saw moving tried to shoot me."

"That happens around here," Igor said before ducking into a doorway.

Nervous, Sandra sat down on a plush couch. She felt out of place here. The main hall wasn't decorated, but the furniture was far better than anything she had back home. Wearing patched and well-worn clothing that showed its age, she felt like a beggar at a royal ball.

There was a whirring noise as something scrambled under the oak table. Sandra edged away from it. More whirring came from up the stairs. This time she saw something scurry from one doorway to another. She didn't get a good look at it, just enough to see it was as big as a cat, shiny, and had too many legs. A pair of small brass and obsidian creations hurried down the hallway, a veritable herd of legs and arms scrubbing the floor as they went. Their movements were quick and jerky, and they soon disappeared into a room. She'd wondered how Moratrayas kept the place running with only one assistant. But if he could build help, why hire it?

Another thought occurred to her. His creations were just cleaning the castle. That suggested one of two things. A) Moratrayas wasn't good at setting priorities if he was using them for something so simple. That seemed unlikely. B) Moratrayas had so many of these strange creations that he didn't mind using some for menial jobs. That seemed more likely, but was also a bit scary. How many of these monsters had he built?

"Good evening," a man said as he stepped out onto the landing. His voice had a commanding presence to it, with a clear, crisp tone that suggested both intelligence and authority. "Allow me to formally introduce myself. I am Doctor Alberto Moratrayas."

Sandra looked up the stairs and finally saw the man she'd come so far to meet. Moratrayas didn't disappoint. The doctor was much younger than she'd expected, tall with an athletic build. His hair was black and cut short, and his skin was tanned. Moratrayas wore black pants, black shoes, a white shirt that buttoned on the left-hand side, and black gloves that reached up to his elbows. Black goggles rimmed with brass concealed his eyes. He carried a brass cane, but didn't seem to need it to walk.

Moratrayas came down the hallway and descended the stairs. His eyes were locked on her the entire time, studying her intently. In stark contrast to his creations, he moved as gracefully as a cat, and with the same expression of casual interest. His steps were smooth, and he practically flowed down the stairs. He carried himself like an acrobat, or a—

"You move like a dancer," she breathed.

Moratrayas froze in mid-step. "I what?"

Sudden realization swept over Sandra. She hadn't just thought those words. She clapped her hands over her mouth and gasped before apologies came flowing out of her lips like a river in flood. "Oh, oh God, I can't believe I said that! I'm sorry, I am so, so sorry, I just, I, sorry, mouth moving faster than my brain for a second! I, I didn't mean to insult you or, oh God that sounded bad. I am so sorry!"

Moratrayas gave her a slight smile as he continued down the stairs. "Over the years I've been compared to many things, most of them cold blooded and covered in slime. I suppose being compared to a dancer is no insult. It is, however, a first."

"Uh, hi, I'm Sandra Sower," she managed to say. She rose to meet him and tried to curtsy, but Moratrayas waved his hands and smiled.

"No need for pointless formalities, Ms. Sower. Let kings and nobles bother with such things." He pointed to the table and said, "Please, sit."

"Thank you." Sandra climbed into one of the large chairs while Moratrayas took the one opposite her. "I've been walking for so long I think my feet might fall off."

"Indeed. I was not expecting anyone so late in the year. You must have desired to reach me very badly to brave the mountains in winter."

Igor hurried down the stairs carrying a silver tray brimming with food. He set it down in front of them and stepped behind the doctor. Moratrayas gestured to the tray and said, "You carry little baggage, and what you do possess appears empty. Allow me to provide some minor hospitality to a guest who has traveled far to get here."

Sandra dug into the food with an appetite that would make a wolf proud. The tray included cream soup, a chicken dish that smelled of wine, sliced apples cooked in honey, and fresh bread slathered with butter. The meal didn't last long enough to cool. Moratrayas watched her devour the food with mild surprise while Igor smiled. Finishing the repast, she realized too late that people with money had all sorts of rules about eating and table manners, and she'd probably broken every one of them.

"Sorry, it's just..."

"No need to apologize for enjoying the meal," Moratrayas said with an indulgent smile. "An empty plate is the best compliment a cook can receive. I take it you have not eaten in some time."

Sandra looked down at the empty tray. "Three days."

"Unfortunate. I assure you that such unpleasantness is behind you now. Those who work for me are treated with the respect they deserve and want for nothing."

"Work for you?"

Moratrayas leaned forward and folded his hands in front of him. "I watched you overcome my traps with great interest. Few attempt what you did, and only one other succeeded. For reasons I would prefer not to discuss, she proved unsuitable for my needs. You used no special equipment, making your victory all the more impressive. I take it you are not what the unenlightened refer to as a mad scientist?"

"Uh, no," she mumbled. "Someone told me you didn't like to be called that."

Moratrayas nodded. "That's quite true. I am a scientist, but I prefer to be considered inspired. Still, it's not important if you don't have the same education and training as I. A woman with your determination and quick wits will be a most valuable asset."

Sandra looked down and tried not to sound as scared as she felt. "There's been some kind of mistake. I didn't come for a job."

"You didn't?" he asked. She shook her head. "Then you know nothing of the message I left when I defeated the wizard Tadcaster."

"Who?"

"The wizard who took over the town of Granite Peaks and ruled it with an iron fist. I defeated him and freed the inhabitants from his despotic rule. I left a message inviting others to join me here."

"I didn't hear anything about a wizard in Granite Peaks," Sandra admitted. "My town doesn't get many merchants or bards bringing news."

Moratrayas' expression darkened. "Didn't hear about it? What about my eradication of the pixie plague threatening the town of Two Rocks?" Sandra shook her head again. Annoyed, Moratrayas asked, "Is it too much to ask if you heard how I defeated the ogre bandits attacking river barges on the Moderately Magnificent Talum River?"

"That one I heard about!" Sandra said excitedly. "You beat four full grown ogres single handedly and opened the river to traffic again."

"On that occasion I also left a message inviting likeminded people to join me in the town of Refuge."

Frightened all over again, Sandra replied, "Nobody told me that part."

Moratrayas slapped his palms against the table. "Three times I saved towns from great danger and no one heard about it! Hundreds of people in those towns promised to tell all they met!" Moratrayas shook his head in disgust. He looked at Sandra and asked, "If you know nothing of my invitations, then what *is* your reason for coming here?"

Before she could answer, he threw back his head and cried out, "Merciful God in Heaven, tell me you're not selling cookies!"

"No! No, I, I'm not," she said and waved her hands. This was bad. He'd been expecting a helper, and she was supposed to join his cause (whatever that was) or swear fealty to him. Instead she was trying to get him involved in her problem. Fearing the response, Sandra told him the truth.

"I'm from the town of Sun Valley. Armed men attacked us a month ago. We don't know who they were or where they came from. They looted the town of our valuables and most of our food. They carried nearly all the men away in chains. There's no one left but women, children and old men. We need help. I, I thought that since you got rid of those ogres on the Talum River, and did that other stuff, you could help us, too."

His reaction was not encouraging. Moratrayas' jaw clenched and his hands balled up into fists. There was a slight tremor in his shoulders and his lips twitched. His faced darkened. Igor looked nervous and backed away from his master.

"I see," Moratrayas said through gritted teeth. "I will *consider* your request."

Desperate, Sandra grabbed his hand. "Please, I'm begging you, don't turn me down! No one else can help. The towns around us said they couldn't send soldiers this late in the year, and that they don't even know where to send them. What else can we do?"

Moratrayas pulled away from her and sank back in his chair. "You will have an answer soon. Igor, show her out."

"No, wait!"

Igor took her by the arm and led her away. "This way, please. Mind your step, the cleaning crew is coming through."

A horde of Moratrayas' creations swept into the main hall and cleaned everything in sight. Made of brass and obsidian with glowing green glass panels, they were as tall as Sandra and looked like spindly men. Moratrayas ignored his creations as they went about their work, and he ignored Sandra's pleas. Stony faced, he remained in his chair.

"You can't do this!" she shouted at the hunchback. "We need help!"

"I know," he said compassionately. "He's like this sometimes. If you try to force him to do something, he'll dig in his heels and fight you every step of the way. I pity the person who toilet trained him."

Sandra pulled away from Igor and stopped before he took her outside the castle. "Igor, please, I'm begging you! These people have my dad and brother. The ones they left behind won't last a year without men to work the fields. I know I'm trying to get him involved in my problem, and I've got nothing to give in return. If Moratrayas wants followers then I'll help him if he does this for me."

"He won't take an offer like that. The doc wants genuine loyalty or nothing at all." Igor patted Sandra on the arm. "He doesn't want to admit it, but he needs a chance like this. Saving those towns was to get the attention of other mad scientists, but they didn't come. Some grand adventure is just what he needs to get the word out about who he is and what he's doing."

"Then what do we do?"

Igor took two silver coins from his belt pouch and pressed them into her hand. "Stay at the inn down in the center of town. This will cover the cost and then some. Give me a day to work on him, two at most, and he'll come to you."

Sandra was on the verge of tears. "These people have my family."

"And we'll get them back," Igor assured her. "The doc does care. Give him a chance and he'll prove he's as good as gold."

Igor opened the main gate and led her out of the castle. "I turned off the traps, so going down will be a lot easier than coming up."

Silently, Sandra left the castle and headed down the stairs. She'd failed. She'd come all this way, endured so much, and she'd failed. Sandra saw that the streets below were empty. No doubt locals in the town had gone inside to avoid the cold. This only added to her feeling of isolation and despair.

Distracted by her experience with Moratrayas, Sandra was almost at the bottom of the stairs when she saw a group of men coming up. There were five of them, wearing chain armor and armed with swords and maces. They had thick winter clothes under their armor and backpacks heavy with supplies. Dirty and poorly shaven, they reeked of body odor and sweat. Even under moonlight, she recognized the men who'd ravaged her town.

One of them pointed a steel mace at her and grinned. "Grab her."

Back in the castle, Moratrayas continued to fume as his creations finished their work and went to clean another room. Whistling cheerfully, Igor returned to take the empty tray away.

"Is she gone?" Moratrayas asked sourly.

Igor sat on a chair and put his feet on the table. "She's on her way."

"Seven months," he complained. "I spent seven months and half my money demonstrating what I could accomplish. I saved thousands of people, and no one knows about it."

Moratrayas slammed his fists on the table. "I knew it would be difficult, but we didn't get a single recruit. Not one! I was sure at least one person in my field would show up, if only for protection and free food. Even a handful of flunkies willing to follow orders would have helped. Instead I get a Girl Scout selling cookies and a woman who wants me to spend even more time and money. Where did I go wrong?"

"Be fair, doc, you knew it would be hard to get another mad scientist to come work for you," Igor reminded him.

"Work *with* me," Moratrayas corrected him, "and we're not mad. Mildly annoyed, perhaps, but that's it."

"Not your fault it turned out like this," Igor said. "There's a lot of big news lately. The new King of the Goblins led the goblins in war and won. That's a first, and one most people aren't happy about. Plus the same guy destroyed the Staff of Skulls and buried the Eternal Army. Big news items like that drown out smaller stories."

"That proves my point!" he yelled. "This Bradshaw person comes from another world, yet rallies goblins, trolls and men to his side, making the world a better place. If he can do it then why can't I?"

Casually, Igor said, "There's another way to make sure people hear about you."

"I am not hiring a publicist!" Moratrayas thundered. More calmly, he added, "Especially not at the rates I was quoted."

"Then you need to do something else to get people's attention."

Genuinely curious, he asked, "The woman's offer?"

"Look at it as an opportunity," Igor replied. He looked off into an imaginary horizon and pointed at some distant threat. "You'll be pitting your creations against hordes of armed men, slavers or worse. Hundred to one odds, and the forces of science prevail! Cheering crowds! Dozens of beautiful women throwing themselves at you! I'll catch as many of them as I can, good friend that I am."

"You said that last time." Moratrayas sank deeper into his chair.

Igor shrugged. "Reputations are like plants. They need constant attention or they wither away. One more big display could do the trick."

Moratrayas tapped his fingers on the table. "It would eat up the last of my reserve funds, plus take me away from my research for weeks or months. And in the end what would we accomplish? We save one town or four or forty. What does it matter if they're in danger again next year?"

"At least they get a year's peace."

An ear-piercing scream split the air, echoing though the castle and shocking Moratrayas out of his depression. He jumped to his feet and grabbed his cane.

"That sounded like Sandra," Igor said.

Moratrayas raced for the castle gates. "She must have run into one of my traps."

"I turned them off!"

The five men attacking Sandra weren't having an easy time of it. She made it halfway up the stairs before one of them tackled her. Sandra dropped her basket when she fell, but landed next to the torch she'd dropped earlier that night. No longer burning, it was still long and fairly sturdy. She grabbed it and swung it into his face, giving him a black eye and forcing him to let go.

"Hurry!" their leader urged. "That scream will bring him coming."

Sandra struck another man across the face with the burned out torch. He swung his sword and chopped the torch in half. A second man came at her from behind and grabbed her. Sandra stomped on his feet as hard as she could and he let go, yelping and jumping up and down. A third man went for his sword, but their leader slapped his hand away.

"We need her alive for questioning!"

Two men tackled Sandra and pinned her down. The group's leader pulled a length of rope from his belt and bent down to tie her up. Sandra kicked the leader in the crotch, and was rewarded with a shrill cry of pain.

"Drag her out of here," another man said. "We have to leave before Moratrayas shows up."

"Oh, it's much too late for that," a menacing voice declared.

All five men looked up in shock as Moratrayas and Igor ran down the stairs. The look of pure outrage on the doctor's face would have made a hungry dragon back away. Igor climbed off the stairs onto a small ledge while Moratrayas went straight for the men.

Still hurting from Sandra's kick, the group's leader gasped, "This is no business of yours."

"No?" the doctor asked, his voice as dark as his expression. Moratrayas pressed a button on his cane. With a hiss it extended to twice its length, becoming a brass staff with a sparking tip. "You come onto my property without permission and bearing arms, attack a petitioner, and a woman at that, and you have the gall to say it's not my business? You, sir, have just invited yourself to a world of pain."

The nearest man drew his sword and attacked. Moratrayas dodged the clumsy overhand swing and whirled his staff around. He jabbed the sparking tip into his attacker's chest, releasing a bolt of electricity that ran through his body and convulsed his muscles. His attacker could only manage a strangled cry as his eyes bugged out and smoke rose up from his chest. Moratrayas pulled his cane away and allowed the smoldering man to collapse.

The remaining four men drew their swords and formed a semicircle around Moratrayas. They attacked more carefully, trying to draw him into attacking one man while a second swung at him from another direction. Moratrayas dodged one attack after another, refusing to give ground but unable to score a hit.

Clank-clank. The arm and pinchers trap rose up to attack, this time with Igor riding it. He'd folded out a small seat at the base, and opened a panel to reveal knobs and levers to control it. Whirring faster and louder, Igor directed the pincers to grab the nearest attacker and pin his arms to his chest.

"Curse you, let go of me!" the man shouted. The arm lifted him as effortlessly as it had Sandra, but under Igor's control it carried him off the stairs and dangled him over the drop-off. "Don't let go, don't let go!"

"I'll think about it," Igor said cheerfully.

Sandra climbed back to her feet, bruised and angry. She wasn't sure what these men were planning on doing to her, but the ideas she came up with were bad. The remaining men had turned their backs on her, proof they didn't think she was a threat with Moratrayas on the field. That was going to cost them.

She'd already lost her knife, cloak, torch and kindling tonight. That didn't leave her a lot to work with. She grabbed her wicker basket. Yes, this would do nicely. She stepped behind the man who'd been giving orders, the one she'd kicked in the crotch. His day was about to get even worse.

Sandra swung her basket overhand and hooked it over the leader's head. He barely had time to say, "What the—", before she pulled as hard as she could. Caught by surprise and pulled backwards, he fell down the stairs, crying out in pain as he rolled down the hard granite steps.

The last two men turned for a fraction of a second to see what happened to their leader, giving Moratrayas the opening he needed. He swung his staff and caught another man with the electrified tip, shocking him unconscious. The last man standing abandoned the others and ran for his life. Moratrayas whirled his staff around and struck him in the back of the knee. He stumbled and fell. The man was about to scream when Moratrayas brought the staff down on the man's neck, shocking him as well.

Igor climbed back onto the stairs. "Nasty lot."

"Indeed." Moratrayas retracted the staff back down to a cane and shut off the sparks. "In three years no bandit or brigand has been fool enough to enter this valley, and approaching my castle is stupidity on the verge of being suicidal. They didn't just want a victim to rob, nor were they after a random woman for vile purposes. They could have gotten either of those more easily by attacking someone in town. They wanted you, Ms. Sower. They must have greatly desired to stop you if they were willing to risk drawing my attention."

"That's not all," she told him. Sandra pointed to one of the downed men. "These are some of the men who attacked my town."

"Then they traveled as far as you did through the mountains in the dead of winter," Moratrayas said. "Why did they so fear you reaching me? This is a question I demand an answer to."

Moratrayas walked down the stairs. "I will retrieve the man Ms. Sower dealt with. Igor, Ms. Sower, bring the rest of the prisoners to the castle for questioning."

The last man awake remained struggling in the pincers' grip. Dangling over the drop off, he shouted, "We'll tell you nothing!"

"To the contrary," Moratrayas began, "you will tell me everything I need to know to find your home base, where you took Ms. Sower's people and who's behind this attack."

Alarmed, Sandra asked, "You're not going to torture them, are you?"

"Of course not," Moratrayas replied. "Torture is for the unimaginative."

He stopped and glanced back at Sandra. "You requested my assistance, Ms. Sower, and you have it. No one brings violence into my home."

Leaving them behind, Moratrayas reached the bottom of the stairs. He found curious townsfolk gathered around the crippled attacker. The people muttered to one another nervously, stopping when they saw the doctor. One of the men said, "Doctor, we heard a woman scream. When we came to investigate, we found this man. He's hurt badly."

"The woman is well," he told them. "This man and four more attacked her. The others are no longer a concern."

People in the crowd grimaced. A man asked, "They attacked her on the castle steps?"

Moratrayas picked up the wounded man and headed back for the castle. "Yes. They have annoyed me."

"Right, we'll start digging graves in the morning," the man said.

"It might not come to that," Moratrayas replied. "I'll keep you informed."

An hour later, Sandra, Igor and Moratrayas had securely tied the five men up in the main hall. Sandra went through the men's backpacks, handing items to Moratrayas for him to study. The doctor sent Igor to the castle's library for maps, although Sandra couldn't see how they'd help.

Four of the men required medical care, which Sandra reluctantly provided. Only one man of the five was able to talk, and he proved unhelpful.

"Where are you from?" Sandra demanded. "What kingdom?"

The man glared at her and said nothing. Angry, Sandra said, "Do you have any idea how much trouble you're in? You could be executed as bandits for what you did tonight."

"We're not bandits," he snapped.

"He's not a bandit," Moratrayas agreed. He studied the man's sword, turning it over in his hands and looking for marks. "This weapon was made less than a year ago. It's human manufacture, hasn't seen much use and is well cared for. All five men are identically armed and by the same swordsmith. The armor is good, too."

Moratrayas tossed the sword aside and examined the man's boots. "Bandits get weapons wherever they can, stealing more when they can get them, holding onto old weapons until they are too dull or rusted to use. To have five bandits this well armed and with the same style is nearly impossible."

Igor walked back into the room with a bundle of papers under his arms. "Got the maps you wanted," he explained before dumping his load on the table. "This is everything we have on the Raushtad Mountains and surrounding kingdoms. Planning a holiday get away?"

"Nothing so dull. The men's boots are new, too, hobnailed, leather, no fur trim. I recognize the style. Representatives from the Peck Merchant House came this spring trying to peddle the same type as mountaineering boots. Peck is new to the region and hasn't reached the north of the Raushtad yet. You're not from far away."

Moratrayas turned his attention to Sandra. "Describe the attack on your town. Leave out no detail."

"They came during the morning," she said. "It wasn't even dawn when ten river barges appeared outside town. We thought they might be merchants late getting out of the mountains before winter. When the barges came to shore, armed men rushed out and attacked."

"How many?"

"Three hundred, maybe four." Sandra shuddered at the memory of that day. "They used clubs and nets on us. They ran us down and beat the men viciously, then tied them up and took them back to the barges. A few people got to their homes in time and barred themselves inside. Those wretches set the houses on fire to flush them out. They took any man old enough to do work and carried them off. Then they took our money and half our food supplies. Then they took our sunstone."

Moratrayas' head snapped up from the backpack he was searching. "You had a sunstone?"

"It's why we're called Sun Valley. We've had it for five generations, using its light to speed up the growth of our crops."

"Yes, they are most valuable," Moratrayas mused. "Continue."

"There's not much more to say. Once they had what they wanted, they got back in the barges and left. We begged them for mercy, promised them anything they wanted if they would just let our people go. They laughed and said there was nothing left worth taking. I don't know why they didn't take the rest of us, too, or take over the town. Farmland isn't easy to come by in the mountains, and ours is worth having."

Moratrayas checked the maps Igor brought in. "That narrows down our enemy's location even more. River barges are large vessels. Most rivers are too rough or narrow for them to travel." He took a wineskin from the man's backpack and handed it to Igor. "You know wines better than I."

Igor took a swig of wine and swished it around in his mouth before he swallowed. "It's sour and smells like the wine barrel it came from had a dead rat in it. Must be from Prenton Vineyards." He took another swig.

"How can you drink that?" Sandra asked.

"It's an acquired taste," Igor said, and drank the wineskin in one long pull. "If that's the only wine you can acquire, you drink it."

Moratrayas took the largest map of the region and began making circles with ink and quill. "Prenton Vineyard only sells locally and to people too poor to buy better wine. That narrows our search down to the middle section of the Raushtad."

The prisoner began to sweat. "We stole the wine. We broke into a farmhouse and took it. It was the only wine they had."

"Keep talking and I'll gag you," Moratrayas warned him. He checked the man's hands next. "You're new at this."

Sandra peered over his shoulder. "What do you mean?"

"He has no scars. A man who fights for a living gets hurt in battles and training accidents. The other men are the same. Their faces and hands are unblemished except from the injuries we inflicted today."

Moratrayas went through their pockets next. He took out a collection of copper coins and dumped them on the table.

"Hey, that's mine!" the prisoner shouted. "I earned it!"

"Igor, if you please?" Moratrayas asked. Igor stuffed an old sock in the prisoner's mouth to shut him up. "Thank you. Most of the coinage is minted locally. I see a few from Granite Peaks, with their particularly stupid emblem of a frightened woodchuck. But these others are new to me, and he has a lot of them. They have a fist imprinted on one side and a starburst on the other."

"I've seen them before," Sandra told him.

"You have? Where?"

"Back at home. Merchants have been passing them around for two years. We hadn't seen them before that, and suddenly a lot of them are going around. The metal's not too pure, but we have to take what we can get."

Moratrayas rubbed his chin. "Interesting. Who would be minting new coins?"

With Sandra and Igor watching, Moratrayas drew one circle after another on the map. Each circle was smaller than the one before and inside the larger one. "Not too far north based on the boots, closer to the middle of the mountains based on the wine...yes. There's still a lot of unanswered questions, but based off the evidence our enemies have provided and which rivers are large enough for their boats to pass, the attack against your village came from the Kingdom of Stone Heart. That's unfortunate."

Curious, Sandra asked, "Why?"

"I was born there."

# Chapter 3

Sandra woke up the next morning on a couch in the castle's main hall. She yawned and sat up, still sore from the fight. The five men who'd attacked her were gone, carried down to the town below to be guarded by the locals. The man Sandra sent spinning down the stairs would also need medical care for his broken arm and leg.

"Ah, you're awake." It was Doctor Moratrayas, coming down the stairs with a tray of food. He looked rested and clean despite last night's battle. Then again, he wasn't the one who got tackled. Moratrayas set the tray down on the table and beckoned her to sit. "Breakfast is ready, and you will find a bathroom with a hot bath up the stairs, second door on the left."

"Thank you."

"My apologies for not providing better sleeping arrangements. I wasn't expecting visitors until spring and don't have rooms prepared. I'd offer you the master bedroom, but it's currently being used for storage."

Curious, she asked, "Then where do you sleep?"

"On a cot in one of my labs. I find it best to stay close to my experiments in case they should get out of hand. If just one of my creations goes on a rampage, I'll never hear the end of it."

Sandra found a veritable feast waiting for her. The tray contained pancakes, syrup, poached eggs, sugared plums and milk. "Thanks for having Igor get this ready for me."

"Igor can't boil water without setting something on fire. He is the first, last and only man I have ever met who could burn a hole in a cast iron frying pan. I prepared this."

"You made this? Uh, thank you. You're the first man I met who can cook."

Moratrayas headed back upstairs. "I developed the skill out of self-preservation. Once you've tasted Igor's griddlecakes, you'll do anything to avoid eating them again. Leave the tray when you're done and something will be along to pick it up later."

After eating, Sandra headed for the bathroom. The bath was made from brass (wasn't everything around here?) and filled with steaming water. She hadn't had a chance to wash during her journey here, and the hot water felt especially good on her sore muscles. She also found something else the doctor had left for her.

Folded up alongside the bath was a set of clothes. The outfit included a white blouse, slacks, boots, gloves, hat, scarf and cloak, all lined with fur and expertly stitched. It was new, warm and fit like a glove. Given how patched and worn her own clothes were she gladly put on the new garments.

One of the tales she'd heard about Moratrayas was that he'd started life as a tailor. No one knew exactly how he went from such a humble beginning to become a mad scientist. He called himself doctor, but no university would admit to training him or granting him that lofty degree. One thing the stories agreed on was to go along with his self-imposed title or risk angering him. Even referring to his days as a tailor wasn't healthy.

"Doctor!" a man called out in the main hall. The voice sounded vaguely familiar, but Sandra couldn't say where she'd heard it before. She left the bathroom to see who was calling. She found a young man with blond hair and wearing winter clothes standing in the hall. Not far behind him a young, dark haired woman hung back by the door.

"We shouldn't be here," the girl said nervously as her eyes darted around the hall.

"I want to make sure she's safe," the man said. He was handsome and muscles bulged under his clothes. He cupped his hands to his mouth and shouted, "Doctor!"

"Hello," Sandra said. She walked over to the stairs. "The doctor is a bit busy."

The man smiled and raced up the stairs, covering steps three at a time. He grabbed Sandra in a bear hug that lifted her feet off the floor. "You're okay! That's great! I thought you might be hurt."

"Ah, bruised ribs!" she gasped. The man quickly set her down. "Ouch, yeah, I'm a bit beat up, but I'll live. I hope this doesn't sound rude, but would you mind telling me who you are?"

"We met outside town last night," he explained.

It took her a second to put one and one together. "Wait, you're Keith the werewolf?"

He smiled and looked down. "Yeah. This is what I look like most of the time. When I got back to town this morning, I heard the men who hit me attacked a woman, and I was worried something had happened to you. Oh hey, where are my manners? This is my best friend, Alicia."

The girl looked thoroughly annoyed. Sandra's guess was that Alicia would rather be Keith's girlfriend than best friend, and really didn't like him showing another woman this kind of attention. In an impressive feat of cluelessness, Keith didn't notice Alicia's discomfort.

"Hi," Alicia said sourly. "Keith, she's okay. Can we leave before the doctor shows up?"

Moratrayas came out of a door, backlit by bright green light. "Mr. Sunter, what's the cause for this visit?"

"Hi, doc," Keith said with a warm smile. "I just wanted to make sure your guest is all right. I hope you don't mind Alicia and me checking up on her."

"Not at all. Your concern for her wellbeing does you credit. Ms. Sower proved most capable in dealing with the men bothering her. I trust you're well?"

Keith smiled. "Right as rain, doc. Those bums knocked me around a bit before they went after her, but I'm okay. Healing fast is the only good thing that came from becoming a werewolf."

Moratrayas nodded. "I'm glad to hear that, Mr. Sunter. I'm currently preparing for a trip, so I'd appreciate it if you and your friend could go back to town. Once I return you may stop by anytime you require assistance."

"Sure thing," Keith said. He ran down the stairs and took Alicia by the hand. Before leaving, he turned to Sandra and said, "Sorry about those guys bothering you. That stuff usually doesn't happen around here."

"It's okay," Sandra said, and waved to Keith and Alicia as they left. Once they were gone, she said, "Nice man. Pity he's as dense as a block of marble."

Moratrayas closed the door behind him and walked up to Sandra. "He's blessed in other ways. Whatever his failings, he is loyal and compassionate, traits not to be despised."

"I know. I'm sorry, that was petty of me."

"Perhaps, but it was also accurate. Alicia is one of three young women trying to attract his attention, and he has misinterpreted all of them."

Sandra laughed. "Three?"

"Sad but true. I've granted him limited access to my castle so I can provide help dealing with his condition. I may have to sit him down and explain a few other things to him." Moratrayas glanced at Sandra and nodded in approval. "I see my replacement garments please you."

"Yeah, they fit fine."

"Good." He headed down the hallway without another word.

Sandra hurried to catch up with him. "I'm not trying to be pushy, but when can we leave?"

Moratrayas walked down the hallway and stepped around a large brass and obsidian hedgehog scrubbing the floor. He opened a door and was bathed in green light pouring from the door. "I need at least two days to pack supplies and weapons."

The answer surprised and disappointed her. Any delay was too long. "Two days? How much are you bringing?"

Sandra followed him into the room and gasped in amazement at the bizarre and chaotic sight. Moratrayas walked in ahead of her and replied, "I intend to bring as many weapons as my barge will carry."

What had once been a storeroom for the castle had been converted into a laboratory of awe-inspiring proportions. The huge room was divided into two sections, the first heavy with tools and parts for his bizarre creations. Saws, vices, hammers, screwdrivers, wrenches, bolt cutters and an assortment of other instruments hung off the walls. There were reams of paper scattered across the room, with every inch covered in writing and diagrams. Workbenches were buried under partially completed creatures of brass, obsidian and glass, some creations as small as mice and others as big as horses. More of the things hung from the ceiling by ropes, partially completed with their innards exposed. The mechanical carcasses reminded Sandra of a butcher shop.

The second half of the room contained a river barge seventy feet long, twenty feet wide and clad in iron plates. It rested in a pool of shallow water with steel doors on the wall at the front of the barge. The barge had a cluster of brass tubes near the back end and no oars or sails. It was loaded down with bundles, boxes and casks, and a tarp covered something enormous that filled the back of the vessel.

"Wow." Sandra was too stunned by the sight to say more.

"Yes, I'm afraid the place is a bit of a mess," Moratrayas said as he walked under a ten legged creation dangling from the ceiling by ropes and pulleys. "One of the reasons I wanted to attract other men and women of science was to assist me. I have to leave many projects unfinished because problems arise that require my attention."

Sandra studied the disassembled creation hanging in front of her. It looked like a giant crab, five feet across with heavy armor plates and larger versions of the pincers that had attacked her on the stairs. The exposed interior sported wires, pulleys, gears and tubing made from brass or glass. Empty glass cylinders connected to those tubes. Obsidian plates and spheres were linked into the crab for a purpose Sandra couldn't even guess at.

"Are your monsters alive?" she asked.

Moratrayas picked through the clutter on the nearest workbench. "I call my creations clockworks. To answer your question, I'm not sure."

"But you make them. If you don't know, who does?"

Annoyed, he replied, "Just because I don't know *now* doesn't mean I'll *never* know." He saw her cringe at his tone. Grumbling, he said, "It is a complicated matter, and with all that's been going on around here it's one I haven't had time to adequately research."

Moratrayas picked up a clockwork centipede three feet long with a score of segmented legs. "When I started this work, I would have told you they weren't alive, that they were constructs that obeyed orders and nothing more. But in the last year I've noticed them display behavior I never built into them. Some are more aggressive than I intended. Others have shown rudimentary cunning. A few have proven willful and mildly disobedient. One of them arranges flowers. I don't know why they do this, nor do I know how to prevent it or enhance it."

"Maybe they have souls, like purple puppet people," she suggested.

Moratrayas set the clockwork down. "They are nothing like puppet people. Puppet people are built with magic. My clockworks are the result of science, of research and hard work, not mumbled words and questionable incantations. But to answer your question, I don't know if they have souls. I haven't had a chance to ask a holy man."

Sandra heard something crawling through the nearest pile of parts. She backed away as the sound inched closer. Moratrayas frowned before he marched over and pointed a finger at the unseen being.

"You have a job to do, Irving, and it's not here. Kindly return to work and leave the young lady be." Whatever lay beneath the debris and parts made a whimpering sound as it tunneled away. "I apologize. I receive so few visitors that my creations, especially Irving, grow curious when one arrives. I told him to stay out of sight when not needed, which he technically did. Honestly, some days they act like children."

Moratrayas marched over to his barge. "The army that attacked your town was three or four hundred strong, a potent force to contend with. We may assume they left behind more men to guard their home base. When we reach Stone Heart and the source of your problems, we will face an army of at least a thousand strong, maybe more."

A two-foot tall upside down terracotta pot slowly slid out from behind a workbench and scooted closer to Sandra. Sounding annoyed, Moratrayas said, "Irving, you're not fooling anyone."

Sandra followed Moratrayas as the pot scooted off. It was hard for her to keep from stepping onto the piles of spare parts that filled the floor like they did the workbenches. Pointing to the barge, she asked, "How many of your clockworks can you carry on that?"

"Less than I'd like. There is room for no more than twenty clockworks in addition to Gertrude, my latest masterpiece. They are a force equal to five times their number."

Twenty times five...hmm. "One hundred against one thousand isn't very good odds."

Moratrayas climbed onto the barge and dug through the tall stacks of supplies already loaded. "Where did Igor put my spare cane? You're right about our chances, Ms. Sower. But one hundred men, or their equivalent, used at the right time and in the right location can work wonders. Force alone won't be enough to free your friends and family. We will have to use stealth, intelligence and careful planning."

Something bumped into Sandra's ankle. She looked down to find a small clockwork shaped like a monkey. Only a foot tall, it gazed up at her with a head that was mostly a smooth obsidian sphere. It held up a small bouquet of tiny white flowers.

"Oh, thank you," she said, and accepted the gift.

Moratrayas glanced up and scowled at the small clockwork. "We've talked about this, Clyde!" The monkey clockwork scurried under a workbench, squealing as it fled. "I built him to fetch my tools, and what does he do? Where did he even find flowers this time of year?"

"They're pretty," Sandra said, and tucked the flowers behind her ear.

Up above them, Sandra heard laughter and a voice say, "Hey, the doc made himself a girlfriend."

Sandra rolled her eyes. "Goblins."

Sure enough, five goblins were climbing around the rafters above the workshop. Goblins were smelly, dirty and thoroughly annoying creatures. The tallest of them was four feet high and roughly man shaped, and all five had exaggerated features. One had gangly arms, another a large nose and a third looked like nothing more than a huge wad of hair with arms and legs stuck on. The fourth had a toothy grin, and the last goblin had what looked like tiny, ineffectual wings sprouting from his back. They were unarmed and dressed in cheap leather clothes.

Goblins had a deserved reputation for being messy, rude and playing nasty pranks on people. They could be found everywhere, and even a town as isolated and small as Sun Valley had a few hanging around. Goblins could get into any building if they put their tiny little minds to it. Thankfully they only did real damage when they were angry, a rare event indeed.

"That will be quite enough of that," Moratrayas told them. "Ms. Sower is a guest and will be treated respectfully."

"Ha!" a goblin snorted. "That would be a first."

"Is it a good idea to let them in here?" Sandra asked. "They could steal your tools or break your clockworks."

The furry goblin stood up straight as an arrow and indignantly replied, "Madam, I resent the implication that we might desecrate this place of chaos!"

"What are you talking about?" she demanded.

"Goblins delight in trouble," Moratrayas explained while he climbed off the barge. "Most of the time they generate chaos and confusion themselves, but if they find someone who seeks to upset the status quo, they either assist or sit back and watch. They cause me no trouble and I return the favor."

"Yeah, what he said," the gangly goblin agreed.

The furry goblin nodded. "We figure all we have to do is sit back and wait. Give the doc a few more years and he'll cause more confusion than we can handle. He's our hero!"

"And we like the guy with the hunch," the large nosed goblin added. "He's an honorary goblin."

The furry goblin pointed at Sandra. "You we're indifferent to. Can you do tricks like the doc?"

"Pull a hat out of a rabbit!" another goblin shouted.

"The goblins and I coexist as well as can be expected," Moratrayas said. He frowned and added, "Although they may be setting a poor example for my creations. The clockworks used to be well behaved."

"We didn't do nothing," the furry goblin replied. He frowned and added, "Okay, there was that one time, but we were hitting the cheddar hard that day."

Sandra shook her head and directed her attention back to the barge. "I know we would get there faster by water, but maybe it's worth it to go by land. You could bring more of your clockworks that way."

"That's not an option." Moratrayas rummaged through a pile of parts until he picked up a glass vial filled with glowing green liquid. "This is the fuel my clockworks require. I can only create a finite amount of it at this time, yet another reason why I sought helpers and colleagues. There's enough on hand to fuel my barge, for emergencies here in Refuge and for powering no more than twenty clockworks for fifteen days. We'd run out of fuel long before reaching the enemy if we went by land."

"Oh." Sandra ran her fingers over a disassembled clockwork man. This wasn't working out as well as she'd hoped. Still, she had Moratrayas' promise to help. She also had another reason to be hopeful.

Sandra had come to get aid from Doctor Moratrayas, but ten other women from Sun Valley were on similar trips. Jennet Foster went to find the hero Julius Craton and get his help. Another woman was looking for the dwarf warrior Tibolt Broadbeard. Women from Sun Valley also went in search of the wizard Elmore, a holy man who called himself Servant, a friendly minotaur named Herd Leader, and five other notable men and women. The eleven had the power to help their town and at least some inclination to do so. Maybe they wouldn't all come, but the hope was that at least half of them would show up. Moratrayas was coming with only Igor and twenty clockworks, but that plus a few of the others should be enough to save Sun Valley.

"Did you see my extra cane?" Moratrayas quizzed the goblins.

The furry goblin shook his head. "Nope. Igor has been bringing in armfuls of stuff every few minutes, but no cane."

Moratrayas glanced over the messy lab. "I'd hire a maid to keep the castle organized if the last one hadn't run off screaming into the night. I told her to stay away from those gears. What happened to her skirt was her fault and no one else's. Help me look for my cane."

Sandra looked through the piles of brass refuse and partially built clockworks, keeping an eye out for gears or anything else moving in the mess. She was a little worried that by getting Moratrayas' help she had a tiger by the tail. He was powerful, but also unpredictable. Between his volatile personality and his bizarre clockworks that had minds of their own, it was only too easy to imagine him making a bad situation worse.

"Will it take long to get to Sun Valley?" she asked.

"Four days, five at the most," he replied. "It took some time to find your town on a map. We'll have to travel through five kingdoms to reach it. Calling them kingdoms is an exaggeration when the largest of them has ten thousand people."

"That many?" she asked in surprise. Sun Valley's population had never been above nine hundred.

Moratrayas dug through another workbench piled high with parts. "That's not a lot of people, Ms. Sower. Kingdoms outside the Raushtad Mountains routinely have populations between fifty thousand and half a million. Of course they have more arable land than we do to support so many citizens."

"Half a million people?" It boggled Sandra's mind just to think about it. "A person couldn't possibly remember so many names. How would they know which people are trustworthy, or who they could count on in an emergency? How do so many people get along without fighting?"

"Generally they trust only family, friends and immediate neighbors," he explained. "Everyone else is a stranger to them. As for fighting, there are plenty of conflicts between both people and nations. I'm told that at Battle Island the population actually bets on wars."

Moratrayas dug through another workbench and came up with a map of the Raushtad Mountains. He held it up, and Sandra marveled at its complexity. Running north to south in a broad strip, the mountains were carved up into dozens of small kingdoms centered around valleys with fertile soil. Along the edges of the map were scores of independent towns, each one too poor, too small or too hard to reach for a king to bother conquering them. Sun Valley was all three.

"I expect little trouble on our journey," he said. "I've traveled through the Raushtad before and everyone's heard of me. I've helped some of these kingdoms, which will ease our passage. The rest know my reputation and should give us no trouble. My only concerns are monsters and an ambush by the army that attacked your town."

"How would they know to ambush us?"

Moratrayas set the map down and continued looking for his cane. "Five of them chased you through the mountains in the dead of winter. They followed you or they deduced where you were headed. Either way, when those men don't come back in a reasonable amount of time, the enemy will assume they were defeated and lay a trap for us."

Sandra leaned on a workbench, careful not to upset the rubbish covering it. "How long do we have before that happens?"

Moratrayas shrugged. "It took them three weeks to get here following you. If they don't return in another three weeks, we can expect the enemy to either send out more men or prepare for an attack on their home base. With luck we'll defeat them and have your townspeople and sunstone back before then."

The furry goblin asked, "How did hot stuff get a sunstone?"

"Obnoxiously put, but a valid question nonetheless," Moratrayas said. "Sunstones are valued at anywhere from five to twenty-five thousand gold coins depending on quality, size and how much light they produce. How did a town as small as Sun Valley acquire one?"

Sandra sat down on a chair, one of the only things not covered in lab equipment, and told them her town's history. "We didn't always have it. Five generations ago my great, great, great grandfather left the valley to earn his fortune. Lots of men did back then. We couldn't support many people since there wasn't much farmland and summers are so short. Everybody figured he'd be gone for good like all the ones that left before him."

She picked up a polished obsidian sphere and held it up for the others to see. "Twenty years later he came back with a wife, three children, the sunstone and more scars than a man should have and still live. The sunstone was four inches across and glowed like the noon sun. He wouldn't say where he got it, just that it was for everyone in the valley and nobody would have to leave home if they didn't want to."

"You used its light in place of the sun to grow crops?" Moratrayas asked.

She nodded and set down the sphere. "My ancestors built a stone tower and set the sunstone in it. We covered the sunstone with an iron pot and old drapes at night or when we had visitors. But when no outsiders were around, we uncovered the sunstone and it poured out light. It extended the growing season by four weeks, enough time to guarantee a good harvest every year. We don't get much surplus, but no one goes hungry."

Moratrayas scribbled figures on a scrap of paper. "A stone capable of producing that much light must be worth a fortune."

"Money doesn't matter," she said. Sandra looked down and tried to hold back her tears. "We've lost our men, the sunstone and most of our stored food. Everyone left in Sun Valley will either starve or leave home for another kingdom. There's not a lot of honest work for widows and single women. We'd have to beg."

"And people say *we're* scum," the furry goblin said.

The gangly goblin nodded vigorously. "We don't do stuff like that to people. Shave their cats, sure, but that's it."

Moratrayas walked over to Sandra and gently lifted her head. "I know what it's like to lose everything. That won't happen to you and your loved ones. You'll get them back and have the peaceful life you deserve."

High above, the goblins giggled and made kissing noises. Without looking up, Moratrayas said, "Another sound out of any of you and there will be violence."

Before Sandra could thank Moratrayas or throw something at the goblins, Igor stumbled into the room burdened down by a mountain of packages. "Almost done packing fuel for the clockworks."

Moratrayas took one of the packages from him and carried it to the barge. "Igor, have you seen my spare cane?"

"You left it in the master bedroom under a pile of dirty socks and the latest issue of *Mad Scientists Quarterly*, the one with the flying clockwork design." Igor set his load down in the barge and headed back for more.

"The publisher needs to change the title of that magazine," Moratrayas complained. "It's feeding people's stereotypes."

Sandra got up and followed Igor. "Is there anything I can do to help? I feel like a fifth wheel sitting around here."

Igor smiled and pointed outside the lab. "Sure! I've got stacks of boxes in the main hall. Loading them will go a lot faster with help. And don't worry, nothing bites unless you turn it on."

"That's...mildly comforting," Sandra said. She followed Igor to the door, but froze in her tracks when a half completed clockwork man hanging from the ceiling waved at her. Her face turned a shade paler and she backed away. "Is that normal?"

"Normal is a relative term around here," Igor told her.

"Normal is also overrated," Moratrayas said. "Extraordinary is a far superior goal."

Looking a bit ill, Sandra waved back to the clockwork and left the lab. Igor was right behind her, but Moratrayas grabbed his arm before he followed her out.

"Igor, how much food and money have you packed for the trip?"

Igor looked up and raised an eyebrow. "Let's see, I've set aside enough to last us months and forty silver pieces for incidentals. You know, bribes, kickbacks, graft, campaign contributions. "

"Triple the food supplies and cash."

Igor didn't question his master, just smiled and nodded. "Right, be a bit of a squeeze getting it all in, but we'll manage. Being in close quarters with a pretty young thing is no hardship, right?"

"Don't start," Moratrayas said sharply. "I've already had enough grief from the goblins on that account."

"Perceptive little things, aren't they?" he said, and ducked out of the lab before Moratrayas could argue with him.

Once they were gone, Moratrayas gazed at the map of the Raushtad Mountains. "Four or five days to reach Sun Valley. Another two days will take us to the land of my birth and source of this problem."

"Spooky," a goblin said. "You scared to go?"

"I am mildly apprehensive. It's said you can never go home. In my case going home is easy. Getting out alive will be the hard part."

With Sandra's help the armored barge was loaded in a day and a half. The sturdy little vessel reminded Sandra of the heavily loaded merchant barges that occasionally came into Sun Valley to trade. She was surprised it could still float burdened down with so many packages, kegs, casks, boxes and coffers, and she wondered if it could move carrying so much weight.

Once it was loaded, Igor turned a wheel by the steel doors in the lab, opening them to reveal a small lake connected to a wide river. It was a clear day and sunlight warmed the chill air. They boarded the barge and took it out onto the river. An engine in the back of the barge made a puttering sound and glowed green, propelling them forward in place of oars or sails.

The goblins waved goodbye from the nearest tower. "Show them who's boss, doc!"

"We'll keep the castle free of rats while you're gone!" the furry goblin said. "Mmm, sweet, sweet rats."

The barge went down the river and stopped by a dock, where twenty men waited patiently for their arrival. Moratrayas stepped onto the dock and stood before the men.

"Doctor," a well-dressed man said formally, and took off his hat.

"Ah, Mayor Blues." Moratrayas shook his hand and nodded to the other men. "Igor and I will be leaving for a while. I trust you and the other leading citizens of Refuge will maintain order in our absence."

"Of course, doctor."

"I shut down my experiments and expect no emergencies, but if one arises I grant you permission to activate the clockworks in town. They will obey your orders in lieu of my own. Use them wisely."

"We will. Thank you, sir."

Moratrayas tapped his cane on his palm. "Now, as to the five men who made the colossally poor choice of angering me. Hold them prisoner for another five days and then release them unarmed outside the valley. By then they shouldn't have enough time to interfere with my mission, and carrying their wounded colleague should slow them further."

"You don't want them executed?" Mayor Blues asked.

"I find it best not to kill my enemies. The smart ones eventually come around to my way of thinking, and the stupid ones do the job for me." Before he returned to the barge, Moratrayas said, "And if another candidate should come while I'm gone…"

"We will house and feed him until you return."

He nodded. "Good man."

With that they set out, leaving Refuge and its people far behind. The barge made good time down the river carrying Igor, Sandra, Moratrayas, twenty clockworks and Gertrude the giant clockwork covered by a tarp on the back of the barge. Sandra didn't believe they would be strong enough to save Sun Valley alone, but if a few other heroes and wizards came then her people had a chance.

# Chapter 4

The barge sped down the river, chugging along with the current and nimbly avoiding obstacles in the water. In two hours they traveled farther than Sandra had in two days of walking. Moratrayas piloted the barge with a wheel at the front of the boat, guiding it between towering cliffs with cracks so large that small trees grew in them. There were a few tree trunks and boulders in the river they had to avoid, but thankfully the water moved too swiftly for ice to form despite the cold.

Their journey was fast but far from comfortable. The barge was loaded down with boxes, bales, casks, barrels, chests and bundles. These contained the tools and weapons Moratrayas would need to save Sun Valley, along with food and fuel they'd need to get there. Little room was left for passengers. Sandra spent the day perched awkwardly on top of a brass cask that sloshed when the barge rose and fell in the water.

"I keep meaning to clear this river for transit," Moratrayas said while steering. "Parts of the river are almost impassible from trees and rocks that fell into the water. Just one more thing I've been putting off for want of help and time."

"You said you wanted other, um, scientists to come here and help you," Sandra said. "How many other people are there who can build clockworks like yours?"

"Not enough," Moratrayas replied. "Those who the masses call 'mad scientists' are as rare as diamonds. Perhaps one in a hundred thousand people enters the field, and I'm sorry to say the attrition rate is high."

Igor saw Sandra's puzzled look and said, "There aren't a lot of them, and most retire or are thrown in jail. Some get chased off cliffs or into swamps by angry mobs. It's funny when you think about it, because that almost never happens to politicians, and it really should."

"That's one of the reasons I settled in the Raushtad Mountains," Moratrayas explained. "There are fewer people here to stop me and no kingdom in the region strong enough to wage war on me and win. I'm also relatively safe from bounty hunters, a necessity since some kings pay a high price for the heads of mad scientists."

The day's travel was uneventful. When night fell, Moratrayas stopped the barge in a slow moving bend of the river. There was no place to land along the rocky shoreline, so they ended up making camp onboard. Moratrayas cooked a simple dinner on a cast iron stove.

"There was something I was meaning to ask you," Sandra said between mouthfuls of stew. "You told me you were born in the town that attacked Sun Valley."

"Yes, Stone Heart." Moratrayas kept eating. "It's a kingdom, though, not a town. When I lived there it had a population of twenty thousand men and women. Goblins were chased out. Dwarfs, elves, gnomes and trolls could come to sell their goods but by law weren't allowed to live in the kingdom, which was foolish as those races could be beneficial."

Cautiously, she asked, "What's it like?"

Moratrayas finished eating before he answered. "It's exactly like the other kingdoms in the Raushtad, mostly mountainous ground with little arable land and little industry. It has one city called Scour and three settlements too small even to be called villages. The city and settlements are dirty, smelly, noisy and unsanitary. There isn't enough farmland to support the number of people living there, so each year a minimum of a hundred men and women migrated out. In bad years the number could rise to a thousand."

Sandra had trouble even trying to consider such numbers. How could a thousand people leave their homes? That was like everyone in Sun Valley just up and walking away from their land and the graves of their ancestors. "It sounds terrible."

"It was," he agreed. "Our king taxed the people heavily, which made a bad situation worse. He lived in a castle throwing balls and banquets for other royalty, while his subjects lived on porridge and sheep's milk. The fool wanted to be respected by kings living outside the Raushtad, the rich ones who ruled real kingdoms and received invitations to the Feudal Awards. Anyone who dared disagree with him was set upon by his royal guard, a euphemism for a sadistic band of armed thugs who delighted in throwing their weight around. Justice, mercy, compassion, these were as rare as gold."

"And you grew up there," Sandra said. Some of Moratrayas' behavior was beginning to make sense. If she'd grown up in a place that awful, she'd probably be just as ruthless as he was in order to survive.

"It's not a fact I'm proud of. My father died in a mining accident, or so I'm told. I was quite young at the time. My mother left the kingdom shortly after to seek work elsewhere. She left me with a tailor she knew. She wrote letters and sent money back a few times, but after two years there were no more letters or coins. When the cash ran out I was apprenticed to the tailor to cover my living expenses."

Shocked, she asked, "No one took you in?"

Moratrayas chuckled. "No one does anything in Stone Heart if they don't have to. My relatives had either left the kingdom long ago or had too many problems of their own to adopt an orphan."

"So what happened to you?"

"I spent the next ten years learning how to make clothes." Moratrayas cleaned out his bowl and put it away. "It wasn't what I wanted to do, but options were limited for a boy without money or connections. I had a keen mind even then and found the work impossibly dull. Fortunately there was a private library in town, and for a few copper coins a month the owner let me read there in my off hours."

Moonlight gleamed off his goggles, and Moratrayas smiled fondly. "Ah those books! Thousands of them, crammed floor to ceiling, dusty, poorly cared for, and more precious to me than all the riches in the world. For a few hours a week I could study them to my heart's content, learning new skills and information. Neighbors laughed at me and said I was wasting my time and money while they drank away their cares. Ha! As if there was something else in Stone Heart worth spending money on."

He leaned in closer and smiled. "That's where I found a book of truly monumental importance, a treasure greater than any other. It was hidden in the back of the library under a stack of farming books. No one knew it was even there. I can't say how long it went buried and unnoticed, like a ruby amid garnets. The book had no title, author or publisher listed. Strange that no one would take credit for such a marvel."

It took Sandra a moment to make the connection. "It showed you how to make clockworks."

"Indeed. You are a bright woman to figure that out. Yes, the book detailed how to make simple clockworks and build a fuel distillery to power them. It took me months of studying to comprehend the instructions. It took years more to build, buy, borrow or steal the tools and parts I needed to make my first clockwork. It was a simple thing, no bigger than a cat, and it could only fetch tools, but I was as proud of it as a new father."

Moratrayas leaned back on a crate. "The book was valuable even if it only showed how to make toys like my first creation. The principles were there to make larger clockworks. I merely had to use what I knew and adapt it to a more ambitious project. That took time, but when I was done I had a far larger clockwork, big enough I could ride on and do real work."

Igor tugged on Moratrayas' sleeve and pointed out onto the water. "I don't want to interrupt story time, but we may have a problem."

Sandra looked at the river and saw rippling fifty feet away. Something was moving down there, something big and coming their way. "How deep is the water?"

"Eight feet," Moratrayas answered. "Deep enough to harbor a wide variety of very dangerous creatures. Everyone stand back."

Sandra and Igor did as instructed. Moratrayas opened a chest and took out a bizarre weapon that looked like a crossbow blended with one of his clockworks. The brass and obsidian weapon began to whir and glow green. He aimed it at the approaching ripples. Bubbles came out of the water and filled the air with a stench like rotting eggs. Igor lit a lantern and aimed the light at the approaching threat.

A monster shot up from beneath the waves with a spray of water. Its head was as big as a grown man and had four eyes on short stalks, and a mouth with thick teeth and a considerable overbite. With light beaming onto it, Sandra could see it had light green scales and sky blue eyes. A long neck festooned with what looked like seaweed held up its head. The monster hissed and swam closer to the barge.

"Oh for the love of...you had me worried!" Moratrayas said. He pressed a button on his weapon, and the green glow and whirring noises died away.

Moratrayas was relaxed, but Sandra wasn't. "What is that?"

The monster slid up against the barge and rubbed its head against Igor. Igor patted it and smiled. "Just a kelp dragon."

The name meant nothing to Sandra. Keeping well back, she asked, "A what?"

"Kelp dragon," Moratrayas repeated as the monster sniffed him. "A river monster that is harmless unless provoked. No relation to a true dragon, of course."

"The big rivers south and west of here are lousy with them," Igor added. "It's odd to see one this far north."

Moratrayas put his weapon back. "They are omnivorous, but the meat in their diet is fish and carrion. They're harmless, and this one's half tamed. Some boy must have caught it when it was a few inches long and kept it in a bucket, then dumped it back in the river when it grew too big to keep. Now it doesn't know to avoid people."

The kelp dragon dipped back underwater and returned with a long waterlogged branch. It dropped the branch on the barge and looked expectantly at them.

"Oh mercy," Moratrayas said. He grabbed the branch and hurled it off the barge. "Very well, I'll play with you. Fetch!"

The kelp dragon swam off with what sounded to Sandra like a gleeful roar. Moratrayas glanced at Igor and asked, "Igor, when you clean out the castle, exactly what do you do with the kitchen scraps?"

"Oh, those," Igor smiled. "Well, I can't bury it without attracting wolves, and we don't want that."

"True," Moratrayas said. The kelp dragon swam back and dropped the branch next to Sandra.

"Seemed wasteful to burn it," Igor continued. "And that makes quite a smell."

Sandra threw the branch as far as she could. The kelp dragon headed after it again.

"And it's not like I can sell the stuff."

"Igor," Moratrayas interrupted, "would you by any chance be throwing our kitchen scraps in the river?"

The kelp dragon returned and dropped the branch next to Igor. "Maybe once or twice. Never more than once a week, and only about a pound each time." The kelp dragon licked Igor and waited to be patted again or for someone to throw the branch. "Seriously, twenty times tops, if you're only counting the big ones."

Moratrayas picked up the branch and tossed it off the barge. "I was wondering why it was so friendly. Try to get some sleep, Ms. Sower. Getting rid of our new friend may take some time."

The next morning, Sandra woke to find that the kelp dragon was gone. She climbed out from under a pile of blankets and saw Moratrayas cooking breakfast. Igor was still sleeping and snoring loudly.

"Good morning, Ms. Sower."

"Where's the kelp dragon?" she asked.

"Igor lured it away with our garbage. We'll be gone before it wakes up and comes looking for another free meal. I realize kelp dragons are harmless, but it's not a good idea to have one quite that attached to us. Some people hunt them, and it could be hurt if it follows us near a town."

"People eat them?"

Moratrayas frowned. "I said they hunt them, I said nothing about eating them. Kelp dragon meat is not only foul smelling but also highly toxic. Fishermen kill them to remove competition, and other more revolting people hunt them for sport."

"That's disgusting."

"You'll get no argument from me." Moratrayas handed her a plate of biscuits and scrambled eggs. He sat down to his own meal and set aside a plate for Igor. "We'll be heading onto the Taum River and into the Kingdom of Eight Peaks. Not long ago I saved them from ogre bandits that were attacking river barges. We should receive a good reception, and I may be able to buy more supplies as well."

Sandra waved her hand over the mountain of boxes and crates on the barge. "This isn't enough?"

"There are things I'm missing that I would pay well to obtain. I may even be able to purchase tools I need for making clockworks and weapons. If we're particularly lucky there could be a few mercenaries in town I can hire. Such men are expensive, but their skill in battle makes them worth the cost."

Feeling nervous, Sandra said, "Um, about that."

"Yes?"

"You, ah, you know we can't pay you. I know we're asking a lot, and you're certainly doing everything you can to help us, and I appreciate it. But...Sun Valley was poor even before we were invaded. We might be able to come up with some kind of a reward later, but right now there's nothing we can give you for helping us."

Moratrayas finished his meal and washed his plate in the river. "Then it's fortunate I didn't ask for payment."

"Oh. Uh, thanks."

"Don't thank me yet," he cautioned her. "There's no guarantee I can help you. In truth my goals are partly selfish. This mission will give me another chance to promote myself, and hopefully gather willing followers and colleagues to my cause."

"I don't mean to pry, but exactly what is your cause?"

"Progress." Moratrayas shook Igor awake and said, "Your food's getting cold. Ms. Sower, my cause is the advancement of the people of Other Place. Your life in Sun Valley was no doubt hard at times. It's even harder in the other towns and kingdoms in the Raushtad."

"And you think you can change that?" she asked.

"I know I can." Moratrayas spoke with passion, like a priest delivering a sermon. "I saw year after year of grinding poverty in Stone Heart, and from my books I learned that the same despair and hopelessness went back countless generations. People were born poor, they would remain poor, and when they died their children would be just as poor. No amount of hard work would change that. What little they could earn through the sweat off their brows or through good fortune was soon taken away, seized by rapacious kings or stolen by bandits and monsters."

Igor rolled his eyes. "Here we go again."

"Finish your food and start the engine," Moratrayas told him before continuing his story. "Once I built my first clockwork, I saw immediate advantages to it. A large clockwork is as strong as twenty men. Imagine how much work could be done with such strength. Road building, quarrying, harvesting timber, construction, the possibilities are endless! The ability to do so much work quickly and safely could revolutionize our world. Imagine it. Stone buildings could go up in weeks instead of months or years. A few men could do the work of hundreds.

"I told you yesterday about the larger clockwork I built. It was eight feet tall and I had to ride on its back to control it. Nowhere near as fast or efficient as my current work, that machine was as big as an ogre and just as strong. It bankrupted me to build it and I became the laughingstock of the whole kingdom, but it worked. I finished it in late autumn when a landslide closed the only road out of the kingdom. Merchants couldn't come in and residents couldn't leave. People said it would take weeks to clear the way." Moratrayas smiled. "I did it in four hours."

"People must have really liked you for that," Sandra said.

"They did. In four hours I went from being a crazy tailor with mad dreams to the savior of Stone Heart. Only hours before people had laughed at me, and after seeing my clockwork in action they admitted they were wrong and praised me. I marched back to Scour at the controls of my clockwork, surrounded by cheering neighbors." He sat back down and paused. "I returned to discover that the king had arrested twenty townspeople while I was gone and thrown them in the castle's dungeon."

"What for?"

"He raised taxes," Moratrayas replied. "Again. Apparently the castle needed decorations for a ball and he didn't have the money for it. Twenty leading citizens petitioned him to reconsider and told him they couldn't pay. His guards arrested them and issued a proclamation that they would be flogged ten times each the following morning for disobedience."

The barge's engine started to whir and glow green. The vessel headed downstream again, this time with Igor at the helm.

"I'd been thinking for some time about other uses for my clockwork," Moratrayas said. "I'd come up with six jobs it would be good for. When I heard news of the arrests, when a crowd of weeping women told me what had happened to their brothers, their husbands, their *grandfathers*, I came up with a seventh."

Moratrayas looked at the horizon. Softly, he continued. "The guards were bullies and thugs, but I will give them some credit. They knew what I intended when they saw me marching toward the castle on my creation. They lowered the portcullis. I tore it apart. They locked and barred the doors. I smashed them down. They came at me together, swords drawn and shields raised. I tossed them aside like rag dolls. When I reached the king, I found him cowering on his throne, his followers fled or defeated. He threatened me. Can you believe that? I'd defeated everyone he had, and he threatened me with imprisonment, torture and execution, all the while shaking like a leaf in a windstorm."

"What did you do to him?" Sandra asked.

There was a savage satisfaction in Moratrayas' voice as he answered. "I pulled him from his throne and dragged him out of the castle. The entire populace of Scour was waiting there, wondering what was happening. I held the king up for everyone to see, and I explained that he was no longer their king, that he didn't deserve to rule anyone. I carried him to the border and set him down. He begged for his life. I told him it wasn't worth taking. I told him I didn't care where he went, but he couldn't stay here. Then I watched him run away."

"And after that?"

Moratrayas glanced at Sandra. "To be perfectly honest, I didn't know what to do next. My actions were driven more by anger than reason. When I came back to Scour, I found the people waiting for me, terrified. I'd taken away their ruler. They had no idea what was going to happen next, and in all honesty neither did I. But with the king gone and his guards either fled or surrendered, there was no one in charge. The situation could go downhill quickly if I didn't take action."

"So he made himself king," Igor said cheerfully from the helm.

"I did not!" Moratrayas said hotly. "Kingships are inherited positions. It would be more accurate to say I became a tyrant, which still sounds more menacing than what I was aiming for. I told the people that I was taking the reigns of power. I would form a council of advisors from the twenty men who'd risked imprisonment and flogging to appeal the king's rulings. I told them that the laws would be fair, that taxes would be lower, that there would be real progress. I meant every word."

Worried what the answer might be, Sandra still managed to ask, "Then why do you live in Refuge?"

Moratrayas stared off into the distance. "I lost. I lost everything I held dear. I had my chance to save Stone Heart and its people from their suffering, and I failed so completely that I was driven away with little more than the clothes on my back. I don't know what happened to my people after I fled. Worst of all, if I'm right and the men who ravaged your town are from Stone Heart, then I may be responsible for the hardships you face."

The next few hours were spent in silence. Moratrayas offered no more of his history and Sandra dared not ask. It was obviously a painful topic, and she worried that further questions might anger him.

The river proved cooperative for the rest of the day. There were no more boulders to dodge or trees sunken just below the surface threatening to tear a hole in passing ships. No monsters appeared except a griffin flying high overhead that showed little interest in the barge or its occupants.

This was the first time Sandra had traveled by boat, and she was enjoying the opportunity. She marveled at the speed, nearly ten miles an hour according to Igor. Sandra had spent her entire life within the confines of Sun Valley, and in mere hours she was seeing more of the world than in the last twenty years.

"We're entering the Kingdom of Eight Peaks," Moratrayas told her. "The capital River City is coming up soon and could offer help for our mission. If we're lucky I can finish my business there in a few hours and we'll be on our way. If not, we'll check into a hotel and the two of you can sleep on beds instead of boxes."

"That'll be nice," Igor said. "Sleeping all cramped up like this is doing my back no good."

There were frequent signs of habitation along the river. Sandra saw many small houses, a patchwork of barren fields, small fishing boats moored to the shore and a few goats pawing through the snow for fodder. She'd expected to find these things, but there were also colorfully painted wood walls next to the river. She pointed at one and asked, "What are those?"

"Advertisements," Moratrayas told her. "Some businesses rent property along heavily traveled roads and rivers to promote their work. It's expensive and not very effective, so I chose not to do it myself. I'm surprised to see them. There were no advertisements on the river last time I was here."

The ads were large and brightly colored to better attract attention. Sandra read them as the barge slid by. One said, '*Not sure where to put that kidnapped princess? Come to Royal Storage!*' Another said, '*Consolidated Looting: We reap mass destruction and pass the savings on to you!*'

"It's kind of seedy," she commented. A third sign showed the silhouette of a man surrounded by flames and said, '*When you don't want it traced back to you, call Plausible Deniability Jones.*' The last sign on the river said, '*Minotaur Home Security: Once you hire minotaurs, you won't go back. We won't let you.*' Feeling a bit worried, she said, "This is getting weird."

Moratrayas scowled. "It demeans the citizens of Eight Peaks to advertise such vulgar businesses on their land. Their king can't be so desperate that he'd take money from such loathsome men."

After another turn in the river they saw River City. It was a small city made of brick buildings, some as high as three stories. People dressed in wool coats hurried along dirt roads. Wood smoke scented with cooking meat rose up from chimneys across the city. Docks littered with fishing and boating gear stretched out onto the river as fishermen brought in their catch.

"Despite that unpleasantness with the ads, I think you'll enjoy a chance to visit River City, Ms. Sower," Moratrayas said as the wind picked up and formed high waves on the river. "I brought enough funds for you to make reasonable purchases while we're here."

"Visiting sounds nice," she said. "Leaving looks hard."

"What do you mean?" Moratrayas demanded. Sandra pointed to a thick iron chain stretched across the river, one end attached to a winch on the docks and the other anchored to the cliff on the opposite side of the river. The chain barred further progress. "This wasn't here the last time I was in Eight Peaks. What madness has seized these people?"

They found twenty armed men waiting for them on the docks. Dressed in scarlet jackets and armed with swords and shields, the men looked bored. Farther back on the dock was a catapult crewed by more men in scarlet. As they sailed near the docks, a man wearing a scarlet jacket and black pants strolled out of a small building on shore.

Igor brought the barge to a stop at the end of the docks while Moratrayas climbed on top of the mountain of supplies to address the soldiers. "Why is passage on the river being blocked?"

"Orders from the king," one of the swordsmen said. "All boat traffic is to be inspected, contraband seized, and good lord it's him!"

The last five words came out as a strangled gasp. The rest of the swordsmen took a closer look at Moratrayas and backed away. Nearby fishermen grabbed their belongings and hurried off.

"I see you recognize me," Moratrayas said. "I am on urgent business and cannot be delayed. Lower the chain so I may pass."

The man dressed in scarlet and black strolled up to the barge and glanced up at Moratrayas. "Officer Billet, why hasn't this vessel been boarded yet?"

The swordsman who'd addressed Moratrayas earlier stammered, "Uh, Lord Balmore, Sir, this vessel is piloted by one Alberto Moratrayas, Sir. He, uh, rules the town of Refuge upriver from here and, uh..."

Lord Balmore, a short man with thin black hair, a weak chin and a nose like a hatchet, waved his hand. "I can see who it is, Officer Billet."

"What's going on here?" Moratrayas demanded.

"It's called 'collecting tolls', Mr. Moratrayas." Lord Balmore spoke as if he were addressing a slow child. "Officer Billet was *supposed* to tell you that river traffic is being inspected, contraband seized and a toll of twenty-five percent of all cargo is being assessed for the right to pass through the kingdom."

Billet backed away from his superior and kept his eyes locked on Moratrayas, scared by what he saw. Moratrayas' face was turning red and his fists gripped his cane so tightly that his knuckles cracked. The fact that Billet couldn't see the doctor's eyes through those dark goggles made him look even more frightening.

"Twenty-five percent?" Moratrayas roared. "Are you insane? I'm willing to pay a reasonable toll, but rest assured I have no intention of turning any of my cargo over to you, much less a quarter of it!"

Lord Balmore sniffed and adjusted the sword hanging from his belt. "No doubt you are considered nobility in Refuge, or as close as the residents can aspire to, but you are in a real kingdom and dealing with a cousin of the king. Here you are a private citizen seeking passage, nothing more. The laws apply the same to you as to anyone."

"Sir, this may not be safe," Billet said. One disapproving glance from Lord Balmore shut him up. He might be silenced, but Billet had the good sense to put more distance between himself and his superior.

The swordsmen behind Billet and Lord Balmore exchanged excited whispers. Sandra overheard a few words, including 'ogres' and 'explosions'. One man used his hands to pantomime someone flying through the air and hitting a tree. Sandra knew that Moratrayas had driven off four ogres that were robbing river traffic, but she hadn't heard the details. Judging by the men's trepidation and snippets of their conversation, the doctor had accomplished the feat in a particularly aggressive fashion.

The rank and file swordsmen recognized what Lord Balmore was unwilling to admit: that a man who could fight four ogres and win could mop the floor with them. The men manning the catapult weren't aiming it at Moratrayas' barge, but instead were edging away from their heaviest weapon. Sandra figured out their reasoning easily enough. If Moratrayas decided to make a fight of it, that catapult was the only real threat to him and bound to be his first target.

"I saved this wretched kingdom mere months ago!" Moratrayas pointed his cane at Lord Balmore and shouted, "Does your king have no sense of gratitude?"

"There is nothing he should be grateful for. You took your sweet time dealing with the ogre infestation. They closed down the river to travelers for months, driving off or looting every boat they could. Toll revenues dried up along with merchant traffic. His Majesty has decreed that boats pay a quarter of their cargo to make up for lost toll income."

Sun Valley had never had a king or noble class. It was too small to support anything that extravagant. Judging by how Lord Balmore was acting, she was happy that they'd never had one. The man was arrogant to the point of being sadistic. Proving that point beyond reasonable doubt, he continued verbally abusing the doctor.

"Whatever minor assistance you offered in the past is just that, in the past. You made no arrangement for free passage or any other payment before rendering service, and you are in no position to demand it now. And if you think a former tailor that overthrew a true king in the least bit impresses the royal house of Balmore, allow me to disabuse you of that notion!"

"Doesn't he know how dangerous Moratrayas is?" Sandra asked Igor in a hushed tone. When Igor nodded, she asked, "Then what is he thinking?"

"I doubt there's any thinking involved in his decision," Igor replied. He sounded cheerful, almost giddy.

At first Sandra thought Igor was being sarcastic, but she realized he was right. Lord Balmore's men were afraid of him. He used his authority like a club to beat down anyone beneath him. But today he faced a man who was legally his equal, since Moratrayas ruled a valley and all the people in it. Lord Balmore could have recognized that fact and made a deal for a smaller fee for passage, or asked for a favor in the future. But that required compromise, for him to stop acting like a big man everyone had to fear, and he'd have to do it in front of witnesses. He wouldn't that.

One of the swordsmen frantically grabbed a bucket of paint and wrote a message on a piece of sailcloth. He raised it up where Moratrayas could see it and Lord Balmore couldn't. It read, '*We're not with him*', and included a large arrow pointing at his superior. Another swordsman clasped his hands together and shook them pleadingly toward the doctor.

This was threatening to turn into a fight Sandra didn't want. She needed Moratrayas in Sun Valley, not beating up some petty bully with a title. While she was sure he'd win the fight, it risked starting a war with a kingdom that hadn't done anything to her people. Sandra wasn't sure if there was a way to stop matters from spiraling out of control. She whispered to Igor, "What should we do?"

The hunchback dug through a stack of supplies until he came up with a bag of peanuts. He smiled and offered it to Sandra. "Sit back, relax and enjoy the show."

Lord Balmore wasn't done talking. "You were run out of the kingdom you stole, driven off to a valley so small no one bothered colonizing it, and you have the audacity to come here and expect to receive remission from tolls? The sheer nerve!" He put his hands on his hips and thrust out his almost nonexistent chin.

"So you would rob me of my creations," Moratrayas said softly.

"They must be worth something, for the value of the metal if nothing else."

Moratrayas bent over, opened a large chest and brought out a weapon. It looked like a brass crossbow with a glass bottle where the crossbow bolt should have been. The bottle was filled with lightning that sparked and shined brightly. With one swift motion, Moratrayas stood up, raised the weapon and aimed it at the catapult.

"You want my creations? Then have one!"

There was a thunderous boom as the weapon discharged. Lightning shot through the air and struck the catapult. The catapult was too close to the river, and spray coming from the waves covered it with a light coating of water. The water helped conduct electricity, and the catapult exploded.

Moratrayas fired again, this time into the dock in front of Lord Balmore. The cousin of the king stood still, mouth gaping like a fish out of water, too shocked to protest or even move. This second discharge drained the weapon entirely, but not before it hit the wet docks and blew off the last ten feet. Lord Balmore was thrown through the air and landed in the icy water.

Swordsmen dropped to the ground. Fishermen on the docks ran away screaming. People farther away from the fight ran over to see what the noise was about. A few men pulled Lord Balmore from the water and set the shivering man on the shore.

Moratrayas selected another weapon and pointed it at Lord Balmore before addressing him with the tone of a judge passing sentence.

"I helped your kingdom and freed the river of ogres robbing those who traveled it. I asked nothing of you in return. I assumed that with the ogres gone you would be able to repair any damage done on your own, but I see I was optimistic. Driving off the ogres was pointless when you are no less rapacious then they were. What merchant will pay such tolls? In your pathetic greed you will strangle off trade and make yourself, your people and other kingdoms along the river suffer."

"You've no right to judge us!" Lord Balmore shouted.

"What would you know of rights?" Moratrayas shot back. "When one inbred, incompetent family of aristocrats can force its will on these people and impose injustices on travelers then there are no rights! Carry a message back to your cousin, the king. I showed him every kindness, and in return he shows stupidity and ingratitude. If he ever again seeks to rob me then he will make an enemy of me for life, and I will reap such a terrible vengeance as to make the damage I did today seem as insignificant as a fleabite."

"You doom yourself!" Lord Balmore bellowed. "Men, attack!"

The swordsmen did nothing of the sort. They took cover behind fishing nets hanging to dry and boats pulled ashore for repairs. A few men peaked their heads up and stared at their superior in disbelief.

Sandra went over to the doctor and put a hand on his shoulder. "Don't get them involved with this. They're just doing their jobs."

"If they follow his orders then they should be held accountable."

Gently, she asked, "What do you want them to do? They know this is wrong, but they can't change their orders and they can't quit their jobs. I'm sure they've got families to feed."

"And gambling debts to pay," Igor added helpfully.

A swordsman stuck his head up and shouted, "Listen to the little guy!"

Moratrayas frowned and lowered his weapon. "Yes, it would be unfair to judge them too harshly. That still leaves the chain blocking our way."

"We'll lower it!" another swordsman promised.

"Not enough," the doctor said. "That lets me pass and no one else. Igor, deal with it."

Igor rummaged through the stacks before picking up a clockwork grasshopper three feet long and equipped with oversized steel jaws. He opened a panel on its back and turned a knob, bringing the creation to life. Glass panels glowed green, and the clockwork rasped and wiggled. Igor set it down and pointed at the chain. With one mighty jump, it leapt off the barge and landed on the chain. Grabbing hold with its front legs, the clockwork lifted its head from the water and chewed through the chain, causing both chain and clockwork to sink beneath the waves.

Moratrayas piloted the barge away from the docks as people on shore watched in shock. Someone screamed when the clockwork grasshopper pulled itself onto a dock by climbing along the severed chain. With a second jump it landed back on the moving barge, where Igor turned it off and put it away.

Slowly and with much effort, Moratrayas regained control of his temper. Speaking formally, he said, “My apologies, Ms. Sower. I hadn’t realized matters had deteriorated so badly in Eight Peaks. We’ll get no help here, and there are no other cities on our route. I’m sorry.”

# Chapter 5

"Infuriating!"

It was almost nightfall, and Doctor Moratrayas had been repeating that word for three hours. Standing at the wheel, he would fume and snarl, then shout abuse against Lord Balmore. When it finally became too hard to contain his anger, he turned to Sandra and Igor and shouted, "I can't believe the arrogance of the man!"

Moratrayas left the wheel and paced the deck, stepping over boxes and barrels. Igor hurried over to take the wheel and steer the barge.

"I'm not taking his side, but you may have started a war back there," Sandra told him.

"Then it's a war worth fighting! Blast it, this wouldn't have happened if I had more help. I swore I wouldn't be like one of those heroes, and that's exactly what I've become."

That made no sense to Sandra. "Isn't being a hero a good thing?"

"Less than you'd think." Moratrayas paced the deck like a caged tiger, too agitated to stop moving. "Heroes ride into towns in danger and save them, then go to the next place that needs help. All well and good, but what happens the next time trouble arises? The hero is gone and the locals have to deal with it on their own. And does the hero ask what caused the problem? Rarely. He confronts the immediate threat without a care what brought it about or what happens after he leaves."

Moratrayas grabbed the deck railing and looked out over the water. "When I was a boy, Stone Heart was under siege by bandits. It took weeks to drive them off. The king's men captured one, and I snuck into the dungeon and questioned him. He was a former soldier from a neighboring kingdom. His king hadn't paid his men in months. So, being armed, combat trained and poor, they deserted and took what they wanted. We drove them off, but the neighboring king caused the problem in the first place. The royal twit was shorting his new soldiers on their pay, so the whole mess could happen again."

"What does that have to do with you?" she asked.

"I swore not make the same mistake. I'd fix problems so they couldn't happen again." Moratrayas stared off into the darkness. "Instead I find myself taking half measures. I should have made a deal with King Balmore before helping him and made sure he kept the bargain, but there wasn't time. I had so many things to do. Build more clockworks, distill fuel, oversee construction in Refuge, attract followers, it takes so much time and there's no one to help but Igor. Instead of making real progress I'm just putting out fires, dealing with the latest emergency before going to the next one."

"That explains why you want help so badly," she said. "But you're pitting yourself against the world, or at least a big piece of it. Would a few more people really help?"

"Yes," he answered promptly. "It takes hours each week to distill fuel for my clockworks. It's a simple task, but it has to be done. A reasonably intelligent woman such as yourself could do it once you were taught to read."

Sandra put her hands on her hips. "Hey, I can read just fine!"

That got his attention. "You can? Most men in these parts are barely literate. Reading and writing are rarely taught to women. How did you come by the skill?"

"Everyone in Sun Valley can read," she told him. "An old man in town gives lessons. The roads are closed during winter, and sometimes even the river freezes. There's not much to do and no place to go, so we read a lot. There aren't many books, and I've read the ones we have a dozen times. I always used to get so excited when someone got a new book. It would takes months to get to me, going from person to person, but what else can you do in the dead of winter?"

"That's a very forward thinking policy," Moratrayas admitted. "I've only just started an education program in Refuge. That should shave months off your training time."

"My what?"

"Nothing," he said. "My point is, it doesn't take an army of scientists mad or otherwise to change the world. It takes one man of my caliber and a host of men and women who want change. You could learn how my fuel distillery operates in days. After that you could handle the chore, freeing me up to do important work. Give me five loyal followers and I can triple the amount of work I do, and with a hundred I can shake the world!"

"You already have hundreds of people in Refuge," she reminded him.

"Good men and women, all of them, but not ready for such work. They want a simple life, to work, worship, raise children and live quietly. They perform important work, but they're not ready for the world changing tasks I have in mind. In time a few of them may grow in desire and capacity, but for now it's me and Igor."

Sandra thought for a moment, trying to come up with a delicate way to phrase her question. "Why do you call the town Refuge?"

"That's a long story."

Sandra swept her arms over the open river. "Do you have something else we need to do for the next few hours?"

Moratrayas hesitated. He glanced at the giant clockwork on the back of the barge, still covered by a tarp. "I suppose I could check Gertrude's legs again, but that task can wait. I see a bit of shore up ahead. Igor, land the barge and I'll answer Ms. Sower's question while we make camp."

Igor stopped the barge at the mouth of a tributary that flowed into the Talum River. The shoreline was sandy and free of ice, and beyond that was a narrow valley lined with pine trees. Igor soon had a large fire burning, and Moratrayas roasted skewered chicken meat. The fire cast flickering shadows where it hit the trees.

"I told you how I came to power," Moratrayas explained while he cooked and Igor put up a tent. "The first few weeks were daunting. Everyone was terrified of me. I needed their cooperation if I was going to be a good leader. Gradually they began to come around, and my advisers and I had productive meetings.

"We needed money, if not for the same reasons the old king did. I sold off tapestries and paintings in the castle, and used the money to buy food and clothing. We passed it out to families in need. That was the first year in living memory that no one left Stone Heart. I freed most of the prisoners, and the few people in the dungeon who deserved punishment I put to work clearing land."

"Is dinner ready yet?" Igor interrupted.

Moratrayas checked the chicken and brushed on spices. "A few more minutes. I also began a program of farm construction. The good land was already being cultivated, so I had unemployed men in the kingdom build terraced farms on the hills, lining the edges of the terraces with stone so the soil wouldn't wash away. When the first farm was ready I held a celebration and gave it to a deserving family from the construction crew. I told the rest of the crew that when the next farm was built I'd do the same thing, giving land to the landless so they'd have a living. I promised the farms would be theirs and their children's for as long as they paid taxes and obeyed the laws. I still can't understand why they were so surprised."

"I guess they weren't use to generous leaders," Sandra commented.

"That was good governing, not generosity. I also built more clockworks and worked on other projects. It took months, but I completed a prototype lightning gun to protect the kingdom. That was also the time Igor appeared."

Sandra laughed. "He just showed up at the front door?"

"Actually, yes."

Igor raised his right hand and solemnly announced, "*Wherever men dream the impossible, wherever dangerous tasks need be done and sanity is only an impediment, there shall an Igor appear*. That's the motto of Igor University. Do you want to hear our college song?"

"I endured that once and I'm still emotionally scarred," Moratrayas said. "Igor heard of my takeover and applied for a job as my lab assistant. I told him there was no such position and I didn't need help, but by that time he already had his bags in a broom closet. Faced with the choice of either dragging him out by his heels or employing him, I opted for the latter."

"That's how most lab assistants get their jobs," Igor added.

Moratrayas handed out the food, and for a while was too busy eating to speak. “It went well for nine months. My council of advisers handled most of the legal cases, and they were merciful and just. I didn’t have an army, so I ordered a few former soldiers and mercenaries to train the townsmen once a week. I made arrangements with merchant houses so we could buy tools we needed and sell off the old king’s trinkets. I kept some of his more interesting possessions, namely his library and a sunstone.”

Sandra almost choked on her food. “You have a sunstone?”

“I used to, which is why I was interested in your sunstone. Mine was much smaller and weaker, generating far less light. Unlike your sensible town leaders, the old king squirreled it away instead of using it.”

Moratrayas paused between mouthfuls of food and pointed a wood skewer at Sandra. “I read in the old king’s library that two sunstones close together produce far more light than when apart. If I’d known about your sunstone back then I could have tested the theory. I always wondered if two sunstones together can produce so much light, what would three do?”

“Did you keep it?” Sandra asked hopefully.

“I know what you’re thinking, Ms. Sower, that a weak sunstone is better than none. I would give it to you if I still had it. I lost that treasure along with the rest of the kingdom.”

“How could that happen?” she asked. “You had your clockworks and trained men and lightning whatever.”

“Lightning gun.” Moratrayas finished his food and tossed his skewer into the fire. “While I was trying to save Stone Heart, the old king was equally busy. He went to neighboring kingdoms and pleaded for help retaking his throne. He had no money or influence, and as you saw earlier, the gratitude of kings lasts as long as a mayfly. Most of his peers wouldn’t even receive him, and none would help him. But that miserable little toad of a man caused enough damage by telling them what happened. One of the neighboring kings named Stoth Voluk heard his tale and decided to take Stone Heart for himself.”

“You couldn’t stop him?” she asked.

“I could have,” Moratrayas said menacingly. “He had three hundred soldiers and an equal number of mercenaries. Thugs would be a better name for them. Not one of them was better than the men I’d already defeated taking the kingdom. The mountain passes leading to Stone Heart were narrow and defendable. I developed a plan to save the kingdom. There would have been losses, but we could have done it. But there was no we.”

“What do you mean?”

“I explained my plan to the council of advisers, former mercenaries and soldiers. They vowed to fight to preserve the justice and peace I’d given them. The men I gave farms to swore they’d defend their land. Friends and neighbors

I'd known for years promised to fight at my side. But on the day we were to gather together and drive off Voluk, no one arrived."

His voice was heavy with disgust. "I begged them to fight. I told them to do it for their families, for their children. I reminded them how bad life was before, and that it would be the same once Voluk took over. Nothing worked. The entire population of Stone Heart stayed in their houses, doors barred, windows shuttered, and nothing I did changed that."

"Two men against an army," Sandra mused. "No wonder you ran."

"We ran," Moratrayas admitted, "but we made them pay for their victory. The two of us held them off for three days and inflicted great damage. In the end it didn't matter. We couldn't be everywhere at once, and they took the capital street by street. They destroyed all my clockworks. We holed up in the castle for a while, but they got a battering ram so close to the wall that I couldn't aim the lightning gun at it. In the last few hours we destroyed everything we couldn't carry. I tore the workings out of the lightning gun, ruining my masterpiece so they couldn't claim it. We fled the castle minutes ahead of our pursuers."

Usually it was hard to read Moratrayas' expression with his goggles on, but this time she could see the terror of that day on his face. "Voluk chased us at the head of fifty swordsmen while Igor and I escaped on the very barge we travel on today. Voluk pointed at me and ordered his men to take me alive. I have a vivid imagination, and could guess what he intended. I had dared to usurp the place of kings, and he meant to make me pay for it.

"We fled for weeks with Stoth Voluk and his men chasing us. He almost caught us twice. We barely fought him off long enough to escape. Eventually we crossed so many kingdoms he lost track of us. We found a small valley, uninhabited at the time, but with ruins of a town and castle. Out of fuel, we had no choice but to settle there."

Moratrayas looked down. "It shames me to admit it, but alone in that castle, my thoughts turned dark. I had done everything in my power to help Stone Heart. They were my people. I loved them with all my heart, and that love was betrayed. I offered to make them partners in justice and prosperity, to live in peace. They sat back and let it slip away so another king could oppress them. My hatred for them rivaled that of the devil himself."

"Doctor, it's not that simple," Sandra told him. "I know you tried to do good for your people, but you asked too much from them. You risked your life fighting for your dream. They were risking the lives of their wives, their children and their elderly parents. If they fought and lost, their families would have no one to care for them, and Voluk may have punished the survivors. They had to think about their loved ones."

Moratrayas sprang up and grabbed her by the shoulders. "Don't you see, that's when you have to fight even harder! They condemned their children to the same suffering they endured. If no one takes chances then nothing ever changes. The suffering and injustice they lived under went on for generations, and they allowed it to go on for generations more! It has to stop!"

The doctor's powerful grip and vehemence left Sandra too shocked to speak. Moratrayas realized he was scaring her. He let go of her and sat down. "I'm sorry, that was...excessive. My feelings get the best of me at times."

"It's okay."

Softly, Moratrayas continued his tale. "I brooded there for months, plotting my revenge. Only Igor remained with me. I don't know what I might have done if that had continued, but one night I saw lights in the valley. People had come, hundreds of them. I left the castle and found men and women huddled together around fires, living in the ruins below the castle. Their leader said he was sorry for coming unannounced and he would have sought an audience with me, but I came before he had a chance. I demanded to know why they were there and what they wanted. He told me they wanted a home. One by one the people told me stories so bitter I was surprised the stones themselves did not weep in sympathy.

"There were farmers taxed off their land by greedy nobles, merchants robbed of everything but their lives by bandits, ranchers that lost their flocks to wolves and monsters. Some fled persecution based on their religion while others fled ethnic strife. They came from a dozen kingdoms and towns in the Raushtad, united only by their suffering. They'd heard of my brief time as leader and tracked me down. They asked me to lead and protect them, promising loyalty in return. I told them how I was forced from the throne after my followers and neighbors abandoned me, and said they should find another leader. I told them I was a failure. Their leader told me, 'so are we'. They were so desperate and without hope that they were willing to trust their lives to me, even though I'd been driven from power."

Moratrayas stirred the fire and stared into it. "I named the town that day. It was my place to escape to and theirs as well. With them by my side I realized why I'd failed. My plans were good, but I had depended on people who didn't believe in them. To them I was only a tailor, a mad one at that. To these people I was their salvation. They believed in me. These were a people I would change the world for, and for the last three years that's what I've been trying to do. I can't let them down."

"I'm sorry," Sandra told him.

"Why? You caused me no harm."

"That's not what I meant. You, you're trying to help people and nobody gets it. It's not fair what the people in Stone Heart did to you and what they call you. You're not mad."

Moratrayas shrugged. "Perhaps I am. I'm trying to save a world that fights me every inch of the way. How do I fix something that wants to stay broken? It's a puzzle that's confounded me for years, and I may be mad to think I can solve it."

Sandra took his hand in hers. The move clearly surprised him. "Sun Valley wants to be fixed. Its people want to be happy and safe again. Maybe you can't save the whole world, but you can save a piece of it."

She stood up and walked into the woods along the tributary. "We're low on firewood. I'll get some and be back in a few minutes."

Once Sandra was safely out of sight of the camp, she started piling up driftwood and fallen branches. "He's not so bad," she said to herself. "He's not a hero, but he's not as bad as everyone says. Just, well, driven. I have to keep him on the straight and narrow for a week or two and everything will be fine. Peachy, really."

The stack of firewood grew quickly, but she gathered still more. Sandra wanted to be by herself after spending so much time cooped up on the barge. She also needed time to think.

Moratrayas was a damaged man, that much was clear. He'd lost his parents and then was abandoned by people he'd thought were friends. That left emotional scars he might never recover from. And he'd shown quite a temper. But deep down he was a good man. She was sure of it.

"What am I going to do about it?" she asked herself. "I can cook, tend sheep, make clothes, read and that's it. He doesn't need a maid or a farmhand. He needs a partner."

Sandra broke a branch off a dead tree and tossed it on the pile. "On the other hand, the rest of the people we're trying to get help from have been working alone for years. Maybe if I introduce them I can get one or two to help him. He could do a lot if he's teamed up with a hero or a wizard. That's way better than anything I could do for him."

Still deep in thought, Sandra picked up a branch off the ground, but stopped before throwing it on the growing pile. It looked like a long, straight branch, but it didn't weigh as much as it should. The texture was wrong, too. Seconds later she realized she was holding a human leg bone. Sandra looked down and saw a grinning skull half buried by snow and pine needles, cleaned of flesh but still bearing a yellow forked beard.

She screamed. She couldn't help it. Sandra threw the leg bone aside and scrambled back as fast as she could. Backing away from the skeleton, she tripped over a large rock. The ground was covered in snow and beneath that were pine needles, which together cushioned her fall. When she sat up, she realized she hadn't tripped on a rock but a long, narrow skull that ended in a wickedly hooked beak. She screamed again.

"Sandra!" Moratrayas came running, his cane extended out to become a sparking brass staff. Igor followed him armed with a log burning at one end.

Moratrayas helped her up and she pointed at the bodies, one human and the other definitely not.

"I'm sorry, I'm sorry, I know they're dead and they can't hurt me but I was surprised and it's dark and oh lord someone was killed here!"

"We need to work on your punctuation," Igor told her. "Simple sentences good, commas good, run on sentences bad."

Moratrayas bent down over the bones and studied them. "There's no flesh left on either of them. Don't worry, Ms. Sower, this happened months ago. The animal was a griffin."

Careful digging through the snow turned up a pile of large bones around the griffin skull. Most of the ribs were broken, and mixed in with them was what looked like a spear made of granite.

"Long ago the elven emperors magically merged giant eagles and lions," Moratrayas said. "It doesn't take a genius to realize such monsters would be voracious and hard to control, or that they might escape into the wild and breed. I wonder what the elves were thinking when they made them."

"Maybe they were *really* drunk at the time," Igor suggested.

"That's a better theory than I've come up with." Moratrayas studied the man's bones, then backed away and exclaimed, "It's a small world after all! I'd recognize that stupid little beard anywhere. Ms. Sower, meet the wizard Tadcaster, scoundrel, villain and for a short time ruler of the town of Granite Peaks before I drove him off. I'd wondered what happened to him."

"You know him, I mean, you knew him?" she asked.

"Not well, of course. He took over Granite Peaks and was busy looting the town and making everyone's life unbearable. One of the residents escaped and asked for my help. I went and met Tadcaster, he attacked and I won. The miserable wizard ran for his life after I prevented him from destroying the town with a landslide. He was a terrible loser."

"What's he doing here?" Igor asked. "Obviously very little, but you know what I mean."

Moratrayas carefully removed litter over the skeleton, making sure not to touch the bones or tattered remains of clothes. "His skull is fractured. If I had to make a guess, I'd say Tadcaster came here after his defeat. The griffin found him alone and tried to make a meal of him. Tadcaster saw it coming and used his magic to create that granite spear to kill it. He actually did a good deed in slaying that beast."

"Will wonders never end?" Igor asked.

"Yes, well, the griffin did the world a service, because it looks like it hit Tadcaster once before dying. He fell and hit his head. Just as well he was stopped before he could spread his evil to another town." Moratrayas put a hand on Sandra's shoulder. "I'm sorry you were startled. Come along, we'll help you with the firewood. Next time someone will go with you."

Sandra pointed at the wizard's bones. "What about him?"

"Bit late for us to help," Igor remarked.

"We can't just leave him here," she said. "We should bury him or pile rocks over him."

"We're not touching him," Moratrayas said. "It's not safe."

Sandra pointed at the bones again. "But he's dead!"

Moratrayas pointed at the skeleton's hand, drawing Sandra's attention to a gold ring. "Powerful wizards typically carry magic items. This ring is magic. I know because he used it to shoot fire at me. When last I saw Tadcaster, he had a magic staff, ring, talisman and for some reason a magic teacup. That's a tempting prize for a thief. Wizards place curses on their magic items to prevent theft and make sure if they're killed no one will benefit from their death. If we touch him, even slightly, we could bring down a curse."

"What would it do?" she asked.

Moratrayas shrugged. "Some form of elemental magic, I suppose. Wizards are creative with magic attacks, and Tadcaster was a filthy sadist. Whatever it is we wouldn't enjoy it. No, he stays where he is."

Moratrayas and Igor walked away. Sandra looked at the dead wizard a moment longer. "That's sad. No one should have to die alone."

"Come along, Ms. Sower," Moratrayas called. "We need to get an early start to reach Sun Valley on time."

Sandra joined the others at the pile of firewood. They loaded up with as much as they could carry and were about to leave when Sandra saw a branch she'd missed earlier, half buried by the snow. She picked it up and brushed it off. It was wood, but it wasn't a branch. It was five feet long, smooth, tapered and covered with ancient runes of power carved into the wood. She'd picked up Tadcaster's magic staff.

Moratrayas and Igor stared at the staff in horror. Sandra dropped the staff and said, "It's official. My life sucks."

The runes on the staff glowed red and a tiny spark of light flew from the tip. The spark soared into the sky and disappeared into the night. Moratrayas and Igor dropped their load, grabbed Sandra by either arm and ran.

"Where are we going?" she asked.

"Back to the barge!" Moratrayas shouted. "We have to get away from here as fast as we can!"

"But nothing happened."

"Nothing happened *yet*!" Moratrayas corrected her. "If we're quick, we can escape before the curse on the staff takes effect."

They were twenty yards from the barge and running fast when the speck of light floated down in front of them. It didn't touch the ground, but slowed down and hovered six feet in the air. Wind picked up and snow was sucked off the ground. The wind and blowing snow temporarily blinded Sandra and the others. When they could see again, a monster made of snow fused into ice was standing in front of them.

The icy beast stood eight feet tall and must have weighed at least a thousand pounds, with stocky legs and arms that reached the ground and ended in long claws. It had no head, instead sporting a gaping maw filled with jagged teeth in the center of its body. Barbed spikes of ice grew out of its back. It reminded Sandra of an ice sculpture, but instead of the smooth finish talented artists put on their work, this beast was roughly cut and had hundreds of pale blue facets that glittered in the moonlight.

"Ice golem," Moratrayas said tersely. "I hate wizards."

The golem headed for them, its jaws snapping. It swung its long arms and cut furrows in the ground with its claws. It had no voice, instead making a crackling sound when it moved.

"Igor, go left, Sandra, go right!" Moratrayas ordered. "Get to the barge and turn on Gertrude. I'll hold its attention."

Sandra and Igor followed his orders. The golem twisted its spiky body left then right, not sure which to attack. Moratrayas lashed out at it with his staff before it could decide. The sparking tip hit its chest and crackled as it poured electricity into the golem. He may as well have spit on it. The staff did no damage and the electricity didn't stun it. The golem lumbered after Moratrayas and swung a clawed hand at him. Moving gracefully, he dodged the attack and hit its knee, a blow the golem didn't even feel.

Sandra and Igor climbed onto the barge. Igor pointed to the chest where Moratrayas kept his weapons. "I need time and the doc needs firepower. Toss him something from in there."

She opened the large chest and was confronted with ten weapons, most of which looked like crossbows blended with bizarrely sculpted pieces of brass and obsidian. "Which one should I give him?"

"Pneumatic saw!" Moratrayas shouted. He ducked under the golem's swing. The golem was so slow that Sandra wondered why he didn't run away.

"Which one is that?" she asked.

Igor ducked under the tarp. "They're labeled."

Sure enough, on the stock of each weapon was a brass plate with the weapon's name. There were other helpful instructions, like 'point away from face', 'hot when in use', and 'objects in mirror are closer than they appear'. "That's convenient."

"Ms. Sower!" Moratrayas shouted. The golem's next swing missed again and accidentally tore open a pine tree. Its attacks were slow and clumsy, but those terrible claws could do a lot of damage if they hit.

"Sorry!" Sandra found the correct label on what looked like an armored glove with a circular saw blade on the back of the hand. She pulled it out and threw it to Moratrayas. The doctor rushed forward and caught it. While the golem lumbered after him, he slid the glove on and pressed a button on the palm. Glass panels on the glove glowed green and the saw spun so fast it whined. Grim faced, Moratrayas slashed at the golem and hit it, the saw's whine turning into a scream. He cut a thin groove into its chest with the saw, and nothing more.

Moratrayas was hurting the golem, but just barely. At this rate it would take him hours to defeat it. Worse, the golem needed just one good hit to kill him. Sandra had to do something.

Desperate, she searched through the weapons' chest. She needed something easy enough for her to use. Dart launcher, pincer glove, anvil cannon, no, they had too many buttons and levers. She'd never figure out how to use them in time. The lightning projector was empty, its power spent earlier that day. Wait, in the bottom row was a bulky thing labeled 'net thrower'. It had just one button. That was simple enough.

"Igor, what's wrong with Gertrude?" Moratrayas demanded. He sawed off the tip off one of the golem's claws and slipped under its counterattack.

"The safeties are on and it's not fueled," Igor answered.

The ice golem tried to kick Moratrayas. He stepped aside and slashed its thigh, then its chest. Sandra lifted the net thrower and braced it on the barge railing. She pulled the trigger and was knocked over by the kickback. But the weapon performed as advertised, firing a net weighted with lead balls. The net spun through the air and wrapped around the golem.

The ice golem was as strong as it looked and effortlessly tore through the net. Sandra struggled to her feet and braced her back against a brass cask. She fired again. A second net whirled through the air and twisted around the ice golem. She fired a third time and wrapped the golem up so completely she could only see its feet.

Moratrayas rushed in and sliced into the ice golem's feet. He hacked off two toes and cut a deep groove into its right leg. But the golem wasn't beat yet. There was a snapping sound, partially muffled by the layers of nets wrapped around it. Moratrayas threw himself to the ground before the nets were torn apart in a shower of razor sharp ice shards. The spikes extending from the golem's back were gone, shattered to free it.

Sandra pulled the trigger on the net thrower again, but this time a small sign popped up on the stock that read, 'please reload'. "No, no, no!"

Moratrayas shouted, "Tadcaster, if you weren't already dead I'd kill you!"

The ice golem headed for Moratrayas. Pieces of the nets hanging off it were sliced up too badly to slow it down. The doctor hacked away at it and cut off one of the golem's fingers. If the golem felt pain it didn't show it, and it swung at him again. This time it scored a glancing blow and sent him sprawling to the ground. Then the golem turned its attention to Sandra.

"Get down!" Moratrayas shouted. Sandra saw the ice golem point its right arm at her. It was too far away to strike, but she dropped flat against the deck all the same. The arm glowed bright blue as cracks ran over it. Then it exploded and sent ice shards flying at the barge. The shards sailed over Sandra's head and pierced containers behind her.

The ice golem headed after Moratrayas again. He got back to his feet and met it. Even one armed, the golem was so big and strong that he was no match for it.

Sandra ran off the barge. She didn't know how to stop the golem, but she had to do something! The net pieces dangling off the ice golem were made of some kind of fiber and might burn. She pulled a burning log off the campfire and hit the golem in the back. The blow didn't hurt it, but as she guessed, it set the tattered nets on fire.

The ice golem panicked. It swung its remaining arm wildly and ran away from Moratrayas and Sandra. The fire wasn't very large, but it terrified the golem more than losing an arm had. When the fires burned out, the golem turned to face them, its mouth opened wide in a furious snarl.

There was a whip crack sound from the barge, followed by another. The tarp over the back of the barge was being ripped off, the ropes holding it down snapping as whatever was concealed underneath broke them like kite strings. A long brass and obsidian tube slid out from under the tarp and pointed at the ice golem. The tube was wide enough that Sandra could have crawled down it, and green light poured from its interior. Gertrude the clockwork bellowed a challenge to the golem, a deep, hateful roar that echoed down the river valley.

The ice golem heard the noise and turned to face the barge. It saw the tube and raised its remaining arm in reply, ready to sacrifice another limb to fire a shower of ice shards at its enemies. But the golem needed a few seconds before it could fire, time it didn't have.

With a roar like an angry dragon, the tube fired something shiny and as big as a wine barrel, something moving so fast that the blast of air from its passing knocked Sandra and Moratrayas to the ground. The kickback nearly capsized the barge. But whatever ill effect it had on them or the barge, it did far worse to the golem. The projectile hit the golem head on and shattered it, sending ice shards a hundred feet in the air. It kept going, digging a trench in the ground for a hundred feet before finally coming to a stop.

Moratrayas stood up and helped Sandra to her feet. "Thank you, Ms. Sower. Igor, you were a bit tardy, but better late than never."

"What is that?" Sandra asked, and pointed at the clockwork still partially concealed under the tarp.

Proudly, Moratrayas said, "That, Ms. Sower, is Gertrude."

# Chapter 6

"Ms. Sower, I'm fine!" Moratrayas protested.

"Hold still! Good lord, I've seen toddlers that were better patients than you."

The morning after their battle with the ice golem was spent checking the barge for damage and loading firewood. Igor retrieved the projectile that had destroyed the ice golem, a brass cylinder with iron bands wrapped around it. He rolled it back onto the barge and placed it under the tarp. Sandra was trying to find out how badly Moratrayas was hurt after the golem hit him, but he resisted her bitterly. When he sat down on the barge to reload the net thrower, she took the opportunity to check his arm and shoulder.

Sandra pressed down where the golem had hit him. "Does this hurt?"

"No, now if you don't mind—"

"Move your arm around."

"That's what I've been doing the entire morning," he replied. The doctor's white shirt included armor plates sewn into the fabric. Those plates had kept him from being cut in half by the golem, but there could be bruising from the hit. Sandra knew a few things about men, and as a rule they refused to admit weakness or injury. Her brothers, father and ex-boyfriend were all that way, and given his pride she was sure Moratrayas was the same.

"Lift your arm and rotate it backwards."

"No." Moratrayas finished reloading the net thrower and sat up. "Ms. Sower, I'm in perfect health. That was far from the worst blow I've taken."

"He's right," Igor chimed in. "The doc can take a hit and keep going. Back in Eight Peaks, those ogres knocked him around pretty good before he lured them next to a barrel filled with explosive fuel byproducts and set it off. You should have seen them go flying."

"Thank you, Igor."

Smiling, Igor began counting off fingers. "And there were those burns Tadcaster gave him, and the cut from his stone spear spell. Then there were the pixie bites he got defending Two Rocks. Those heal slowly. Plus there was the whole business at Stone Heart where he really got his—"

"You made your point," Moratrayas said firmly. "I've been in many fights worse than this and come out alive. The day an animated piece of ice defeats me in battle is the day I retire. Now if you're finished poking and prodding me, we must be on our way. Time is not our ally."

The day's travel went much better than yesterday. The weather was clear, as if all the winter storms had hit while Sandra was on her way to find the doctor and not on the way home. They encountered no cities or even towns that might offer help or hindrance. The few people living in the isolated farmhouses they passed seemed eager to avoid attention. Most stayed far from the river, and some even ran indoors when they saw the barge approach.

"They think we're river pirates," Moratrayas explained. "Merchants don't travel this late in the year due to bad weather and icing over of slow moving waters. Anyone traveling these rivers so late in the year are either desperate or predatory."

"I can't blame them for being scared after what happened to my hometown," Sandra replied. Hesitantly she said, "I'm sorry about yesterday."

"If you're referring to Tadcaster's ice golem, you did nothing wrong. I didn't recognize the staff, so I can't blame you for making the same mistake I did. If anything, Tadcaster is to blame for placing a curse on his staff. He had no business casting a destructive spell that might last beyond his death and hurt innocent people."

"How long would it take the golem to grow back its arm?"

"It wouldn't. Golems in general and ice golems in particular are temporary things, made to do a job and die in the effort. If the battle lasted much longer, or it thought we were escaping, it would have detonated the rest of its body in the hopes that the resulting shrapnel would kill us."

"Gruesome," she said. "Is the staff safe to touch now?"

Moratrayas shrugged. "Perhaps. Tadcaster may have placed several curses on the staff, and we have no way to know how many have already been triggered. Tadcaster's gear may be a threat for years to come. When I'm done helping your town, I'll have to contact someone experienced in magic to neutralize the curses. One more thing to do. I recall hearing there is a wizard in the Raushtad Mountains who is less self-serving than the rest. What was his name? Elfman, Ellitor, something like that."

"Elmore," Sandra said.

"You've heard of him? Do you know where I can find the man?" Moratrayas smiled when Sandra nodded. "Good, that will save some time in dealing with Tadcaster's last mess."

Sandra pointed to the tarp and the bulky clockwork hidden beneath it. "Next question, exactly what have you got under there?"

"Ah, that would be Gertrude!" he said excitedly. "My finest work yet. My lightning gun proved less valuable than I'd hoped. It was so heavy I couldn't move it. Gertrude is my solution to that problem. It's the largest clockwork I've ever made, a self-propelled weapon capable of firing the shells you saw with phenomenal speed and destructive power. Gertrude isn't as powerful as my old lightning gun, but makes up for it in speed and versatility. It's also developed a bit of a temper and is a force to be reckoned with even after the projectiles are fired."

"Uh huh," Sandra said. "Why did you give it a woman's name?"

"Igor won the coin toss," he admitted. "I wanted to call it the Self Mobile Assault Clockwork King. He said it was too wordy. We argued. I flipped a coin to settle it and he won. I know the name is less than ideal, but the results are impressive."

Sandra looked back at the tarp covering the giant clockwork. "But you keep it shut off and unfueled. Can't you control it?"

"Gertrude has proven more aggressive than I'd intended," Moratrayas admitted. "I had to install extra safeguards to keep it from pursuing enemies without my orders."

Igor smiled and added, "The old girl lives by three rules. Find enemies. Crush them. Find more enemies. And it's got a wide definition of the word enemy. One time there were these squirrels—"

Moratrayas stepped in front of Igor. "That regrettable incident occurred months ago. There's no point bringing it up when the farmer accepted our apology, and I'm confident it won't happen again without provocation. Ms. Sower, while Gertrude is hard to control, rest assured it will perform when needed and defeat the foes of your people."

"It sure did the job on the golem," she agreed. "How did it do that?"

"I'm glad you asked. You see..."

Sandra spent the rest of the day listening to an endless monologue by Moratrayas on clockworks, how they work, fuel fluid dynamics and the effect of magnetism on throwing very big objects. She understood less than one part in a hundred of what he said. If Moratrayas noticed her confusion, he didn't let it slow him down. He seemed eager to tell someone about the marvelous new toy he'd made, and Sandra was too polite to ask him to stop.

The following day was blissfully uneventful. Moratrayas guided the barge up a smaller river that fed into the Talum. At last they came across landmarks Sandra was familiar with. Home wasn't far away. Once they arrived, she could rejoin her people and let the heroes, wizards and other important people save her town.

The river slowed down and became shallower as it approached Sun Valley. Pine trees lined the shore, the result of her people's tree planting campaign decades ago to provide firewood and building materials. The landscape was still snowy and bleak, but Sandra's heart leapt at being back on familiar ground.

"Hello!" A person bundled in wool clothes stood on the riverbank. He, or maybe she, was waving and shouting. Moratrayas slowly brought the barge closer to the person, who called out, "Sandra, is that you?"

"Margaret! Doctor, this is my cousin, Margaret Dinsel. Margaret, hello!"

"I wonder how many other members of her family we're going to be introduced to?" Igor asked.

"All of them, I imagine," Moratrayas said in a resigned tone.

"Is this the doctor?" Margaret asked.

"Yes, he agreed to help us. Margaret, go on ahead and tell the others."

Margaret hurried off over a hill. Moratrayas followed the river and its many turns and twists, taking far longer than Margaret did on foot. With night fast approaching, they came around a steep, tree-covered hill and floated into Sun Valley.

The sight crushed Sandra's earlier enthusiasm. Sun Valley had never been large or prosperous. There were only 110 homes and as many small barns crowded together. The streets were packed dirt, without cobblestone or timber sidewalks. The fields were bare this late in the year, and the livestock were hiding in barns to keep out of the cold. Simple to the point of being crude, Sun Valley had never been a place that attracted visitors, and that was before it was attacked.

Damaged buildings in Sun Valley had been repaired as well as the women and old men could manage, but there were still noticeable signs of the raid the town had suffered. Some houses had boarded over windows, while others had fresh timber covering holes cut into walls and doors. Several homes were blackened from fires that had driven their owners into the waiting arms of their attackers. Five buildings had been reduced to charred foundations. The stone tower that once held their sunstone was little more than a heap of rocks after the attack.

The entire population of Sun Valley gathered by the river. Two hundred women, four hundred young children, and thirty old men came bundled against the cold to see the man who'd come to save them. Their reaction was muted, partly because they feared Moratrayas like Sandra used to. But there were other reasons. They were underfed, bedraggled, exhausted from hard work and worry. Sandra loved these people, knew them all by name and had grown up with them. It hurt to see them in such misery.

Wait, something was wrong. Sandra recognized *everyone* here. Where were Julius Craton and Tibolt Broadbeard? Where was Herd Leader the minotaur and Servant the holy man? If they were staying in someone's house then surely they would have come to see who'd arrived in town. Sandra felt a cold, empty feeling deep inside her as fear began to grow in her heart.

At the head of the group was an older woman who bore a strong resemblance to Sandra. Simply dressed, the grim faced woman led a boy of about twelve years who huddled close to her side. When the barge stopped, Sandra charged out and hugged the woman and boy together.

"Doctor, this is my mother, Angela Sower, and little brother Tad," she said. "Mom, this is Doctor Alberto Moratrayas. He's come to help."

Moratrayas got off the barge and walked up to Sandra's mother. The crowd backed up as he approached, but Angela stood her ground. Moratrayas shook her hand and said, "Mrs. Angela Sower, allow me to present myself and my assistant, Igor. May I assume you lead this community in the absence of your men?"

"I do," Angela replied. "Doctor, on behalf of the people of Sun Valley, I thank you for coming. I apologize for not offering a better reception."

"Apologies are unnecessary given your circumstances. May we retire indoors? I wish to discuss matters with you. My assistant can look after the barge."

Angela nodded. "Of course. If you'll follow me."

Angela and Moratrayas went into the Sower family home, a humble building that had taken a lot of damage. Sandra hurried to follow them, mindful of the doctor's temper. She didn't think her mother would do anything intentionally to drive him off, but if Sandra was around she could defuse potential problems.

Like magic, Jennet Foster appeared in the crowd and ran for the Sower home. The little vixen had been through everything Sandra had but somehow still managed to look incredible. She had long shapely legs that looked good despite her ragged clothes, and a figure that even layers of wool clothes couldn't conceal. Long blond hair blew out from under her fur hat. Like a moth to a flame, she smiled and headed straight for Moratrayas.

"Oh no you don't," Sandra whispered. Slipping through the crowd, she exchanged brief greetings with friends and neighbors as she caught up with Jennet just outside the house. Sandra grabbed Jennet by the arm and said, "Jennet, go get Julius."

Jennet stared at Sandra with those doe eyes that men kept falling for. "Who?"

"Julius Craton, the hero, the man you were supposed to bring back! Go get him so they can get started."

Jennet frowned and bit her lip. "Uh, I can't."

Struggling to keep her temper, Sandra demanded, "Why?"

"Um, cause he's not here?" Jennet had the maddening habit of making statements into questions. Sandra suspected it was because Jennet was as dumb as a bag of hammers.

"You were supposed to bring him back! Where is he?"

"I don't know," Jennet whined. "I went to the town where he was supposed to be and he wasn't there. So like, I asked around, and everybody said he used to be there but he went away to fight monkey snakes in another town, and that was like months ago? When I got there, they said he killed the monkey snakes and went somewhere else, and then somewhere else after that, and after that nobody knew where he went."

"Great. Listen, I need to talk to Moratrayas and my mom alone."

"I want to see the doctor," Jennet whined some more. God, she was annoying!

"We'll be busy for a while," Sandra told her. "Tell you what, why don't you go talk to his assistant on the barge. They've got lots of cool stuff."

Jennet smiled, no doubt because she hadn't seen Igor yet. "Okay."

Jennet ran off to the barge, and Sandra suppressed the urge to hit her once her back was turned. Sandra was about to follow her mother inside when she saw Moratrayas waiting for her at the door, one eyebrow raised. He'd heard the entire conversation.

"She stole my first boyfriend," Sandra explained.

"Ah. If you're finished protecting me from your archenemy, perhaps we can get out of the cold."

With that settled, Sandra and Moratrayas went indoors. Her house was in a little better shape than when she'd left weeks earlier. Smashed windows were boarded up, and there were old pieces of furniture taken out of storage to replace what had been destroyed in the attack. Her brother Tad stood quietly in a corner along with both Sandra's younger sisters. Sandra quickly introduced Moratrayas to her siblings and took a seat to his right.

Moratrayas sat at the table opposite Angela Sower. Without preamble, he asked, "How many people did you go to for help?"

"Including you, eleven," Angela replied. The strain was evident on her face, and Sandra saw wrinkles she was sure hadn't been there four weeks earlier. "When no kingdom would help us, we sent messengers to eleven men and women known for their bravery, their abilities and their willingness to help those who have no one else to turn to. I hoped they might save us when our neighbors would not."

"How many came?"

"So far only you. Some could not be found, like Julius Craton."

Moratrayas leaned back in his chair. "That's the problem with heroes, the demand always exceeds the supply."

"So it seems," Angela said. "We found Tibolt Broadbeard in bed with two broken legs. Weeks earlier he'd saved a caravan from a rogue stone golem and paid the price for it. The wizard Elmore had left for a magician's conference days before our messenger arrived and won't return for weeks. As for the others, we don't know. The women I sent to them haven't returned."

"Nor will they." Moratrayas pointed at Sandra and explained, "Your daughter was pursued by five armed men she identified as being part of the attack on your town. They were desperate to stop her, and nearly succeeded. We must assume an attempt was made to intercept the rest of your messengers as well."

"Maybe they were slowed down by bad weather," Sandra suggested.

"Possible, but if the enemy knew Sandra was coming to me then it's likely they knew about the others you sought aid from." Moratrayas tapped his cane on his palm. "Whether your messengers were caught or delayed, I fear I must start without them. It's clear our enemy expects us, and giving them more time is a mistake."

"You can find the fiends who did this to us?" Angela asked.

"Definitely. Your daughter has already provided me with a detailed description of what happened to your town. I believe I know who is responsible and I can leave early tomorrow. But first, Sandra told me you lost most of the town's food supply."

"Half our food and all our money," Angela replied. "We're getting by on half rations. I sent women to plead for help from other towns, but our neighbors say that while they feel sorry for us, sorry only goes so far."

"Indeed, silver goes farther." Moratrayas took a leather pouch from his pockets and handed it to Angela. "This should buy enough food to support your people until spring. In addition, I have four tons of food on my barge. Igor will assist you in unloading it."

Angela's expression softened. "Thank you. This helps us greatly."

"You asked me to save you. I take that responsibility seriously."

"Is there anything we can do to help?" Angela asked.

"I need more information," he told her. "Have there been more attacks against this town or neighboring ones since Sandra left to find me?"

"Not against us or anyone living nearby, but we only receive news from a few communities," Angela replied. "We're cut off from the world here in Sun Valley, partly by the mountains and partly by choice. We didn't want strangers coming who might see our sunstone and try to steal it. If anything happens farther than a week's journey from here, it's unlikely we'll ever hear about it."

"I understand," he said. "I must also ask a favor from you. I'll need Sandra's help in this mission."

Angela and Sandra simultaneously demanded, "Why?"

"I'm trying to save hundreds of men I've never met. I won't be able to identify them, while Sandra can. Your men won't know me, either, or if they do only by my less than stellar reputation. They won't trust me, but they will recognize and listen to Sandra. Lastly, you daughter has proven herself capable in dangerous situations, and has asked me an enormous number of questions. If I took another person from Sun Valley, they might not be as capable and I'd have to answer the same questions again."

Angela looked at her daughter. She'd just gotten Sandra back from a dangerous journey, and she was being asked to send her on another. However much it pained her, Angela said, "You've already risked so much for our town. I'm sorry, Sandra, but I have to ask for more."

Sandra hesitated. She would be going into the land of the people who'd ravaged her town. She'd already come close to death more times than she wanted to remember. This was a job for heroes and wizards, not a farm girl! But Moratrayas had a point. He needed help to save her people. In the end, what choice was there?

"I'll go."

Angela took Sandra's hands and gripped them tightly. "Thank you. Help him in any way you can. Doctor, I'm entrusting you with her safety. If you wish you may spend the night here before leaving."

"Thank you, but no," Moratrayas said. He stood up and shook Angela's hand again. "There are things I need to check on my barge before I leave tomorrow. Don't fear for your daughter's wellbeing. I will return with her or not at all."

Moratrayas bowed at the waist and then left. Sandra hugged her mother and followed him into the cold night. When she caught up with him, he said, "You didn't tell me you summoned other helpers."

"I was worried," she confessed. "Finding them was so difficult we might not reach them, and I didn't know how many would agree to come. I thought we'd get a few of them and together you could save us. And I thought, well, maybe if you knew we were asking lots of people for help, you'd figure one of them could do it."

Moratrayas kept walking, showing none of his fiery temper. "Given that only I arrived, I suppose the situation is no different than what you described when we first met. I can't be angry with you. In your place I'd have made the same decision. I must admit I would've enjoyed meeting a few of the other notable people in the region. It would have been...interesting."

"Thank you."

"Your mother is a formidable woman," he said. "She's made good decisions and difficult ones without flinching from what had to be done. Your town did well to put her in charge."

"Maybe, but she wishes they didn't. She cried before she sent me to find you. All the bad things that could have happened scared her. She'll be happy when everything's back to normal."

"That's the way with leadership," he told her as they walked back to the barge. "The best leaders don't want the job."

The town was a flurry of activity. Igor was already unloading food off the barge with the help of an old man and twenty women. They were dividing the food into bundles of equal size and passing them out one to a family. The women and children were happier now, and much of their fear had melted away.

One woman wasn't happy at all. Red faced and so angry she was baring her teeth, Jennet Foster marched up to Sandra. Jennet pointed an accusing finger at Igor before saying, "*That's* who you wanted me to meet?"

"I thought you'd be perfect for each other," Sandra said innocently.

Igor sneaked up behind Jennet and wrapped an arm around her slender waist. "Where are you going? I was about to show you my collection of teeth."

Jennet screamed and ran off. Igor called after her, "Don't be like that. They're other people's teeth!"

Sandra helped divide and deliver food the rest of the night. She managed to slip away and personally give food to her family. Her siblings ran over and hugged her when she came in alone.

"Help me with this." Sandra passed bags of food to the children. "Let's see, we've got dried beans, dried peas and thirty pounds of flour. Tad, you take that one. There's a jar of cooking oil and some salted bacon. There you go, that should last you for a while."

Her mother hugged Sandra next. "I'm sorry, dear. It's not fair what I've made you do. I wanted to keep you here with me, but I couldn't ask other women to send their daughters for help if I spared my own the danger. And now I've done it again. I pray one day you'll forgive me."

"It's okay," Sandra said softly. "It worked out all right. I know why you told me not to leave home before now. It's awful out there. There are monsters and bad magic and worse kings."

"Before you were born, your father and I traveled for three months looking for land we could settle and start a family where it wasn't so crowded. We almost died four times and finally decided to come back." Angela sat down. "Tell me, is Moratrayas the monster rumors say he is?"

"He's not. Mom, I think he wants to be a good man, but he's messed up. He does good things and he wants everybody to be safe and happy. I think with someone to help him stay on the right course, he'll be a good leader and make things a lot better."

Angela looked out the window at her people, happy for the first time in weeks. "Any other time I'd be glad to hear that. Lord knows there are enough bad men in the world that I should be grateful one of them is actually good. But as much as it hurts me to say this, we don't need a good man. We need someone as ruthless as the stories say. We need someone so terrible that he'll crush the men that did this to us and make sure they never do it again. God forgive me for saying this, but we need a monster on our side."

Sandra hugged her mother again. "I should sleep on the barge in case he leaves before dawn. Don't worry, mom. We won't let you down."

Sandra went back and slept comfortably under a pile of blankets on the barge. It was less cramped with so many supplies offloaded, and she could stretch out and sleep soundly.

Moratrayas spent the evening double checking his creations with Igor's help. Before he went to sleep, he looked down at Sandra. "There's something I don't understand about what happened here."

Igor kept his hands busy mending a clockwork spider as big as a grapefruit. "What's that?"

"Stoth Voluk had his men attack this town and seize their sunstone. That makes perfect sense for a thief like him. He'd take anything if he thought he could get away with it, and a sunstone so large and bright would be worth a king's ransom. But Stone Heart has more people than it can feed. Why take Sun Valley's men?"

"It's a puzzle," Igor agreed.

"If he plans on selling them into slavery, the mountain passes and rivers are too dangerous this time of year to take them to the nearest kingdom engaged in that despicable trade. More than that, why take only the men?" He looked down at Sandra again. "If I were the sort of man who'd attack a defenseless town—"

"Which you aren't," Igor said.

"And I was taking prisoners, then, err, I would be, um, inclined to take everyone, especially the women. You met Ms. Foster earlier."

Igor stopped working and smiled broadly. "Sure did. What a looker!"

"Err, yes, well, were I in their place, I doubt I'd leave her behind."

"Or Sandra," Igor said, and nudged Moratrayas in the ribs.

"Um, no." Eager to change the subject, he said, "The men would also be far stronger and more likely to rebel. Why take only the people best able to resist? If they took their families they could use them as hostages, but without them the men would have every reason to fight back. I'd give my eyeteeth to know what Stoth is doing."

Igor took a pouch from his belt and handed it to the doctor. "You want eyeteeth, I got plenty. Better yet, when we get to Stone Heart, take Stoth's eyeteeth, and a couple molars while you're at it."

Moratrayas stared hard at the pouch. "That is a most disturbing hobby."

"Not really. I find most of them at dentist offices and barroom floors after a good brawl."

Moratrayas, Sandra and Igor left the next morning so early that the people of Sun Valley were still asleep. They needed the extra time because a winter storm developed during the night, and by morning dropped an inch of snow an hour. The storm lasted the entire day and slowed their progress to a snail's pace. Moratrayas couldn't see far enough ahead to avoid obstacles in the river and had to keep the barge moving slowly. The only mercy was that weather this bad kept monsters in their lairs.

The next day proved little better. The river narrowed and the current sped up. Moratrayas worked hard to keep the barge moving slowly enough that it didn't hit an obstacle in the river, forcing the clockwork engine that drove it to spend an enormous amount of fuel. The river wound between high cliffs, and rushing water kept trying to slam the barge against the rocks.

On the third day, the weather cleared and the river let up its fury. The cliffs gave way to rolling hills thick with pine trees. At noon they saw the first person to cross their path in days, a broad shouldered dwarf in shabby clothes. He was fishing on the bank, but when he saw them he put down his fishing pole and waved his arms. "Hey! Hey, you!"

Moratrayas reached under the tarp and brought out a short rod with a mesh box on one end and a wire on the other that led back under the tarp. He spoke into the mesh box, and something under the tarp magnified his voice to a roar. "Yes?"

The dwarf stumbled back, surprised by the strength of Moratrayas' voice. He got back up and shouted, "There's a split in the river up ahead! Go left!"

"Why not right?"

"That way leads to Stone Heart," the dwarf explained. "A merchant I worked for went that way and was robbed of everything but his clothes, beaten up and thrown in the dungeon. I barely got away."

"Thank you for the warning," Moratrayas said. He put the strange devise back under the tarp and continued down the river. "I can't believe Stoth is robbing merchants. Once word gets out what he's done, no merchant will come here again, and he'll never keep his people fed without someone bringing in supplies."

"Maybe he's robbing merchants as well as towns," Sandra suggested.

Moratrayas frowned. "He's greedy, but he's not stupid. Something is going on in Stone Heart that he can't let anyone know about, something he's so desperate to hide that he'd risk alienating merchants he needs."

Moratrayas stopped the barge that night by a bend in the river. Tall pines hid the barge from sight, and the ground was too rough to support farms. Igor anchored the barge and they ventured onto land carrying a pile of equipment.

"Ms. Sower, welcome to Stone Heart," Moratrayas said. "The land is every bit as inhospitable as it looks, and as hard as it is to believe, the people are worse. We should be safe from detection this far from the capital and settlements, but remain alert."

"What do we do now that we're here?" she asked.

"Gather information." They came out of the woods and onto a steep hill blown clean of snow. Moratrayas unpacked his equipment and took out a clockwork dragonfly two feet long. He poured a small dose of green fuel into the clockwork's mouth, bringing it to life. "This is one of my older creations, a scout that records what it sees."

Sandra marveled at the giant dragonfly. It was made of brass and obsidian, like all the doctor's creations, but this one was a work of art. It had large turquoise blue eyes and six legs folded up under its body. The wings were hard as steel, but thin and clear like glass. The body and wings were etched with fine lines to form graceful patterns. She picked it up and cradled it in her hands. "Oh, it's beautiful!"

Moratrayas took it back. "Don't let it hear you say that! This clockwork is particularly willful and already has a swollen head without your praise."

"I still think it's pretty. Why can't all your clockworks look so nice?"

The dragonfly flapped its wings and buzzed out of Moratrayas' hands to land on Sandra's shoulders. Annoyed, Moratrayas plucked it off and pressed buttons hidden on its tail. He threw the clockwork into the cold night air and watched it fly off as fast as a hawk.

"It shouldn't take it long to survey the settled parts of the kingdom and return," Moratrayas told her.

"Then what?"

"Then, Ms. Sower, we develop a plan. I doubt my winged creation will find your missing sunstone, but hiding captured men is a harder task. Saving them takes top priority. After that we try to recover the sunstone, and if the opportunity presents itself we do as much damage to Stoth Voluk and his army as possible."

"I don't want to hurt innocent people," Sandra told him. "I know you're angry with them, but please, we have to make this between us and Stoth's army, not everyone living here."

"That may not be possible," he cautioned. "I'll do what I can to limit damage to civilians. They were once my people, after all, and despite their betrayal I don't want them dead any more than you do. But we may find ourselves in a position where we need to do a great deal of damage to free your men, and some of that is bound to spill over on bystanders. I can't promise you a war without tears."

"We might be able to get some of our old stuff back from Stoth," Igor said.

Moratrayas frowned. "That's the lowest possible priority. I've written off what we used to have here, and so should you."

"Even your sunstone?" Igor pressed. "Or that really cool dolphin statue?"

"Blast it, man, why must you tempt me?"

The dragonfly clockwork was back in an hour. Moratrayas tried to catch it as it landed, but the dragonfly veered off and set down in Sandra's hands. Giggling, she handed it back to him. Moratrayas hooked it up with wires to a rounded glass panel edged with brass. The panel lit up and a grainy gray storm danced across it.

"Come on, show me what you saw," Moratrayas urged. Instead of a picture, the screen displayed the words, '*low fuel*'. "Don't give me that! I gave you a full tank before you left."

The words '*low fuel*' flashed on the screen again. Grumbling, Moratrayas took a bottle of green fuel and dribbled more into the dragonfly's mouth. When he tried to take it away, the dragonfly grabbed the container. A new message appeared on the screen, '*leave the bottle*.'

"I'll do no such thing!" Moratrayas thundered. "You'll show me everything you saw and you'll do it now, or I'll break you up for parts!"

The dragonfly hissed at him, but relented and followed instructions. The glass panel lit up and formed a fuzzy gray picture of when Moratrayas threw the dragonfly into the air. There was no sound, but Sandra still watched it with rapt attention, amazed as the panel showed everything the clockwork saw from its own eyes. It flew over pine trees and rock outcroppings, passing log houses with smoke coming from their chimneys.

"Ha!" Moratrayas exclaimed. "Blasted wizards think they're so special with their magic mirrors. Whatever they can do with magic, I can do with science."

The panel continued to show the dragonfly's journey. It flew over a small cluster of houses with sheep pens, roads clear of travelers and granite quarries empty for the night. More hills went by, and barren farmland long since stripped of anything edible. The dragonfly flew higher until it came upon the bustle and bright lights of the capital city Scour.

The walled and gated city was a beehive of activity even this late at night. People filled the cobblestone streets. The castle in the center of Scour looked exactly the way Sandra pictured a castle, with tall towers and bright lights. On every street corner hung banners with an armored fist over a starburst. The castle was just as active, swarming with hordes of people crowded around a podium decorated with more banners.

An appalling number of the people were soldiers, easily one in three. The dragonfly's picture was grainy and in shades of gray, but it was clear the men wore chain armor and carried shields, spears and swords. They marched through the city, lined the castle walls and stood guard at the podium where someone gave a speech to cheering people.

Moratrayas pointed at the man on the screen. "Say hello to Stoth Voluk, usurper of my homeland."

The view changed as the clockwork flew on. Outside the city were two camps, both fenced and guarded. In one camp were thousands of armed men. They wore chain armor, but had crossbows, swords, shields and battleaxes. More people cooked, cleaned and entertained these men. The second camp contained crude buildings guarded by dogs and men with swords. Here the fences had sharpened tops, and the doors to the buildings were barred from the outside.

The dragonfly flew over the city again. It hovered over a town square filled with empty wagons, and near them were huge numbers of siege weapons in neat rows. There were catapults, ballista and battering rams covered by frames with stone tiled roofs. Not far away, blacksmiths' forges coughed up clouds of black smoke, and men carried out swords by the dozen.

"What is this?" Moratrayas asked. "This isn't right at all."

A large river flowed by the city. Sandra spotted the ten barges used in the attack on Sun Valley. They were moored to a dock, along with thirty more vessels identical in size and design. Next to the river was a dry dock containing four more barges under construction. It was a formidable fleet for the small kingdoms in the Raushtad.

"This isn't a city," Igor protested. "It's an army base."

"There must be ten thousand soldiers, maybe more," Sandra whispered. "And all those boats and weapons."

Moratrayas stared at the images in horror. "Voluk, what have you done?"

# Chapter 7

The next morning was bright and warm, a terrible contrast to Sandra's situation. The men of Sun Valley weren't held captive by a thousand soldiers. Their enemies numbered many times that, and they had siege weapons, a fleet of river barges and an armory brimming with weapons. However marvelous the doctor's creations were, what could they do against such odds?

They'd spent the night back on the doctor's barge, and at first light Moratrayas led them through a dense pine forest. Igor brought along a box of equipment and Sandra carried a brass telescope.

Moratrayas was silent during the trip. He hadn't spoken much since last night, too shocked by the transformation of his homeland into an armed aggressor. He led them through the forest to a high hill overlooking Scour and its castle. There he took the telescope and mounted it on a tripod. He studied the city while Sandra and Igor kept watch.

"What are you looking for?" Sandra asked.

"Your people. One of the camps outside the city is built to hold prisoners or slaves. I need to know how many soldiers guard it, when they change shifts and if possible how many men are held there. Stoth could have raided other towns, and we may have to rescue people besides your own."

He adjusted the telescope and waved her over. "Look in here and tell me if you recognize anyone."

Sandra peered in the telescope's eyepiece and saw poorly dressed men lined up in front of the camp. They were chained together and carried picks or shovels. A few men had axes and saws instead. Soldiers with swords and crossbows guarded them, and snarling dogs on long leashes barked at them.

"Those are the men from Sun Valley," she told him. "There's my dad, my brother, my cousin, my neighbors, everybody. I recognize all the men there. If they kidnapped people from another town, they're not here."

Sandra's people were marched to distant hills covered with tree stumps and farther on pine trees. Men with axes and saws were put to work cutting down trees, while those with shovels and picks began the difficult task of removing stumps. They moved slowly, and were prodded by soldiers whenever they tried to rest.

"What are they doing?" Sandra demanded. "This isn't the time of year to take out stumps. The ground is frozen as hard as rock. It's twice as much work now than it would be in springtime."

"That's the point," Moratrayas told her. "You saw all those soldiers last night. With so many men under arms, there aren't enough people left to work. For the first time in its history, I believe Stone Heart has a labor shortage. They took your men to do their work for them. But it takes time to make free men into slaves."

Sandra looked up. "What do you mean?"

Moratrayas looked through the telescope. "You were right when you said it's harder work now than in spring. The point of this abuse isn't to get work done, but to break the men's will. Day after day of backbreaking labor, not enough food, not enough sleep, constant abuse, and sooner or later they'll be too exhausted to resist. Eventually they'll give up hope and do as they're told without trying to escape. Any work done during the process is a bonus."

"My dad and brother are down there," she lamented.

Igor patted her on the arm. "Not for long."

Moratrayas took the telescope and studied the other camp outside the city. He gestured for Sandra and then Igor to look at it. "This offers both risk and opportunity. I recognize these men by their reputation. They're the Blue Sashes mercenaries."

Sandra looked in the eyepiece and saw armed men wearing blue sashes across their chests. "How original," she said sarcastically.

"They aren't known for their creativity," Moratrayas replied. "They're known for hard fighting and hard drinking. In ten years no army that's hired the Blue Sashes has lost a war. Dealing with them will be a problem. They're experienced, heavily armed and well led. The last I heard, their price was a silver coin per man per week plus provisions, and they're worth it."

"I see at least three thousand mercenaries," Sandra said before letting Igor use the telescope. "They must be costing Stoth a fortune."

"Who are those people with them?" Igor asked. The Blue Sashes camp was evenly split between mercenaries and noncombatant men and women.

"Camp followers," Moratrayas explained. "They cook and clean for the Blue Sashes, mend their clothes, sharpen their weapons, and handle pack animals. Some of the women are, err, good friends with the officers."

Sandra rolled her eyes. "Oh come on. They bring their girlfriends with them when they fight?"

Igor and Moratrayas exchanged glances. Clearly Sandra's life was even more sheltered than they'd thought. Moratrayas replied, "That's not quite what I meant. But I digress. If you look carefully, you'll see that the soldiers and townspeople avoid the Blue Sashes camp. Whether this is by order or because they simply don't like them is beside the point. They don't know those people well. With a little work we can disguise ourselves and sneak in pretending to be with the Blue Sashes, and there should be few questions."

Igor looked in the eyepiece and added, "I see camp followers going into the city. Maybe they're buying food and whatnots."

"Good." Moratrayas opened the box Igor had brought. He took out clothes and jars of makeup. "I can't disguise Igor's hunch, so he'll have to stay here and continue observations. Ms. Sower, you and I will explore the city and see what we can discover."

Sandra waved him off. "Hold on a minute. Disguise or no, you can't just walk in there. These people grew up with you! A change of clothes won't fool them. For that matter, a lot of soldiers saw me when they attacked Sun Valley. We'll be caught before we even get to the city gates."

Smiling, Moratrayas took wigs, fake beards and a bottle of hair dye from the box. "When I'm done your own mother won't recognize you. Ms. Sower, have you ever wondered what it would be like to have blond hair?"

Two hours later Sandra studied herself in a small hand mirror. The doctor was right, for her mother wouldn't recognize her now. She didn't recognize herself!

Sandra's hair was dyed blond and tied back in a ponytail. She wore a blue and silver dress that, while warm enough, struck her as altogether too impractical. The material was lightweight, the skirt too tight and too short, and the design needlessly elaborate. The outfit came with a silver necklace set with faceted garnets, two silver rings and a copper bracelet. There were also silver earrings, but Sandra left them behind since she didn't have pierced ears. Rounding out her gaudy attire were boots that came up to her knees and a purse made of fine linen containing a few coins. The cover story Moratrayas had her memorize was no less irritating. As if she'd date a mercenary!

"You're kidding," she said.

"Not at all." The doctor was even more unrecognizable than Sandra. His goggles were gone, which automatically made him look strange. He wore workmen's clothes made from sailcloth, sturdy and well worn. He had a beard and long gray hair courtesy of a fake beard and wig. A fake scar ran from his right eye to his chin. To complete the disguise, he carried a bag of blacksmith's tools, a leather apron slung over his shoulder and thick leather gloves in one pocket. Sandra would have felt more comfortable if she was wearing his disguise. "Does the dress pinch anywhere?"

"It fits. I just feel ridiculous! Where did you even get a dress like this?"

"I made it before we left my castle. I felt we should both have disguises ready."

Her eyes narrowed. "You hate tailoring! You said so yourself."

"I said I hate it. I never said I was bad at it." He took her hand and led her behind a hill. "I have other outfits for you, but this one is best suited for the situation. We can get in close without anyone seeing us. Once we're near the Blue Sashes camp, we'll head to the city gates and go in."

"And then what?"

"We listen," he told her. "People say a lot without thinking, especially when they feel safe. We will walk around the city and eavesdrop on conversations. I'll also be on the lookout for new construction and buildings that have been renovated, places where our enemies may be storing weapons, valuables and important equipment we need to destroy."

They ducked behind a hill and came closer to Scour. The city gates were wide open, allowing farmers, craftsmen, soldiers and mercenaries to enter and leave at will. Moratrayas scoffed. "Their security is ridiculous! There should be a pass system and soldiers checking incoming packages and wagons. I know they don't expect enemies to come in winter, but this is sloppy."

"It works in our favor," she reminded him. "Do you think you'll find friends in Scour who can help us?"

Moratrayas' expression hardened. "They turned away from me when I offered them everything. I doubt anyone will feel like changing sides now that I have little to give and oppose a powerful army. It's unlikely we'll find a person with a serious enough grievance against Stoth to turn traitor."

The soldiers at the gate looked at them only briefly before waving them in like everyone else. Moratrayas nodded to them and Sandra smiled. She didn't like the way the soldiers watched her.

Inside the city was a veritable sea of people. The narrow streets were choked with men, women, children and the occasional pack animal such as donkeys and oxen pulling carts. Without exception the crowd was human. The people were simply dressed, loud, smelly and rude. Men and women got through the crowds by pushing. This led to arguments, but no fights broke out. Sandra guessed it was because there were so many soldiers guarding buildings, marching through the streets or conducting business. No one wanted to start a fistfight when men with cold steel were close at hand.

The city itself was nothing to write home about. The buildings were constructed from wood or quarried bricks, poorly built and not nice to look at. Most houses and shops were two stories tall and very narrow. Every house flew the armored fist and sunburst banner, and some flew flags with the same images. The streets were paved with cobblestone and slick from homeowners dumping chamber pots onto the street. There were also generous helpings of dung left by pack animals. Needless to say it smelled terrible and could only get worse in warm weather.

Moratrayas pointed to an outdoor café with tables and few patrons. "We'll meet back here in an hour. Remember, listen more than you talk."

With that Moratrayas disappeared into the packed crowd, slipping between people instead of pushing them aside. Sandra followed his example and headed for a marketplace.

Sandra picked her way through several outdoor markets. Most of the shops and peddlers carts had little to offer. There were preserved foods like dried apples, sauerkraut, smoked meat and the like. A few peddlers had fresh fish from the river and bread right out of the oven. Some stalls sold metal tools like knives and shovels. Customers haggled over prices, and with good reason! The cost for everything was higher than Sandra could imagine.

"A copper coin for an apple?" a man snarled at a shopkeeper. "Do you take me for a fool?"

The shopkeeper matched his customer's voice in both volume and venomous reply. "If you think you can get them cheaper somewhere else then go ahead and try, you stinking miser! At least I won't have to look at that pug ugly face of yours anymore."

"Can you believe these prices?" a woman complained to another. "It's a full time job trying to keep my family fed."

The other woman smiled. "A few more months and it'll be no problem. We'll be a proper kingdom."

Sandra desperately wanted to know what the woman meant by that, but Moratrayas' warning kept her from asking. A woman going shopping brought little suspicion, while one asking about what should be common knowledge to the locals would draw attention. Instead Sandra kept moving, following people and listening to what they said.

"I couldn't be prouder of my boy," an older man bragged.

A storekeeper smiled back. "He made officer, then?"

"Lieutenant of the royal lancers, first company," the old man beamed. "It's only been nine months since he enlisted, and he's giving orders!"

The shopkeeper laughed and slapped the old man on the back. "Congratulations! I knew he had it in him."

Sandra filed this away for later. She tried to keep an eye on the crowd and see if anyone noticed what she was doing. A few men watched her with leers on their faces. She didn't worry about them. Soldiers watched her, their expressions betraying jealousy. One deliberately stepped in her way and folded his arms across his chest.

"You're one of the Blue Sashes' women. Why are you here?"

Sandra smiled. "I'm doing a little shopping."

The soldier snorted. "Your man couldn't think of anything better to do with you than send you out for lunch?" Leering, he said, "I could show you around town, show you some things your man never could."

"I don't think that's a good idea," she said demurely. "He's the jealous sort, and he'd find out. I don't think he'd like it, and I know I wouldn't."

Before he could reply, she slipped around him and fled into the crowd. The soldier fumed and his face turned red, but he didn't follower her. Moratrayas had said the Blue Sashes had a reputation. It looked like it was enough to scare off local toughs.

What surprised her the most about these people was how ordinary they were. She expected them to be ugly, to have warts and scars, hooks for hands, dragon tattoos and wear black clothes. Instead they looked normal, talked normal. They were more obnoxious than the people of Sun Valley, but if you planted one in her town they'd look no different than the locals. It would almost be better if they were monstrous or disfigured.

She wanted to scream at them! They'd taken her neighbors and family members and were working them like oxen. It couldn't be a secret when they were penned up right outside the capital. How could these people go on chatting and haggling as if nothing was wrong when their kingdom had done something so terrible? It took all her willpower not to grab the nearest man by the shirt and shake him, try to wake him up to what was happening. Instead she kept moving, kept listening.

She managed to find two Blue Sashes wandering the marketplace. The men were impressive in a rough sort of way. Powerfully built and tall, they were poorly shaven and had plenty of scars. They looked fierce in their armor and were equipped with swords, shields and daggers. Locals were polite but kept their distance, and the crowd made room for them as they walked. The mercenaries checked stalls selling alcohol, but left empty handed.

"You believe this?" one mercenary asked the second. Sandra pretended to study a cart selling food while she listened. "One tankard of beer can't cost this much!"

"Not much to buy even if we had the money," the second groused. "If we don't ship out soon, we'll drink this city dry."

The first mercenary snorted derisively. "If we can afford it! My pockets are as empty as a beggar's stomach. They're barely keeping us in food and giving us nothing to drink but water. Five weeks we've been here and not a single coin to show for it! I don't care what they promised the general, either we get paid soon or we should try our luck somewhere else."

The mercenaries walked on. Once they left, a peddler said, "Good riddance. I'm glad we'll only need them for a little while."

A neighboring peddler put a hand on his shoulder. "Keep it to yourself. Other people are listening."

The peddlers glanced at Sandra and scowled. She was going to leave, but stopped when an old woman manning a cart grabbed her by the wrist. "You've been standing in front of my cart for five minutes doing nothing! You're keeping real customers away. What's the matter, you hothouse rose? My food not good enough for you?"

Startled, Sandra opened her mouth and tried to come up with something to say. She'd been so busy listening to the mercenaries she hadn't even looked at the goods for sale. A quick glance showed it was mostly pickled fish and hardboiled eggs. The food had an odor so foul she could smell it even over the street's sewer stench. Sandra's peasant upbringing made her hate the idea of food going to waste, but this slop gave her pause. There were tags listing prices. One look at those made her jaw drop.

"You're charging a copper piece for three eggs? If you're worried I'm keeping customers away, don't be. You're doing that on your own."

The old woman's eyes narrowed and her grip on Sandra's wrist hardened. "That's a good price, taxes being what they are. Who are you, anyway? Never seen you before."

Oops. Sandra was attracting attention. More people looked at her and the old woman. Sandra had to end this without arousing their suspicion. Fortunately she was strong from hard work and had no trouble breaking free of the old woman's grip.

"I'm with the Blue Sashes. My boyfriend is an officer."

Sandra hoped the lie would shut up the woman like it had the soldier. No such luck. Pouting, the old woman demanded, "Then what are you complaining about prices for? We pay a mountain of gold in taxes each month to pay for your men. You ought to be swimming in cash."

Peddlers and bystanders chorused in agreement. Remembering what she'd heard the mercenaries say earlier, she replied, "You may be paying it, but they're not getting it yet, and if my man doesn't get paid then he hasn't got anything to give me. What he does have goes for liquor."

The old woman's expression softened. "Ha, typical. Men are the same no matter what they do. Their women always come last."

Women in the crowd nodded and laughed. The men scowled and went about their business, not willing to admit anything of the sort.

The old woman seemed convinced by the disguise, which gave Sandra the confidence to ask a question. Moratrayas believed he had no friends here, but it was possible he was letting his anger blind him. Asking the old woman wouldn't make her suspicious since she already believed Sandra wasn't a local.

"I heard a doctor used to rule here," Sandra said.

The old woman scowled and scrunched up her face like she'd bitten into a lemon. "Oh, that fool. Yes, there was a tailor who overthrew our old king. Mad as a hatter, that one. Our new king drove him off, and good riddance! We don't take orders from a tailor."

Nods and mummers of agreement followed from everyone in the crowd, proving the doctor was right. Sandra tried to make a quick exit and pick up gossip elsewhere. Before she left, the old woman grabbed her sleeve and asked, "Hey, your man, what's he like?"

Thinking fast, she said, "He's great when he's sober."

Sandra disappeared into the crowd. She didn't hear more interesting conversations, but people repeated things she'd already heard. Prices were high, taxes were high and a lot of men were soldiering. In spite of their hardships, the locals expected good times to come. Sandra headed back to the café by the gate and sat at a table until Moratrayas returned.

He didn't keep her waiting. Ten minutes later he sat next to her and set down his bag of tools on the table. He also brought a loaf of bread and a block of cheese. Softly, he asked, "Did you have any problems?"

"Nothing serious." She told him what she'd heard and kept an eye on their surroundings. Moratrayas seemed mildly interested until she mentioned that the Blue Sashes hadn't been paid yet.

"That is surprising," he murmured. "Military campaigns are conducted in the summer and autumn when travel is easier and food is plentiful. Most mercenaries wait out the winter and live off their wages. Could that be what they're doing?"

"A peddler said they needed them, just not for long. That doesn't make sense if they're waiting for spring."

He studied the crowd before answering. "No, it doesn't. They're here for a reason. Stoth built a large army and did it quickly. A newly enlisted soldier promoted to lieutenant in nine months is far too fast. These men are well armed and numerous, but they're not experienced soldiers. The Blue Sashes may be here to toughen up Stoth's army when he goes on the offensive."

"But who is he after?"

"If I'm right, everyone." A soldier came too close, and Moratrayas fell silent. Once the soldier moved on, he said, "Most kingdoms in the Raushtad have a few hundred soldiers, at most a thousand. This army is far larger than it needs to be to attack their nearest neighbor. With so many soldiers and siege engines, he could take on half the kingdoms in the Raushtad and win. Stoth already took one kingdom. It appears he wants more."

Sandra tried to imagine what a war that big would be like. Stoth's soldiers treated her people brutally, and she had no reason to think they'd be merciful the next time they went on the march. But this time they wouldn't be terrorizing nine hundred frightened farmers. They'd be attacking kingdoms with ten or twenty thousand people. Those men and women were no different from Sandra's kin, and they'd be robbed and enslaved.

"There's more," Moratrayas told her. "I checked the forges before soldiers made me leave. Stoth's blacksmiths are making weapons and armor as fast as they can. There's an armory filled to capacity, enough to equip another thousand soldiers, and they're still making more. Don't ask me where Stoth expects to get the men, but he's going to make his army even bigger. He also has warehouses filled with animal fodder and rations."

Moratrayas tore the loaf of bread in half and handed her a piece. Between mouthfuls, he said, "There's one thing that bothers me. Stoth has made preparations for war, but there's no way he can reach another kingdom this late in the year. Even those river barges can't carry more than two thousand men. Add in the equipment and food they'll need and it becomes impossible. He can't march until the mountain passes melt clear in spring, but by all appearances he's set to go this minute."

Moratrayas looked up and saw Sandra hadn't touched her food. "Go on, eat. You need your strength, and the day's not over yet."

"I can't, not after what I saw. My father, brother and so many friends are being kept like dogs in a kennel, and these, these people who did it to them, they're happy. They're proud of themselves." She looked down at the bread. "How can I eat when everyone I love is being treated like that?"

"You do it because you have to," he replied softly. "The only chance they have is us, and if you're weak from hunger or worry that makes saving them harder. Eat. Keep up your strength for them."

Sandra picked at her food. It wasn't much to begin with, bland and burned around the edges. Her bad mood made it seem worse. "I never left Sun Valley until we were attacked. We did business with traveling merchants and stayed at home where it was safe. I keep thinking if we'd traveled more maybe we would have come here and seen them building their army."

"It wouldn't have helped if you did see their army," he said. "You couldn't know where they were going to attack. Even if you did, what could you have done to stop them? Your people couldn't have fought off an army this big even if they'd known they were coming, no more than I did when Stoth came for me. Your only hope would have been to flee. Sandra, what happened isn't your fault."

She ate quietly. When she reached for the cheese, Moratrayas stopped her. "Not that. We'll need it for tonight."

"Why?"

He smiled. "I don't want to spoil the surprise. Come, let us leave this wretched place and see what Igor has learned."

They grabbed their belongings and headed for the city gate. Before they reached it, they saw people hurrying out of the way. Moratrayas pulled Sandra into an alley moments before ten Blue Sashes mercenaries marched into town. They followed a man in magnificent plate armor polished so it shined like a jewel. The man carried his helmet instead of wearing it, displaying his scarred face and shaven head. His scowl made him look even more intimidating.

"Who's that?" Sandra asked.

Moratrayas frowned. "General Addaxes Thane, leader of the Blue Sashes. He is a man to be feared."

Sandra could only imagine how terrible Thane must be if a mad scientist like Moratrayas was afraid of him. "He doesn't look happy."

"No, and I think someone's going to feel his wrath rather shortly."

Thane marched through the city, his men keeping the rabble at a respectable distance. They didn't have to work hard, for Thane's scowl was enough to get soldiers and civilians out of his way. Stoth's soldiers cast jealous glances at his fine equipment. As far as Thane was concerned, they were as beneath his notice as the merchants and farmers scurrying to avoid him.

Soldiers guarding the castle gate stood at attention when they saw him. Slackers. He saw them flirting with local women when he was three blocks away. If they were serving under him, he'd have them whipped and knocked down a pay grade for being that sloppy. It was inefficient and unobservant men like that who lost wars.

"General Thane, you're not expected," one of the soldiers said when he approached. That translated to 'we didn't send for you, so go away.' The fools didn't even salute him, a general! None of these farmers in armor saluted, a show of disrespect he found irritating. Doing his best to ignore the insult, Thane marched up to the soldier before speaking.

"Announce me to the King."

"His Majesty—"

"Announce me and grant me entrance within the next five minutes, or I go in, by force if need be, and give my report to the King. The first option involves less bloodshed."

The soldiers gulped. One hurried away and returned two minutes later. "His Majesty will see you. If you'll come with me?"

Thane marched into the castle, leaving his men at the gate. That was partly good manners. To bring his men suggested he expected trouble from his employer. The other reason was because if Stoth did do something stupid, Thane was confident he could handle the problem alone.

The interior of the castle was lavishly decorated with paintings, tapestries and embroidered rugs. Thane could make a fortune looting the place. The walls were whitewashed, the floors swept clean and an army of servants worked hard to maintain the illusion of wealth without limits.

But that was all it was, an illusion. Stoth must have spent piles of gold to make his castle look so fancy, and that was a huge drain for a kingdom as poor as Stone Heart. The barges and siege weapons were built here rather than purchased, and so were most of the weapons. That was cheaper than buying them, but even so, their manufacture must have been expensive. Thane knew his employer's treasury was nearly empty, and Stoth's debts made the situation even worse. But that might change soon, so Thane and his mercenary army remained loyal, for now.

Thane followed the soldier through the gaudy castle until they came to a library with a chandelier and padded chairs. The library was small and many of the shelves were bare. Stoth Voluk, his employer, sat calmly reading while the captain of his royal guard stood behind him.

Stoth was tall and of medium build. His face looked simple, his brown hair was cut short, and his skin smooth and free of blemishes. Out of his fancy clothes, Stoth would look so ordinary that he could blend in with a crowd and never be noticed. He wore a purple robe over a white shirt and blue pants, and black riding boots finished the outfit. Stoth's jewelry included a gold crown set with rubies and rings studded with diamonds. He sipped brandy from a crystal goblet, not seeming to notice Thane's arrival.

The captain, a fool named Tinley, was younger and in better health. He had the hard build of a man used to work. His plate armor was high quality and so was his sword, but neither had seen much use. That and the purple cape he wore told Thane this man gave orders rather than fought.

"Ah, Thane, do sit down," Stoth said smoothly, his voice relaxed and cheerful. "I'm in the middle of a fascinating book. Can't say I understand half of it, but the rest is captivating."

Thane frowned. "My armor would damage the chair."

Stoth looked up from his book. "So it would. You know, you don't have to dress like that around me."

Thane kept his temper. Most of his employers were twits. Somehow the stupidest people always ended up with lots of money. It was a balancing act to get as much cash from them as possible without killing them in frustration. Thankfully for Stoth, it was a skill that Thane mastered long ago.

"I'm told there's something you want to get off your chest," Stoth said.

"My scouts say the towns in our path are preparing for war."

Stoth went back to his book. "Really?"

"I told you this would happen," Thane said. "You sent your army out too soon. The attack on Sun Valley gave away your intentions to make war. The people you didn't capture spread the news, and now your target towns and kingdoms are alerted."

"Fascinating."

How else could Thane put this so the inbred fool would take him seriously? "They're repairing their city walls, training men and buying or making weapons. Some are hiring mercenaries of their own. I've even heard talk that the kingdom of Two Peaks wants to hire a wizard. It's going to be a lot harder to fight this war."

Stoth turned a page on his book. "Oh I very much doubt that. Do try to calm down, Thane. You need a hobby. I'd lend you a book, but as you can see there aren't many here. I'm sorry to say the last owner took most of them when he left. That was a sign of genius on his part, you know. Moratrayas took the real source of power in this castle. This is one of the few books he left behind, a lab notebook of his. Would you like to see it?"

Thane leaned in close. "I know why you ordered the attack on Sun Valley. Your men had no combat experience. It was a quick raid to boost morale and get slaves. But why didn't you take the women? You don't leave witnesses to a sneak attack!"

Tinley bristled at the criticism. “Our men are ready and eager for war.”

“They might be eager, but they’re not ready,” Thane retorted.

Before a war of words could break out, Stoth looked up from his book and at last met Thane’s eyes. “You think that’s what I wanted? A couple slaves and an easy win? Thane, you’re so shortsighted. I can’t blame you. After all, it wasn’t that long ago I would have been thinking just like you. But I don’t anymore. I’ve seen the light. Ha, bit of a pun there.”

“The sunstone?” Thane asked. He’d heard that Stoth’s men stole a large sunstone during their raid. He knew how close Stoth was to bankruptcy in spite of the trappings of wealth. Until now Thane worried where Stoth would come up with the money to afford the Blue Sashes’ fee. For a second he felt relief. “Then you can pay us!”

“Yes, but not with that. You’re right, that shiny rock is worth a bundle. My treasurer estimated its value at fifty thousand gold pieces.” Stoth took a handkerchief from his pocket and handed it to Thane. “Here, you’re drooling. No, I won’t be pawning it to pay your men. You’ll get your money once the campaign starts. The banking cartels already loaned me the gold.”

Stoth held up the notebook so Thane could read its title. ‘Electromagnetic Theory and its Applications in Offensive Clockwork Design.’ “Quite a mouthful, isn’t it? In laymen’s terms, it describes how to build a machine that harvests lightning from the sky, stores it and shoots it. Judging by your expression you’re doubtful, but take it from me, Thane, it’s real. I should know. I was almost killed by one. There are bits of it upstairs, but Moratrayas crippled the machine in a regrettable act of vandalism.”

“I don’t understand,” Thane admitted. “Are you saying you can fix this weapon?”

“Oh I wish! The idea appeals to me very much. Sadly, while this notebook is a marvel, it’s volume one of three. Even if the other two were here, I doubt anyone in my service is bright enough to repair that delightful little toy. We can’t get it to fire again, but we can get the controls that turn it to function. That’s all we need.”

Smiling like the cat that caught the canary, Stoth plucked a second book from the shelf. “I’m told this one was here before Moratrayas took power, and thankfully a book he didn’t have time to steal. Using this together with the notebook, we will become unstoppable. Let my enemies build higher walls or hire men to round out their armies. Let them hire a wizard for all the good it will do. It won’t matter, Thane. No army in the world can stop us. Not with these two books.”

Thane took the book from Stoth’s hands and looked at the title. It read, ‘A Wizard’s Study of Sunstones.’

# Chapter 8

Sandra and Moratrayas left Scour an hour before nightfall. Their exit went as unnoticed as their entrance, prompting disgruntled remarks from the doctor. Once they disappeared into the wilderness outside the city, they removed their disguises and put on their original clothes. They returned to their camp in a clearing surrounded by pine trees, where Igor kept a small fire burning to warm himself and allow Moratrayas to cook dinner.

Sandra sat by herself and poured hot water over her hair. The water came out yellow from hair dye washing out. "This is the third rinse. How many more times do I have to do this before my hair is back to normal?"

"That's a good question," Moratrayas said. "I've never used the stuff myself."

Sandra pointed an accusing finger at him. "If I'm stuck with this color until my hair grows out, you're in big trouble, mister."

Moratrayas plucked a bottle from his box of disguises and tossed it to her. "This should wash the dye out, if you can handle the smell."

He headed over to Igor and found the hunchback still watching the city and castle through a telescope. Igor had a notebook on his lap, where he scribbled page after page of writing and the odd doodle. "What have you learned?"

Igor handed him the notebook. "I've got the guards' schedules, the routes they patrol and where they go to slack off where their officers can't see them. Once they have the slaves back in the camp, they bring in four dogs and post two men at the front gate. Four more men patrol the inside. None of them look happy to be outside when it's so cold. I should add there's a pretty lady living in a third floor apartment in the castle."

"Voyeurism is beneath you, Igor."

"I've been stuck out here for hours with a telescope. What did you expect me to do?"

Moratrayas considered the question for a moment. "I suppose it was a predictable course of action. For the sake of group harmony, don't tell Ms. Sower."

Sandra walked over to them, her hair smelling like a chemical leak but back to its original color. She handed Moratrayas back her disguise and said, "Next time I want a say in what I'm disguised as."

Moratrayas put the disguise away in a box, but paused before closing it. "Where's the jewelry?"

Sandra smiled nervously. "Uh, is there any way I can keep it? I never had anything pretty like that before. Please?"

"Fine, it's yours," he replied. "Just put it somewhere safe."

Sandra hugged him. "Thank you! Nobody ever gave me something this nice. Did you make it?"

"I received some of the jewelry as payment for saving a merchant's life. Igor brought me the necklace, and I was sensible enough not to ask how he came by it."

Smiling and running her fingers over the jewelry, Sandra stepped up to the telescope. "What are you guys talking about?"

Igor smirked. "Heavenly bodies."

Before Sandra could ask for an explanation, Moratrayas coughed and said, "This is no time to discuss astronomy. We've learned a lot of information on our enemies, but it's all recent intelligence. There's no telling what they did before we came. I need to know what's been happening in the last few months if I'm going to develop an escape plan. I'm going to gather informants. You two stay here and maintain observation on the camp."

Moratrayas grabbed the block of cheese and a ball of twine from his supplies before marching out into the cold night. Igor kept watch with the telescope, leaving Sandra unsure what she was supposed to do.

Sandra felt comfortable around the hunchback. He wasn't much to look at, but then again the soldiers who'd devastated her town looked normal. Besides, anyone who was fighting to save her family and neighbors was a good man as far as she was concerned.

"Did anyone see you while we were gone?" she asked.

Igor smiled and looked up from the telescope. "Not much chance of that. I took three courses in skulking and hiding at Igor University, and passed them with flying colors. Nobody sees me unless I want them to."

Sandra chuckled. "They teach classes in that?"

"There do, and they're packed. No Igor worth his salt graduates without passing them all."

Puzzled, she asked, "Wait, there are lots of students named Igor?"

Igor leaned in closer. "You never heard?" When she shook her head, he grinned and said, "Igor's not a name. It's a title. Towns have their butchers, their bakers, their holy men and their Igors. We fill a vital role in society, doing the nasty things people don't want to admit they need done. Part of the job is calling yourself Igor. It adds to the mystique, and it's a union rule."

"And you need to take classes in hiding to do it?"

"You have to be discrete when you work for a mad scientist," he said. "Doesn't matter if he's trying to save the world, cure diseases or hunt down dangerous monsters, everybody assumes the worst. You'd be amazed how fast torch wielding mobs form when they find out where you live. An Igor is no good to his master if he's seen."

"I see." Looking at Igor, it was hard to imagine how he could do anything without drawing a crowd. Tentatively, she asked, "I know it's not my place, but can Moratrayas fix your back?"

"Don't know," he said as he peered into the eyepiece. "Didn't ask. Wouldn't want him to if he could."

That surprised her. "You wouldn't?"

"Nope. It used to bother me a lot when people teased me about the way I look. But when I went to Igor University, nobody cared. Everybody there had some kind of a problem or another. I talked to the university chaplain once, asked him why God would make a man that looked like I did. He told me an ugly body won't keep you out of heaven, but an ugly soul will. Changed my life."

"I never thought of it that way," she said.

"If someone hates you because of something you didn't cause and had no control over, it says more about him than you."

Sandra smiled at him. "A lab assistant and a philosopher."

"I'm good at all sorts of things. Most of them you'll never hear about. That's rule number three at Igor U, *keep them guessing what you really do*."

That made her laugh. "What's rule number one?"

"*Don't let your master get killed*, which is harder than it sounds."

Moratrayas was facing thousand to one odds, and Sandra was the one who'd involved him in this mess. "I might break rule number one for you."

Igor looked up from the telescope. "Don't tell me you're worried about this! The doc was in trouble this bad or worse long before you showed up, and he'll be in as much trouble long after you go home. He's a mad scientist, flirting with death is what he does."

He sat down on a rock and pointed to Moratrayas, who was slowly returning to camp. "Most people fail at what they do, not because they're stupid or lazy, but because they never try. They're so sure they'll lose that they never begin anything. Now the doc, he's a mad scientist, whether he likes the name or not. Knock him down a hundred times and he'll get right back up and try again. His confidence gets him through hard times. He loses his home, his friends abandon him, he's facing an army, so what? He can work around that. Sometimes that confidence gets him in trouble and he won't admit he's in over his head. The work I do in the lab or out here is secondary. My main job is pulling him out of danger at the last minute."

Moratrayas returned with half the block of cheese left. "Igor, Ms. Sower, has anything happened?"

"We were just talking about life," she told him.

"I've developed some very interesting theories on the subject since I began building clockworks."

Eager to forestall a lecture, Sandra asked, "What were you doing out there?"

"Setting the table for our friends." Moratrayas sat on a tree stump next to her and pointed at a branch stuck in the ground. There was a thin slice of cheese on it hanging just above the snow, and farther on another slice of cheese was suspended from a pine tree by a length of twine.

"You've been hinting about this for hours," she said. "What's going on?"

Fifty yards away there was a blur of motion, something small and moving fast. Sandra would have missed it entirely if she hadn't already been looking in that direction. She heard no sound, no crunch of snow being stepped on or rustle of branches. Alarmed, she asked, "What was that?"

"Did you know goblins eat cheese?" Moratrayas asked.

"No," Sandra admitted. "Now that I think about it, that explains why no one in Sun Valley makes cheese. We drink milk and eat yogurt, but the only time we have cheese is if we buy it from passing merchants, and then we eat it right away."

Moratrayas took a knife from his pocket and cut a thin slice of cheese off the block. "That's not surprising. Goblins love the stuff. They can eat any organic matter and generally prefer things no other race can stomach. I've seen them eat worn out boots, torn shirts, rotten meat, spoiled milk, shed antlers and more. Many communities tolerate them only because they act as living garbage disposals, consuming waste that might otherwise clutter the land or attract wolves and scavenging monsters. But cheese is one food that no goblin can resist."

Something small and as silent as a ghost swung on a rope between the trees. It was a goblin dressed in black and moving fast. He swung directly at the suspended slice of cheese, gobbled it up in midair and disappeared into the inky night.

"Cheese factories have security approaching that of treasuries," Moratrayas continued. "Goblins will do anything for a taste, and it takes magic and mechanical traps to keep them out. If anyone made cheese in Sun Valley, your resident goblins would devour it long before you ate a bite of it. Normally that's a problem, but tonight I want as many goblins as I can get."

"You baited a trap for them?" she asked.

"Not a trap," he corrected her. "A meeting."

The branch with cheese on it trembled ever so slightly before sinking into the snow and disappearing, cheese and all. This time Sandra was close enough to hear someone chewing, and a soft voice say, "Oh that's good."

"Didn't you say men chase goblins in Stone Heart?" she asked.

"They do," Moratrayas said. "To be blunt, they try to kill them, just one more example of needless cruelty. But I digress. Yes, the residents of Stone

Heart will attack any goblin they see. That doesn't mean there are no goblins, just that the goblins are careful not to be discovered."

Moratrayas held up the piece of cheese he'd cut and tossed it in the air. A goblin rose up from out of the snow and caught it in his mouth. Slowly more goblins began to filter in. They were every bit as short, dirty and weird looking as the goblins in Sun Valley and in Moratrayas' castle. A crowd of thirty goblins gathered around the camp, dressed in camouflage clothes, disguised as brush piles and tree stumps, or digging their way up through the ground with shovels and picks.

"Thank you for coming," Moratrayas said to the goblins.

"It's Al," one of the goblins said. "Al's back!"

The goblins blinked and squinted at Moratrayas. They smiled in recognition and charged toward the doctor, cheering and hooting, "Al!"

Sandra looked at Moratrayas and asked, "Al?"

Moratrayas shrugged. "Al, Alberto, it's an abbreviation. They're goblins. Did you really think they would address me by my full name?"

A goblin dressed in black shook Moratrayas' hands. "Al, we missed you. Where have you been, buddy? It's been years."

Moratrayas smiled and spoke to the goblins like they were old friends. "Too long, I know. I've been busy south of here since I lost my home."

Sandra leaned over to Igor and asked, "Why do they like him so much?"

"Stone Heart used to pay bounties on goblin heads," he explained. "When the doc took over he ended that."

Somehow the news didn't surprise her. "I keep thinking my opinion of these people can't get any lower, and then it does."

A goblin walked up to Sandra and said, "Hey, Al brought a new friend. Does that mean you're a mad scientist like him and make nightmarish creations to unleash on an unsuspecting world?"

"Uh, no," she stammered.

"Too much to ask that you'd be cool," the goblin pouted.

Other goblins kept chattering away around Moratrayas. One asked, "Did you come back to take over?"

"Is there any more cheese?" another asked.

"Have you seen my socks?" a third goblin quizzed him.

"I'm not here to take control of Stone Heart, there is more cheese and your socks are hanging from your belt," he told them. "I need your help. Stoth Voluk, the man who drove me off, has taken hundreds of men prisoner and is using them for slave labor."

"We know," a goblin dressed as a tree stump said. "We've been watching them for weeks. It's painful even to be around that kind of abuse. We've tried, but we can't get in close enough to help."

Sandra's opinion of goblins went up a notch. "Wait, you want to free them?"

"Of course," a goblin said. "We owe Stoth and his people plenty for what they've done over the years. Letting their slaves go would start to even the scales and really make Stoth angry."

"We tried and failed," the goblin in black said. "There are too many soldiers and dogs, and the soldiers have crossbows. Even if we busted someone out, he'd get shot before he reached cover. We're digging an escape tunnel for them, but it will take two weeks to finish."

"It's good that you tried," he told them. "I came here to free them and do as much damage to Stoth as I can. That's why I invited you here tonight."

"Speaking of which," a goblin prompted him.

"Ah, yes." Moratrayas sliced up the cheese and tossed it into the crowd, where hungry goblins snapped it up. "Now then, I know you watch men from the shadows. I need to know what's been happening in the castle and city during the last few months."

"Lots of elves in fancy clothes and pretty jewelry came a few weeks ago," a goblin told him. "Everybody was excited, and they threw a party for them. I heard a guy say they were bankers."

Moratrayas rubbed his chin. "That explains where Stoth is getting the money for his war. How long did they stay?"

"Two days," the same goblin said. "They left after another big party."

A goblin with a shovel added, "River barges came through last summer, sometimes five a week. The men on them said they worked for something called the Peck Merchant House. They sold Stoth all sorts of stuff. Tools, weapons, clothes, armor, you name it."

The black clad goblin grabbed Moratrayas by the hand and tugged. "Al, listen, you're in trouble. We all are. There's some bad magic going on in the castle."

Moratrayas bent down close to the goblin. "Explain."

The goblin pointed at the distant castle, lit up with lanterns so it practically glowed in the dark. "There's something going on in the tower where you kept your sparky gun."

"My lightning gun? I crippled it before I left. There's no way that fool could get it working again," Moratrayas said defiantly.

"It's not the sparky gun, it's something else," the goblin said. "Three times this week the tower lit up bright as day. Your sparky gun never did that."

"The sunstone!" Sandra exclaimed. "That's where they're keeping it."

"There's more to it," a goblin armed with a shovel said. "One time the light reached out of the tower down to the ground. We went to check it out after it stopped. The snow was melted away, the plants were gone and the ground was baked hard as rock where the light hit."

The black clad goblin tugged on Moratrayas' hands again. "We've been listening to people, and all of them say Stoth doesn't have a wizard working for him. We know Stoth isn't a wizard, either. But if he's trying to do magic and he messes up, there could be big trouble."

Another goblin added, "Most of us goblins already left Stone Heart. Some went to the new King of the Goblins and others just headed out for any old place. We're not planning on staying much longer ourselves. If Stoth tries to do strong magic he's not trained for, there might not be a kingdom left when he's done."

Moratrayas shook their hands. "Thank you. You've given me much to think about. I intend to free the slaves as soon as I can. Can I count on your help?"

The black clad goblin nodded. "We'll do it, but after that we're packing our bags and taking off."

"So are we," Moratrayas told the goblins. "We're going back to the river where I have my barge. Come to me tomorrow night and we'll begin. Sandra, Igor, we must leave."

Moratrayas led his followers away and the goblins melted back into the forest. Sandra hurried to keep up with him and asked, "What did he mean there might not be a kingdom left?"

"I read up on magic after my battle with Tadcaster," he explained. "Wizards spend years studying how to cast spells, and much of that training involves controlling the power they summon. If a wizard taps into a source of energy and loses control, the effects will be bad."

"Destroy a kingdom bad?" she asked. Sandra had heard how dangerous wizards were, but how could anyone be that powerful?

"Possibly. If a wizard makes a mistake casting a spell, the energy doesn't disappear, but instead it's released locally. If a wizard tries to light a campfire and his spell fails, he could burn himself or a friend. If he tries to destroy an enemy with fire and makes a mistake, he could kill himself or start an uncontainable wildfire. The more powerful the magic, the more devastating the result of failure."

It wasn't hard for Sandra to follow his reasoning. "So if Stoth's not a wizard and he's trying to do strong magic, there's a really good chance he'll fail. And if he fails, it will be big."

"Very big," Moratrayas agreed. "Sandra, goblins are perhaps the most resilient race on Other Place. Fires, floods, droughts, blizzards, earthquakes, hurricanes, none of those disasters bother them, but they're fleeing Stone Heart. In all recorded history they've rarely fled a kingdom, and only before disasters of epic proportions.

"It's clear Stoth is using your sunstone to cast this strange magic. If the spell can reach down from the castle to the land below then it's very powerful indeed. We have to stop him and quickly. When, not if, he loses control, his failure may consume the castle, the city, the slave camp and who knows how much more in a matter of seconds. He can't be allowed to keep your sunstone. It galls me to say this, but to save your people we'll have to save Stone Heart as well."

The castle of Scour included eight short towers and one central tower twice as high as the others. At the top of the tallest tower was a room containing the remains of Doctor Moratrayas' lightning gun. It was also the prison of one Jeremy Rostenburger.

Jeremy was a small man of slight build. At fifty his hair was almost gone. He tried to compensate by growing a mustache, but it looked like a brown fuzzy caterpillar clinging to his lip. His clothes were simple workman's attire, sturdy and functional. He wore glasses and a perpetual look of fear.

This room had been Jeremy's prison for months, a cot in the corner, a chest containing his clothes and a chamber pot his only furnishings. A bored soldier watched Jeremy so he could neither flee nor destroy the monstrous contraption that took up most of the room.

The outlandish machine in front of him was his personal nemesis and the source of his suffering since arriving. The lighting gun was a massive contraption, a bewildering machine of titanic proportions. There were seven huge glass cylinders with copper rods in them placed in a circle around the room. Something resembling a giant tuning fork could be raised through a hole in the ceiling to catch passing lightning and channel it into the cylinders. Large wood shutters on all eight walls could be raised to let the horrible weapon fire onto the land below.

Then there was the gun itself, a monolithic weapon carved entirely from granite. The barrel was fifteen feet long, the base twenty feet wide, and dozens of gears (which resembled a jigsaw puzzle of mind-boggling complexity) rotated the base and lifted or lowered the barrel. There was a seat next to the gun, and on that seat were hundreds of switches and a collection of glass lens that could be folded out of a brass box. When used together, the lens allowed a person to see for miles.

When Jeremy was first thrown in here, he was told how this monster of granite and glass once fired lightning. If that was true, it didn't anymore. Cables connecting the component parts were broken, and so were the glass cylinders. Most of the granite gears were missing when Jeremy was first imprisoned here, but with much hard work new ones were made to replace them. Jeremy discovered delicate inner workings to the giant tuning fork and gun, all of it smashed so badly it was impossible to figure out what they did. Heaven help the man trying to fix the thing!

Which unfortunately was Jeremy's job. He sat timidly on the edge of the seat next to the cannon and flipped a switch. Nothing happened. Did that mean the switch was broke, or was the thing it controlled broke? It could be either or both. Another possibility was that the switch only worked if he flipped another switch at the same time. Sometimes he had to flip three switches at once to have an effect. He pasted notes to the controls he'd figured out so he wouldn't forget what they did. What little he understood about this mad machine was that it was dangerous, and best left to a man with more intelligence and fewer reasons to live. His halfhearted tinkering could only make things worse.

There were newer components to the gun, parts he could control even if he didn't want to. Three granite spheres hung in the barrel. The spheres could be opened to reveal the treasures inside, a move so risky Jeremy sweat profusely every time he tried.

"Jeremy!" a friendly voice called. It was Stoth Voluk, goblet of brandy in one hand and notebook in the other. He came up the stairs with his lapdog Tinley three steps behind. "How's my super weapon doing today? I see it's not up against the ceiling anymore."

"I managed to lower the platform it's attached to," Jeremy said nervously.

Stoth smiled like a cat with a cornered mouse. "Good to see you fixed the problem you caused. You had me worried for a while there, and you know I don't like being worried."

"It's these controls," Jeremy protested. "There's no mention of them in the notebook. The only way I can figure out what they do is by trial and error. Sometimes they do things I don't want them to."

"You know the basics, and that's enough for now. The last test went well, Jeremy, so well that I need you to do it again for my speech tomorrow. This demonstration will have to be bigger, but I'm sure you're up to it."

"The gun will fire," Jeremy promised.

"Good man," Stoth said with false cheer, and casually tossed the notebook on the floor. "Once that's done, I'll need you to disassemble the gun."

"What?" Jeremy sputtered, "But, but why?"

Stoth waved the half-empty goblet toward the closed shutters. "Jeremy, use your head. The gun's useless here. It's a defensive weapon, and I most certainly am not going to be on the defensive!"

"What good is it in pieces?"

"That's going to be a temporary situation. The gun, or at least the parts of it you bothered to fix, is too big to move. Once you've disassembled it, the parts can be taken down the staircase. The barrel and base will be lowered down with ropes. Then we'll put the pieces aboard a river barge, which I'm assured is large enough to carry it, and reassemble the gun when and where I need it in the coming war. Simple, no?"

"No, not simple!" Jeremy cried. "I can't do it!"

Stoth stared at him, his expression displaying mild interest. "You refuse me?"

"It's not that," Jeremy said hastily. He knew better than to disappoint Stoth. "It's, it's just what you're asking for is impossible."

"Impossible," Stoth repeated.

"Please, I'm a clockmaker," Jeremy said. "I build clocks! This, this monster you've put me in charge of, I don't understand it. I read the notebook and I listened to the men who saw this madman Moratrayas build it. I've tinkered with it for nine months. None of that helped. I barely understand how to work it, and you want me to take it apart and then put it back together?"

"That was the idea," Stoth said blandly.

Praying he wouldn't anger Stoth, that for once the man would see reason, Jeremy went on. "I am telling you as plainly as I can, I'm not sure how to take it apart, and once it's in pieces I can't promise I can put it back together so it will work. I'm not trying to trick you. It's just what you're asking for is beyond me. I, I've done all I can for you. Please, let me go home to my family."

Stoth stared at Jeremy for a moment before he flipped a switch on the control panel. The wood shutters rolled up into recesses in the ceiling, giving them a 360-degree view of the kingdom. At this height they could see for miles. Frigid air poured into the room. Jeremy flinched from the cold. Stoth didn't. He walked up to the edge of the tower and looked out over his kingdom.

"Jeremy, do you ever look at Stone Heart? I mean, really look at it, closely. You're from where again? Granite Peaks? I bet back when you were traveling through the mountains on that silly boat of yours trying to sell clocks, you never thought you'd see a sight like this."

"I could have lived without it," Jeremy replied.

"Oddly enough, so could I. Captain Tinley, help Jeremy over here, would you?"

Tinley twisted Jeremy's arm behind his back and forced him to the edge of the tower. There was a slight lip, no higher than five inches, and after that a terrible fall to the ground below. Jeremy struggled in vain to break free.

"Look at it, Jeremy," Stoth said. "It's so much larger than the kingdom I came from. Back home there were only five thousand people. That's even fewer than Granite Peaks, isn't it? But it was a kingdom, and it was mine. Yes sir, my very own personal dung heap of a kingdom. Dirt poor, and I mean that in both the figurative and literal sense. So when the opportunity came to conquer Stone Heart, I jumped at the chance."

For a moment Stoth looked at the flickering lights below. “Captain Tinley, give Jeremy a closer look at my kingdom.”

Tinley threw Jeremy over the edge. For one terrifying moment he fell before Tinley grabbed him by his heels. Tinley grinned and left Jeremy hanging there, screaming for dear life. Calmly, Stoth asked, “You want me to let you go? Did I hear that right?”

“Pull me up!”

Stoth shrugged. “Some people can’t make up their minds. Captain Tinley, oblige the clockmaker.”

Tinley dragged Jeremy up and set him on the floor. Jeremy sat there, gasping for breath. His heart was beating so hard he thought it would burst from his chest. Stoth bent down next to Jeremy and swirled the brandy in his goblet. When he spoke, it was as if nothing had happened.

“I left my kingdom to my younger brother. I figured, so what if you never see that miserable stinking place again. But once I was here, I realized this place is just a bigger dung heap than my old kingdom. The same poverty, the same dirty illiterate peasants always complaining, the same everything. You know what real kings call me? A kinglet. That’s a real word, you know. It means a small king, a king of a lesser country. I traded one worthless kingdom for another.”

Stoth walked over to the gun and ran his free hand over the barrel. “But there was a consolation prize. My predecessor left this marvel behind and clues how to fix it. If I was careful and patient, I could take this work of genius and make it even more dangerous than it was before. Once I was finished there’d be no stopping me. I could conquer any kingdom I pleased. Keeping what I took would be hard, of course, so I’d have to limit my ambitions. But once it was working I’d be a power to be reckoned with. No one on Other Place would dare look down on me.”

Stoth sat down on the floor next to Jeremy. “You made the gun work, sort of. I appreciate that. There will be a reward for your services. I’d like to give you a royal apartment with proper accommodations, but I can’t. I mean, be fair, the only reason you’re here day and night under guard is because you tried to run away. What was I supposed to do? But that’s neither here nor there. The gun is only useful to me if it’s mobile. Take it apart. Bring it down to the river. Then put it back together again. I know it’s a challenge, and doing it in thirty days won’t help.”

“Thirty days?” Jeremy gasped.

“Thirty days, no more. I’m afraid my timetable isn’t flexible. Then we go on a little cruise to visit the neighbors and show them that there’s a new man in charge. When this is over I was thinking of putting you in charge of Granite Peaks in appreciation of your help. You’ll rule it in my name as a baron, your wife a baroness. That sounds nice, doesn't it? All your hard work and time away from your family will be amply rewarded."

Stoth got up and walked to the stairs with Tinley following close behind. Before leaving, the king smiled and said, "Don't fail me, Jeremy. If you disappoint me, I'll have to let you go...all the way down."

# Chapter 9

The next morning promised snow, with clouds billowing and blotting out the sun. Moratrayas, Igor and Sandra sat on the doctor's barge planning their mission to liberate the men of Sun Valley. They were still moored to the same spot on the river, hidden by rough ground and high trees.

"The snow will help," Moratrayas told them. "It will reduce visibility and make following us harder."

"Won't it make it harder for us to get away?" Sandra asked.

"Not the way I plan on escaping." He took out a map he'd drawn of Scour and the surrounding land. "I've marked the slave camp with an x. The armory, depot for the siege weapons, troop barracks, storehouses and other buildings I'd like to destroy are also marked. But what we really need to remove are the river barges."

"That's how we're getting my people out," Sandra said.

"Exactly. The docks are close to the slave camp, and there are low hills between them that will hide our approach when we bring your people there. We'll take as many barges as we need and flee, burning the others so Stoth's army can't pursue us."

"What about the sunstone?" Igor asked.

Moratrayas shook his head. "I'm sorry, but I've tried day and night to find a way to recover it. It can't be done without fighting through Stoth's army and the Blue Sashes, and it's too risky to sneak in and steal it. The best I can do is make sure Stoth can't use it against us."

Moratrayas looked at Gertrude, still covered by a tarp. "Once we're away I'll use Gertrude to destroy the tower containing the lightning gun. Don't ask me how, but he's using that in unison with the sunstone to work his magic. I'm confident we can destroy both the tower and lightning gun. As for the sunstone, I'm less sure. My apologies, but it will either be destroyed or remain in Stoth's possession if it survives the attack."

"Getting my people back is more important," she told him.

Moratrayas stabbed the map with a feather quill, marking the siege weapon depot. "The goblins can sneak in and set these on fire, which should disable them and confuse Stoth's army as to the real threat. Given time I can arrange accidents for the other buildings. After that we sail home. Stoth will still be a threat, but a bearable one."

"Al!" The three of them looked up and saw the black clad goblin running through the dense forest. "Al!"

"What's wrong?" Moratrayas asked.

The goblin doubled over and gasped for air before he answered. "There's a rally starting in the city. All the bigwigs are there, and most of the people, too."

"Curse our luck!" Moratrayas shouted. "This would be the perfect time to rescue your people, and we're not ready."

"What's the rally about?" Sandra asked.

The goblin stood up straight again, still breathing hard. "I don't know. Stoth has lots of rallies. Most of the time he whips the people up into a frenzy with hate talk, but this time he's promising something big."

Moratrayas rubbed his chin. "It might be worthwhile to find out what's going on."

"You want us to listen in on it for you?" the goblin asked.

"No, I need to hear this for myself."

"Why?" Igor asked him.

"Something's going on here," he said. "Stoth's army is ready to move today. If he sends the army out, he may take Sandra's people for forced labor. I need to see as much of this as possible with my own eyes to adjust my plans."

"Not the disguises again," Sandra begged.

Moratrayas climbed off the barge and walked over to the goblin. "I know you have ways of getting into the city. Are any of them big enough for me to fit?"

"Sort of," the goblin replied. "There's a tunnel big enough for goblins to run through. You'd fit if you crawled."

"Good enough," he declared. "I'll be back soon."

"We'll be back soon," Sandra said.

Moratrayas frowned. "Ms. Sower, you don't have to come with me this time."

"Stoth's going to be there," she said. "He's responsible for everything bad that's happened to my people. I want a good look at him."

Moratrayas looked to Igor for support and got none. "Hey, don't get me involved in this."

Moratrayas waved for Sandra to follow him. "Fine, but you need to be careful and follow my orders without question."

The tunnel leading into Scour was dank, dark and cramped. Wood boards lined the tunnel, but dirt leaked in between them and coated the floor. Sandra crawled on her hands and knees with Moratrayas ahead of her and a goblin leading them both, the tunnel lit by one of the doctor's glowing green orbs held in his right hand. The tunnel entrance was half a mile from the city wall, meaning they had a long way to crawl.

"Doctor?" Sandra asked

"What is it?"

"How come the goblins get to call you Al and I don't?"

Moratrayas stopped crawling and looked back at her. "What brought this on?"

"I'm just curious. I've been traveling with you and helping you all this time, and I still call you doctor. Why can't I call you Al?"

"Keep moving," the goblin urged them.

Moratrayas crawled forward. "It's rather informal, isn't it?"

"There's nothing wrong with being informal. I wish you'd call me Sandra instead of Ms. Sower. That's what everyone calls my mother. It makes me feel like an old woman."

"That's how you're supposed to address a lady."

"Says who?" she asked.

"It's how they address women in the books I read growing up," he explained.

Sandra stifled a laugh. "That's how you learned to act around women?"

"There's nothing wrong with that! It's not like there was anyone to teach me. The tailor I was apprenticed to was rude and frequently drunk, hardly a man I should model my behavior on."

"I can buy that, but didn't your girlfriends explain this to you?"

Moratrayas paused before answering. "I didn't have any."

"You're kidding."

"Does that sound like something a man would joke about?" he said tersely. "Ms. Sower, half the women I grew up with thought I was insane and the rest were sure of it. Since I fled Stone Heart I've met a great number of women, most of whom run away screaming when they see me. The rest try to sell me cookies, or," he added dryly, "they want something from me."

"Ouch. I had that one coming. I know I already owe you a lot, but is it asking too much to be called by my first name?"

He grumbled before saying, "I suppose not. Sandra it is, then. And if it means that much you can call me Al, just not around other people. It spoils the air of mystery and danger I'm aiming for."

"And you wonder why women don't like you."

"Igor tells me women are attracted to danger."

The goblin stopped at the end of the tunnel, where a ladder led to the surface. "Hate to interrupt this lovers' quarrel, but we're here."

They climbed the ladder and pushed aside a loose board to enter a toolshed. The shed was dark and cluttered with rusty farm implements. Outside, they could hear the low rumble of thousands of people talking at once. The goblin pulled a board off the wall to reveal peepholes.

Sandra and Moratrayas bent down and looked through the peepholes. They saw a wide square filled with excited men and women in front of the castle. Soldiers in the center of the square surrounded a large wood podium liberally hung with armored fist and sunburst flags. General Addaxes Thane stood on the podium flanked by two mercenaries, the three men clearly annoyed to be there.

"Where's Stoth?" Sandra asked.

"He always keeps them waiting," the goblin told her.

Moratrayas grunted. "A pointless display of power over others. Why does that not surprise me? Are there more holes we can look through?"

The goblin pulled off two more boards hiding peepholes facing different directions. Moratrayas checked each one before returning to the first.

"What are these rallies like?" Sandra asked the goblin.

"Weird," he said. "Most of it doesn't make sense. 'Everyone hates you, everyone's against you,' and it can go on like that for hours."

"I hate him, so he's got something right," Sandra said.

"You and me both, but we have good reasons to," the goblin said. "I've traveled some, and I've never heard anybody say bad stuff about Stone Heart. They don't hate them. Most people don't know they exist. You'd think telling people the whole world looks down on them would drive them off, but the crowd eats it up. By the time he's done talking, they're ready to kill the first foreigner they see."

"He's developing a scapegoat," Moratrayas said. "It's common enough in politics. An outside group no one likes is responsible for all the people's problems. No matter what goes wrong with Stoth's plans, he can blame it on foreign enemies. It stirs up bloodlust for his war and lets him off the hook if his plans fail."

Suddenly there was a cry, and the crowd's murmur turned into exuberant screams. Men and women surged toward the podium and would have overrun it except soldiers kept them back. More soldiers took their places near the podium before Stoth appeared. The crowd's screams doubled in intensity when they saw Stoth. He waved to them and smiled, bathing in their adoration.

"We should have brought a crossbow," Sandra muttered.

"Don't think I didn't consider it," Moratrayas replied. "The problem is he has followers and family members that could take his place if he dies. Picking him off would delay the war, not stop it."

"He looks so normal," Sandra said.

"Being ugly isn't proof of evil," Moratrayas said. "Stoth is proof that beauty isn't proof of goodness."

Stoth let the crowd cheer for a while before holding up both arms. The crowd died back down to their original murmur and then became dead silent at his command. When he spoke, his voice echoed through the square, listened to by thousands of attentive ears, his every gesture and expression followed by thousands of bright eyes.

"People of Stone Heart, brave people, noble people...*my people*," Stoth began. The crowd broke out into cheers again. He left them howling in joy for a while before gesturing for silence. "My people, you have suffered long and hard, but not for my grand mission. No, you have suffered all your lives. Year after year you toiled away in your meager fields, scratching a living from thin soil. You mined and quarried these mountains for little gain. You did this unnoticed, unappreciated. How many of your brethren died in those mines? How many men grew old working those fields with nothing to show for their labor? Too many!"

The crowd cheered again. Some of them shouted out their hardships as if Stoth could hear them over the roar.

"That's over," Stoth announced. "In the three years since I came to you, I asked for a different kind of sacrifice, a sacrifice that would end in time. You hardened your bodies and honed your senses. You spent long hours training for battle. It was a hardship, but soon you will know it was worth it."

Stoth walked over and threw an arm around General Thane's shoulders. "Your sacrifice of money allowed us to build mighty weapons of war and hire noble warriors to fight by our side. In the coming months you will know what that sacrifice was for. Together with our trusted allies, we will sweep over the many kingdoms of the Raushtad. The greedy merchants who cheated you, the arrogant kings who belittled you and ignored your suffering, the landowners who kept the best cropland and pastures for themselves, they will know the true power of the people of Stone Heart. They will know when we batter down their castle walls, kick in their doors and demand what's ours!"

The crowd's applause and roars of approval were deafening. Sandra covered her ears to keep the noise out. It barely helped.

"I offered them peace, progress," Moratrayas said, his voice lost in the roar. "They scream for plunder."

"He wants them to kill people, and they're cheering for him?" the goblin asked incredulously. "Are they insane?"

Moratrayas watched in disgust. "They don't have that excuse."

Stoth wasn't done. "The Raushtad will be a land of one kingdom, not dozens. There will be one people, our people! All other kingdoms will be ours. Their treasures and lands will be the rightful spoils of war. All other people will have a choice to join us as brothers, serve us as slaves or die by our swords!"

The king waited for the crowd to tire itself out cheering. The people looked at him in ecstasy, hungry for more. He gave it to them. "The coming battles will test you. It will be risky, but your lives have always been risky. How many of your brothers and sisters took the risk of leaving their homes to seek a better life elsewhere? How many of you risked hazardous work to earn the money you needed to feed your families? Was that not a risk?"

"Yes!" the crowd screamed as one.

"Was it fair?" he asked them.

"No!"

"Other people will work for us from now on," he promised them. "Once we have conquered the Raushtad, you won't even have to risk your lives in battle. But if you fear, if you doubt, put your minds to rest. Your sacrifice made the impossible a reality. Because of your perseverance, your faith in me, your belief in total victory, I have made a weapon so powerful no army, no wizard, not even a dragon dare oppose us."

Stoth pointed at the city gates. Soldiers opened them to reveal the wintry land beyond. "Do you see those mountain passes in the distance?" Stoth asked. "They are the only safe route for an army as grand as ours to take. They're covered in ice and snow, impassable for a lesser army, for a lesser people, but not for us. People of Stone Heart, loyal people, my people, behold the power that will lead you to victory!"

A soldier held up a lantern and waved it high in the air. Another lantern flashed in reply from the castle's highest tower. The tower was still and silent for a moment before a light as bright as a bonfire poured out. A second light appeared next to the first, smaller and weaker.

"One of those is the sunstone Stoth took from me," Moratrayas said.

The two lights came together to form a single brilliant and radiant light so great it rivaled the noon sun. Then a third light appeared next to these two and began shifting toward them. The third light was as strong as the first two together.

"That's the one he took from us," Sandra said.

Moratrayas watched the three sources of light come together. "Then he has a third sunstone, one he didn't get from either of us. But that means...oh no."

The light from the three sunstones came together, and when they did their brilliance was a hundred times greater. There was a high-pitched tone from the tower, like a single musical note played at incredible volume. The light dimmed for a moment, then shot out with a terrible scream. A shaft of light fifty feet across radiated from the tower and hit the snowy road leading from Scour to the mountain passes.

The beam of light melted all before it. Roads were clear close to Scour, but farther out snow three feet deep covered the cobblestone road. The beam evaporated snow and ice with a single pass. In seconds it cleared five miles of road and kept going. The beam stopped and the light died back after only nine seconds, but that was enough to blast clear eight miles of road. The cobblestones steamed. Grass alongside the road was gone, and ashes were left in their place.

For a moment the crowd was too awed to speak. Stoth spoke for them. "Behold the power and the majesty of the Sun Gun. The way is clear, my people. Our enemies think they're safe until spring. Fools. I will burn a path to our enemies, and then I will use the awesome power of the Sun Gun on their cities, their armies and their ships! With this weapon, victory is in the palms of your hands. Will you take it?"

The crowd went mad with delight. Only the presence of armed men kept them from sweeping forward and lifting Stoth on their shoulders. Stoth smiled and shouted encouragements the crowd couldn't hear and didn't need.

"You were right," Moratrayas told the goblin. "This is very bad magic."

"Can you stop him?" the goblin asked.

"I have to. It's my fault this is happening."

Sandra was still looking through the peepholes when one of Thane's mercenaries pointed at the toolshed they were in. "I think we've been spotted."

The mercenary shouted something to Thane, his words lost in the crowd's braying. But he kept pointing at the shed, and Thane's eyes opened wide in surprise. He and his two followers climbed off the podium and forced their way through the crowd.

"He spotted the peepholes!" the goblin exclaimed. "Nobody's done that before!"

Moratrayas lifted the board covering the escape route. "We have to leave. You two go first."

Together they climbed back into the dark tunnel. Moratrayas put the board back over the exit and followed them. "Hurry! Thane and his men won't be long."

They heard the shed door splinter apart. "How long do you think it will take them to find the tunnel?" Sandra asked.

There was another crash as the board covering the tunnel entrance was smashed apart. They heard Thane's commanding voice shout, "They went through here! The tunnel is too narrow to go through with your armor. Take it off and go after them."

"Sir!" two men shouted in unison. Armor clanged as it hit the floor. Sandra, Moratrayas and the goblin fled as fast as they could. Behind them, two Blue Sashes mercenaries, swords in hand and stripped down to their street clothes, followed them into the darkness.

"Faster!" Moratrayas shouted. The goblin didn't have to crawl and easily outpaced them. He got to the end of the tunnel and opened the concealed door. Sandra and Moratrayas crawled out. The goblin closed the door behind them and wedged a board in the door's hinges.

"That'll slow them down a bit," the goblin said.

"Thane will send men out the front gate, too," Moratrayas told them. He scooped up the goblin and set him on his shoulders. "My apologies, but you're too slow to do this on your own. Run as fast as you can, Sandra. Your life depends on it!"

They fled into the barren fields around the city. Thane's men were soon on their trail, but slowed by their heavy armor and not sure what they were looking for, they never came close.

"Let me get this straight," Stoth asked after the rally. He was back inside the castle, seated on his throne. The throne room was the largest room in the castle. Tiled with marble and with marble pillars along the walls, it was used as a ballroom during parties. Paintings and tapestries hanging from the walls showed scenes of war as glorious instead of bloody. The throne was a work of art, made of wood with gold and ivory inlaid panels, and placed next to a towering window.

"Sire," Tinley began. He was in the throne room alongside ten guards, General Thane and two Blue Sashes mercenaries. This scared Tinley more than the threat of battle. There were only two reasons why Stoth would have so many people here. The first possibility was so they could carry out his orders right away. The second was that Stoth was angry enough to have these men kill Tinley on the spot. Stoth's face was unreadable, and his voice held the same tone of mild interest it always did. There was no way for the captain to know if he'd leave this room alive.

"No, no let me get this out." Stoth swirled his usual goblet of brandy. The mercenaries eyed the potent drink enviously. He spoke calmly and said, "I'm giving my grand triumphal speech, displaying my super weapon at full power, and someone was spying on me. Someone, we don't know who, dug a tunnel into the city. We don't know how long it's been there, what was brought through it, or how many enemy agents could be inside Scour right now plotting to assassinate me. Is that close?"

Tinley began to sweat. "Yes, Sire. But the tunnel was the right size for goblins. That must be who was spying on you. They're no threat."

Thane rolled his eyes. "The tracks leading from the tunnel were too big for goblins! Goblins may have made the tunnel, but it was men or elves using it."

"Lovely," Stoth commented. "I should add it wasn't you who found it, Captain Tinley. As captain of my royal guard you have two duties, to protect me and keep the castle and capital safe. I call it two duties, but be fair, there's a lot of overlap. You failed in your responsibility, and on the eve of our march to war someone got in under your nose. Our dear friend General Thane had to spot them for you."

"Thane's men didn't catch the spies," Tinley said.

Stoth took a sip of brandy. "That's not his job. He and his men went above the call of duty today. I'll send a barrel of brandy to your tent, Thane.

It's my way of saying thanks for taking care of problems made by my men's stupidity. I appreciate it."

"It's what you pay me for," Thane said. "When you pay me."

"Be patient," Stoth told him.

"Now's not the time of patience," Thane replied. "I'll send patrols to find the spies. With luck we can catch them before they flee to their homeland and warn their superiors."

"You'll do nothing of the sort," Stoth said. Thane's expression started at shocked and quickly turned to anger. Before he could argue, Stoth said, "As I said, it's not your job. Captain Tinley?"

Tinley bowed. "Yes, Sire?"

"You failed me, Captain Tinley, and when you do that you make me look weak. I can't afford that. You made this mess, and you'll clean it up. I want half the royal guard sent after the spies. Use dogs. Use horses. Use your wits for a change. I want them found no later than sunrise tomorrow."

Tinley saluted. "Thank you, Sire. I won't let you down."

"You won't let me down *again*," Stoth corrected him. "You had nothing before I came here. You were a dirt grubbing peasant with a miserable strip of land to farm. I gave you everything you have. Your money, your authority, it's all from me, and I can take it away as easy as not. You're the third captain of the royal guard I've had since I came here. I can always have a fourth. Make no mistake, if I remove you, I won't send you back to your farm. I'll bury you in it. Are we clear on this?"

The threat was delivered in such a bland, conversational tone that Tinley needed a second for the full weight of it to sink in. "Very clear, Sire."

Stoth pointed his goblet at Tinley. "Good man. And off you go."

"This is my fault," Moratrayas growled under his breath.

"What do you mean?" Sandra asked.

Sandra and Moratrayas were back at the barge while the goblin left to join the others of his kind. Tracking them would be harder with night falling fast, but not impossible. Moratrayas prepared his weapons in case they were pursued. He set one of his bizarre weapons on the barge's deck and loaded it with darts while Sandra filled in Igor on what happened.

"It's my lightning gun he's using," Moratrayas snapped. "I built it and I left it behind, crippled, or so I thought. But somehow that snake of a man has got it working again using three sunstones as a power source. He's using my weapon, Sandra, and my plans, too!"

"You left the plans for a weapon that powerful behind?" she asked.

"Partially. I'm missing some of the notes I used to construct it. Not enough for him to repair the lightning gun, but today showed it was enough for him to do far worse. I've figured out what he's done, and I showed him how to do it." Moratrayas brought out a second weapon and poured green fuel into it. "Years ago when we were fleeing Stone Heart, the last few hours were a nightmare. All around us Stoth and his men were getting closer. Our defenses were crumbling. Would the castle doors hold for hours or minutes? We didn't know."

"Bad times," Igor said.

"The worst in my life, at least until now. Sandra, we had no idea how much time we had to escape. Igor and I loaded my barge with everything we could, but there was only so much room. We left so much behind to make space for food and fuel for the engine. I left chests of gold because I couldn't fit them! I left my *sunstone* behind. I thought it was just a bauble, a bit of petty magic I could do without. One more jewel lost mattered little as we took the important things. Ha! Shows what I know."

Moratrayas set the weapon down and pointed angrily at the castle. "If I took the sunstone he wouldn't have his blasted Sun Gun, would he? What's worse, I left behind valuable books in the rush. They were smashing the doors in. I had to hurry. I took as many books as I could carry and abandoned the rest. One of them was a book on sunstones."

"You told me you read about them," Sandra recalled.

"If that was all I did we'd be in no danger. I made notes in the book, Sandra! The author said putting two sunstones close together made them more powerful than if they were alone. I wondered what would happen if there were three sunstones together. I theorized they could be used as a weapon. Fool that I was, I wrote it in the margins. Now we know I was right, don't we!"

Moratrayas' hands trembled in rage. He looked down and his lips twitched. "I made this possible. The terror that engulfed your town and now threatens dozens more is because of me. If I hadn't made the lightning gun, if I hadn't lost to Stoth, if I'd taken the sunstone with me, if, if, if! This is happening because of my decisions! Thousands of people are going to die and tens of thousands more put in chains because of my creations, my plans! I wanted to save these people. Instead I've doomed them!"

Moratrayas threw back his head and howled. He pounded his fists on the barge's armored hull, striking it again and again. Sandra ran to him and threw her arms around him. Struggling, she managed to pin his arms to his side and stop him from hurting himself. He could have broken free if he tried hard enough. Instead he screamed again and sank to his knees.

Sandra kept her grip on him in case he lost his temper again. Igor watched, worried but willing to let Sandra handle this for now.

"This isn't your fault," she said softly. "You didn't do this. Stoth did."

"They were my ideas," he muttered.

"But he's the one who carried them out. He chose to build the weapon. He chose how to use it. He takes the blame for what's happened."

Sandra turned Moratrayas around and tried to look him in the eyes. As usual the only thing she saw were his dark goggles. She pulled them down and let them hang against his chest. His eyes were brown and had a haunted look. Sandra pointed back to Scour. "Those people take the blame, too. You saw what I did. They're a part of this, not victims of it. If Stoth didn't have their support he'd get nowhere."

"They cheered for him," he said mournfully. "He wants to kill thousands of people and they cheered for him. I grew up with them. I'm related to some of them. With all my heart I wanted to help them. They want Stoth and his war instead."

"They made a choice, Al. They proved they don't deserve whatever you could give them. They don't deserve you. The people in Refuge and Sun Valley deserve you and your help. Please, don't let them down."

Moratrayas stood up and put his goggles back on. His voice regained its usual strength and determination. "I will not fail them or others menaced by Stoth. I lack the strength to remove the threat entirely, but I swear when this is over, Stoth will weep when he thinks of what he's done."

Moratrayas went back to preparing his clockworks and weapons. Igor sauntered up to Sandra and asked, "You're calling him Al?"

She shrugged. "We had a breakthrough on the way there."

"Help!"

All three of them spun around and saw the black clad goblin running through the woods toward them. More goblins burst out of the snow and brush, running as fast as their short legs could carry them.

"Soldiers are coming!" a goblin warned. In the distance they heard men shouting and crashing through the woods.

"I haven't refueled the barge's engine," Igor said. "We can't escape before they get here."

Moratrayas grabbed his cane, and with the flick of a switch extended it to staff length before slinging a crossbow-like weapon across his back. "If we can't hide or flee then we fight. Those soldiers can't be allowed to report our presence. Come. Let them pay for the course they've chosen."

Moratrayas stalked off the barge and headed straight for the approaching soldiers. Igor grabbed a bottle and rag and then disappeared into the woods left of the doctor. Sandra picked up a crowbar and headed after them. The goblins stopped running when they saw Moratrayas going to confront the soldiers, then regrouped and brought up the rear.

"I can't believe we're doing a goblin hunt this late at night," a soldier complained. He pushed his way through fallen branches and dead undergrowth laden with snow. Seven more men came behind him. Two men carried lanterns that reflected light off the snow. They were bundled up against the cold and looked miserable. Armed with swords and wearing chain armor, they made a lot of noise and not much progress through the woods.

"It's not supposed to be a goblin hunt," another soldier told him. "Captain Tinley says we're looking for men or elves."

The soldier in the lead snorted. "Tinley's running around like a chicken with its head cut off. Look, it was a goblin tunnel, right? Men or elves would have made something bigger. We go out, grab some goblins, make an example of them and everything's settled."

"Tinley wants a man. He won't like it if we come back with a goblin," a soldier carrying a lantern said.

"Well Tinley can go suck a—"

Moratrayas stepped out from behind a tree and jabbed his sparking staff into the soldier's chest. The chain armor conducted electricity exceptionally well, and the man was shocked unconscious. The rest of the squad shouted and drew their swords. Panicked, some of them charged Moratrayas and the rest backed away. Their attack had no coordination and very little skill.

One soldier swung his sword and missed as Moratrayas gracefully ducked under the swing. The sword hit a pine tree instead and stuck deep in the wood. The soldier couldn't pull it free before Moratrayas shocked him.

It was hard for the soldiers to see who they were fighting in the dancing shadows cast by their lanterns. But one soldier got a good look at Moratrayas and screamed, "It's the mad tailor!"

"It's scientist, you idiot!" Moratrayas screamed. "Mad scientist! And yes, I'm very angry!"

The soldiers backed away from him. Terrified beyond words, they didn't notice Igor sneak up behind a man in the back of the group and slap a rag soaked in chloroform over his mouth. The man gasped and struggled, but Igor held onto him tightly and eased him into the shadows without the rest of the squad noticing.

The goblins struck next. They threw rocks and smashed the lanterns, plunging the battle into shadowy darkness. The black clad goblin tripped a soldier and screamed, "Dog pile!" Thirty goblins piled onto the soldier and pinned him to the ground.

"Take him!" a soldier shouted. He was amazed when the remaining three members of the squad ran off and left him to face Moratrayas alone. He made a show of it and held Moratrayas off for a few heartbeats before he was taken down.

Igor tackled another soldier and knocked him out with chloroform. Sandra attacked a second and tripped him with her crowbar. She hit him again and again, making sure he wasn't going to get up any time soon. The last two men ran for their lives. Moratrayas threw his staff like a javelin and hit one of them with its electrified tip, bringing him down. The doctor unslung the weapon on his back and went after the last soldier. Igor and Sandra joined him. The soldier ducked between trees and disappeared into the gloom.

"Where did he go?" Sandra asked.

"I can't hear his armor jingling," Moratrayas said. "He's staying put, trying to hide from us and hoping we miss him in the dark."

The goblins tied up the man they tackled and spread out into the forest after their enemy. Igor checked the man Sandra attacked to see if he needed to be tied up, but the soldier was in no position to resist. Igor glanced at Sandra and asked, "Just once can you leave a man able to walk after you're done with him?"

"Not if I can help it."

They searched through the forest, around towering trees and tangled dead wood that looked malevolent under the dim light. There were plenty of tracks on the ground, both from the soldiers and the goblins they were chasing, which made following the lone soldier difficult.

There was a jingling noise to Sandra's right as the last soldier lunged out from behind a tree. Moratrayas fired a stream of white tipped darts at him. Sandra swung her crowbar but missed. The soldier grabbed Sandra and put a knife to her throat. He pinned her arms to her side with one arm and spun her around to face Moratrayas.

"Nobody move! I'm getting out of here and I'm taking the woman with me. Anybody does something stupid and she gets it."

He sounded scared. Sandra could use that. "You'll die before I will."

"Shut up!" The soldier was in a bad position and he knew it. Moratrayas kept his weapon trained on him and the goblins surrounded him, clubs and rocks at the ready. Angry and scared, he shouted, "Back off, all of you! I'm giving you to the count of ten to back off or she dies."

"Go ahead," Sandra said. "Ten seconds after that the poison kicks in."

That got him. "What poison?"

"The poison on those darts, dummy. Three of them are sticking out of your arm."

The soldier looked down at three white-tipped darts stuck in his chain armor. Calmly, Sandra said, "It's in your blood by now. First you get a tingling sensation, then you arm gets weak. Your vision blurs, you feel queasy. After that the really gross stuff happens. Twenty minutes from now there will be nothing left of you but a puddle of goo."

"P-puddle of..."

"Goo," she finished. "Yellow with bits of red in it. The kind of stuff even rats and wolves won't touch, something so poisonous the ground won't grow grass for fifty years on that spot. And the agony you'll be in! It's going to make losing an arm feel like a headache."

The soldier holding her trembled and his eyes rolled back into his head. He dropped his knife and fell over backwards, releasing Sandra. She walked away from him and noticed Moratrayas staring at her before he said, "That's a paralytic poison, and it needs ten minutes to take effect."

"So I exaggerated a little."

"He passed out," Igor marveled.

"Ms. Sower," Moratrayas began, but he stopped when Sandra held up a finger. "Sandra, if you can bluff like that, maybe you should consider taking up gambling."

Igor picked up the soldier. "Help me get these guys tied up."

"Stoth will know something's wrong when they don't report back," Moratrayas said. "We have hours, perhaps less before he realizes there's a real threat out here and not just goblins or spies. We're not ready to liberate your people, Sandra, but if we don't do it tonight he'll increase security, send out more soldiers and maybe move your people inside the city. Ready or not, we have to do this now."

# Chapter 10

Moratrayas, Igor and Sandra left their camp within the hour as the goblins scurried off into the dark forest to prepare for their part in the coming battle. They left their prisoners tied up around a blazing fire to keep warm. As the barge sailed down river, Igor told the soldiers, "We'll send someone for you when this is over."

"When will that be?" one asked.

Igor shrugged. "Who knows? Could be months."

"Igor, stop taunting them and take the wheel," Moratrayas said. Igor did as ordered and left the doctor to prepare his minions for battle.

The barge's piles of packages were greatly reduced after Moratrayas donated food to Sun Valley, but many containers remained. He unlocked steamer trunks in the front of the barge and pulled out large brass and obsidian clockworks. One by one he set them on the deck until there was no room left to walk between them.

Sandra marveled at them. There were six clockwork men, faceless except for their obsidian eyes. They had smooth bodies and thick arms and legs like she'd seen on the strongest of men. After them came three clockwork hounds wearing fake furs and sporting terrifying jaws. The giant grasshopper she'd seen earlier was back with a veritable horde of smaller clockworks. There were spiders as big as grapefruits, crabs with razor edged pincers and cats that looked positively menacing despite their size. Lastly the dragonfly filled out the brass and obsidian menagerie.

Moratrayas poured green fuel into them, emptying two brass casks in the process, and then turned them on. The clockworks came to life with whirring noises and green light that shined from between cracks in their armored skins. Their movements were awkward for the first few seconds but quickly smoothed out. They climbed to their feet and faced their creator, except for the dragonfly, which flew into Sandra's hands and purred for attention. Moratrayas ducked under the tarp to prepare Gertrude and then returned.

"There we are, everyone's up and ready for work," Moratrayas said reassuringly. "We've got a big night tonight, and I know I can count on all of you. We're going to be helping Sandra Sower by—"

The human clockworks looked at Sandra and gave out piercing wolf whistles. Sandra's eyes opened wide as teacups, and she blushed so bright a shade of red that Moratrayas and Igor could see it under the poor light.

"That'll be quite enough of that!" Moratrayas yelled at them. "I expect better from you. We'll be working closely with her tonight, and you'll take her orders as seriously as my own. It will be dangerous work, but Gertrude will back you up."

Moratrayas nodded at the tarp, which shifted as something very large moved underneath it. "Gertrude is in perfect working order and will play a major role in tonight's battle. Unfortunately that part will be near the end. For the first half of the fight you will shoulder most of the responsibility. Are you ready?"

The clockworks came to attention, and the ones built like men saluted. From under the tarp came a low, bestial growl from Gertrude. The tarp began to shift and tear, surprising Moratrayas as much as it did Sandra. Gertrude wasn't just voicing its readiness. The giant clockwork was getting up to fight right now.

"Gertrude, no, no! Bad!" Moratrayas scolded it like a disobedient lapdog. Four brass claws as thick as ax heads sliced openings in the tarp. Gertrude's growls grew louder and more inhuman, a promise of untold levels of violence and aggression to come. "Blast you, Gertrude, behave yourself!"

The giant clockwork froze in place, its growls silenced as it settled down under the tarp. Muttering, Moratrayas ducked under the tarp again. When he came out, he said, "I had to put the safeties back on. My apologies, Sandra, but Gertrude is proving more willful than normal tonight. It takes threats against me personally. It will perform as needed when the time comes, but for now we have to keep it turned off."

He clapped his hands together and said, "But that is a minor problem, and we face large ones. Gather around and I will explain everyone's part in tonight's performance. Stoth put on quite a show today, and I mean to upstage him."

The barge slid through the water with its lethal cargo of clockworks. Clouds overhead blotted out the night sky and dumped so much snow that the barge was covered and blended in with the white hills. In spite of the darkness and cover provided by the storm, Sandra kept watch for more search parties. Igor steered the barge while Moratrayas set out his collection of unearthly weapons in anticipation of the battle.

If Stoth or his men knew they were in danger, they hid it well. The capital and castle were lit up brightly, and so was the Blue Sashes camp. There were few guards and no extra security since their earlier visits. Their two targets tonight, the slave camp and the docks, were lightly defended.

The slave camp consisted of a high wooden fence surrounding ten barracks made of pinewood. The fence posts had sharpened tops and rusty nails sticking out of them. Climbing over the fence would be impossible. The barracks were barred from the outside, windowless and raised up on blocks so they didn't touch the ground. At the back of camp were latrine pits that smelled foul even in the cold weather. Next to the pits was an eleventh building, smaller and unbarred.

"That's were they keep their tools," Igor explained.

"Pathetic," Moratrayas spat. "The soldiers guarding the camp aren't even at their posts."

Sure enough, the men who should have been patrolling the camp's interior huddled around a fire behind one of the barracks. There were only four men and four dogs inside the camp while two men stood guard outside the gate.

"We're in for it if those dogs start barking," Sandra said.

"Don't worry about them," Moratrayas told her. "Now everyone knows their parts, so let's be quick about this."

Igor landed the barge and climbed off, hurrying to the docks and their fleet of river barges. Moratrayas and Sandra got off and led the clockworks to the slave camp. Moratrayas carried two of his strange weapons and Sandra was armed with his net thrower. The clockworks carried no weapons, but Sandra doubted they'd need any.

They reached the camp's fence unnoticed and far from the derelict guards. Moratrayas put his pneumatic saw on his right hand and powered it up. The glow and hiss from the weapon didn't attract attention until he touched the saw to the fence. It sliced through the soft pine with ease, but made a whining sound. Guard dogs in the camp heard it and came running.

"Right on schedule," Moratrayas said. He turned off the saw and pulled a bottle from his pocket. He opened it and covered his face from the fumes drifting up from the cap. The dogs charged at them, their jaws snapping. Moratrayas splashed them with the bottle's vile smelling contents, and was rewarded with the animals' cries. All four dogs fled, whimpering and rubbing their noses in the snow.

Sandra covered her mouth and nose with her cloak to keep from throwing up. "Good lord, what is that stuff?"

"Ammonia, various sulfur compounds, poison ivy extracts and a collection of loathsome animals Igor found living in a bog. Stir, bottle and store under the stove for a month, and you have a perfect animal repellant. As much as you hate it, dogs have a better sense of smell and will suffer more and longer."

Moratrayas put the rest of the vile solution away and finished cutting through the fence. Passing off the saw to a clockwork man, he led the charge into the camp. They sneaked through the shadows to the fire where the soldiers huddled. The soldiers were bundled up against the cold so much it was hard to see their armor, much less their faces under their cloaks and coats. The men watched the dogs try to rub off the noxious repellant in the snow.

A soldier covered his nose and asked, "What did they get into?"

"Smells like they fell into the latrines," another said. "How did we get stuck with the stupidest dogs in the world?"

"Same way we got stuck out here on a night this cold," the first said. "Bad luck and lots of it."

The soldiers watched the dogs' suffering instead of paying attention to their surroundings. The first clue they had that they were under attack came when Moratrayas jumped between them and swung his electrified staff into a soldier. He stunned a second man as his clockworks tackled the other two. Clockwork hounds kept their savage jaws directly over the men's necks.

Moratrayas leaned over and looked the two men in the eyes. "Choose your next words carefully. They may be your last."

"We surrender," one of them whispered. The other nodded.

Moratrayas smiled and tied the soldiers up. "A wise decision. Now for the men at the gate."

The two soldiers at the gate did their best to stay awake. It was late and they'd been at their posts for hours. On top of that the cold was making them sleepy. They'd bribed their way out of this duty before, but they'd run out of coins to pay off their officers.

"Wouldn't be so bad if we had some rum to keep ourselves warm with," one said to the other.

The second soldier snorted. "Good luck finding any you can afford. Those filthy mercenaries are drinking up all our stocks. Nothing left for us working stiffs."

Two soldiers march up to them from inside the slave camp. They paid no attention to either since they were clearly the men patrolling the inside of the camp. Hard to see under all those clothes, but who else could it be?

"What's wrong with the dogs?" the first guard asked.

The soldiers walked up to the gate and beckoned for the men to come in.

"I said what's wrong with the dogs? They're making a racket like someone's killing them."

The two soldiers pointed inside the camp where the dogs were rolling around. Then they pointed at latrine pits dug inside the camp.

"Oh come on, tell me they didn't chase some critter in there!" the second soldier said. He saw one of the silent soldiers in the camp hold up a bottle and shake it. The guard's eyes opened wide. "You got booze? Why didn't you say so?"

The two soldiers opened the gate and went inside. The first man slapped what he thought was a fellow soldier on the back. "That's right kind of you. We were just saying how we could do with a drink. Must have cost you a day's pay to buy that bottle and you're sharing it. You're a real pal!"

Once the soldiers were inside the camp and out of sight, the two human clockworks knocked them out with quick blows. Moratrayas and Sandra hurried from behind a building and dragged the men away. Two clockworks picked up the soldiers' weapons and then took their place guarding the gate. Minutes later four clockwork men and three clockwork hounds patrolled the inside of the camp, mimicking the route of the soldiers. Wearing the soldiers' armor and coats, they were indistinguishable from the real thing.

"They look the part," Sandra admitted, "but what happens if someone walks up and asks a question?"

"Clockworks can only make simple noises. Growls, whines, err, whistles." Moratrayas was still embarrassed how his clockworks had treated Sandra earlier. "You're right, though, they can't talk. One more reason we need to move quickly and not draw attention to ourselves."

They ran to the nearest barracks and unbarred it. The door was locked as well. Cursing under his breath, Moratrayas used his saw to cut the lock off. They went inside and closed the door behind them before Moratrayas turned on one of his glowing green spheres. He held it up and illuminated the building's interior.

Inside they found a hundred men in dirty clothes sleeping on bunk beds set three high. They were covered in thin sheets and had a wood stove in the center of the room to keep them warm. The men slept deeply and missed Sandra and the doctor's entrance. Even the light didn't wake them.

Sandra walked down the row of bunk beds looking for her father and brother. It was hard for her to recognize any of these people. The men ranged in age from their teens to sixties. They'd lost a lot of weight since she'd last seen them, and many had scraggly beards. When she did find her father, she almost didn't realize him.

"Dad, dad wake up," she said. She shook his shoulder.

The older man grumbled before he opened his eyes. "Sandra? Oh mercy, they got you too?"

"No, dad, I'm here to help. You have to get up and wake everyone. We're leaving."

Sandra's father sat up and pulled off his sheet. He was in his fifties and strong as a draft horse from years of hard work. His hair was thinning and he looked like he'd lost a few pounds, but what worried Sandra most were two scars on his face he didn't have before his capture.

"Sandra, you have to leave right now. Whatever you're planning won't work. I saw Stoth's magic clear the road, but only to the pass. We'll never get out that way, and even if we did, we don't have food for the trip home."

"Who said anything about taking the pass?" Moratrayas asked.

Smiling, Sandra said, "Dad, this is Doctor Moratrayas. He's here to help. Al, this is Ulysses Sower, my dad."

Other men in the barrack began to wake up. One of them heard the introduction and asked, "Moratrayas the mad scientist?"

"I'm not mad," Moratrayas corrected him. "Horribly disappointed with my homeland, but not mad. Mr. Sower, you and your people are leaving tonight. Take your sheets for warmth and let's go."

Sandra's father lifted his right leg high enough for them to see the shackle on it. "We're chained to our beds at night."

"Where's the key?" Moratrayas demanded.

"In the castle. After they lock us up they take the key there and bring it back in the morning."

"That will slow us down," Moratrayas said. He put the pneumatic saw on his right hand and turned it on. "Sandra, bring in the grasshopper clockwork from outside and have it chew through the chains. Don't worry, Mr. Sower. Your trip home is delayed but not denied."

The mood was somber in the Blue Sashes camp. Thane brought the barrel of brandy Stoth gave him and shared it with the men, but it was only enough to give everyone a sip. He spent a fair amount of his own money buying more alcohol and served it. The men had gone without a good drink for weeks, and Thane was willing to part with some gold to improve morale.

It didn't help. The men spent too much time talking in hushed tones. Thane couldn't order them to be cheerful, and given their situation he couldn't blame them for their poor disposition. Week after week of inactivity, poor food and little liquor left them restless, and that was before what happened today. Best to let them talk it over and arrange for a few hours of sparing and marching in the morning to let them work off their anxiety.

The camp included a cluster of canvas tents, penned up draft animals, nearly empty supply wagons and a stockade fence around the edges. A few fires provided light and warmth, but no cheer. Men wandered around camp and guards stood at rigid attention. Thane stood by a fire as he looked at Scour and its castle.

One of Thane's officers marched up to him and came to attention. "Permission to speak, general."

"Granted."

The officer hesitated. He'd served with Thane for years and survived more battles than either man could count. It was clear the officer wasn't happy with the situation, but he didn't like complaining to the general who'd led him to victory time and again. "Sir, the men are worried by what happened today. It's the Sun Gun."

"It's quite a weapon," Thane said.

"That's just it. If King Stoth has a weapon that powerful, then why hire us? Sir, there's also some concerns about how he means to use it. We haven't been paid yet and won't be until the fighting starts."

Thane looked back at the castle, the highest tower in particular. “They’re worried if Stoth can’t pay us, or decides he doesn’t want to, he might use the Sun Gun on us.”

“Yes, sir. We fight a few battles for him, we demand our pay instead of ask for it, and he might use that thing to turn us to ashes. The men aren’t cowards, sir, but they’re not comfortable with magic that powerful.”

“Neither am I,” Thane replied. “Spread word to the men, unofficially, that I’m working on a plan in case things turn sour. We’ll be paid one way or the other.”

The officer came to attention. “Yes, sir.”

Thane opened his mouth to say more, but was interrupted by a commotion from the city gate. It was a goblin dressed in black and running out of Scour as fast as he could. The little critter held a large Stone Heart flag in one hand and a dagger in the other. The goblin shouted exuberantly and fled into the night.

“Ha ha! I got your flag! I got your flag!”

Cursing and shouting soldiers chased after the goblin. They ran out like an angry mob instead of an armed force, bumping into neighboring soldiers and getting in each other’s way. They spotted the goblin and made a beeline for him. The goblin had short legs and wouldn’t be able to run fast in the snow. His head start wouldn’t last long, but the little pest screamed with wild abandon instead of fear.

“I got your stupid flag, and you know what I’m going to do with it? I’m going to go to the bathroom and wipe my bottom with it!”

The soldiers shouted death threats in reply and closed the gap between them. Rather than speeding up, the goblin instead began running in a zigzag pattern. Thane couldn’t figure out what the foolish pest was thinking. Goblins as a rule were crazy, but this one was going to get himself killed. Blue Sashes mercenaries and camp followers gathered to watch the spectacle. Some placed bets on how long the goblin would last.

The soldiers chasing the goblin got within ten feet when suddenly the four closest soldiers fell to the ground. Men behind them ran into the fallen soldiers and fell over as well. A soldier skidded to a halt, only to have more men ram into him from behind. One soldier dug through the snow and found a trip line tied to two stakes. The trip line was hidden by snow, effectively invisible until someone ran into it.

Soldiers struggled to their feet and went after the goblin again. They hit more trip lines, followed by shallow pits under the snow, and another line of traps after that.

“It’s like watching an army of clowns,” Thane said.

The officer laughed. “Good one, sir.”

Thane was going to explain that he wasn't joking, but he saw men and women all over the camp laughing and pointing at Stoth's soldiers. The soldiers saw this and knew they were being made fun of. They got angry and tried all the harder to catch the goblin. More soldiers joined in the chase. They didn't want to look bad in front of the mercenaries, unaware that it was much too late for that.

By this point Thane was willing to do anything to cheer his men up. He pointed at the fleeing goblin and said, "Now that's a real soldier. A hundred men after him and there's not a scratch on him. Stoth should hire him!"

The whole camp erupted in laughter. A mercenary shouted, "Hire him nothing! Make him a captain!"

More jokes followed at the expense of Stoth's soldiers and loud enough for everyone to hear. Humiliated soldiers still chased the goblin in a vain attempt to salvage their pride. It was clear the little fellow was going to make a clean escape, but they kept after him anyway. Then another twenty goblins emerged from cover and threw snowballs at the soldiers, a scene so bizarre Thane laughed until he fell over.

"Watch it," a man said nervously. The clockwork grasshopper chewed through the chain around his leg, its oversized steel jaws making a grinding sound as they bit through the chain. "Careful. I'm very attached to that leg."

"Don't worry, it hasn't made a mistake yet," Sandra assured him.

The man could barely hear her over the noise. Sandra was busy directing the clockwork to free one man after another while Moratrayas used his saw to cut the men's shackles. They'd already freed everyone in the first barrack and were busy in a second. The freed men were excited as could be and peppered Moratrayas and Sandra with questions. Others looted the toolshed and came out with axes, hammers and picks, which they used to break chains on their own. In a few more minutes everyone would be free.

It was more than mere excitement flowing through the growing crowd. For the first time in a month they had hope. They smiled and thanked Moratrayas and Sandra. They talked about going home to families and friends they thought they'd never see again. Seeing soldiers who'd tormented them tied up, gagged and locked in a barrack along with their miserable dogs only added to their glee.

Two men studied the clockwork grasshopper as it freed a third man. "Funny looking thing. Never thought I'd be grateful to see a mad scientist."

"Any port in a storm," the other man said.

"Mr. Sower, I have a question," Moratrayas said as he worked. "These barracks hold a hundred men apiece, but there are only three hundred of you forced into three buildings. What is the purpose of the extra barracks?"

Ulysses Sower scowled, his expression even more intimidating because of his scars. "They got us first, but weren't going to stop with us. The way they talked, they'd be kidnapping and shipping in hundreds more men to work their fields this spring."

"That won't happen," Moratrayas told him. "Once we're done, Stoth won't cause trouble for you or anyone else."

Sandra ran in with a young man who bore a striking resemblance to Ulysses. "Dad, I found Jason!"

"Good girl," Ulysses said. He hugged his grown son and smiled. "Well boy, our little girl has shown us both up."

Jason Sower smiled fiercely. "Sandra's one in a million. Now that we have our chains off, where do we go next?"

Moratrayas smiled. "To the docks. Igor should be done by now."

The docks were quiet. Ship builders who usually made this place ring with hammering and the hiss of saws were gone for the night. A few soldiers guarded the river barges, dry docks, building supplies, storerooms and toolsheds. Like the soldiers at the slave camp, these men were lax in their duties after months spent protecting the docks from enemies that never came. Two of them huddled next to a small fire and talked.

"I haven't seen Charlie in a while," one said.

"I thought Captain Tinley sent him into the woods," the second replied.

"No, he was here an hour ago by the dry docks."

The second man shrugged. "He probably sneaked off somewhere warm. It's not like anyone's going to catch him. Tinley must have sent two hundred men out on a wild goose chase and left the city guard real light."

Concealed by the darkness, Igor dragged Charlie the unconscious soldier between two barges. He'd used his chloroform soaked rag on the man and three others guarding the docks. Once his latest victim was safely tied up, he slipped back into the shadows.

"Weird stuff going on lately," the first soldier said. "There was that goblin tunnel they found today. Who knows how long that was there? And the dogs were making a racket in the slave camp a little while ago."

"Not our job, not our problem," the second soldier said. "Let the guys on slave guard duty take care of it."

Igor slipped through the shadows, moving closer to the two men. They were the last threats to his part of the plan, but if either of them screamed they could bring in dozens of soldiers in a hurry. This would require delicacy.

Roars of laughter came from the Blue Sashes camp, prompting both soldiers to scowl. The first spit and said, "They're laughing at us. I know it."

The second soldier waved his sword at the Blue Sashes camp. "Filthy foreigners, always looking down on us. Who do they think they are?"

The first soldier took a step away from the fire and pointed an accusing finger at the mercenary's camp. "The ugly one called Thane keeps saying we should be doing more drills and marches, like he's got some right to order us around. You know what's going to happen? When the war starts, those no good parasites will fight as little as possible and take every bit of loot they can lay their hands on."

The soldier was so angry and focused on ranting against the mercenaries that he didn't notice Igor sneak up, chloroform his companion and drag off the unconscious man.

"What are they fighting for, anyway?" he demanded. "We're fighting for our rights, for respect! Them, they're just a bunch of money-grubbing thugs going from war to war, standing for nothing except the next payday. Once we finish taking over the Raushtad there won't be a place for men like that! We'll chase them like dogs after foxes and kill the lot of them. They wouldn't be laughing if they knew what was coming their way, would they?"

The soldier turned around and saw Igor standing two feet away, a cheerful smile plastered on his face. "No, I guess not," Igor said, and then slapped the rag over the man's mouth and chloroformed him.

With the soldiers on guard duty dealt with, Igor took oars and sails from the storerooms and placed them on eight barges. It was hard work, but Igor was far stronger than his bent body suggested. With that done he dumped rags, sawdust, wood chips and sailcloth on other barges as fuel to burn them.

Igor finished all the work, which was both good and bad. Everything was ready for when Moratrayas brought Sandra's people. But according to the plan, Igor was supposed to do this work with their help. Since he'd finished without them it meant they were running very late.

"Doc's behind schedule," he said nervously. "Come on, don't keep a friend waiting."

Sandra and Moratrayas finally had all the men freed and assembled outside the barracks. They were eager to leave, but without instructions their escape could turn into a disaster. Worse, they were armed with tools that could double as weapons, and they were angry enough to attack their tormentors if they got a chance.

Moratrayas stood in front of them and said, "Gentlemen, if I can have your attention. We have a means of escape thanks to Stoth's fleet of barges. Who here has experience sailing?" Ten men raised their hands. "You ten will be in charge of handling the barges' rudders, and the rest of you will man the oars. I know you're tired, but with a little more work you can be home soon."

"What about food?" someone asked.

"I have my own barge with provisions aboard," Moratrayas told them. "It won't go far with so many men to feed, but it will only take two days at most to make our escape. You may be hungry before you get home, but you will get home."

Ulysses Sower laughed. "We've been hungry for a whole month. What's two days matter?"

"That's a good attitude," Moratrayas said. "We need to leave quickly, quietly and along a route that won't expose us to detection. Follow Sandra Sower or myself when we leave. My clockworks will take up the rear and protect us. If you have questions now is not the time to ask them. Move quickly, follow instructions and we'll get out of here and make sure Stoth and his army won't be able to follow us."

Moratrayas cut a wider hole in the fence so the men could leave more quickly and then led them out into the snow. It would take time to reach the barges, especially since the men were exhausted from hard work and the abuse inflicted on them. The clockwork menagerie guarding the back of the group would buy them that time.

"What about the clockworks pretending to be soldiers and guard dogs?" Sandra asked Moratrayas.

"I need to leave them in place for as long as possible to maintain the appearance that everything is normal. Once everyone's aboard the barges I'll recall them." Moratrayas pulled a brass whistle from his pocket. "Dog whistle. They will hear it and come when ordered."

"We're going to be fighting alongside those fools?" a mercenary asked derisively. The Blue Sashes were still chuckling at the soldiers' humiliation.

Thane shared their disgust, and with good reason. A company of Stoth's men was still after those goblins somewhere in the woods, as if they had any chance of catching them. They'd lost to goblins, for crying out loud! Mind you, years of travel and combat gave Thane a healthy respect for what goblins could do if properly annoyed. They made great saboteurs, and when there were enough of them they were passable fighters. Still, to embarrass a hundred men was outrageous!

"I'll suggest our employer schedule more drills and a joint exercise with us," Thane said. "That might help a little, or at least show them that they're not as good as they need to be."

"You've asked for that before, general," an officer pointed out.

Thane nodded. "Captain Tinley protested at the time, but I think the good captain won't be a problem for much longer. His replacement might be more receptive."

"Stoth's got a bunch of green recruits he calls an army, but they're not all bad," the officer said.

Thane raised his eyebrows. "Really? I haven't seen a man in Stone Heart worthy of my respect."

"He's got a good bunch guarding the slaves for a change. Attentive, aggressive, checking the doors like they should instead of sneaking off to hide by a fire. I know that's not much, but it's better than most of them."

"Really," Thane repeated, but thoughtfully this time. The soldiers at the slave camp were as a rule lazy and easily distracted. He'd seen them ignoring their duties not two hours earlier and was tempted to go over and put the fear of God into them. They made a 180-degree change that quickly? Something was wrong. "Show me."

The officer led Thane to the edge of the mercenary's camp and pointed at the slave camp. Sure enough, the soldiers on guard duty patrolled with the efficiency Thane expected from his own men. The officer said, "That's them. Maybe we can hire them away from Stoth before we leave."

Thane's eyes narrowed. This wasn't right. Not one soldier he'd seen in weeks living here showed that much professionalism. There were other things that didn't make sense, either. There was the goblin prank that lured away so many soldiers, and the goblin tunnel with men or elves escaping from it. So many odd things happening in one day worried him. In his experience, when life didn't make sense it meant you were about to get hurt.

Struggling to see in the poor light and through falling snow, Thane squinted as he studied the slave camp. "Wait a minute, there are only three dogs inside the camp. Where's the fourth one?"

The officer frowned. "I don't know. They had it earlier."

Thane pointed to the officer and ten nearest mercenaries. "You men, with me."

Thane marched to the slave camp with his men at his heels. They didn't understand his concern, but they respected him too much to question his orders. Thane stopped thirty feet from the slave camp's gate. The two soldiers saw them and came to attention. They looked normal enough, bundled up against the cold so no skin showed. Then they saluted.

It was an understandable mistake. When general and officer approach a soldier, he should salute them. The clockworks didn't know how much the soldiers hated the mercenaries and how much the feeling was returned in kind. Moratrayas himself hadn't realized how deep the hatred ran or he would have warned his creations. Politeness and military protocol aside, Stoth's men never saluted mercenaries no matter their rank. The second Thane saw that, he knew they were intruders.

Thane drew his sword. "We've been invaded! Sound the alarm and summon reinforcements!"

# Chapter 11

Thane and his men attacked the clockworks guarding the gate to the slave camp, not suspecting what they faced. At Thane's direction, one mercenary ran to alert the Blue Sashes camp and another went to warn the soldiers in Scour. Thane, one of his officers and eight mercenaries drew their swords and attacked the two clockworks, fighting with the competence and fierceness that made the Blue Sashes renowned. Five against one were good odds, and defeating the two invaders should have been child's play.

Should have been and wasn't. The first clockwork swung a sword with enough strength to hack a large piece off a mercenary's shield. The second clockwork parried a blow and grabbed a mercenary by the arm. With one fluid motion, it threw the man into the fence around the slave camp.

"They're not men or elves," the officer said. A mercenary got a lucky hit and slashed through a clockwork's clothes and armor. Ignoring the damage, the clockwork responded with a circle kick that sent his attacker flying. Startled, the officer cried out, "They don't bleed!"

"Nether do golems, but hit them hard enough and they'll fall," Thane snarled. He tried to cut his foe's legs out from under him, but the clockwork leaped into another Blue Sashes mercenary, knocking both of them down. The clockwork got back up and looked Thane in the eye before beckoning him to try again.

Thane smiled and pointed his sword at his enemy. "Finally! After months of doing nothing I have a decent fight! Before this is over I'll either kill you or hire you!"

Moratrayas and Sandra heard the sound of battle from the slave camp. Men shouted and cried out in pain. Swords rang like bells when they struck. Moratrayas said, "We've been discovered. Everyone get to the barges. Help anyone who trips!"

Men ran through the snow to the lit docks. The menagerie of small clockworks took up the rear, whirring and clicking as they bounded through the snow. The docks were two miles away, a lot of ground to cover to reach safety. Fear gripped the crowd and then doubled in intensity when they heard alarm bells in the Blue Sashes camp. Mercenaries poured from the camp like ants from a hill that had been kicked, and they headed straight for the slave camp. Once they reached it, they'd spot the fleeing men's tracks.

"Can nothing go right tonight?" Moratrayas asked. He shouted to Sandra, "Keep them headed for the docks! I'll be right behind you."

Moratrayas allowed the crowd to run by him. The clockwork menagerie caught up to him and stopped. He blew his dog whistle to summon the other clockworks from the slave camp, and told his smaller creations, "Delay our pursuers as long as possible, then join me."

The small clockworks saluted before digging into the deep snow. Anyone following the escaping men was going to have a very nasty surprise indeed. Moratrayas left them and hurried to catch up with the others.

At the docks they found Igor waiting. He directed men to the barges he'd prepared for them and away from ones he'd turned into floating powder kegs. When Moratrayas arrived, Igor said, "Fashionably late, I see."

"It's one of those nights, Igor. Any trouble?"

Alarm bells rang from Scour and the castle. Soldiers came out, more slowly and disorganized than the Blue Sashes, but they came. Igor watched them and frowned. "Not yet, but I'd rather not extend our stay."

"Agreed. Get my barge and I'll oversee matters here."

The fight outside the slave camp was confusing as six clockwork men and three clockwork hounds fought a growing army of mercenaries. Human clockworks had enough of their disguises hacked off to show that they weren't men. Thane and his men had no experience fighting mad scientists and their creations. They didn't know what they were up against except they fought hard, were stronger and heavier than they looked, and could take abuse that would drop an ox.

A clockwork man pulled a bottle out of its tattered coat and threw it at a band of approaching mercenaries. It hit a man's shield and shattered, splashing them with Moratrayas' animal repellant. Men gagged at the foul odor, but they didn't flee.

Clockwork men fought against impossible odds and held their own, relying on their strength and durability to get them through the fight. Clockwork hounds bounded through the snowy battlefield, bowling men over and moving on to the next mercenary. They moved so fast that it was impossible for the mercenaries to surround them. Despite their small numbers, this was proving to be a real fight.

In spite of the clockworks' incredible performance, there was no question how the battle would end. Two hundred Blue Sashes were already present and the rest were coming fast. Once the men got into formation, it didn't matter how strong the clockworks were, they'd be outnumbered, surrounded and cut to pieces.

Thane was beside himself with delight. He'd scored four hits on the same clockwork man. He'd cut open its armored skin to reveal the tubes and spinning gears within, but it wouldn't fall. With all that damage it fought every bit as hard as in the first minute the battle. After so much inactivity this was the kind of exercise he needed!

A mercenary ran into the slave camp and hurried back. "General, the slaves have escaped!"

"So that's what this is about," Thane said to the clockwork. "The goblins were a distraction while you got the slaves out. You're good."

The clockwork bowed in reply, and with its next swing nearly skewered Thane. He parried the blade, but it still came within inches of his chest

Stoth's soldiers came running to the battle. They stopped and bunched up, gaping at the sight.

"Your slaves escaped!" Thane roared at them. "Get moving and cut off their retreat!"

The soldiers recognized the clockworks. They knew who made them and what they were capable of. Worse, so many clockworks meant Moratrayas couldn't be far away. One of them cried out, "It's the mad tailor's inventions! He's here! He's come back to destroy us!"

All the soldiers backed away in horror. Together with the mercenaries already present they outnumbered the clockworks a hundred to one, but it didn't seem to matter. Terrified beyond reason, they either started to flee or stood as still as statues.

Thane landed a solid kick and knocked over the clockwork he was fighting. Before it got up, Thane pointed his sword at the soldiers and bellowed, "You cowardly, yellow bellied, fire tending, good for nothing nobodies! Your slaves are gone and these things are responsible!"

The clockwork sprang back to its feet and attacked again. Thane parried its swing and added, "You're nothing but a bunch of frightened old women! You men say you're soldiers instead of farmers? Ha! If you don't want to be farmers again you'd better get those slaves, or come springtime you'll be back to grubbing in the mud!"

Insults worked where reason and discipline didn't. Stoth's soldiers ran after the fleeing slaves, red faced from shame as much as anger.

But they didn't leave alone. As one the clockworks raised their heads, up as if listening to a sound only they could hear before they fled to the docks. Fleeing was the practical thing to do since they were outnumbered and the mercenaries were getting organized. Thane approved. The question was where were they going and what would they do when they got there?

Thane pointed his sword at the man who told him the slaves escaped. "Which direction did the slaves go?"

"Their tracks head to the river and docks. Should we go after them?"

"No, let Stoth's men do that," Thane replied. He saw the disgust on his men's faces when he gave the order. "They're heading for the river barges to escape, that much is clear. Stoth's men can harry them, but we need to be where they're going, not where they are now."

A plan formed quickly in his mind. His entire army was present and ready for battle, giving him the manpower to end the fight. He pointed at his officers and put them into motion. "You three, take your men downstream and attack them if they come. You three take your men upstream and do the same. The rest of you get ropes, grappling hooks and crossbows from camp. Bring them to the upstream and downstream groups. They won't get away from us."

"Come on," Sandra urged her people. "We need the same number of rowers on each barge."

She was trying to sort the men out and make sure each barge was equally crewed. There was no wind to speak of, so they needed to use the oars. If one ship had too few rowers it wouldn't move fast enough and could be left behind.

The freed men moved as fast as they could, which wasn't fast enough. Hard work, long hours, malnutrition and frequent abuse by their captors left them weaker and slower than they once were. The damage would heal with time and good food, but they needed to escape now. The eight barges they were stealing were still moored to the docks as the men took their places by the oars.

Sandra saw lights in the distance moving toward them. She heard armor clang and angry voices cry out. Hundreds of armed men were coming their way. It didn't matter whether it was Stoth's soldiers or his mercenaries. Either one could stop the barges before they left. Sandra figured her people had ten minutes or less before the enemy was on them.

Moratrayas ran up to her and asked, "Are they ready?"

"Another minute or two, but they'll move slow going upstream," she told him.

"Once they're in the water that won't matter. Igor is coming with my barge. Wait for him and do whatever you can to slow down Stoth's men." With that he ran off to the remaining barges.

"Where are you going?"

"To make sure we're not followed!"

The barges loaded with Sandra's people cut their mooring lines and slowly edged out onto the river. They turned and headed upstream under oar power. Sandra was used to the speed of Moratrayas' barge. Compared to that, these barges moved like turtles.

Farther down the docks, she saw Moratrayas light a torch from a fire and step aboard a moored barge. Seconds later the barge lit up the night with flames. He ran off and boarded a second barge, which soon became a floating bonfire.

"They're burning our ships!" an approaching soldier screamed. "Move faster, you louts! Stop them!"

Sandra knelt down and braced her back against a toolshed before firing the net thrower. She pulled the trigger three times, the kickback from the gun bruising her shoulder. As before, the weapon flipped out a tab reading 'please reload', but it did the job. Three weighted nets spun through the air and hit the soldiers. Each net was wide enough to wrap around three or four men and leave them helplessly tangled on the ground. Unlike the ice golem, the soldiers didn't have the strength to rip through the fibrous net and were trapped until someone else freed them. More men tripped over their fallen comrades, slowing the attack down and weakening it, but not stopping it.

"Faster!" a captain urged his men.

The soldiers almost reached Sandra when the snow exploded around them. The clockwork menagerie jumped out of snowdrifts and attacked. Most of the clockworks were small, but surprise and ferocity made up for their size as they stopped the charge on their own.

"Not in the face!" a man shouted when a clockwork cat jumped at him. It hit him, jumped off his head and slammed into another soldier. The clockworks moved quickly, hitting one man and moving to a second before the soldiers could react. They weren't hurting anyone very badly, but the shock of having a hissing, twenty-pound brass clockwork charging into them scared the men.

Damaged clockwork men and hounds caught up with the soldiers, running through the frightened men, knocking them aside and adding to the confusion. If the soldiers kept their cool and maintained a formation they would win the fight quickly enough, but panic and inexperience eliminated any chance of victory.

"Sandra! Doc!" It was Igor, coming down river at the wheel of Moratrayas' armored barge. The river was wide enough for him to go around the fleeing river barges loaded with the men of Sun Valley. "Come on, we have to go!"

Sandra ran over and climbed onto the barge once Igor brought it to the docks. Torch still in hand, Moratrayas came off a third river barge, leaving it a blazing inferno. He hesitated and looked at the barges still moored to the docks. There were so many left.

"Doc, come on," Igor said. "I saw the Blue Sashes heading upriver. They're trying to cut us off. We leave now or we don't leave!"

Snarling, Moratrayas ran down the nearest dock and leaped onto his barge. "We didn't do nearly enough damage," he said bitterly.

The dragonfly clockwork fluttered down into Sandra's hands. They'd left it behind when they went to free the slaves, and judging by its loud buzzing it wasn't happy about that. Moratrayas seized it and placed the lit torch into its legs. Pressing buttons on its tail, he threw it into the air. The dragonfly soared into the snowy night, flew over the moored barges and dropped the torch on a fourth barge, setting it alight.

"That's eight barges taken and four destroyed," Moratrayas said when the dragonfly returned to roost on Sandra's shoulders. "They still have dozens more to follow us with."

Igor smiled and steered the barge to follow the others fleeing Stone Heart. "Well, yes and no."

Back on land, the clockworks broke off and fled again, leaving Stoth's men more disoriented than defeated. Captains gradually got their men heading to the docks. They found many barges missing and four burning brightly. The river was too cold and deep to swim, leaving the remaining barges the only way to catch the escaped slaves. One of Stoth's captains stared in shock for a moment before shouting, "Uh, you men, put those fires out! Uh, uh, the rest of you get on the other barges and go after them!"

Soldiers trying to stop the fires weren't having much luck. There weren't any buckets handy, so they used their helmets to scoop icy water from the river and throw it on the fires. It was slow and not very effective. Other soldiers ran to the remaining barges and got on them, only to find no oars or sails to propel them. They checked nearby buildings and found them empty.

"Where are the oars?" the captain demanded. "We can't go anywhere without them."

"They're over here!" a soldier by the river answered. The captain ran over and found all the oars not taken by the fleeing slaves. They were stacked up on the barges Moratrayas had set fire to, and they burned like logs in a fireplace. No one was going to follow Moratrayas by water.

The captain stared at the flames, too stunned to react. "I'm going to get blamed for this. I just know it."

Back in Scour, the scene was pure pandemonium. No one knew quite what was going on, including Captain Tinley. He was already a nervous wreck from the threat Stoth had made against him. Earlier that evening Tinley had sent out half his men to look for the intruders. Then a hundred more went after the goblins that promised to desecrate their national flag. Now he was getting conflicting reports that something was going on at the slave camp, or maybe the docks. No two soldiers told him the same thing.

Tinley paced back and forth next to the armory and square where the siege weapons were parked. Soldiers ran by on errands while others milled around, not sure what was going on or what they should do. Complicating matters, townspeople were coming out of their houses, confused by the commotion and wanting answers.

"What's going on?" a housewife demanded.

"You'll be told when it's important for you to know," he snapped back. She opened her mouth to argue, but ran off when he drew his sword. "Blast it, what's going on around here?"

A soldier ran up to him and reported, "Captain Tinley, it's the mad tailor, he's back!"

Tinley grabbed the man by his shoulders. "You're sure?"

"Positive. He's here, and he brought his brass monsters with him. They're fighting the Blue Sashes to a standstill."

"So much for the professionals," Tinley spat. He spotted a handful of soldiers milling about waiting for orders. "Right, go tell King Stoth. As for the rest of you, prepare two catapults and take them to the docks. We'll see how much that fiend likes facing real weapons!"

The soldiers ran to the catapults, but they pulled away when they set their hands on the first one. Tinley marched up and demanded, "What's wrong with you? Get moving!"

"Sir, something's wrong with the catapult," a soldier said. "It's sticky."

Confused, Tinley set a gauntlet-covered hand on the catapult. His hand stuck to it, not so much that he couldn't pull it free, but that wasn't the point. The catapult was fine this morning, clean and ready for use. Tinley sniffed the goo left on his gauntlet. Puzzled, he said, "It's pine resin."

One of the soldiers stepped back and looked at the rest of the siege weapons. "They've all got it on them. Look, they shine."

He was right. Now that Tinley was paying attention to them, he saw resin dripping off the rest of the siege weapons. Under the weak light of the soldiers' torches, they seemed to glisten like they were coated in slime.

"They weren't like this in the afternoon," Tinley said. "Someone did this in the last few hours. Wasn't someone supposed to be guarding them?"

"Hey, Tinley!" a squeaky voice shouted.

Tinley and the men spun around to find three goblins sitting on the roof of a house. The roof was lined with empty buckets smeared with pine resin. The goblins smiled and waved sticky brushes and lit torches. Hopping from foot to foot, a goblin jeered, "Looks like you finally figured out which end of a sword you're supposed to hold it by. Only took you a year."

"You filth!" Tinley shouted back. "You did this!"

"Clever boy," a goblin said.

The neighboring goblin nodded. "With a mind like that you'd never guess he used to grow potatoes for a living."

"Resin won't stop us!" Tinley snapped at them.

"Yeah," a goblin agreed. "But pine resin isn't just sticky. It's also flammable."

The goblins laughed and threw their torches, each one aiming for a different target. Tinley desperately swung his sword and knocked a torch aside, but the other two hit their targets. Two catapults burst into flames, the dry wood and resin burning bright enough to light up the courtyard. The goblins lit more torches and threw them.

But the second attack didn't go as well. Soldiers swatted aside the torches with swords and blocked them with shields. Worse, the soldiers fought back, throwing anything they could at the goblins. The three were knocked off the roof and landed on bags filled with straw they'd left there earlier. Soldiers ran after them, but the goblins ducked into a small hole in a stable.

Fires from the catapults grew brighter and higher. Tinley swore and shouted, "Move the other catapults away from the burning ones! Hurry, or they'll catch fire and spread down the row!" He saw worried townspeople gathering. "Clean the siege weapons. Get soap and hot water. Run!"

Tinley kept the disaster from growing out of control. Within minutes the fires were contained, but the two burning catapults were going to be a total loss. By morning there'd be nothing left of them but ashes.

"Ah, Captain Tinley." Stoth said calmly. He walked into the courtyard flanked by ten soldiers. He looked at the burning catapults with mild interest. "My men told me there was a problem, and I find my precious siege weapons burning like campfires. This is coming out of your pay, captain."

"Bill me if we live that long!" he retorted. "Moratrayas is back, and he's in league with the goblins. He's hit us here, at the slave camp and maybe the docks. I'm not sure about the last one. Your hired thugs are fighting him and losing."

Stoth's eyes opened wide and he smiled eagerly. During his speeches Stoth occasionally looked excited, but that enthusiasm was fake, a mask he put on for the crowd's benefit. This time his glee looked genuine. "He's here? You're sure?"

"The men saw his brass monsters. That's not a sight they'd mistake."

Stoth clapped his hands together. "Magnificent! Leave your men to clean up this mess and come with me to the castle."

Confused, Tinley pointed his sword at the city gates. "But, but he's out there."

"Oh don't be a fool," Stoth said. "I beat Moratrayas last time by the skin of my teeth, and that was when he only had nine months to build his army. Well he's finally back for his revenge, and he's had three years to prepare for it! Swords and spears won't stop him."

Stoth smiled and looked up at the castle's tallest tower. "But we've got something better."

"We're behind schedule, but we're moving in the right direction and we haven't lost anyone," Moratrayas said. The fleet of fleeing barges gradually made their way upstream. Towering trees grew on either side of the riverbank.

Heavy snowfall made visibility low, but they forged on. "Another hour and we'll be beyond Stoth's grasp."

"Going to be a rough hour, though," Igor said.

Moratrayas looked behind them. "Stoth still has the Blue Sashes and the Sun Gun. Gertrude won't have a clear shot at the castle tower until we get out of the forest and reach a clearing. Once we do I'll put an end to that horror."

Everyone on the barges was nervous, and with good reason. The eight stolen barges were making poor progress, and the men aboard lacked armor and proper weapons. It would be disastrous if they got into a fight. Moratrayas' armored barge brought up the rear of the fleet to offer what protection it could. Farther back onshore the clockworks followed on foot. Once the battle was over Moratrayas could stop and bring them aboard, but for now that was time he didn't have.

They were close enough to the last barge to hear the men rowing. The man at the rudder shouted, "Stroke, stroke, stroke", and men struggled to row fast enough. Some of them grumbled, but they didn't stop.

"I should be with them," Sandra said.

"They need you here," Moratrayas told her. He reloaded the net thrower and handed it back to her. "I'll need your help if we have to fight our way out of this."

"But I don't understand how any of this stuff works," she protested.

"You know more about it than they do. You've already fought several battles and won them all. What you do here and now will determine whether these men get home. Do your best, follow my orders and we'll succeed."

Just then they heard snaps and crashes in the woods. It sounded like a crowd was moving through the forest and trampling through snowdrifts and fallen branches. Four hundred men came out of the forest and stopped along the shoreline, roughly in the middle of the fleeing fleet of barges. It was the Blue Sashes.

The mercenaries attacked with precision and efficiency rivaling that of Moratrayas' clockworks. They threw ropes with grappling hooks and caught two barges with two grappling hooks each. Twenty men pulled on each rope and slowly dragged the barges to a halt. More mercenaries fired crossbows, forcing everyone on the barges to keep their heads down. Slowly, inexorably, the snared barges were pulled toward shore where armed men waited.

"Row harder!" a man on a snared barge shouted. The rowers pulled for all they were worth, but they were fighting both the current and dozens of strong mercenaries.

Moratrayas took the wheel of his barge and got behind the first snared boat. He pressed the bow of his vessel against the back of the barge and then put all the power he had into the engine. The two barges began to move and at the same time dragged the mercenaries on the ropes toward the water.

"Let go or you'll go in the river!" a Blue Sashes' officer ordered. The men gave up on the ropes and the barge moved on its own power again. Stymied, the officer shouted, "Fire on the one in back!"

Crossbow bolts rained down on Moratrayas' barge. Most of them broke against the barge's armored side, but a few stuck into empty boxes and barrels. Sandra, Moratrayas and Igor kept down and tried to make sure none of them stopped a crossbow bolt the hard way. Sandra fired the net thrower twice and tangled up a few of their attackers. Igor took the wheel, leaving Moratrayas to grab his dart launcher and pepper the men on shore with white tipped darts.

Igor deftly piloted the barge to the second snared ship. This one was almost dragged to shore, and the men aboard were panicking. They were coming on a bend in the river, and there wasn't enough room to push the caught barge free. Muttering under his breath, Moratrayas seized his pneumatic saw and fiddled with its controls. He turned it on and aimed it at the ropes. This time the saw's familiar buzz was replaced by a shriek before the saw blade shot through the air. It cut the ropes holding the barge, then skipped across the water before embedding itself in a tree. The mercenaries pulling the ropes fell over and the barge went free.

"That's it for the saw," Moratrayas said, and tossed the weapon aside.

The Blue Sashes weren't done yet. A team of men with axes hacked away at a tall pine tree next to the river. Working at a feverish pace, they cut into the tree until it fell across the river. The tree landed on Moratrayas' barge, and no sooner had it struck then men climbed over the trunk.

"Sandra, the net thrower," Moratrayas ordered. Sandra fired once and wrapped two mercenaries against the tree.

"That's everything I've got," she told him.

Under Igor's control the barge began to move forward, dragging the tree along with it. More men climbed on it and tried to board the barge. Moratrayas pointed to a large box in the middle of the barge and said, "I'll keep them off. There's a handle on the box. Fold it out and turn it."

Moratrayas extended his staff to full length and swung at boarders while Sandra ran to the box. The strange box was two feet across and made of brass. She found the handle, unfolded it and began to turn it. The box played 'pop goes the weasel' as she turned the handle. She kept turning, and when the box played the last note, the lid flew off and a shower of razor edged brass daggers shot into the air toward the mercenaries.

"Take cover!" a mercenary shouted. The mercenaries got behind rocks, trees, shields, whatever they could before the daggers landed. Many of the daggers fell uselessly in the river, but the rest pierced anything left unprotected and kept the Blue Sashes from boarding the barge. The barge pushed past the tree and continued on.

The clockworks caught up with Moratrayas and the river barges. They hit the Blue Sashes from behind, catching them by surprise and battering a good number of them to the ground. As before, the clockworks sought to fight their way through their enemies rather than trying to destroy them. Within minutes they broke through and followed their creator to freedom.

At last both the clockworks and barges broke clear of the forest and entered a wide clearing with no trees on the riverbanks. They had a good view of the castle and the tower containing the Sun Gun. The Blue Sashes followed them, but too far away to pose a threat. Moratrayas was about to congratulate Sandra and Igor when a light as bright as the noon sun lit up the night sky.

"No!" Moratrayas screamed.

Stoth ran into the chamber housing the Sun Gun, where he found the guard waiting for him and Jeremy puzzling over the controls. "Ah, Jeremy, have you started disassembling the gun?"

"No, I—"

"Good, I couldn't be happier," Stoth said. He rubbed his hands together and marched up to the gun with Tinley at his heels. "Power it up, Jeremy. We've got a fight on our hands."

"B-but, the barrel's still hot from using it this afternoon," Jeremy protested. "It's not safe to use it again so soon."

Stoth ignored him and went to the lens on the gun. He didn't know how to use most of the controls, but these made sense to him. He flipped lenses down until he had enough magnification to see the river far below.

"Ugly sight, isn't it, Jeremy? Someone down there took my property and destroyed even more. Now let's see, where are they? Ah, that must be my property fleeing for their lives. Not nice of them to leave without saying goodbye, don't you think?"

He adjusted the lenses to focus on the fleeing barges. "Now, if I were a raging madman—"

"If?" Jeremy asked.

Stoth pretended not to hear him. "Where would I be? Yes, that one in the back! It looks like a barge mixed with a blacksmith shop, and it's glowing green in the back. Moratrayas just has to be on something that ridiculous."

"I don't understand any of this," Jeremy said.

Stoth patted Jeremy on the back. "You don't have to understand. Just cut that boat in half port to starboard with as narrow a beam as possible."

"Do you ever listen to me?" Jeremy asked. "The barrel's too hot! If we fire it now, it could damage the machine beyond use."

"Ah, look, more targets," Stoth said cheerfully, and pointed to Moratrayas' clockworks coming out of the forest. Turning his attention back to Jeremy, he said, "I think I've already established what a bad idea it is to argue with me. If I haven't been clear enough on that point, Captain Tinley will be glad to reintroduce you to the concept of gravity. We're four hundred feet up, Jeremy. Have you ever seen a man fall from that height? Do you want to experience it firsthand?"

Jeremy's face became as white as a sheet. Stoth pointed at the Sun Gun.

"I'm waiting."

"Igor, take the wheel!" Moratrayas shouted. He ran to the back of the barge where Gertrude waited. "Sandra, there's a knife in the chest by your feet. Cut the ropes holding down the tarp! Quickly!"

The light was coming from the highest tower of the castle, and it grew brighter with every passing second. Worse, the Sun Gun was powering up much faster than it had at the rally that afternoon. Even at this distance they could hear its high-pitched cry.

Sandra found the knife and cut the first rope holding down the tarp. Moratrayas lifted the edge of the tarp and went underneath it. He stopped for a second and saw the Blue Sashes taking cover while his clockworks hurried after their master. He reached for the first of three levers extending out from a huge brass and obsidian form, but was too slow.

The Sun Gun fired and filled the air with its terrible scream. The river and clearing became as bright as noon on a summer day. A beam of light fifty feet across shot down from the tower and hit the clockworks. It only touched them for a second, but that was enough. The snow they were running through evaporated, dead grass and young trees around them burned to ashes, and with screams that reminded Sandra of boiling tea kettles, every last clockwork fell motionless to the ground.

The beam of light then shrank to a circle a foot across before sliding onto the river. Water boiled at its touch and clouds of steam billowed into the air. The beam swept over the barge, setting fire to it and cremating boxes and packages it touched. Sandra closed her eyes and covered them with her hands, but she could still see the blinding light.

When the beam passed, Sandra opened her eyes to find the barge still intact. The armor plates were red hot, but they'd held. The wood underneath smoldered, and she saw flames licking up through the armor. What hit her next was the delicious scent of cooking fish. She looked over the railing and saw dozens of fish floating on the surface of the river. They'd been boiled alive by the strength of the beam.

Igor spun the wheel to no effect. "The controls aren't responding!"

Moratrayas worked on Gertrude, trying to remove the safeties keeping it shut off. “Just a few more seconds…”

The terrible light returned. The beam appeared next to the barge and swept over the same spot as before. The armor plates were already red hot, and when the beam hit them again they melted through, cutting the barge in half. Sandra and Moratrayas were on the back half and Igor was stranded on the front. For just a second they floated on before both halves began to sink.

“Sandra, swim to shore and head for the forest,” Moratrayas told her. “Igor, go to ground!”

Sandra hesitated, staring into the swirling, steaming water. “It’s too hot!”

“Staying isn’t an option,” he told her. Moratrayas grabbed her by the shoulders and jumped off with her. The water was hot, like a good bath. Together they swam to shore. Sandra didn’t see what happened to Igor. One second the hunchback was on the sinking front half of the barge, and when she looked back he was gone.

Sandra and Moratrayas reached shore and climbed out of the water. The clockwork dragonfly survived the barge’s destruction and flew over their heads. Moratrayas plucked it from the air, pressed buttons on it and sent it off.

Gasping for breath, Sandra said, “We’re soaking wet. We’ll freeze if we don’t get a change of clothes or make a fire.”

“Bigger problems,” Moratrayas said. The Blue Sashes were back and in hot pursuit. “Run!”

They didn’t get far before five mercenaries surrounded them and drew their swords. Moratrayas extended his cane to a staff and lashed out at them, but these men were more dangerous than the soldiers Stoth employed. They dodged his blows and circled around him. One of them was going to hit Moratrayas from behind. Sandra jumped on the mercenary’s back and wrapped both her arms around his neck as tightly as she could.

It helped, but only for a second. Two more mercenaries grabbed Sandra and pulled her off. More Blue Sashes arrived until Moratrayas was surrounded by a dozen of them. One of them hit him across the face with a punch that shattered his goggles. Another swung his sword and cut the brass staff in half. Moratrayas pulled more weapons from his pockets, but he was tackled and knocked to the ground before he could use them.

Sandra and Moratrayas were tied up and set on the ground. General Thane marched out of the woods followed by a thousand more mercenaries. Thane looked dubiously at the still steaming river.

“Not a bad raid,” Thane admitted. He looked up the river where the remaining eight barges rowed on. “I actually broke a sweat fighting your monsters, and you got the slaves away. You’ve got talent, but you’re way out of your league.”

"Orders, sir?" a mercenary asked.

"I've received word that King Stoth wants those brass contraptions, whether they work or not." Thane pointed at Sandra and Moratrayas. "He wants these two alive. I'm told he wants to question the man personally."

Sandra and Moratrayas were lifted up and dragged back to Scour. More mercenaries carried the broken clockworks, making sure not to leave a single piece behind. As they were taken away, Moratrayas smiled weakly at Sandra and said, "That could have gone better."

# Chapter 12

Sandra and Moratrayas were taken to Scour. Their captors were silent during the trip, not complaining how the battle went or insulting their prisoners. When Sandra and the doctor began to shiver from the cold air and their wet clothes, the mercenaries covered them in blankets. While Sandra was grateful for that, she knew it was not done out of kindness, but to keep them alive as prisoners.

They reached Scour and found the city as active as in full day. Word got ahead that the Blue Sashes had Moratrayas, and the townspeople came out in droves. Every man, woman and child packed the streets for a chance to see their enemy. The mercenaries had to clear a path to get in the gates and forced their way to the castle. Once the crowds saw Moratrayas, they began to cheer and howl insults at him.

"We got him!" a woman cried out. "We have the mad tailor at last!"

"Three years of waiting, and we can finally punish him!" a man agreed. "You're not so big anymore, are you, tailor?"

Moratrayas gave insults as good as he got them. "Vultures! Carrion crows! You wretches won't commit evil, but you're happy enough to profit when others do evil in your name! I should have burned this place to the ground when I left as an act of civic improvement!"

Townspeople threw rocks and rotten fruit at Moratrayas. Their aim was poor and they hit his captors more often than the doctor. Gritting their teeth, the Blue Sashes raised their shields against the foul rain of garbage. A man ducked in between the Blue Sashes and drove both his hands into Moratrayas' pockets, saying, "What's he got? He has to have money!"

The man screamed in pain and ran away. Sandra saw chattering brass teeth clinging tenaciously to his fingers. He howled and jumped around, momentarily amusing the crowd. When the spectacle grew old, they screamed abuse at Moratrayas and threw more debris. Their aim was no better the second time. Irritated mercenaries drew their swords. The move stunned the crowd to silence, and they backed away.

"That'll be enough of that," Thane said, his voice echoing through the streets. "King Stoth Voluk wants this man brought alive to the castle, and I'll not let you kill him before he's executed. And the next one of you that throws a rotten egg at me gets it in the face!"

They made good progress to the castle after that. The crowd followed and cheered, hurling insults but not projectiles. The mercenaries and townspeople stopped at the castle gate, where Stoth and Tinley waited for them at the head of a large body of soldiers. Judging by their cocky expressions and clean uniforms, none of these men had been anywhere near this evening's battle.

"General Thane," Stoth said calmly. "I see you've captured the man responsible for this night's atrocity, indeed, the man responsible for all this kingdom's hardships going back many years."

Thane bowed. "It was done with His Majesty's invaluable assistance."

"You're too kind," Stoth said. "Captain Tinley, take custody of the prisoners and place them in the deepest, darkest cells of our dungeon. Let them wait there for my judgment. It will be harsh and not long in coming."

Tinley directed his soldiers to take Moratrayas and Sandra. The crowd roared in approval and chanted Stoth's name while Thane and his mercenaries left the city.

Sandra's first impression of Stoth's castle was that it was much prettier than Moratrayas'. Banners, paintings, murals, statues, vases, it was all so beautiful. But the scene changed abruptly for the worse when they were taken to a side passage and down a flight of stairs into the dungeon.

The name said it all. The dungeon was dark, cold, damp and infested with swarms of revolting vermin. The walls were brick and caked in filth, and the floor so dirty the stones were black. Guttering torches provided poor light and lots of smoke. Sandra and Moratrayas were led past instruments of torture so vile their names alone invoked pain, and more crude machines whose twisted forms and metal spikes could only be designed for suffering.

Soldiers untied them and took everything Moratrayas had except his clothes, a move that nearly cost a man his finger when a second set of chattering teeth in the doctor's pockets bit him. They stole Sandra's jewelry and argued over who got which piece. Then Sandra and Moratrayas were taken to cells in the back of the dungeon and locked inside, each in their own cell and opposite one another. The soldiers marched away without another word.

Once they were alone, Moratrayas asked, "Are you hurt?"

Sandra wrapped her blanket tightly around herself. "Not much, no."

"Good." Moratrayas stretched out his arms and legs, testing his muscles. Satisfied that nothing was injured beyond repair, he brushed the worst of the grime off the floor and lay down. "Strange as this is going to sound, make yourself comfortable and try to get some sleep."

"Sleep?" she asked incredulously. "Here?"

"I *did* say it would sound strange. You'll need your strength later, and very little is going to happen for a while. Trust me, I'm an old hand at this. Compared to some of the dungeons I've been in, this one is almost homey."

Sandra scrapped a spot of floor clean, or as clean as it could get without water, soap and possibly fire, before she sat down. "Al?"

"Hmm?"

"I just wanted to say thank you."

Moratrayas looked over at her and waved his hands around their squalid surroundings. "You're thanking me for this?"

"Not this part, but yeah, I'm thanking you. My dad and brother are free, and the men from Sun Valley. That's what I wanted when I first came to you, and I got it. I, I knew it was going to be dangerous when my mother asked me to find you, and I accepted that because so many people were counting on me. And we're in a prison and Stoth is going to torture us and starve us and publicly execute us and oh God some of those things look painful out there and –"

"Breath, Sandra."

Sandra stopped and took a deep breath. "And I'm not looking forward to that. But, but I was ready for this when I went to find you. I mean, I wasn't really risking anything since everyone in Sun Valley was pretty much doomed without our men and sunstone."

She looked at Moratrayas. His clothes were dirty and torn. His goggles were broken and one of the dark lenses was missing. His cane was gone and in pieces even if he got it back. His armored barge was sunk and his clockworks were ruined. His clothes included armor plates sewn into them that spared him from much of the damage he would have taken tonight, but he was still hurt. And it was her fault.

"This wasn't your fight. I got you involved in it. You should still be in your castle, making clockworks and watching after your people. Instead you're stuck here with me. So I wanted to say thank you, and I'm sorry."

"Is that what's bothering you?" he asked. "I'm surprised there's room for you to fit in your cell with all the guilt you're carrying. Pot calling the kettle black, I know."

Moratrayas sat up and looked at Sandra. "You're not to blame for what happened tonight. We would have won if I'd had just one more trustworthy person in my service. It's another case of me trying to do too much with too little. As for getting me into this mess, yes, you did, but Stoth wants to forge an empire from the Raushtad Mountains, and that includes Refuge. Sooner or later he'd have come for me or I'd have gone after him. You made our battle happen sooner than it would have, but he and I would have locked horns eventually with or without your participation."

Sandra was silent for a moment. "Now what?"

Moratrayas took off his goggles and cleaned the remaining lens on his sleeve. "Stoth suffered a heavy blow tonight. He'll spend a few hours figuring out how much damage we've done, and in spite of what our current condition suggests, we've done a lot. He'll leave us sitting here for a while, letting our fears prey on us while we wait. Eventually he'll show up to gloat and announce some terrible punishment. The whole process should take a day or two."

"So we just sit here until then?" she asked.

"We sit here and plan. Sandra, as desperate as this must seem to you, it's not that bad. I've been in worse situations before and often."

"It gets worse than this?" Sandra asked. Moratrayas nodded. Stunned, she asked, "How can you deal with it? Losing everything again and again, being betrayed by people you did good for? How do you keep coming back from that?"

"Part of it is pride," he explained. "I refuse to lose to these ignorant, destructive thugs. I may be willing to lose to a better man, but not to these cretins. Another part of it is my mission. I believe I can save the world, or at least part of it. I can make life better for thousands if not millions of people. If I fail then the world fails with me, and I won't accept that."

Moratrayas pointed at torture devices in view from their cells. "The rest of the answer lies there. More than anything else, these abominations show the sort of enemy we face. Stoth either brought them from his homeland or commissioned their construction once he arrived in Stone Heart. How many people has he used them on? I find the question too offensive to consider. How many more people will he use them on? None if I can help it.

"Stoth seeks to bring untold suffering to the people of the Raushtad. Terrible as your people's hardships have been, it's dwarfed by what he's planning. Hundreds of thousands will die, be enslaved or made refugees fleeing his evil. Stone Heart has lost many people to emigration, and most of them settled in surrounding kingdoms. Stoth's armies will kill many who are their cousins, nephews and siblings in this war. Thane and his mercenaries are hardly better, willing to commit any act of violence if the money's right.

"We deal with it because we have to, Sandra. We come back from every defeat, every failure, every betrayal. We do it because if we don't, Stoth and men like him will win. That can't be allowed to happen."

The throne room should have been a place of celebration. Moratrayas the mad tailor was caught! The man who'd once seized control of Stone Heart with his brass monsters now resided in the castle's dungeon, his creations destroyed, his barge sunk. But there was no celebration.

Stoth sat on his throne, calmly surveying his men under the harsh glare of lantern light. Captain Tinley stood at the head of a dozen other captains and stayed on Stoth's right. To the King's left were Thane and some of his officers. All the men looked nervous, and a few of the captains sweated profusely.

"Where to begin?" Stoth asked. "There was the oafish performance of my soldiers. A handful of the mad tailor's toys humiliated you. That is, they humiliated you after you finally got up the nerve to fight them. You lost three hundred slaves, twelve barges, two catapults and your dignity."

When the captains said nothing, Stoth turned his gaze on Thane and his officers. "Or should I start with the great General Thane of the mighty Blue

Sashes? You're renowned throughout the land. I wonder what people would say if they saw your poor performance tonight. Your men fought the same clockworks and didn't kill any of them. You attacked the stolen barges and escaped slaves, and you failed to recapture them. You fought Moratrayas, a hunchbacked freak and a woman, and you lost. He'd have gotten away except for my intervention. Thane, you keep asking me for your pay, and I'm forced to ask what, if anything, you've done to earn it."

"We caught Moratrayas," Thane said.

"So you did," Stoth agreed. "Well done, that. I am moderately pleased by your performance in that regard. Thane, you did capture him, eventually, so we'll call it even. Captain Tinley, I wanted whoever was spying on me. I think we can assume it was Moratrayas, so you're off the hook."

Stoth leaned back in his chair and beckoned for a servant to bring him a goblet of brandy. He took a sip and swirled the remainder. "This day is just too much to deal with sober. Yes, well done on grabbing Moratrayas. No executions for anyone, hurray. Everyone here still performed terribly. I wouldn't bet money on you in a fight, and not just because of what Moratrayas did. Need I remind you *how* I lost my catapults, or the debacle at the gate? A hundred men went after one goblin and failed. Goblins humiliated you. I'll repeat that so it sinks in. *Goblins* humiliated you."

The men were shamed, and that would make them easier to control for a while. That was important to Stoth. Men in power knew how easy it was to lose power, and men with swords were the greatest threat to them. Large armies were nice, but created the risk that an ambitious officer or general might decide he'd like to wear your crown. Another risk was that Thane might decide to turn against Stoth and make himself king. Mercenaries were never very loyal, and a mercenary army this large and experienced was as big a threat to Stoth as it was to his enemies.

Shame would prevent any one man from rebelling for a while, but it was important to make sure they didn't cooperate against him. After all, coups were much easier when several officers worked together. To prevent that from happening the officers had to hate and fear one another. Stoth had worked hard for months to make sure his men despised the Blue Sashes, and that part of the plan worked like a charm. Now it was time to add to the distrust and paranoia.

Stoth smiled. "So, whose fault was this?"

Thane, Tinley and all the captains and officers shouted and screamed abuse at one another in a desperate bid to avoid taking the blame.

Out on the riverbank, soldiers searched through the snow and mud looking for remains of Moratrayas' barge. Most of the men had gone home, but three squads totaling twenty-four men remained to salvage Moratrayas' treasures. They worked feverishly in spite of the cold and pitch-black darkness.

Spread out along several hundred feet of the river, they carried lanterns and prodded the water with spears in an attempt to locate anything of value.

A two-man team probed the spot where the barge went down. The first said, "This isn't working. The good stuff floated downstream or sank to the bottom."

"We got some of the mad tailor's belongings," the other man said. "With the bounty King Stoth promised for this stuff, we've got enough to double our pay this week."

"This junk?" the first asked, pointing his spear at a pile of debris. It wasn't much to look at. Most of it was bits blasted off the barge when the Sun Gun hit it. Brass tubes and broken gears made up most of the pile, plus a few instruments neither of them could guess a use for. "We'll be lucky to sell it to a scrap metal dealer."

The second soldier nodded. "I know. The King is paying the biggest bounties for the mad tailor's books and brass monsters. But that's where we've got an advantage. Those brass monsters weigh a lot."

"So?" the first asked. Neither of them noticed a shadowy form slip out from a cluster of trees and duck back into cover.

"So they'll sink, dummy! The current won't move them when they weigh a couple hundred pounds. They'll be right here where the barge went down, and we can get them."

The first soldier frowned. "How sure are you that you want to find one? What if they're still alive? They're as tough as they look."

The second soldier shuddered. "Yeah, I saw the men who fought them. Poor guys looked like they'd wrestled bears. But for a bonus worth a month's pay I'd wrestle a bear or one of those crazy brass critters."

The soldiers prodded the water with their spears, trying to locate salvage hidden near shore. They missed the shadowy figure dart between trees and rocks. They also missed the fact that the other teams searching the riverbank were gone. But when something flew over their heads, they noticed it.

"What was that?"

The second soldier peered into the darkness. "Owl?"

"Too loud." The light from their lantern caught something metallic and shiny clinging to a tree branch. Before they could get a good look at it, it flew to another branch farther from the river. "There, you see it?"

The two men followed it, spreading out and moving slowly. "Don't spook it. I see it. It's one of the brass monsters, and it's still working."

The second soldier licked his lips. "King Stoth will pay plenty to get it. Small enough it can't hurt us, either."

"Small enough to get away if we're clumsy," the first said. "Go to the left and I'll go to the right. Looks like a big old dragonfly, don't it?"

The soldiers crept closer to the clockwork dragonfly. It clung to a pine branch and didn't seem to notice their noisy approach. Under the lantern's light it shined as if it were made of gold instead of brass. The soldier with the lantern set it down along with his spear and held his hands out.

"Hit it with your spear if it tries to fly away," he told his fellow. "It's worth more working than broke, but it's worth nothing if it gets away."

"Don't you worry none about me," the second soldier said. Neither of them noticed the fact that they were far enough from the river that no one could see them, or that the dense forest muffled sound so that no one could hear them unless they screamed. And the shadowy figure coming ever closer? They were too focused on the clockwork to spot him.

"Careful," the first soldier said as he moved closer to the clockwork. "That's it, you keep sitting there nice and pretty, Mr. Bug. Bet you're tuckered out from flying around. Hold still, just a little more...got you!"

The soldier lunged forward and snagged the clockwork. It flapped its wings and nearly pulled away, but he clutched it against his chest and held on tight. Seconds later it fell silent. He turned around and triumphantly held up his prize. "I got it!"

His expression changed from joy to confusion when he saw his brother in arms passed out on the ground, and a smiling hunchback carrying a bottle and a rag that smelled of chemicals.

"Good catch," Igor said, and tackled the soldier. Pressing the chloroform soaked rag against the man's mouth, Igor muffled his cries for help and knocked him out. Igor brushed himself off and set the clockwork on the ground. "That's two more to tie up and leave by the fire."

The clockwork buzzed in reply. Igor smiled and said, "And we get all the goodies they collected. We'll need them. It's going to be hard work breaking the doc out, but we have help."

Igor's gaze slid back to the spot on the river where the barge went down. Clockworks need air to burn their fuel, but they can function without it for short periods of time. Being underwater didn't hurt them, either, no matter how long they stayed down or how cold the water was. This meant Gertrude the giant clockwork was alive and well resting on the river bottom, waiting for Igor to swim down into the frigid waters and turn off the safeties.

"Don't worry, doc," Igor said softly. "I'll be there when you need me."

The next morning found the men of Sun Valley resting on a riverbank. They hadn't left the kingdom, in part because they were too exhausted to go on. They also didn't know which way to go. The river forked, and Stoth's soldiers had blindfolded them the last time they came this way. Tired, cold and hungry, they built fires and sat on shore while a few men stood guard.

Ulysses Sower stood on the riverbank looking back the way they'd come. He held a pickaxe in his hands. It was a dangerous weapon as well as a tool, but it was useless against the horror he'd seen the night before. The mad scientist's barge was covered in armor plates, and that terrible beam had sliced it in two. What good was a pickaxe against that? He was free, for now, but it cost him his daughter. He gripped his weapon tightly, wanting to lash out but lacking a target for his rage.

The rest of the men were angry, too. They'd escaped, but only after a month of imprisonment and abuse. They'd never gotten a chance to strike back against their captors for the indignities they'd suffered. They were also famished, and hunger made them more irritable.

Ulysses saw his neighbors gather around him. One put a hand on his shoulder. "We're sorry about what happened to your daughter. We were in the last barge, but they were too far away for us to help. We'd have been caught if we'd stopped, or shot with that gun."

"I'm not blaming you," Ulysses said.

"We saw them swim to shore."

Ulysses didn't move. "Then Stoth and his boys have them, and they're in the same fix we were."

The man nodded and looked away. "Yeah, they are. We're going to send a few men out to scout the rivers and see where they lead."

"What for?" Ulysses asked. "Say we find the way home and row there, what happens then? You heard what the men guarding us said. They're planning on taking over the whole Raushtad. What good does it do to go home if they're going to come and get us again in a couple weeks?"

"We could keep going," his neighbor suggested. "Take everyone back home with us and keep sailing."

Ulysses pointed at the barges left moored to the riverbank and under guard. "There's enough room on the barges to carry all of us and maybe another two hundred people. That's not enough to bring our families, not to mention our livestock and possessions. Some of us can get away, but not everyone."

Another man walked up and said, "We could do it in stages, take half the people on one go and then come back for the rest later."

"And go where?" Ulysses asked. He didn't notice it, but the rest of the men were listening, and more gathered around him. None of them saw a tiny speck circling high overhead. "We can leave our land behind, but that's the only valuable thing we have left. Once we've lost that we've got nothing. What kingdom will take in nine hundred refugees? Even if they do, what do we do once we get there? We'd be farmers without any land."

"So what do we do?" Ulysses' son Jason asked. He drifted into the conversation with five other men. "They've got thousands of soldiers and the Sun Gun. We can't fight that."

"Yes you can," a cheerful voice said. Everyone looked around and saw Igor leaning against a tree. The men on guard stared at him in amazement, unable to see how he'd gotten by them.

"You're that little guy that helped the doctor," Ulysses said.

"It's 'helps the doctor', present tense. He's alive so I'm still on the job. Nice speech, Sower, and you're right. You are screwed, and me and everyone else in these mountains. Once Stoth gets going he'll march right over us."

"What do you expect us to do about it?" Jason Sower asked. More men gathered around Igor and Ulysses. A tiny speck circled above them and lazily descended. "They're soldiers and we're farmers. There's nothing we can do to stop them."

Igor smiled. "The thing is, they're farmers, too. Well, not the Blue Sashes, but Stoth's army used to be just like you a few years ago. They're not very good soldiers. Trust me, I took out two dozen of them last night."

"Are you forgetting about Stoth's super weapon?" another man asked. The speck came closer. It only looked small because it was so far away. "What are three hundred men supposed to do to stop it?"

"That's where the doc comes in," Igor explained. "I recovered some stuff from his barge. Actually somebody else did and I mugged them, but let's not squabble over details. The doc didn't have time to bring out his biggest toy. It's still down there waiting for someone to turn it on, and it's every bit as dangerous as the Sun Gun."

"So turn it on and be done with it," Ulysses said. The speck in the sky grew overhead.

"I can't get to it without someone stopping me. I took down twenty-four men to get their loot. Stoth's men are as dumb as they come, but after that they're going to expect me. It doesn't help that the doc's best clockwork is underwater, very cold water I might add. Getting to it will be difficult, dangerous and time consuming. I'll fail unless someone's watching my back, namely you. One last point is while the clockwork is as tough as nails, it'll go down if enough men start jabbing it with pointy bits of metal."

"You need us?" a man asked incredulously.

Igor smiled. "In a word, yes. You said it yourselves, you can get away, but for how long? Stoth is going to move his army sooner or later. Can you run far and fast enough to get away? Then there's the topic of revenge."

The men perked up when they heard that. Although they were kind-hearted people, they still ached for a chance to get even. Igor said, "Let's have a show of hands. Who wants to see Stoth hoisted by his own petards?"

Most of the crowd raised their hands, except for a few holdouts and one man who asked what a petard was. "Come on," Igor urged them, "be honest." More hands went up until nearly everyone showed support.

A dissenter said, "Hey, I want to hurt him as badly as the rest of you, but we're not up for this! We've never fought a war. Let someone else stop Stoth, someone who knows what he's doing."

"Nobody else is coming after Stoth, and there's no one we can warn who could get here in time," Igor said. "Once Stoth start marching with the Sun Gun in tow he'll be unstoppable. We do this and we do this now, or that army is going to come after Sun Valley, neighboring towns and everybody around here. It's not going to be easy and it's sure not fair, but it has to be done and we're stuck with the job."

One of the men on guard looked up and saw the growing speck in the sky. He pointed a sledgehammer at it and shouted, "Griffin!"

The griffin swooped down over the crowd of men and shrieked. Everyone threw themselves to the ground or ducked behind trees. The griffin flew by a second time and screamed again, trying to panic the men like it would a herd of sheep. It landed near the water's edge and charged.

The griffin was a magnificent predator and a fine example of its species. Big as an ox, it had the head and wings of a giant eagle and the body of a lion. It was covered in gold feathers tipped with black. It's beak and claws were razor sharp. Proud, strong and dangerous, it cried out again to frighten its prey and scatter them so it could pick off stragglers at its leisure.

But the men didn't run. Instead they gathered together with their weapons raised. Puzzled, the griffin stopped. It screamed at them again and raked the air with its claws. Still there was still no panic.

The men stood their ground and stared hard at the griffin. They were angry after the abuse they'd taken for a month. All that time their captors had laughed at them, insulted them, hit them, and why? They'd never done any harm to the men who enslaved them, never even met them before they were attacked. And now this monster was trying to frighten them and hurt them. They weren't going to take it. Terrifying as the griffin was, they were too angry to be scared.

They were also hungry.

"Lot of meat on that bird," Ulysses said. His neighbors nodded and licked their lips.

If the griffin was confused before, it was shocked when three hundred men screamed a battle cry and charged it, hammers, picks and axes in hand. It took a moment for the griffin to realize how much danger it was in and try to fly off. It made the decision two seconds too late.

# Chapter 13

Sandra woke up to find a soldier reaching into her cell and shoving a bowl of oatmeal in front of her face. She took it and the soldier stepped away. He placed another bowl in Moratrayas' cell, careful not to get too close to the doctor. Moratrayas woke and looked him in the eyes.

"Your name is Simon Ledger," Moratrayas said. The soldier blinked and backed away. "You lived on Potter Street when I was last in Stone Heart. I saved your cousin when I took power. He was to be publicly flogged, and I set him free."

"That was a long time ago," the soldier said.

"Four years by my reckoning," Moratrayas replied. "What crime did I commit against your family that you ignore my act of mercy?"

The soldier stared hard at Moratrayas before leaving the dungeon. Moratrayas shrugged and picked up the bowl. "Too much to expect him to reciprocate, I suppose. Breakfast, now that is a surprise. I didn't think Stoth would feed us."

"They didn't give us spoons," Sandra said.

Moratrayas scooped up the oatmeal with his fingers and ate it. "Worried what I might do with it, or perhaps just another way to demoralize us. Rather contrasts with feeding us in the first place."

Sandra ate, grateful for anything to fill her empty stomach. After the first mouthful she froze. "What if it's poisoned?"

Moratrayas finished his meal and set the bowl down. "I doubt it. Stoth is certainly capable of that, but why poison prisoners when the tools of torture are close at hand?"

"Gee, thanks for reminding me." Sandra ate more of the oatmeal. She didn't feel any ill effects, and Moratrayas looked okay. "This is my first time in prison. Is it normal to get fed?"

"No. This was an act of generosity on Stoth's part, and that's not like him. If he's trying to be nice to us, even in a small way, then he expects something in return that he can't take by force. I expect he'll be along shortly to make his demands."

"He's good," a man said from the shadows. It was too dark to see him. "Cynical, but that comes with the territory when you're in charge."

Sandra recognized the voice. "Stoth," she hissed.

Stoth walked into the light, followed by Captain Tinley. They brought a third man with them, a frightened, balding little fellow who shook like a leaf. Stoth held up a crystal goblet and raised it in a toast. "Moratrayas. I understand you go by the title of doctor these days, but I'd think twice before asking you for medical advice. Do you mind if I call you Al?"

"I would mind a great deal," Moratrayas replied. "It's an honor you haven't earned."

Stoth shrugged and sipped his brandy. "Doctor it is, then. And this was generous on my part. You have no idea how tight our supply situation is with winter set in and having to feed the Blue Sashes. Seriously, the way Thane and his men eat, it's like watching hogs at the trough. Of course we don't have to feed three hundred slaves anymore, so that gives us a little to spare."

Stoth walked up to their cells. "Anything else I can get you?"

"A dagger," Sandra said.

"Your head," Moratrayas answered.

"Or a rock, anything I could throw," Sandra continued.

"Walked right into that, didn't I?" Stoth said indulgently. "Still upset that I ousted you?"

"I dislike you for a wide variety of reasons," Moratrayas explained.

The answers hardly seemed to bother Stoth. "Can't please everyone, I suppose. I see your taste in help has gone up a notch. When you were king here you had a circus freak as your right hand man. Whatever help he offered was more than offset by having to look at him. Be fair, though, she's better, but you're still settling for second rate."

Sandra put her hands on her hips. "Hey!"

"That was always your problem," Stoth said. "You settle for less than you deserve. That freak, this kingdom, your wench, they're all second rate. Why is that? Why does a man with your abilities settle for garbage?"

Moratrayas remained sitting and folded his hands on his lap. "I demand the best, Stoth, and I get it. You're too blinded by appearances to see what has real value. Take that preening peacock beside you." Tinley bristled, but at a gesture from Stoth he remained silent. "The armor and weapons are good, the uniform a bit less so, but the man? He's cowardly and disloyal. Placing trust in him is like pouring water into a cracked jar. It's not a question of if he'll fail you, but when."

Stoth took a sip of brandy and swished it around in his mouth. He swallowed and said, "Can't say I agree with you. Tinley's ambitious. I like that in my followers. They go that extra mile to get more for themselves. I can use that. The whole kingdom is the same way. They're hungry, desperate for more of everything. Just a taste more, even the promise of it, and they'll do anything I say. But that's not enough."

Stoth swirled his brandy. "Do you remember when we first met?"

"Rather hard to forget your invasion," Moratrayas said dryly.

"Invasion? If that's what you want to call it. There I was, commanding an army of soldiers and mercenaries, poised to conquer a kingdom many times larger than my own. My men who'd sneaked in months earlier opened the city gates for me, and what do I see? You, riding on the back of a ridiculous brass contraption trying to close the gates! The stupid thing was eight feet tall and had arms that almost reached the ground. It made a noise like there was a beehive inside it. You came running straight at the vanguard of my army, screaming insults! You looked so stupid!"

Stoth broke down laughing. If he expected a reaction from Moratrayas, he wasn't getting one. The doctor sat quietly, his expression showing idle curiosity, as if he was studying an unusual bug. Stoth kept laughing for a while and Tinley smirked. When the King finally quieted down, he looked more thoughtfully at Moratrayas.

"And then you ran that stupid thing over the best part of my army. It was a sobering experience, like watching a terrier attacking rats. An entire platoon of spearmen went down and a platoon of swordsmen after that. My crossbowmen had just enough time to load before you reached them. They shot that walking scrap pile of yours so many times it looked like a hedgehog when they were done. And still you got away."

"Is there a point to this trip down memory lane?" Moratrayas asked.

"I'm getting there," Stoth promised. "My advisers told me it would take hours to finish you off. It took three days...three days of you sending one walking nightmare after another at me. You blew up my supply wagons with your lightning gun, almost killing me in the process. Every time my men turned a corner, you or that freak were waiting for them with your brass monsters. More of those things waited in ambush inside buildings, charging out at the worst possible time."

Confused, Sandra asked, "Does he expect an apology?"

Moratrayas shrugged. "If so, he's in for a disappointment."

Stoth smiled. "When we finally took the castle, what did I find? Nothing. You'd stripped it of valuables to fund the creation of your brass army. I needed the little you left behind to pay my mercenaries, and I might add they weren't going to take an IOU after a beating like that. Stone Heart proved to be not worth having. It took a fortune just to redecorate the castle. But what stuck in my mind was how the real treasure got away...you."

"Me?" Moratrayas didn't try to hide his surprise.

"You." Stoth smiled more broadly, enjoying Moratrayas' puzzlement. "A king's job isn't to do anything. He gives orders and other people work for him. I saw your brass monsters, and I was in awe. They were magnificent, a sight to chill men's hearts in battle. I wanted them so badly, but I couldn't find anyone to make them for me. You could have conquered any kingdom you wanted with them, but you didn't. You stayed here in this miserable, dirty, stinking little kingdom. You lack the vision to use your talents! But I see what you're capable of, and I want it."

Moratrayas stared at Stoth for a moment before bursting out into hysterical laughter. Sandra had never seen him laugh before. He rocked back and forth, nearly tipping over backwards. Stoth's only reaction was to finish his brandy.

"You," Moratrayas said between chuckles, "you have got to be the stupidest man alive. You (ha, ha), you invaded my homeland, destroyed my creations and forced me to run for my life. You turned my people into a bloodthirsty horde, and now you want to hire me? Stoth, your talents are wasted. Go into comedy!"

Still smiling, Stoth walked over to the little nervous man he'd brought with him. "You keep calling it an invasion. Odd, that. But I'm afraid I must insist on gaining your services. I haven't introduced my friend. Meet Jeremy the clockmaker, a worthless little failure of a man who came to my kingdom some time ago. I was already planning my war of conquest, but with more modest tools. My men constructed the catapults and other siege engines before he came. But his arrival made the impossible happen."

Stoth pointed his now empty goblet at Moratrayas. "After you fled, I spent months combing the castle for clues how to make your brass monsters, but there were few left. I couldn't repair the ones I'd destroyed or make new ones. I placed Jeremy in my service and found he couldn't do it, either."

"This wasn't my idea," Jeremy whimpered.

"I know," Moratrayas replied.

Stoth grabbed Jeremy's shoulders tightly. "When I want you to talk, I'll ask for it. Anyway, where was I? Ah yes, Jeremy couldn't fix them, but he could repair parts of your lightning gun. Sadly, those weren't the parts that shot lightning, missing the point entirely. But I found one of your notebooks on the lightning gun and a most fascinating book on sunstones."

"And you already had one," Moratrayas said.

"Right you are. It was the most valuable possession I had before coming here. It's the size of a raisin and produces as much light as a lit torch. And I had the one you left behind. According to the book and your notes, all I needed was a third. The book said I couldn't get another sunstone by dividing one of the two I had. It seems cutting sunstones destroys them and they stop generating light. Months later my spies heard rumors of a sunstone in an insignificant little valley."

Sandra stood up and shouted, "That's my home you're talking about! You ruined our lives!"

"Someone in this world must care about your problems," Stoth said. "It isn't me. After a brief visit there, I got my third sunstone and Jeremy put them together. The effect was as magnificent as you promised. It was so strong it melted everything we tried to house it in. The power was useless if we couldn't control it. But your lightning gun is carved from granite. I gather it had to be to survive the energy it fired. It was the perfect tool for the job and the only thing that could contain the sunstones' power. With a little prodding Jeremy got it working. Well, sort of working."

"A question," Moratrayas said. "When you attacked Sun Valley, why did you take only the men?"

Stoth looked puzzled. "Because I needed work done. Harvesting timber to building my barges isn't easy, and if I had to make my soldiers do it then they wouldn't have time to train. It would be bad for morale, too. It's hard to make farmers into soldiers. If I tried making soldiers into lumberjacks there could be a rebellion. So I took the men I needed to get the work done and left their horse-faced wives and brats behind so we wouldn't have to feed them. If they're still around when I begin my war I suppose we'll take them."

"And you want me to be a part of this," Moratrayas said.

"That's one of the places you come in," Stoth told him. "Make no mistake, I still want my army of brass, but right now I need the Sun Gun working reliably. Jeremy can't do it, can you, Jeremy?"

"I'm trying," Jeremy begged. "I swear I am."

"Yes, I know you are," Stoth said soothingly. "And I'd hate to think you might be, oh, I don't know, stalling."

"No, no!"

Stoth kept smiling. "You already spent some time down here for disobeying me, Jeremy. Do you need to spend some more?"

"Send the clockmaker away, Stoth," Moratrayas said. "His suffering earns you nothing except my disgust."

"Yes, let's see what he can do now that he's properly motivated." Soldiers emerged from the shadows and took the trembling clockmaker away. Stoth turned his attention back to Moratrayas. "And that brings me to you. I know how to motivate people. It's part of being a king. I understand you have a nice little hideaway south of here. After I conquer the Raushtad, you can keep it and rule it as my subject. I've heard about your petty self-promotions. I can make people help you. You'll have unlimited resources. Money, manpower, rare materials, whatever you want, I can get it for you."

Moratrayas laughed.

"You want more land?" Stoth asked. "I can give you a second kingdom to rule. You want women? I can give you a harem that makes this wench look like an old maid in comparison, which isn't hard, by the way."

"And the hits just keep on coming," Sandra said.

Moratrayas chuckled. "If I wanted any of that I'd have it already. Do you know why I didn't conquer a kingdom with my clockworks? Because I don't want one and I wouldn't be able to hold it, and neither will you. You're trying to take over dozens of kingdoms covering a thousand square miles. Your army will be stretched too thin to keep what you take, and the Sun Gun can only be in one place at a time. You'll win battles and lose the war."

Stoth nodded. "Well put, if totally wrong. You say I don't have enough men? I told you I like my men hungry for more, doctor, and if you haven't noticed that describes a lot of people in the Raushtad. There are plenty of soldiers who were denied promotions, land hungry farmers, third and fourth sons of kings who know they'll never inherit their fathers' thrones. I've contacted them, promised them wealth, power, position. They're coming for a party tonight where they will swear allegiance to me. When I march there will be a hundred men inside every kingdom ready to support me. And once I start winning I expect plenty of new recruits. Everybody wants to be on the winning side, especially considering the alternative."

"And what of the bankers who fund you?" Moratrayas asked.

"You know about them? Oh well done, I am impressed. Yes, they're being very generous, aren't they?"

"They'll own your kingdom," Moratrayas said. "Their loans must be coming with high interest payments. You'll be bankrupt in a year and they'll take everything you have."

Stoth laughed. "I keep forgetting how green you are. You only play at being a ruler. Here's a lesson from a real king, doctor. Only poor people pay back loans. The bankers aren't getting a single coin back, and if they demand payment, I have the Sun Gun to keep them respectful."

Moratrayas looked at Stoth and shook his head. Sadly, he said, "And you think I would play a part in this madness? After everything you've done since invading my kingdom, you expect me to help you inflict this horror on other lands? Even a goblin couldn't be so stupid."

"I didn't invade Stone Heart," Stoth said.

"You marching in with an army! What *would* you call it?" Moratrayas screamed.

Stoth chuckled. "The mighty genius still hasn't figured it out after three years. That's rich. I didn't invade your kingdom. I came by invitation."

Dumbfounded, Moratrayas stared at him. "Explain yourself!"

"It's simple. A messenger came to me after you took over Stone Heart. It wasn't the idiot king you overthrew, by the way, but a man claiming to represent the people of Stone Heart. He asked for help getting rid of you."

"You lie!"

"Quite often, to be honest, but not this time," Stoth replied. "I have to hand it to you, all the things you did after your coup were impressive. Free food, cutting taxes, giving farmland away, freeing prisoners, it was magnificent, a masterpiece of political theater that I am in awe of. You know, anywhere else it would have worked. But these people weren't fooled. They knew what was coming."

"What are you talking about?" Moratrayas demanded. He was getting angry, and in Sandra's experience that was a bad thing.

"I'm talking about revenge. These are small-minded, petty people. For years they'd insulted you, laughed at you, ignored you. You put on a good act, but they knew it was only a matter of time until you felt safe enough in your position to get even with everyone who'd abused you."

"Not a word of that is true," he protested. "They were my people. I'm related to some of them! I would never hurt them!"

Stoth snorted. "Please, there's no audience to pander to down here. They decided to hit you before you hit them. They told me your plans, smuggled my spies into the kingdom and even made payments for my mercenaries. When I came they stayed indoors because I ordered them to, and they were grateful for it. They welcomed me as a liberator."

Moratrayas sat back in his cell, an expression of shock frozen on his face. "My people."

"They were never yours," Stoth gloated. "They never wanted to be yours, and if by some miracle you retake the throne, they won't waste a second trying to get rid of you. You think they'd take orders from a tailor? They're pathetic, greedy, ignorant thugs who'd sell their own grandmothers if the price were right. They didn't want you and your grandiose plans, but I do."

"Get out," Moratrayas growled.

"You *will* help me. I'd prefer if it was willingly, but as Jeremy proved I can make you cooperate." Stoth snapped his fingers, and a brutish man wearing black leather clothes and a hood over his face stepped into the light. "Meet my torturer. He's been in my service for years, breaking men's will. I find I don't need him very often, but when I do he's invaluable. It took him a week to break Jeremy, and he barely touched him."

Moratrayas bared his teeth. "Send him in. I'm in the mood to hurt someone, and he'll do until I can reach you."

"Your optimism is refreshing and so out of place. Maybe I should have him spend a few hours working on your woman first."

Sandra's first instinct was to protest being called Moratrayas' woman, but once she figured out what Stoth was threatening her with she scooted back. The torturer stepped up to her cell and rested a hand on the bars.

"Stoth," Moratrayas hissed, "if you hurt her in any way I will kill you. These bars won't stop me. Your torturer won't stop me. That preening peacock won't even slow me down. When I get my hands on you, your death will be the stuff of legends."

"Is that a threat?" Stoth sounded amused.

Moratrayas stared at Stoth. "Of course it's a threat! What else would it be?" Throwing back his head, he screamed, "Merciful God in heaven, I have an idiot for an enemy!"

Stoth smiled and walked back into the shadows. “I’ll give you a few hours to think it over. I have an important party tonight and you’ll be there. Whether it’s as a guest of honor or a prisoner proving my strength is entirely up to you.”

The torturer followed Stoth out of the dungeon, but Captain Tinley remained. “Preening peacock?”

“It fits,” Moratrayas said.

Tinley took off his helmet and scowled. “Do you even remember me?”

“You’re Christopher Tinley. When I came to power you had nothing, no land, no hope, no future. You were going to leave for another kingdom. I gave you a terraced farm and asked nothing in return but your loyalty.”

“That’s right, you wanted to make me a farmer.” Tinley spat. “You’d be living in a castle and I’d be grubbing in the dirt trying to make a living! No gold, no luxuries, no power, you’d get all that.”

“Your life would have continued to improve,” Moratrayas told him.

“Sure it would,” Tinley sneered. “Maybe in a decade I’d get a shiny new shovel. I don’t need your help or your charity. I earned this rank, and I’ll earn even more! The King promised to make me a baron.”

“Make you a baron?” Moratrayas asked skeptically. “And how many people will you kill to get that lofty rank?”

“Doesn’t matter. They’d do the same if they got the chance. I’m just making sure it’s me hitting them and not the other way around.”

Moratrayas stood up and walked to the edge of his cell. He looked Tinley in the eyes, his contempt for the captain made clear by his expression. “Tinley, you are a monster, and worse you choose to be one. You have no excuse for what you’ve become. The only pleasure I take in seeing you like this is the knowledge that one day Stoth will recognize you as a threat and destroy you. The pity is you’ll do so much harm before he puts an end to your worthless life.”

“Captain Tinley,” Stoth called from the distance. “We’re leaving.”

Tinley sneered and walked off. “Enjoy the gallows, tailor.”

Tinley followed Stoth and the torturer out of the dungeon. They stopped at the door separating the dungeon from rest of the castle. Four soldiers stood guard and saluted.

“He tried to subvert a soldier before I spoke to him,” Stoth said.

“Don’t worry, that won’t work,” Tinley assured him.

“Captain, all it takes is one man with a guilty conscious and Moratrayas will be free to reap as much damage as he can. Whatever your failings may be, I know you can figure out who he’ll come after first. Keep your soldiers outside the dungeon. My torturer will handle him alone.”

Tinley bowed and smiled. “May I tell the men he’s on the job?”

"By all means. It will be good for morale." Stoth turned and looked approvingly at the torturer. "Bravado aside, this is going to be difficult. I need the good doctor taking orders from me within the month, sooner if possible, and men like Moratrayas tend to break before they bend."

"I like a challenge," the torturer said. "And the girl?"

Stoth took a moment to consider the question. "He seems to like her. No accounting for taste, I know. Threaten her all you like, but hurt her only as a last resort."

The torturer nodded and headed back into the dungeon.

Stoth smiled and rubbed his hands together. "Now that's taken care of, I do believe it's time for lunch."

"Al?" Sandra asked. Moratrayas sat in silence, brooding. Every so often his lips twitched. "Al, I'm sorry. I know that must have hurt."

"All this time I thought they stayed indoors because they didn't think we could win. I thought they were cowards. Now I discover they betrayed me. All I did for them, all I was going to do, and they plotted against me. I can understand their fear at first, but after nine months of only doing good, why didn't they have faith in me?"

Moratrayas leaned back in his cell and tapped on the stone floor. "I can do so much, yet they still call me a tailor. It boggles the mind. After everything I've accomplished they only see what I was, not what I've become."

They heard a door close somewhere in the darkness. Moratrayas smiled and said, "Finally, they're gone."

Puzzled, Sandra asked, "Who's gone where?"

Moratrayas' voice became serious. "The men Stoth left to watch us. I suppose they were trying to be stealthy, but short of playing drums I don't know how those mouth breathing idiots could make more noise standing in one place."

Sandra hadn't heard anything. "How long were they there?"

Moratrayas scrapped filth off the cell floor. "Since we arrived. They changed shifts twice, each time after five hours. This time only three hours went by, so I assume they're gone while Stoth's torturer plies his trade. Either they have weak stomachs or Stoth is worried one of them might show some humanity."

Suspicious, Sandra asked, "You knew we were being watched? How much of what you said was an act?"

"I did nothing to deceive them or you. I find the truth is the most effective way to get my point across. My apologies for not fully explaining our situation, but if I'd said anything they'd know they'd been spotted."

"The soldiers are gone for a little while, but how does that help us?"

Moratrayas lifted a brick off the floor. It swung on hinges and made no sound. He reached into a compartment under the brick and pulled a lever, and his cell door popped open. "With them gone we can escape."

"You could have gotten us out any time you wanted to!"

He took items from inside the compartment and stood up. "The cells, yes, but the soldiers would have prevented us from leaving the dungeon."

"How did you know the lever was there?"

"Sandra, this was my castle before it was Stoth's. When I owned it, Igor suggested I modify the cells so I could escape from inside if need be. At the time it seemed pointless, but as always Igor gives good advice. Now, the brick two feet to your left and a foot up will open your cell. No, the next one over. Yes, that's it, lift it on the right side...your right, not mine."

Sandra lifted the brick and found a compartment underneath it with a leather pouch full of coins, a set of brass keys, a lever that opened her cell and what looked like four brass rings fused together in a row. She opened her cell, collected the valuables and tools, and joined Moratrayas. Holding up the strange set of brass rings, she asked, "What's this?"

"Brass knuckles."

"I should have guessed," she said. "What is it with you and brass?"

"Do you have four hours to discuss the topic?"

"Right, we're on a timetable. We're out of our cells, we're armed, kind of, and we've got spending money. What do these keys open?"

"Every door in the castle," Moratrayas told her.

"That's if Stoth hasn't changed the locks since you left. But even if we get out, Stoth has the Sun Gun and his army."

"Both are serious threats." Moratrayas slipped the brass knuckles over his fingers. "The timing isn't perfect. I'd hoped to do this when the soldiers were changing shifts at night, but if Stoth has set his torturer on us then your life is in danger, and I can't allow that."

Sandra kissed him on the cheek. "That's sweet."

The kiss stunned him for a moment. "Err, well, I have too few friends to risk losing them. Come, we have to get out of here."

"It's still us against everyone here," she said. "What do we do?"

"The Sun Gun has to be destroyed at all costs," he told her. "After that, we do as much damage as we can before leaving. It's a tall order, but as I see it we have three advantages over Stoth. The first is that Igor is still out there doing everything he can to help us. The second is that I know the layout of the castle and town, including things Stoth doesn't know about."

"And the third?"

Moratrayas smiled at her. "Stoth doesn't realize what you're capable of. You're going to play an important role in destroying him, and he's too blind to see it."

They heard a squeaky door open in a distant part of the dungeon and close with a bang. A light appeared in the gloom, and there was the sound of footsteps coming slowly toward them. Moratrayas took Sandra by the hand and led her into the shadows.

It was the torturer, a lit torch in one hand and a whip in the other. He took his time walking to the cells in an effort to build fear. "You're supposed to be something special, tailor, but I've broken tougher men than you." He marched up to Moratrayas' cell and peered in. "What the—"

Moving silent as a ghost, Moratrayas drifted in behind the torturer and whispered, "It's doctor." The torturer spun around and swung his whip, but Moratrayas was faster. Two lightning fast blows sent the torturer to the floor. He struggled to his feet, but Moratrayas pressed the advantage, striking hard with every word he spoke. "Doctor Alberto Moratrayas!"

The torturer dropped stunned to the floor. Standing over him, Moratrayas said, "There would be a lot of irony and more than a little justice in strapping you to one of these machines and putting you through the same punishment as your victims. Fortunately for you, I have neither the time nor the stomach for such brutality."

Sandra and Moratrayas dragged the groaning man into a cell. Moratrayas slid the brick back into place, hiding the escape lever. They walked out and closed the cell door behind them.

"Think he'll figure out how we escaped?" Sandra asked.

"Not before we're long gone."

Sandra and Moratrayas headed for the exit. Before they got far, they heard a woman cry out, "Sandra, is that you?"

Sandra followed the voice and found a passage with more cells imprisoning seven women and three older men. "Joy? Joy, thank God you're okay! Al, Joy is from my village. She was sent to find Servant the holy man. Joy, are you hurt?"

Joy clutched the bars of her cell. "A little. Sandra, I'm sorry. Soldiers caught me before I found Servant and stuck me down here. They made me tell them about the rest of you and where you were going for help. They got almost everyone we sent, and it's my fault."

Sandra could only imagine what Joy had suffered through down here. "It's okay. Who are the men with you?"

One of the men took off his hat and said, "Marcus Talent, at your service. My friends and I are traveling merchants. We came here months ago selling spices. We were seized and our goods stolen. We're not strong enough to cut down trees, so they stuck us down here. Please, sir, I beg you, free us! We can't reward you in our current condition, but I swear one day we will pay you our weight in silver."

"I ask for no such price," Moratrayas said. "If I'm leaving so are all of you. Mr. Talent, if I may direct your attention to the floor a step behind you and to your right...your right, Mr. Talent, not mine."

The soldiers guarding the dungeon sat around a table outside the door. Bored, they passed the time by gambling. Two of them drank what little beer they could afford and the other two ate crackers.

"I raise two," a soldier said. "How long do you think the tailor can hold out?"

A second soldier tossed two copper coins onto the pile. "I'll see that. He's a tough one. I give him a week."

"Are you kidding?" another asked. "Three days tops."

The next soldier tossed a ring onto the pile. It was one of the pieces of jewelry taken from Sandra. "I don't know, he fought an army for three days. I say he'll be in there for ten days before he breaks. The ring's got to be worth ten. Meet it or fold."

"I thought you were going to give that to your girlfriend?" the first soldier asked.

"Like that's going to happen."

It was standard procedure to lock the door to the dungeon. The men working inside didn't carry a key, so if they were overpowered the prisoners couldn't escape. Soldiers and the torturer were let in on specific timetables, no exceptions. This made the soldiers' surprise even greater when the door swung open and slammed into the table.

Moratrayas burst out of the dungeon and struck men unconscious with rapid blows. One of them almost raised a cry for help, but Sandra grabbed a chair and clubbed him with it. Once all four men were defeated, Moratrayas bent down and retrieved Sandra's jewelry.

"Yours, I believe."

"That's the second time you gave me something nice, even if it's the same gift."

Moratrayas took a soldier's sword and stuffed the keys in his pocket. "The keys work, more proof that Stoth didn't spend time or money changing locks. I left behind several secret caches of money and equipment in case of emergency. I didn't have time to recover them when I fled here years ago. Some of the caches may have been discovered and looted, but if even a few remain we can make Stoth's party a truly memorable event."

The other prisoners came out of the dungeon with equal parts fear and excitement. Moratrayas pointed to the soldiers groaning on the floor. "Help me lock them in the dungeon. After that I'll try to get you out of here, and then make sure Stoth's plans go up in flames before the Raushtad does."

# Chapter 14

"This is where the barge went down," Igor told Ulysses Sower. He and the rest of the men of Sun Valley stood around the riverbank. The men now had gold feathers tipped with black sticking out from behind their ears, and a few of them were still eating roast griffin. They were acutely aware of how close they were to Scour, but by hiding in the trees they were relatively safe. It was early in the morning, still dark and cloudy, which might help them avoid discovery.

The men hadn't taken long to return. They'd rode the barges and let the current carry them close to where they saw Moratrayas' barge destroyed. Twenty men stood guard in case enemy patrols arrived, and another ten watched the barges.

"How long will it take to get it moving?" Ulysses asked Igor.

Igor dug through the pile of Moratrayas' equipment he'd recovered. Most of it was junk, but there was a light-producing orb. "Don't know. I have to find it, turn off the safeties and hope it's not trapped under the back half of the barge." Igor took off his cloak and handed it to Ulysses. "I could be a while. Get a fire going so I can warm up between trips."

With that Igor turned on the orb and dove into the river. Men stared in disbelief that anyone would risk the freezing waters. Ulysses pointed at them and said, "You're rested and fed, now let's get moving!"

A hundred soldiers stood straight as arrows outside the walls of Scour. Some of the men were filled with shame because of their defeat. The rest were incensed that they were taking the blame for the failure of others in their company. Their officers stood stiffly in front of them while their captain bawled them out.

"I was given an honor!" the captain shouted at them in the cold morning air. "The honor to recover the mad tailor's belongings and present them to the King as the spoils of war. I assumed three squads could do the job, that twenty-four of my men would be enough to gather up some wreckage!"

"A real honor," one of his men said quietly.

A fellow soldier smirked. "For him, anyway. Who'd you think would take the reward money for the tailor's stuff?"

The captain missed the snide and totally accurate comment, and went on shouting. "Three squads were defeated, tied up and left around a fire. The treasures they recovered were stolen. One deformed parody of a man defeated twenty-four soldiers! The King has lost all confidence in you, and so have I. There's been talk of disbanding this company and sending you back to your fields. In his graciousness, His Majesty has granted you dogs a chance to redeem yourselves."

"And save your career," a soldier whispered.

"I wonder what happens to him if we go back to being farmers?" another said.

"Nothing good, I'll wager."

The captain drew his sword and pointed it at the dense forest along the river. "Somewhere out there that freak is hiding with the loot he stole. He can't have gone far when he hasn't got a boat or animals to carry it. We're going to find him, kill him and get back the loot. If it's not in the King's hands by tomorrow morning, you'll be stripped of your rank and position. If the King's particularly annoyed, he might come up with a more inventive punishment. After all, he'll need to make an example of failures like you, and his torturer won't be busy with Moratrayas forever."

The captain sneered at his men and swung his sword toward the forest. "Move out!"

Igor popped back to the surface and swam to shore. Two men helped him over to a blazing fire they'd made under the pine forest's canopy. Igor turned off the glowing orb and plopped down next to the fire. Three times he'd dove into the icy water, coming back alive but without Gertrude. Ulysses walked over and asked, "Well?"

"I found it," Igor said as he rubbed his hands together. Men gathered around him and barraged him with questions. He waved them off and said, "It's in one piece and it's not caught under the barge. I'll turn off the safeties and bring it up on the next trip."

"Good, because we're going to need it," Ulysses said. "We've already been here too long. No one spotted us yet, but our luck can't last."

Igor dried his hair with a rag. "Give me a little time to warm up and we'll have Gertrude up and running."

A man on guard duty rushed over to Ulysses. "There are soldiers coming, lots of them!"

"Have they seen us?" Ulysses asked.

"I don't think so. They're digging around in the snow and brush. One of them said something about treasure."

Igor ran back to the river. He shouted over his shoulder, "Hide if you can, but stall them if they come this way!"

Still shivering, Igor dove into the cold water again. The men grabbed their tools and took cover by the edge of the woods. Ulysses put his finger to his lips, and the men fell silent.

They heard voices in the distance, accompanied by crashes and the sharp crack of dead branches snapping. Chain armor jingled and the voices became more distinct. Birds flew away from the noise and a deer ran by. The forest was so thick and the land so hilly it was impossible to see more than a few yards, but judging by the noise the soldiers were heading their way.

"He may have buried the loot," a voice in the forest said. "Look for disturbed dirt or snow."

"Stay together and make them come to us," Ulysses told his neighbors.

The men waited. The noises grew louder and they could make out more voices. Bright lights from the soldiers' torches shined in the gloomy forest. A few soldiers walked into sight, slowly moving around the trees. At first the soldiers didn't see the men hiding, but one saw the glint of steel from an ax and shouted, "Who goes there?"

"What's going on?" their captain demanded.

"There's someone by the river," the soldier said. "Wait, there's a crowd of men!"

"So much for hiding," Jason Sower told his father.

Ulysses shrugged. "Life hasn't been easy so far. Why should it change now?" He stood up and shouted, "Make them pay, boys!"

The soldiers drew their swords and charged. The trees were so close together that they couldn't come in a formation, and instead came in twos and threes. The men of Sun Valley stood up and met them, ganging up on the first few men and knocking them to the ground. Unaware of how badly they were outnumbered, Stoth's men fought fearlessly if not very well.

More soldiers came led by the company's captain. The captain managed to organize his men into a line so they couldn't be surrounded. They pushed the men of Sun Valley back onto the riverbank. More men could attack the soldiers in the open, and the two sides fought to a standstill. Ulysses led his people and swung his pickaxe with enough force that he smashed a soldier's shield.

Igor crawled back onto the riverbank, shivering and out of breath. Jason Sower saw him and dragged him to the fire. "Tell me you got that thing working!"

Water swirled and bubbled in the center of the river. Waves splashed high into the air and sent icy drops onto both farmers and soldiers. Surprised and confused, the two sides stopped fighting and separated. The river seethed like a boiling pot. Whatever was causing the ruckus was moving toward the bank.

"What is that?" a soldier asked.

"Kelp dragon?" his captain offered weakly.

Igor smiled. "You should be so lucky."

Water surged up onto the bank in a wave so large it swept over the men's boots. Steam billowed into the air and green lights shined in the river. A gleaming mass of brass liberally set with carved obsidian plates and glowing green panels rose up and put its front legs on dry ground.

Like most of his creations, Moratrayas based Gertrude on an animal. In this case he chose a snapping turtle, but one of monstrous proportions and weighing thirty tons. Gertrude's shell was twelve feet tall at the top and twenty feet long, with its tail and neck adding another ten feet to the length. Its head was five feet long and ended in a set of snapping jaws big enough to fit a grown man inside. Its eyes were black and glowed green along the edges. Gertrude's legs were as thick as tree trunks and sported thick claws.

As imposing as Gertrude was, the threat it posed didn't end with its enormous strength or ferocious claws and jaws. A wide barrel sprouted out of the clockwork's back and reached out over its head. The base of the barrel included a slowly rotating cylinder, each of its six chambers containing a shell the size of a wine barrel.

Gertrude studied the battlefield with hate-filled eyes. It clawed the ground and twisted its head to study the terrified people in front of it. Slowly it opened its mouth and issued a deep, malevolent growl.

"Gertrude," Igor called. The giant clockwork twisted its head around to look at the little man. Igor smiled and pointed at the men of Sun Valley. "Friends, Gertrude, friends."

The enemy captain backed up. "Uh oh."

Still smiling, Igor pointed at the terrified soldiers. There were so many interesting orders he could give Gertrude, ones it would follow to the letter without Moratrayas present to contradict him. So many amusing scenarios played out in Igor's mind, but in the end he opted for something far less brutal than the soldiers deserved. "Enemies, Gertrude. Fetch."

Gertrude roared a battle cry that echoed throughout the kingdom, magnified by speakers mounted next to the gun barrel. Thirty tons of brass, glass, obsidian and pure rage charged into the soldiers, bowling them over, smashing into and through the trees along the edge of the forest. Soldiers threw down their weapons to run faster, but the giant clockwork got ahead of them and chased them back to the river. In seconds Gertrude herded the screaming men to Igor, where they fell to their knees and pleaded for their lives. Igor patted Gertrude's armored head and looked at Ulysses.

"Worth coming back for?" Igor asked.

Ulysses stared at the giant clockwork. "Oh yeah. I like it a lot."

Back in the castle, Moratrayas led Sandra and the people they'd freed from the dungeon through a bewildering series of backrooms and passages. They traveled through secret doors and empty hallways, avoiding servants and soldiers bustling through the busier parts of the castle.

"Tonight's party is a bit of good luck," Moratrayas told Sandra. "Most of the staff will be busy cooking and preparing rooms for the guests. We should go unnoticed so long as we stay near the edges of the castle."

They ducked into a storeroom empty except for a few crates filled with bars of soap. Once inside, Moratrayas felt along the floor until he found a hidden compartment and opened it. He took out servant's clothes and more weapons.

"Another good sign. Our host neglected to change the servants' attire." Moratrayas stripped off his shirt and put on a manservant's uniform. He dusted himself off, took off his goggles and brought out a wig and fake moustache. He presented himself to the others. "Getting around just became easier."

"For you," Sandra said.

"True. I'll get our friends out of here the first chance I get, then see about finding more appropriate clothing for you."

Two women's voices approached the room they were hiding in. Moratrayas ran to the door and waited with weapons at the ready in case they entered.

"Can you believe how these people behave?" one of the women asked as she walked by the closed door. "The dirty little foreigners act like they own the place!"

The other woman clucked her tongue. "They come here hat in hand, begging for our help, and have the nerve to put on airs. They're no better than King Stoth said they were."

The voices receded into the distance, and Moratrayas lowered his weapons. "It's just as well they moved on. They might be missed if we'd tied them up, and soldiers would come looking for them. It appears Stoth's guests have already arrived."

Sandra scowled. "Sounds like he's found a bunch of vipers as bad as he is."

"They may be scoundrels, but we can use them. So many strangers in the castle will make it harder for Stoth's men to spot someone who doesn't belong. Come, there's a secret escape tunnel nearby. We'll send our friends out and then be about our business." Moratrayas rolled his shirt around the sword to conceal it and led them on.

Not far from Moratrayas, Stoth and Captain Tinley greeted their guests at the castle's main gate. Maids stood by with trays of wine and perfumed water while servants took coats and cloaks from the guests.

The route leading to the castle was heavily decorated. Bright banners hung between houses and proclaimed a joyous welcome to the King's new allies. Townspeople cheered the richly dressed guests as they arrived. The fact that these men were here to plot treason against their homelands was conveniently ignored.

A parade of ambitious men came in to be saluted and treated like royalty by the castle staff and soldiers. The men came in ones and twos, distrustful of one another and sticking close to their bodyguards, servants and wives. Some were rich and dressed in silks and soft furs. Others wore the uniforms of officers from a dozen different kingdoms. A few men had far simpler attire and were self-conscious of how little they had compared to the other traitors.

Stoth smiled at a petulant young man in rich clothes, escorted by a guard and an attractive young woman. "Ah, Prince Henry Balmore, such a pleasure you could make it. I see the bad weather didn't keep you away. Your father won't miss you?"

"Miss me? He wouldn't notice if I fell dead at his feet. Why should my absence draw his attention?" The prince saw a less prestigious guest approach the castle. He sneered and demanded, "Why are they allowed to use the same entrance as myself? I assumed I would be treated better than the dregs of society you've enlisted."

"Oh come now, Henry, there's no need for this hostility. These people will prove useful in the coming years. Save your anger for your father and older brothers. They're the ones keeping you from what's yours, not these worthies." Seeing that the prince still wasn't satisfied, Stoth added, "The celebration will begin in five hours, more than enough time to rest and refresh yourself. Accept my hospitality and enjoy yourself. I will deny nothing to so valuable a man. Please, suffer through these minor indignities on the way to inheriting your throne."

Prince Henry nodded curtly. "Very well."

Once the prince was inside the castle, Tinley murmured, "He'll be trouble once we've won."

Stoth smiled as the next traitor approached. Softly, he replied, "The prince will serve his purpose and be gone, as will all these fools." More loudly, he addressed his guest and said, "Captain Toffit of Granite Peaks. It pleases me to no end to see you again. And this must be your radiant wife."

Toffit, a man in his thirties, bowed in return and his wife blushed. They were nowhere near as rich as Prince Henry and their clothes showed it, but they carried themselves with more dignity. "King Stoth, the pleasure is mine. Know that I, my family and the men I command are at your disposal."

Stoth put his hand on Toffit's shoulder and solemnly announced, "When I hear you say that I feel as if I've gained an army of ten thousand men. Please, come inside dear captain, or should I say general?"

"Save the honors until I've earned them, Your Majesty, and earn them I shall," Toffit said before going inside with his wife.

Tinley drew in closer to Stoth and asked, "What do you mean?"

"It's simple, Tinley. Traitors are wonderfully effective in war, but they have very short life spans. An appallingly large number of them are going to die carrying out their sabotage missions. The few who survive will be pariahs, despised by their people. No one will care when I do away with them. They're like torches, use them when they're needed and toss them aside when they're spent. No need to tell them, of course."

"Then none of them will get what you promised?"

Stoth gestured for a servant to bring him a goblet of brandy. "Not a one, including General Thane. Oh come now, Tinley, I've promised to give these men money I don't have and positions they're not ready for. Even if I wanted to keep my word, I've already promised many times what I could deliver. Maybe one or two will survive and prove useful, which I doubt, but the rest are going to die or at the very least be ruined. Besides, how can I make you a baron if I give the job to someone else?"

Stoth smiled again and stepped forward to greet the next rogue. "Master trader Yaldin, how good to see you!"

Tinley smiled, too, but it was the grin of a predator sensing weakness. These men weren't competitors for the rank he desired. They were dupes and would get nothing for their trouble. The fact that the same fate could befall him was lost on the captain.

It took hours for Moratrayas and Sandra to reach the secret exit. They had to be careful not to be seen, and they spent lots of time hiding in side chambers waiting for castle staff and soldiers to pass by. But they eventually reached their destination, a broom closet at the south end of the castle. Moratrayas stepped inside and lifted a brick on the floor to reveal another lever. Pulling it opened a secret door leading to a dark, stone lined tunnel.

Moratrayas pointed down the tunnel and handed the men and women he'd rescued a torch from the wall. "Go down there and you'll find a door at the end with a bar across it. Remove the bar and you'll be in an outhouse outside the city walls. Get outside and take cover. If I don't come for you by morning, try to escape without me."

"Bless you, sir," Joy said. She hugged Sandra and led the others to freedom.

"What do you mean if you don't come?" Sandra demanded once the others were gone.

"We're in great danger, Sandra," he explained. "I can't guarantee either of us will escape, but I'll do everything I can to keep my promise to your mother. I will stop Stoth, but the cost may be higher than either of us would like."

"Oh no you don't," she said sharply. "You're not getting yourself killed tonight, Al! Not happening, end of story. We've gone through too much for you to throw your life away. I'm getting out of here and so are you, and that's the last I'll hear of it."

Moratrayas opened his mouth, but before he could speak, Sandra said, "Stoth has gotten away with too much already. He's done terrible things to so many people, and it's not fair. He's not going to kill you after the good you've done."

"You're forcing me to be optimistic?" he asked with a smile.

"Yes," she said. "Now come on. We've got a party to crash."

A scream came from the tunnel, followed by a loud conversation. Moratrayas raised his sword, but lowered it when he saw a short figure run down the tunnel toward them. "Igor!"

"Doc, it's good to see you. I met the strangest people on my way here." Sandra hugged him tightly, prompting him to say, "I need to come to the rescue more often."

"What news do you have?" Moratrayas asked.

"Straight to business." Igor set down a bulging bag, and opened it to reveal a pile of the doctor's weapons and equipment. "Gertrude is up and chomping at the bit. I left it with Sandra's people a few miles away."

"They didn't get away?" Sandra asked.

Igor smiled. "They didn't want to miss this. These are the weapons I salvaged from the barge. I got your spare cane, plus some of these little wonders."

Igor handed the doctor small brass spheres with what looked like obsidian whistles sticking out of them. Moratrayas smiled as he shoved them in his pockets. "This is a bonus."

"What are they for?" Sandra asked.

"They tell Gertrude where to fire when they're activated. Place one, turn it on and back away. Well done, Igor. Where would I be without you?"

Igor said, "You'd be dead, in jail or working as a tailor."

"Quite possible." Moratrayas slapped Igor on the back and took the spare cane. Tossing the sword aside, he said, "Filthy things, I can't abide them. Come, let's see what damage we can do."

Moratrayas led them in a search of the outskirts of the castle. They checked several storerooms and found most loaded with food and spare furniture. Two more secret compartments yielded up a replacement pair of goggles and armored gloves for the doctor. They found one locked room that held destroyed clockworks piled up in a corner. The doctor ran over and checked the nearest one. Sandra stood next to him and put a hand on his shoulder.

"I didn't think you had so many," she said. The pile of broken clockworks looked larger and the designs more varied than what he'd had aboard his barge.

Moratrayas rummaged through a clockwork man's innards. "Not all of these are ones I brought with us. There are the clockworks here I lost when Stoth first drove me from Stone Heart, as well as the ones destroyed by the Sun Gun. He must have saved them in the foolish hope he could repair them."

"How beat up are they?" Igor asked him.

"My more recent creations aren't too bad off. The Sun Gun boiled away their fuel and lubricants, breaking some tubes in the process. With the right tools, spare parts and enough time I can fix them. Had he kept the beam on them longer, they would have melted completely."

"Are they dead?" Sandra asked. She felt awful seeing the clockworks broken and silent after they had fought so hard to free her people.

"My clockworks have suffered damage this bad or worse before and been fine once I repaired them," Moratrayas replied. "They are inoperative, but not dead."

Sandra ran her fingers over a clockwork hound struck by the Sun Gun. Its fake fur was burned off and the brass shell underneath was blackened. "If that's what it does to clockworks, what would it do to people?"

"Men, elves, dwarfs, even trolls would be killed instantly. Armor would be no defense against the Sun Gun, and I doubt protective magic could resist it, either. We'll find no help here."

Another storeroom was under guard by a bored soldier. When he saw Moratrayas approach alone disguised as a servant, the soldier asked, "What's your business here?"

Moratrayas smiled and extended his cane out to full length. The soldier had only enough time to gasp before the doctor shocked him unconscious. Igor and Sandra came from around a corner and helped Moratrayas drag the soldier into the storeroom.

Inside they found two wagons loaded with barrels. Igor climbed on top of a wagon and broke a hole in one, letting strong smelling liquor drip down. He drank straight from the barrel and then whistled.

"Stoth is keeping the best stuff for himself. This is good brandy, Winchester Vineyards I think. It's worth at least fifty gold pieces a barrel."

Sandra counted the barrels and rolled her eyes. "He's bought a fortune in booze. This is what he's spending money on when he's about to invade every kingdom in the mountains?"

"He's ambitious," Moratrayas said. "No one said he was practical. It must have come recently if it hasn't been unloaded yet. Igor, I believe we're close to the stables. Come, I have a mission for you."

It took a little time to find a pair of draft horses and hitch them to one of the wagons. A few servants watched, but they assumed Moratrayas was what he pretended to be and didn't interfere. Getting the wagon outside was also easy. They used a side passage reserved for servants and supplies entering the castle. A few guests and soldiers noticed them, but none reacted to servants doing their work. Within an hour, Igor left the castle and then Scour itself at the reins of the wagon, his short body wrapped in heavy winter clothing and a smile plastered across his face.

It was getting dark at the Blue Sashes camp. General Thane watched the city warily as one traitor after another entered Scour. There was going to be a celebration in the castle tonight, and Thane wasn't invited.

"It's an insult," one of his officers told him. "We're eating bread and cheese while they feast. You should be there after catching Moratrayas."

"I should be there judging the worthiness of our new allies," Thane corrected him. He and his officers stood beside a fire in the camp, watching traitors from kingdoms all over the Raushtad entered Scour. "We need to know how reliable those men are. Any of them could be a double agent. We'd spot them sooner than Stoth or his men."

"Assuming they'd spot them at all," another officer said.

The first officer to speak added, "These fools don't know what they're doing. To leave you out in the cold proves how little they respect you. What happens when you give advice in battle? Will they ignore you then, too?"

"And what was that ruckus in the woods?" another demanded. "Stoth's lapdogs said they'd find out what it was. I wouldn't trust them to find their way home with a map, a guide and a trail of breadcrumbs! General, with all due respect, we're taking unnecessary risks and aren't getting anything but food and water in return."

Thane nodded. "Our employer is disrespectful and a fool. We've run into that before and survived. We'll ignore the insult and bide our time."

A mercenary walked up to the gathering and saluted. "Sir, a supply wagon has arrived from the castle. The driver says he's delivering fresh water."

One of the officers said, "We have enough water for three days."

Thane's eyes narrowed. He marched to the camp entrance with his men following, and found a wagon loaded with barrels waiting by the entrance. "What's this about?"

A little man wrapped up tightly against the cold was driving the wagon. "It's exactly what it looks like. My mates and I drew lots for the job, and I got stuck delivering water."

"It's not time for a delivery yet."

The little man rubbed his eyes. "Look, it's late, it's cold, I'm tired and I don't need this grief. All I know is my boss told me to make a delivery and I'm doing it. Can you please take this stuff so I can go home?"

Thane waved on a few of his men to unload the wagon, but something odd happened as they did so. Once they climbed on the wagon, they sniffed the barrels and caught a scent that made them grin wickedly. They unloaded the wagon in record time. The little man drove back to the castle, leaving Thane wondering what was going on.

Once the wagon was out of earshot, Thane said, "All right, out with it."

A mercenary grinned at him like a maniac. "These aren't water barrels, general. They smell like brandy!"

He may as well have dropped raw meat in a pool of sharks. Men came running from across the camp, and the few who didn't hear his shout came when they saw the commotion. Thane removed the stopper from a barrel and sniffed the contents. He tipped the barrel to pour some into a leather cup offered by one of his men. One sip told him the truth. "By God, it's Stoth's private stock!"

The men cheered. One of the officers exclaimed, "There are thirty barrels here! Stoth's staff must have made a mistake and sent it to us instead of water."

"I'm not going to tell him!" Thane roared. He'd had a bellyful of Stoth's arrogance and stupidity. If he couldn't get cash from his employer, he'd settle for good booze. "Come on, lads, you've gone too long without a drink. Let Stoth have his celebration and we'll have ours!"

The mercenaries cheered and drank cup after cup of brandy. They were too busy drinking themselves into a stupor to notice Igor abandon the wagon outside Scour and flee into the night.

Sandra and Moratrayas stood in a side passage of the castle near bathrooms reserved for important people. Richly dressed men and women went in and out while Moratrayas studied them from the shadows.

"What are you looking for?" Sandra asked.

"Your disguise. Nothing I have in storage will fit you, so we must be inventive. Be patient and a donor will appear."

Castle staff and guests walked by them. Sandra and the doctor caught snippets of conversations indicating that the party was a hit and Stoth was planning a speech.

"That will be when we strike," Moratrayas said. "I need to prepare first and get you in place."

"What about Igor?" Sandra asked.

"He'll make sure Gertrude performs as needed, then lead it and your men in." Moratrayas spotted a young woman enter the ladies' room. She wore a gaudy burgundy dress and carried a silk purse. He nodded. "Yes, she'll do nicely."

When the woman came out again, Moratrayas stepped up alongside her. Careful to make sure no one was about, he smiled and said, "Excuse me, madam, but if I may borrow a moment of your time?"

The woman sniffed and walked away. "I beg your pardon! I don't talk to servants."

Striking with the speed of a cobra, Moratrayas wrapped his left arm around her waist, pinning her arms to her side, then clasped his right hand over her mouth. She let out a muffled cry as he dragged her into a dressing room.

"I serve no one, and I most certainly do not beg," he told her. "Sandra, meet the woman who is providing your disguise."

Moratrayas waited outside the dressing room for an hour, tapping his fingers on the wall. The delay annoyed him. He leaned over to the dressing room door and asked, "Will this take much longer?"

"Just a minute," Sandra said from inside. "What are all these straps for, anyway?"

"Do you need a hand?"

"No! Give me another second or two...and there we go."

Sandra stepped out of the dressing room and spun around slowly to give Moratrayas a good look. The fine silk dress clung to her, too thin for her liking and too short. Impractical as it was, she was sure it must have cost a fortune. "Did I miss anything?"

It took Moratrayas a moment to answer. "No, uh, no, I believe everything's just...magnificent."

"Stop staring."

"I'm trying."

"I can't say much for the design, but it's a perfect fit," she told him. "How did you know it would fit me?"

Moratrayas spun his cane and answered, "I did used to be a tailor. How is the young woman doing?"

Sandra peered in the dressing room. "Tied up, gagged, wearing a towel and not happy about it."

Moratrayas slammed the door closed and hung a 'do not enter' sign on the handle. "Life is full of disappointments."

Sandra and Moratrayas made good time through the castle, neither one attracting attention. Guards and servants bowed when Sandra walked by. A richly dressed man with wine on his shirt put a hand on Moratrayas' arm and said, "Boy, take me to my room, I need to change."

"This man is already seeing to my needs," Sandra said. "My apologies, but you will have to find another servant."

"I say!" the man exclaimed, but Sandra turned her back on him and walked away.

Moratrayas followed and suppressed a smile. Once they went around a corner, he said, "I believe you like being a noblewoman."

"It has its perks."

"Now to business," he said. "The only rooms large enough for so many people are the throne room and main hall. Inside the main hall are stairs leading to the central tower, where you'll find the Sun Gun. It's the biggest threat to us. Gertrude and your people can win the day, but not if that horror is turned against them. Since we're already in the castle, it makes the task of retrieving the sunstones rather than destroying them a possibility. Once you're in the main hall, I'll create a distraction so you can get up the stairs and steal them."

"Risky for both of us," she said. "Where's the kitchen?"

"Why is that important?"

"I need a weapon, and I think I can find it there. It won't take long." Smiling, she added, "Don't make me pull rank on you."

Moratrayas looked at her curiously. "Very well, this way."

The kitchen wasn't far off. Most of the staff was away delivering meals, but a few women prepared rich desserts for the guests. Sandra peeked inside and saw what she needed in a spice rack. She grabbed hold of Moratrayas' cane and said, "They won't just let me waltz in there and take what I need. How does this thing work?"

"Press the button on the middle to extend it. Press it again to retract."

Smiling, Sandra took the cane and walked into the kitchen. The room was filled with piles of dirty pots and pans used in making the night's feast. Three older women looked up from their work and stepped in front of her. The oldest and most disgruntled of the three said, "Guests aren't allowed in here, ma'am."

"How about spies?" she asked, and with a press of a button extended the cane. She swung it in a wide arc, catching all three women and stunning them. Once they were down, she retracted the staff back into a cane and took a jar of ground pepper and a small jar of cooking oil. She loaded them into her purse and left. Moratrayas looked curious but said nothing when she handed him back his cane. "I'm good. Let's go."

They reached the main hall and stopped. The room was packed. Long tables on the edges of the room were covered with platters of rich food. There were roasted meats garnished with mushrooms, bowls of hot soup, trays of bread and cheese, and an assortment of dishes so bewildering that Sandra could only guess what they were. More tables bore cakes, pies and pastries dripping with frosting and sugared fruit. Seeing so much food made Sandra angry. These traitors gorged while the people of Sun Valley were near starvation. For that matter the commoners of Stone Heart didn't eat half as well.

Guests sat by tables in the center of the room. Servants brought them generous helpings of food and filled their wine goblets whenever they emptied. Sandra couldn't help but notice the best-dressed people were at the front of the room, and the farther back the tables were the less expensive the guests' clothes and jewels became.

"There's got to be a hundred traitors in there," Sandra said.

"And each one no doubt represents many more where they came from," Moratrayas replied. His fierce expression softened, and he added, "There's no one here from Refuge."

Sandra smiled at him. "You have a good bunch over there."

"The best."

"Are you ready?" she asked.

"Not yet." Moratrayas retreated from the main hall and found an empty room. Ducking inside, he took off his servant disguise and put his shirt back on. His replacement goggles and armored gloves came next. He extended his cane to full length, momentarily studying the sparking tip. He looked at Sandra and said, "I refuse to fight in disguise. Whether we succeed or fail, I will do it as myself. Now I'm ready."

# Chapter 15

Stoth Voluk checked his clothes before going out to address his newest followers. The very riches and power that made them useful meant he had to handle them carefully. Many of these fools were obsessed with fashion and appearance. They'd notice if he wasn't perfectly dressed, and it would lower their opinion of him. He'd gone to great lengths to reach this point. It wouldn't do to fail now.

He had conquered Stone Heart and raised an army from its peasants. He'd convinced the most feared mercenaries in the world to serve him in return for the promise of gold they'd never get. He'd built a fleet of barges, wagons and a host of siege weapons, paid for with loans from bankers who'd never see their money again. And now he had the last piece of the puzzle, an army of men willing to betray their kingdoms for rewards they wouldn't live long enough to see.

Stoth stood at the entrance to his throne room and glanced at Captain Tinley before putting the final touches on his masterpiece. "There ought to be a law against duping men this stupid."

Tinley snickered in reply. "They're signing up to die, and all they're getting for it is a free meal."

"Yes, a lot of idiots are going to die for nothing. I like to think of this as improving the species," Stoth said pleasantly. "Let's see if we can't spice up the show. Send word to the torturer that I need Moratrayas up here in an hour, gagged, chained and suitably beaten."

Stoth stepped before the crowd and smiled. They sat in ranked tables before him, well fed and cheerfully oblivious to the fact that most if not all of them would be dead in a year. Servants closed the doors to grant them privacy and make sure none of the guests wandered off in search of a bathroom during his speech. The guests clapped for him, with the exception of a few high-ranking fools who thought themselves partners in Stoth's conquest and not pawns in it.

"Honored guests, thank you for coming," Stoth began. "You risked traveling through the mountains in this harsh winter, no small challenge even to men such as yourselves."

Sandra sat in the audience near the back of the main hall. No one paid her any notice when she went in, no doubt assuming she was a guest. Sandra saw the staircase Moratrayas described off to one side and guarded by two soldiers. She couldn't get up there until Moratrayas provided his distraction. Until then she sat back and did her best to look attentive.

She was scared. Everyone around her was an enemy. If even one person realized she didn't belong here she was doomed, surrounded by soldiers and with no escape route once the doors closed. Admittedly the chances of someone figuring out who she was were slight. The guests didn't know one another, so they likely wouldn't spot anything out of place about her. Then again, someone here was missing a wife, girlfriend or mistress, and Sandra was wearing the woman's clothes.

A woman broke Sandra's concentration and said, "Dear, I simply adore your dress."

"Oh, thank you. I got it special for tonight."

"You *must* introduce me to your tailor."

Sandra smiled. "I'm sure that can be arranged."

Both of them were shushed by the crowd of traitors as Stoth continued his speech, drawing Sandra's attention off her worries and onto the venomous lies he was spewing. Listening to him was almost more than she could bear, and sitting next to these villains was no better. The traitors laughed and congratulating one another on being part of a plot that would bring about so much suffering. It was like being in a nest of poisonous snakes. Stoth had done so much evil, and with their help he'd do a thousand times more.

"I'm going to tell you the story of my life," Stoth said as he walked between the tables. "It's going to sound familiar, because it's your life's story, too. Since I was a young man, I saw neighboring kings wasting fortunes every year. The rich and powerful looked down on me and treated me like a rat while they squandered riches I deserved.

"It infuriated me. Why did these fools with no talent and no skill get the good things in life? What right did they have to their riches? The short answer is they don't have any right. They take their power and position for granted, assuming this is the way it *is* and the way it *should be* and the way it always *will be*."

Sandra couldn't make any sense of this. Stoth was a king even before he conquered Stone Heart! She doubted he'd ever missed a meal in his life, but he spoke like he was a starving beggar. He was one of the men on top! But the crowd was eating it up. Most of them were rich and powerful, yet they acted like they had nothing at all. Some of them actually drooled at the prospect of starting a war that would kill so many people.

"Some men would be content to just get by, to live unnoticed in the shadows on whatever morsels came their way, but not us," Stoth said. "We take chances."

Moratrayas stood outside the main hall holding a brass sphere to signal Gertrude. He had six spheres, one for each shell the clockwork could fire. Casually he tossed a sphere in the air and caught it.

It was tempting to start his attack immediately, but he waited and listened to his enemy's speech. There was no telling what plans Stoth would reveal to his co-conspirators. There could be parts to his schemes that Moratrayas didn't know about. And so he waited and listened through the door, hoping Stoth would reveal some new element of this plot that Moratrayas could uproot and destroy.

A manservant walked by and saw the doctor. "Hey, who are you?"

"I'm busy," Moratrayas said, and shocked him unconscious.

Stoth's muffled voice came through the closed doors. "I defeated the mad scientist who ruled here. No one else thought it could be done, but I drove him off in three days! But is one kingdom enough? Would it be enough for any of you? No, this was a beginning, nothing more.

"We're here tonight to build on that beginning. There are dozens of kingdoms out there just waiting to be taken. They're corrupt, their leadership is incompetent and their armies are a joke. Only one of these kingdoms worried me, the one ruled by the same mad scientist I defeated to take Stone Heart. But that man sits in my dungeon, a threat no more!"

The audience applauded. Stoth waited for them to finish before he said, "You're here tonight because you want more. You want the honors refused you, the positions denied you, the inheritance that should be yours but instead goes to another because of an accident of birth."

Back in the main hall, Stoth walked among the audience, smiling and talking. "You have ambition. You have drive. You have a hunger than can't be satisfied by the crumbs off someone else's table. That's why I invited you here tonight."

Sandra tried to keep out of sight. The only person here who'd had a good look at her was Stoth, and he was drawing closer. For a moment she thought he'd missed her. He walked by, smiling, and without any warning he grabbed her right arm.

"I don't remember inviting you. It seems we have a spy among us," he said pleasantly. Guests gasped and backed away. Soldiers marched in to take her. Stoth looked pleased with himself until he recognized Sandra. In a flash his expression changed to panic. "Wait, you're Moratrayas' woman!"

Sandra closed her eyes tightly and took a deep breath before she pulled the jar of pepper from her purse with her free hand and swung it in the air. The stopper popped out, sending a cloud of finely ground black pepper across the room. The cloud swept over Stoth, filling his eyes, nose and open mouth. He let go of her and collapsed in a fit of coughing and sneezing. The pepper cloud spread over the rest of the room and had the same effect on the guests and soldiers. Men shouted and women screamed. Sandra escaped in the panic and ran up the stairs.

Outside, Moratrayas heard the screams and realized Sandra had been spotted. He turned on the first brass sphere and tossed it in the corner by the doors. The sphere made a tiny whistling noise, a call to arms for the doctor's most dangerous creation.

Igor stood outside of Scour with the men of Sun Valley and Gertrude the clockwork. They hid by the river in a grove of pine trees that offered them cover and kept them out of the wind. The men were agitated, talking to each other and pointing their tools at the brightly lit city.

Igor had awakened these men's anger and was having trouble keeping it under control. Complicating matters, Gertrude growled in agreement and pawed the ground. Even the clockwork dragonfly buzzed angrily overhead. With both men and clockworks itching for a fight, Igor didn't know how much longer he could keep them from attacking before the time was right.

"We saw those rich people go in and didn't attack any of them," Ulysses told Igor. "Letting them go wasn't easy. They're going to help that monster! We've got the men and your clockwork. What's holding us back?"

"The doc hasn't given the signal yet," Igor said.

"How much longer do we have to wait?" Ulysses demanded.

Igor was going to tell Ulysses to calm down when he saw Gertrude lift its armored head and listen. He couldn't hear anything, but he knew what had the clockwork's attention. He grinned and said, "Sower, if you want a fight, you're about to get one."

Gertrude braced its legs against the snowy ground. The cannon barrel lifted and a shell loaded into place. The barrel glowed green and began to spark.

"Duck your heads and cover your ears!" Igor shouted.

Gertrude fired with a deafening blast. The shot drove Gertrude back a foot, its clawed feet digging deep ruts into the ground. Men near the clockwork were knocked over, and snow shook off the trees. The shell screamed through the air over the city wall and hit the castle dead on. Stone walls offered no defense against it.

The shell smashed through the castle's outer wall, through three interior walls and some furniture, and then took off the front of the main hall. A cloud of dust and powdered masonry filled the room. People screamed in panic and cowered in the corners.

In the main hall, a woman temporarily blinded shouted, "Is there a doctor in the house?"

There was a moment of silence after the blast. Those blinded by pepper and dust gradually got their sight back. They looked around, frightened and confused. Then they heard footsteps slowly approaching. A lone man walked through the dust cloud and came to a stop next to the sundered doors. He wore a white shirt, black pants and boots, a pair of gloves lined with iron plates and goggles over his eyes. He carried no sword, and instead was armed with a brass staff that sparked at the tip.

"I couldn't resist an opening line that good," Moratrayas said. "Stoth Voluk, you took everything I had and made it ugly, and I have come for satisfaction. Courtesy demands I give you a chance to surrender before I unleash the fullness of my wrath."

Tears blurred Stoth's eyes so badly he could barely see, but he knew Moratrayas' voice. Still coughing, he waved his hand toward the sound and ordered, "Guards, kill him! Kill him now! He's a monster!"

Moratrayas tossed a brass sphere ahead of him. "I was hoping you'd say that."

Stoth's soldiers drew their swords and advanced. They hadn't gotten ten feet when a whistle announced the arrival of a second shell. This one punched through the walls as easily as the first and kicked up a new cloud of dust. Moratrayas headed for Stoth, unperturbed by the chaos he caused. He tossed another sphere and brought down a third shell from Gertrude.

Stoth, the guests, his servants and soldiers fled into the throne room. More shells followed one after another until all six were fired. Moratrayas made sure he didn't shell the stairs so Sandra could come down again. The shells made holes in the walls big enough for a man to walk through. Whole sections of the outer and inner walls collapsed. Through it all, Moratrayas walked remorselessly after Stoth.

Stoth recovered enough of his vision to see Moratrayas coming. He pointed an accusing finger at him and shouted, "I beat you twice before! I took your brass monsters apart and sank your boat. I beat you, and I can do it again!"

Soldiers ran forward and formed a line between Stoth and Moratrayas. More soldiers came in from other parts of the castle. Moratrayas paid them no attention, focusing instead on his nemesis. "They're called clockworks, Stoth, and you didn't get them all."

Clack snap pop! Strange noises came from behind Moratrayas. More pops and clanks followed. An iron hoop rolled across the floor and stopped at the opposite wall while others rolled in front of Stoth. Then, moving slowly, the brass shells Gertrude fired at the castle unfolded, plates shifted, gears turned and panels lit up green. The shells transformed into six large clockwork men. They stood seven feet tall and had hands that ended in studded brass fists. The clockwork men climbed out of the rubble and stood alongside their creator.

Moratrayas whirled his sparking staff. "You had your chance."

Outside the city, the men of Sun Valley cheered wildly. Gertrude's attacks blew a line of holes in the castle. The cylinder on the base of the barrel rotated, loading one shell into place after another until the six were fired. Clouds of dust rose up from the castle, and even from this distance the men heard alarm bells ring across the city.

Ulysses was the only man not celebrating. "All of you, quiet! Igor, it hit the castle, that's well and good, but it didn't break through the wall around the city! How are we supposed to get in there?"

Igor patted the giant clockwork's head. "Gertrude, the nice man wants to get inside and help the doc." Gertrude growled in response. "Can you help him get inside?"

The clockwork roared and charged toward Scour while Igor and the men of Sun Valley ran cheering after it. Gertrude lumbered across the snowy landscape, trampling anything in its way. The few people out so late screamed and ran for their lives. Soldiers manning the city gate saw the clockwork coming. They closed the gate and lowered a portcullis. When Gertrude and the men got close to the city wall, Igor shouted, "Gertrude, there's a door next to the gate! Claw it open!"

Gertrude either didn't hear the order or was too angry to obey, instead slamming into the closed city gate. The wooden gate bent inward when thirty tons of angry brass and obsidian hit it.

"Uh, no, the door's to the left," Igor said. Gertrude screamed a battle cry and bit a hole in the gate. It put both its front feet into the hole and pulled the gate apart in a shower of splinters and bent nails. The portcullis still barred its path, but not for long. Gertrude broke through it as if it were made of matchsticks. The clockwork charged into the city, screaming in rage. The men of Sun Valley followed it in and screamed almost as loud. Igor stood by the shattered defenses for a moment. "Well, whatever works."

Sandra ran up the stairs leading to the Sun Gun. She heard Gertrude's shells hitting the castle and hoped she could disable the gun before it killed the giant clockwork. She followed the spiral stairs higher and higher, racing by torches set in the walls and windows that showed a dust cloud rising over the castle. When she reached the top, she saw Jeremy the clockmaker huddled in a corner, a confused soldier by the stairs and an incredible machine that could only have been built by Moratrayas.

The soldier drew his sword and demanded, "What the devil is going on down there?"

It took a second for Sandra to realize he thought she was a guest. She pointed down the stairs and cried, "Please, save me! It's the mad tailor! He's coming this way!"

The soldier pushed her aside and stood at the head of the stairs, sword raised menacingly over his head to face a threat that wasn't coming. Sandra got behind him and ran into him, knocking him down the stairs. She heard his armor clang, and the soldier cried out in surprise and then pain as he tumbled down the stairs.

"That's getting to be a habit with me," Sandra said. She walked over to Jeremy and helped him up. "Come on, I'm taking the sunstones and getting you out of here."

Jeremy looked at her in confusion before he smiled broadly. "You're the woman from the dungeon. I, we're going home?"

"You, me, Al, everybody's leaving. Shake a leg, Jeremy. Once the Sun Gun is out of commission we're gone."

Jeremy staggered to his feet and led her to the Sun Gun. "It's not hard to do. The sunstones are contained in granite spheres in the barrel. I can open the spheres and take out the stones or release the spheres still sealed."

"Take the spheres or it'll be too bright for us to see."

Jeremy sat at the controls of the Sun Gun and began throwing switches. While he worked, Sandra looked down at the city below. She saw the gate ruined and Gertrude rampaging through the streets with her people following behind it.

But that's not all she saw. There was the courtyard where Stoth kept his siege weapons, and his fleet of barges moored on the river. There were supply wagons and the armory brimming with weapons. Before Jeremy could disable the Sun Gun, she grabbed his hand and said, "Hold on, we still need this."

"What do you mean?"

Sandra pointed to the weapons and transports Stoth had amassed. "The Sun Gun won't work if we take the sunstones, but Stoth has other weapons, enough to let him take over a couple kingdoms. We have to destroy all of it or he'll still be a threat."

"You don't understand," Jeremy said. He pounded his fist on the edge of the control panel. "No one listens to me! The Sun Gun is too dangerous. The barrel is still hot from when Stoth made me sink your boat. I had to open the shutters on the walls to let in cold air, but it's not cooling the gun fast enough. If we fire it too many times, we'll destroy it."

"Isn't that a good thing?"

"Not that way! The closer the sunstones get to one another, the greater the energy they produce. When the stones are eighteen inches apart they become weapons instead of sources of light. If the Sun Gun breaks, or God forbid it melts, the sunstones could come even closer together. I don't know what that would do and I don't want to know!"

The goblins thought the Sun Gun could destroy the whole kingdom if it went out of control, and Moratrayas agreed with them. Jeremy was right, using it was a terrible risk. But leaving Stoth with those weapons put many kingdoms in danger. The people in those kingdoms were strangers Sandra had never met and likely never would, but she couldn't expose them to the suffering she'd known. "How many times can we safely use it?"

Jeremy threw up his hands. "I don't know! Anything more than four times a day could destroy it."

"Then we'll settle for four," she said. "Power it up. I'm going to make sure no one stops us."

Nervous, Jeremy readied the Sun Gun while Sandra took the bottle of cooking oil from her purse. She spread it on the stairs, making sure anyone who tried to reach the Sun Gun would have a hard time of it.

The Sun Gun lit up and made the room impossibly bright. Jeremy handed Sandra brass rimmed goggles and put on an identical pair. "I found these in the tower when they imprisoned me here. Put them on or you'll be blinded."

Jeremy sat by the controls and brought the Sun Gun to full power, filling the tower with light so bright it made Sandra's skin tingle. "Lower the gun ten degrees."

"How?"

"I labeled the controls."

Sure enough, many of the buttons had pieces of paper glued to them with instructions listing what they did. "That's convenient."

Sandra and Jeremy picked out the correct switches among the controls. The controls were similar to the ones Moratrayas used on his weapons and clockworks, so Sandra had some familiarity with them.

"What do you want to shoot?" he asked.

"Let's start with his fleet."

The Sun Gun turned under their control to face the fleet of river barges. The tower lit up even brighter, and the Sun Gun sang a single note as it fired a blazing beam of heat and light. The beam swept over the fleet and construction yard, setting fire to everything it touched. Twenty-eight river barges and four more in dry dock were turned into bonfires in three seconds.

"What's next?" Jeremy asked.

Back at the Blue Sashes camp, the mercenaries watched the display of firepower with a mix of awe and fear. They saw Gertrude shell the castle and then charge into Scour. The Sun Gun fired in reply, but instead of hitting the giant brass monster, it destroyed the entire fleet of river barges.

The Blue Sashes should be running to defend Scour and put this threat to flight. They had some experience fighting clockworks and wouldn't be beaten by them a second time. But they feared the Sun Gun and didn't want to go near it, especially when it couldn't seem to tell friend from foe.

They held back for another very good reason. Every last person in the Blue Sashes camp was so drunk they could hardly stand. The mercenaries hadn't been getting much alcohol for weeks, and when confronted with so much potent booze, they couldn't resist the temptation. They'd drained every drop of brandy from the thirty barrels Igor had brought them.

Thane watched the barges burn. "Stoth lost control of the Sun Gun," he said. It was hard not to slur his words. "I knew that thing was trouble."

A mercenary sitting on an empty barrel said, "That...that has got to be expensive."

"Lots of money going up in smoke," an officer agreed. They saw Gertrude rampage past the destroyed gate, a crowd of soldiers fleeing its wrath. "S-sir, I, I don't believe we're getting paid enough to fight a monster that big."

Another tipsy mercenary added, "We haven't been paid at all."

Thane watched the Sun Gun fire again. This time its blazing beam struck the courtyard and set fire to the siege weapons, destroying them as easily as it had the barges. "You make a good point. I, I have to say, looking at this, it's going to cost a fortune to fix it. Makes me think Stoth isn't ever going to have the money to pay us."

"That's a shame," an officer said. "So, what do we do?"

It took Thane a few seconds to collect his thoughts enough to answer. "I've been giving that some thought these last few days. And it seems to me, in a situation like this, we should grab anything worthwhile that's not nailed down and leave."

"I like this plan", the mercenary sitting on the barrel said before he passed out and fell over.

Inside Scour, Gertrude charged through the city on its way to the castle. Frightened people fled before it and the men of Sun Valley followed it. The clockwork crushed stalls and carts in its way, roaring challenges through speakers on its back the whole time.

Those challenges didn't go unanswered. Most of Stoth's army was asleep in their barracks when the attack began. Soldiers poured out as they put on armor and tried to figure out what was happening. They couldn't see what the Sun Gun was hitting and assumed it was repelling an attack. When they heard Gertrude's roars inside the city, they formed up into ranks and sought out their enemy.

The first company that saw Gertrude panicked and ran for their lives. Two more companies managed to hold their place when it came for them. Soldiers raised their shields and spears into a wall. They could effectively block the clockwork's path in the narrow streets of Scour, and the men of Sun Valley couldn't get around it to help.

Gertrude attacked the wall of spears. It backed away when spears pierced the thinner armor around its knees and base of its neck. It snapped at the spears and broke a few, but the men pushed forward and hit the clockwork again. It couldn't get close enough to attack the men without being badly damaged. Gertrude was forced back.

"That's it!" a captain urged his men. "Aim for the joints. Keep at it!"

Igor climbed up Gertrude's tail, ran across its armored shell and sat down on its neck. He leaned in close to the clockwork's head and whispered to it. Gertrude's eyes narrowed. It pushed itself upright and grabbed onto the nearest building. More spears struck it, but the clockwork didn't back up. Instead it pulled with all its might until the front of the building peeled off and came down on the spear wall. Most of the spears broke when the wall landed on them, and the few left intact were pinned to the ground.

"Orders, sir," a soldier whimpered.

Gertrude growled. The captain gulped and cried, "Run!"

The soldiers broke and fled. Gertrude ran after them until it came to a street that led straight to the castle. Igor pointed at the gapping holes in the castle's wall. "The doc is in there. Come on!"

Gertrude roared and ran to the castle. The men of Sun Valley cheered and followed. The holes blasted through the walls were too small for Gertrude to fit through and join the battle. The men of Sun Valley had no such trouble.

Moratrayas parried a soldier's sword in the throne room and stunned the man with his brass staff. He stepped over the fallen man to engage the next soldier. "I'm coming, Stoth!"

"Kill him!" Stoth screamed. His calm, dispassionate voice was gone, replaced with terrified shrieks as Moratrayas came ever closer. Stoth cowered on his throne and watched the battle in horror. He and his guests were trapped in the throne room, the only exit blocked by Moratrayas and his six clockworks. Soldiers fought desperately to break through, but to no avail. They steadily lost ground to Moratrayas' attack.

A soldier picked up a chair and threw it at Moratrayas. It would have struck him, but a clockwork grabbed the ungainly projectile and threw it back, bowling the soldier over. More soldiers tried to gang up on the doctor, only to be kicked and punched by the clockworks. One soldier stabbed a clockwork and drove his sword through the brass contraption's belly up to the hilt. The clockwork grabbed him by the collar and slapped him before throwing him into a wall. Moratrayas pulled the sword out and tossed it aside.

Moratrayas couldn't be surrounded with his clockworks supporting him. No more than two men could come at him at a time, and the same was true for the clockworks. This battle would be decided by quality more than quantity.

Moratrayas struck a soldier in the knee and drove him to the ground, then stunned him. He felled another soldier with a savage kick to the chest followed by a jolt from his staff. Soldiers began to back away from him rather than risk his fury. They were afraid of him. They had good reason to be.

Moratrayas' face betrayed the great anger building within him. He knew the men he was fighting. Every one of them was a neighbor, relative or a man he once called friend. More than that, he knew what they could have become, the greatness they could have achieved. He knew how much good they could have accomplished in a world that so badly needed help. He saw the wasted potential in them, and his hatred grew tenfold.

"Prison bars didn't stop me!" Moratrayas raged. He blocked a sword with his armored gloves and punched the soldier in the face. "Castle walls didn't stop me! The Sun Gun didn't stop me! What makes you fools think you'll succeed where all else failed?"

Fear gripped Stoth's men. Soldiers ran away when they could find an opening. The few who fought back did so in a panic, too scared to work together. Soon only twenty men stood between Moratrayas and Stoth.

More soldiers came from elsewhere in the castle and attacked the clockworks from behind. Caught between two forces, Moratrayas and his creations were halted. The doctor stunned men with his staff and his clockworks kicked and pounded men aside. A few soldiers scored hits on the mechanical men and cut into their armor. But like their smaller cousins, these clockworks could take an enormous amount of punishment. They took the hits and kept coming, kicking men aside and throwing them into walls.

A bright light shined in through the holes Gertrude had blasted in the castle, and Moratrayas heard the Sun Gun's now familiar scream. He looked outside, terrified that the Sun Gun was destroying Gertrude, or worse, killing Sandra's people. Thankfully it unleashed its fury against a different target. Its terrible beam swept across the wagons that would have hauled supplies for Stoth's army. One touch of the beam burned them like kindling.

Moratrayas smiled. "Sandra, you keep surprising me."

The Sun Gun was being consumed by its own power. The gun's granite barrel was so hot it steamed. Granite gears that turned the gun creaked and moved more slowly than before. Even the control board was hot when Sandra touched it.

"The stone is expanding from the heat," Jeremy said. "We're reaching the gun's limits."

"Can we get one more shot?"

"One more and that's it," Jeremy told her. "I can't be held responsible for what happens after that."

Sandra looked down on the city. "One is all we need. You see that building down there?"

Jeremy adjusted the lenses next to the gun, lining them up to see more closely. She pointed at a large brick building next to a row of blacksmith shops. "What is it?"

"That's the armory," Sandra told him. "It's not made of wood like the other targets. Can we still destroy it?"

Before Jeremy answered, two soldiers ran up the stairs. One shouted, "Turn the blasted thing off or we'll kill you!" Both men drew their swords and then stepped on the stairs Sandra had oiled. The pair slipped and tumbled screaming down the stairs.

"I'm ashamed to admit it, but I found that deeply satisfying," Jeremy said.

"Can we burn the armory?" she demanded.

"The Sun Gun can destroy anything if used long enough," he told her. Sandra and Jeremy flipped more levers, causing the Sun Gun to laboriously turn to face the armory. The Sun Gun fired for the last time ever and hit the armory's roof. Its beam stayed on the building for ten seconds, burning through even stone until it reached the weapons. Wood handles burned to ash and steel blades melted to form a molten pool that dripped into the foundation.

Jeremy wasn't exaggerating when he said the Sun Gun might destroy itself. Dense clouds of steam rose from the gun, and drops of molten rock dripped from the barrel. The wood shutters began to smolder simply because they were too close to the unstable weapon. Notes pasted to the controls caught fire and burned away. Jeremy turned off the Sun Gun and switched one last lever to seal the three sunstones in granite spheres. He put on heavy leather gloves and handed a second pair to Sandra, then took the spheres out by handles. Jeremy carried two and handed the third to Sandra.

"Come on, we have to go," she told him. "Watch the first few stairs."

"Tailor!" Captain Tinley bellowed. He pushed his way to the front of the panicked crowd and led the remaining soldiers. Bad as his situation was, Stoth's forces still stood a chance. There were a lot of soldiers and Moratrayas had only six clockworks. More soldiers hurried in to save their King, and they replaced every man who fell. They could win this.

Tinley ignored the clockworks and headed straight for Moratrayas. A savage swing of his sword struck the doctor's staff and forced him to his knees. More swings followed that the doctor barely blocked.

"I won't lose, tailor!" Tinley screamed. He swung again and again, the strength and fury of his blows keeping Moratrayas on the defensive. "I've risked everything for a chance at greatness! I won't let you take it from me! I won't go back to being a farmer!"

Tinley raised his sword for another swing, but it never landed. Ulysses Sower slammed into Tinley and knocked him to the ground. Tinley looked up, not sure who these ragged people were coming through the holes in the castle. Ulysses looked down at Tinley and asked, "What's wrong with being a farmer?"

It was Sandra's people. The men of Sun Valley poured in and hit the soldiers from behind. They lacked experience fighting, but they had surprise and superior numbers on their side. Three hundred men vented their fury on Stoth's forces, while outside the castle Igor and Gertrude fought off any soldier foolish enough to approach them.

The army of farmers pressed Stoth's men on one side and the clockworks struck from the other. Soldiers were terrified of Moratrayas and the vengeance the farmers were sure to take. Worse yet, they were trapped. Their discipline broke, and with it any chance of victory. Captain Tinley tried to rally his men, but Moratrayas tripped him with his staff. "I'm not done with you," the doctor said savagely.

The battle reached a fever pitch around them. A clockwork grabbed a soldier and threw him through a hole in the wall, then lost an arm to another soldier's sword. Undeterred, it picked up the arm and clubbed the soldier with it. Two men from Sun Valley tripped a soldier and kicked him on the floor. Tinley managed to land a blow on Moratrayas and tore open his coat, but the armor plates sewn into it prevented him from drawing blood. The clockwork dragonfly swooped in and rammed Tinley in the face, driving him back.

Fierce though the fighting was, there could only be one outcome. Moratrayas and his allies had superior numbers, surprise and strength. One by one, Stoth's men went down. They were surrounded, pulled to the ground, disarmed, defeated. Tinley lashed out like a rabid dog at everyone around him. Ulysses swung his pickaxe and punctured Tinley's shield, then pulled it from his hands as Moratrayas stabbed him with his electrified staff. Tinley dropped to his knees. He remained awake long enough to look Moratrayas in the eyes.

"I was going to be a baron," Tinley gasped.

"You were going to be a murderer," Moratrayas told him, and silencing him with another shock.

The fight was over. Stoth and his frightened guests huddled together at the end of the throne room. They saw sections of the city burning through the large window behind the throne. In the distance, the Blue Sashes left Stone Heart burdened down with whatever loot they could find. Stoth trembled on his throne, his eyes fixed on Moratrayas.

Moratrayas took deep breaths until he regained control of his temper. He pointed at Ulysses and his men, and said to Stoth, "Generations ago, these good people came into possession of a sunstone worth a fortune. Of all the things they could have done with it, they used it to grow crops. You stole it from them and turned it into a weapon. You turned my homeland into a nation of warmongers. How is it you corrupt everything you touch?"

Moratrayas and Ulysses Sower walked up to Stoth. The doctor looked at Ulysses and said, "This will be the second time I've pulled a man off this throne. Mr. Sower, if you'll lend a hand we can make sure it doesn't happen again."

Both men grabbed Stoth by his arms and threw him to the floor. Stoth covered his face, waiting for the killing blow he would have delivered in their place. Instead he heard grunts followed by a creak. He looked up and saw Moratrayas and Ulysses lift the throne off the floor and hurl it through the window to smash apart on the ground below.

Sandra and Jeremy ran down the stairs. They stopped in front of Moratrayas and lifted up the granite spheres. "We got the sunstones," Sandra told him.

Moratrayas smiled. "Expertly done, Sandra. I see you found an old pair of my goggles. They look quite nice on you. Jeremy, you also have my thanks. I'm impressed by your work and would like to offer you a job."

"I just want to go home to my family," Jeremy begged.

"Easily done, but not compensation enough for your suffering." Moratrayas plucked Stoth's crown from his head and handed it to Jeremy. "Sell this and you'll be rich for the rest of your days."

Ulysses pointed his pickaxe at Stoth. "What about him?"

"That's the wrong question," Moratrayas said. He pointed his staff out the broken window at Scour. "What about them? Your daughter pointed out to me that the people of Stone Heart weren't forced to help Stoth. All that transpired here was done with their support. What we've done tonight will prevent them from being a threat for a long time to come, but there must be a reckoning for their crimes."

"What are you going to do?" Sandra asked.

Moratrayas spun his staff. "That depends entirely on them."

# Chapter 16

Moratrayas led Sandra, her people and his clockworks from the castle. They dragged Stoth along, the defeated king helpless in the men's iron grip. The guests stayed back, not sure why they'd been spared. Moratrayas found Igor and Gertrude on guard outside the castle. The giant clockwork wagged its tail like a happy puppy and bounded up to the doctor. Moratrayas smiled and patted its head.

"Your work was exceptional, Igor," Moratrayas said.

Igor climbed off Gertrude's neck and shook the doctor's hand. "Always a pleasure. The Blue Sashes did a bit of looting while we were busy, but they missed some nice stuff."

"Leave it," Moratrayas said. "We're only taking what matters."

Outside they found the city silent. The soldiers had fled, and most of them had thrown down their armor and weapons, littering the streets with swords, armor and helmets. Every building in the city was closed tight, their doors barred and windows shuttered. The only sound to be heard was the crackling fires from burning siege weapons and wagons.

"Oh no, I'm not letting you off easy a second time!" Moratrayas said ominously. He opened a panel on Gertrude's side and took out a short metal rod with a mesh box on one end and a wire attached to the clockwork on the other. When he spoke into the rod, his voice came out of the speakers on Gertrude's back many times louder than normal. "Get out here! Get out here and face me, or so help me I'll bring this city down on your heads!"

Startled by his threat, Sandra tried to reach him. Igor put a hand on her arm and stopped her. "Let him," Igor said. "He needs this, and they earned it."

"I won't let him kill them!"

"He won't. We know him better than that."

"Now!" Moratrayas bellowed through the speakers. Slowly and with the greatest reluctance, doors opened across Scour and people came out. They gathered in the courtyard in a mass of terrified men, women and children. The crowd stood in the cold night air and looked down at their feet, waiting for Moratrayas to pronounce his judgment against them. A few men coughed from the smoke, but none spoke.

"I once called you my people," Moratrayas told them, his voice echoing through the city so loud that none could ignore it. "You were my neighbors, my friends, my family. I risked my life for you. I gave you peace, progress, justice. All I did, all I created, my whole being was for you and your betterment."

At Moratrayas' direction, the men of Sun Valley threw Stoth to the ground. Moratrayas marched up to him and pointed his brass staff at the defeated king. "You threw it away. This is the leader you wanted. You chose Stoth Voluk and his dreams of blood and conquest. He wanted to bring the horrors of war to neighboring lands, to kill thousands and enslave tens of thousands, hundreds of thousands! How many men would you have killed at his command? How many women would be left widows? How many...how many children would be orphaned by your war?"

The people cringed, none daring to look Moratrayas in the eyes. Scowling, he went on. "If you'd fought him, resisted even a little, I would understand. It's hard to face men with swords when you only have farm tools. But you didn't fight him! You asked him to come. You invited him, welcomed him, going so far as to become a part of his schemes. You saw men put in chains, and you cheered!"

Moratrayas looked at the crowd, his eyes darting from one person to another. They looked at their feet. Some of them trembled. No one refuted him. When Moratrayas spoke again, his voice was heavy with scorn. "So be it. I once called this place home, but no longer. I renounce you. I'm leaving, and these good men are coming with me. My friends and I will take enough food and warm clothing to get home. I'm taking the sunstones and all my creations destroyed because of you."

The people in the crowd looked up in surprise. They were expecting far worse. Moratrayas retracted his staff back to a cane and pointed it at them. "You spent your time, effort and money for years to bring death and destruction on your neighbors. We ruined your ambitions and freed the men you enslaved. But you're fools if you think that's your only punishment!"

Moratrayas pointed his cane back at the castle where Stoth's guests stood in the shadows listening to him. "I know what you planned tonight. I'll tell everyone in your home kingdoms about the treason you plotted. I suggest you leave these mountains forever, because if you go home your own people will kill you.

"Stoth," Moratrayas said venomously. Stoth sat on the ground, too shocked to speak, not sure how his plans could fail so suddenly. Moratrayas prodded Stoth with his cane to make sure he had the defeated King's attention. "You ruined this kingdom even if you didn't do it alone. Your old kingdom won't take you back after such a failure. You've no army left, no weapons stockpiled and no hope. Of all the things I can do to you, leaving you here is the most fitting punishment. Run away and live like a vagabond if you wish, or stay here and try to hold onto power without the means to do so. Either way, your life will be an unending series of disasters from this day on.

"And you!" he roared at the crowd. "To call you my neighbors and relatives hurts like driving a knife through my heart, but that's what you are. No matter how much you disgust me, I can't bring myself to deal out the punishment you deserve. But what I *will* do is let the kingdoms in these mountains know what you were going to do to them! If you so hunger for war, then war you shall have."

The doctor led his creations and the men of Sun Valley from Scour. They loaded up two wagons, filling the first with destroyed clockworks and the remaining books in the library. They loaded the second wagon with food and clothing for the journey home. They tied both wagons to Gertrude, who had no trouble pulling them. The crowd parted and let them pass in silence. None of the people spoke, and few would even look at them.

Once they were outside the city, Sandra ran up to Moratrayas. "Al, you can't do this!"

Moratrayas kept walking. "I showed more mercy than they deserve."

"You don't understand. Before I disabled the Sun Gun, I used it. The barges, the wagons, the armory, the siege weapons, I destroyed them all."

"I know. Impressive work."

"I'm not looking for praise! Al, they can't fight anymore, not even to defend themselves. The Blue Sashes left, their army is defeated and most of their weapons are gone. They can't even hide inside the city anymore now that the gate's broken and the castle has holes in it. If you tell other kingdoms what they were going to do, they'll destroy the place."

Moratrayas stopped and gently took Sandra by the shoulders. "Sandra," he asked softly, "did any of those people apologize to you?"

She was surprised by the question. "No."

"They committed unspeakable acts against you and your people. Did they drop to their knees and plead for mercy? Did they swear never to do such deeds again? Did they vow to repay you for what they did? Did even one of those men or women tell you they were sorry?"

Sandra looked down. "No."

"Even after what my people have done, there's still some love for them in my heart. I had to know if Stoth was lying when he said they asked him to come. They didn't deny his claim. I gave them a chance to offer reparations to your people, to seek redemption. They wouldn't take it. They didn't apologize because they're not sorry. They only regret being stopped. They would not ask for mercy, so they shall have justice instead."

"So we just leave them like this?"

He looked out into the darkness around Scour. "There are a few others we need to collect."

Joy and the other women of Sun Valley came out of hiding with the merchants. After they joined up, the thirty goblins left in Stone Heart emerged from tunnels and gathered around Moratrayas.

"Al, we're sorry," the black clad goblin said. "We did the best we could."

"That's all I ask. Come."

Curious, the goblin asked, "Where are we going?"

"I'm taking everyone worthwhile with me, and I count you among them." The goblins smiled and fell in behind Moratrayas. Satisfied, he said, "Now we can leave."

Men, clockworks and goblins left Stone Heart never to return. Out of fuel, the clockwork dragonfly landed on Sandra's shoulders and shut down. She smiled and stroked its brass shell.

Worried, Sandra said, "We've got another problem."

Moratrayas looked over at her. "What is it?"

Sandra held up the granite sphere. "Our sunstone is worth a king's ransom. We kept it for so long because no one knew we had it. Now everyone will know about it, and they'll know it can be made into a weapon. Thieves will come for it, or even armies. We've got our sunstone back, but I don't think we'll be able to keep it."

"The same thought occurred to me," Moratrayas said. "Sun Valley is too far from Refuge for me to protect you. I couldn't come in time if you were attacked, and I can't leave enough clockworks to defend you. Your people don't have the skills or tools to fuel them, much less fix them when they're damaged. For that matter I have precious few clockworks for my own needs until I fix these damaged ones."

"So, what do we do?"

Moratrayas walked on in silence for a moment. Hesitantly, he said, "I know of a secluded valley. It's uninhabited and has good soil. It can only be reached by taking a path in Refuge. The only reason no one lives there is it's so isolated...that and there's a mad scientist living next door."

Sandra smiled. "No kidding? What's he like?"

Moratrayas waved his cane around. "He's trying to be a good man. It's not easy, and he lets his anger get the best of him at times."

Sandra wrapped an arm around his waist. "Some things should make you angry. So, would he mind having nine hundred people living next door?"

"I think he'd like that," he said, and put an arm around her shoulders.

Six months later, Refuge was full of life. Fields grew wheat and oats, orchards flowered and set fruit, while people tended sheep and chickens. Terraced farms on the mountainsides raised more crops. Greenhouses on the highest and most rocky ground grew a bewildering array of tropical plants known for their sweet fruit or medical value.

Men and clockworks built roads and houses. The clockworks looked like men except for one as big as an ogre. Igor rode on the back of the large one and led the rest of Doctor Moratrayas' creations in their labors.

There were many new homes and farms since the previous year, but the largest new building in the kingdom was a lighthouse. It rose high over the fields and bathed the land in artificial light. Weapons no more, the two smaller sunstones were housed in the lighthouse, placed so close together that their light rivaled the noon sun and promoted crop growth. The largest sunstone was in the neighboring valley and served the same function.

The inhabitants were happy. They included a large number of people from Sun Valley as well as a steady stream of refugees from other kingdoms in the mountains, drawn in by the hope of prosperity and peace. Well dressed, well fed and many of them well educated, they finally felt like they'd found a home.

This would normally be inspiring to Mantu Sako, mad scientist and master alchemist. Unfortunately he was huddled behind a collapsible wood shield, protecting himself from a seemingly endless stream of white tipped darts.

Mantu was a tall man, his features sharp and his skin so dark he seemed to be carved from ebony. His custom leather clothes contained many pockets holding clear capsules, and he wore a bandoleer with more capsules sewn into it. He carried a steel staff and the folding shield that was protecting him from a storm of darts.

This was not the first threat Mantu had faced trying to reach the castle. He'd defeated the moving stairs by gumming them up with glue. He rendered the pincer arm helpless when he found a concealed shutoff switch. Now, mere feet from the castle door, a brass cylinder rose up from the floor and shot at him. He'd tried outlasting it, but every time it ran out of darts, more slid into place and it resumed firing. Waiting it out was not an option.

Mantu took a capsule from his bandoleer and loaded it into a slot on his staff. Taking careful aim, he pulled a trigger on the staff and fired the capsule. He hit the cylinder, releasing a spray of powerful glue that splattered over the dart firing ports. This rendered the last trap helpless. The brass cylinder whirred in protest but could do nothing more to stop him.

Satisfied the threat was over, Mantu plucked out the darts embedded in his shield and folded it up. He climbed the last few stairs and swung the knocker on the castle door. It rang loud, a sound that echoed through the valley below and prompted cheers from the people. The door opened to reveal a young woman with brown hair wearing a simple cotton dress.

"Welcome to Refuge and Fortress X," she said pleasantly. "Please, come in."

"Do you always treat guests like this?" he asked without rancor.

"I'm afraid so. I've spoken to my husband about it. He said we need the protection, and he didn't want to insult you by making the test easier for you than for others."

Mantu's mind drifted back to his last home and the angry mob that destroyed it. Holding back a shudder at the thought, he said, "I can't argue with him being careful about intruders. Is your husband...?"

The woman smiled and held up her hand to show off a gold ring. "Sandra Moratrayas, and yes, my husband founded Refuge. He would've greeted you himself, but he was controlling the defenses. If you'll come with me, I'm sure you'd like to meet the others."

Excitement gripped Mantu's heart. "How many came?"

"Including you there are five."

Mantu followed Sandra through the castle. He was filled with joy. He'd been alone for so long, running from a seemingly endless stream of enemies. So many times he'd tried to build a laboratory and do groundbreaking work, only to be forced out by angry mobs, bounty hunters or vengeful kings. The chance to work in peace with men who shared his goals was a lure too powerful to resist.

Sandra brought Mantu to the castle's main hall, where he found the rest of the mad scientists waiting for him. Alberto Moratrayas entered through another door and greeted his newest ally warmly. Shaking his hand, he said, "Mantu Sako, builder of clockworks and accomplished alchemist, welcome to Refuge. I heard of your deeds long ago and hoped you would join us. It's a pity what happened to you in Tresca, but difficulties like that are temporary and can be overcome."

"That's part of the reason why I came." Mantu said. "I heard your offer, and how you defeated an army."

Moratrayas took Sandra's hand. "I had considerable help with that accomplishment. You've already met my wife. She does much of the daily running of the kingdom and dealing with guests. I must admit she has an edge over me in dealing with people."

Sandra nudged her husband in the ribs. When he didn't get the hint, she whispered, "Introductions."

"Ah, yes," he said. "Allow me to introduce you to the other members of our cabal. I'm sure you've heard of the renegade mathematician Alexander Zerokov. He built the observatory in the kingdom of Middleta. It was a marvel before it was burned down. A tragic loss, and an unnecessary one."

A man with a long black beard, bushy eyebrows and a head of frizzy hair sat at the table and nodded in acknowledgement. He wore flowing black robes and a red belt loaded with pouches and pockets.

Moratrayas went on to the next man seated on a couch. "Professor Improbable needs little introduction. He's called nearly every kingdom on Other Place home at one point or another, and was well received by none of them."

The professor was as bald as an egg and wore a monocle and crisp cotton clothes of the highest fashion. He smiled at Mantu and said, "My sincerest condolences on the loss of your laboratory. Don't worry, we'll get you up and running in no time."

"And the last of us— " Moratrayas began.

"Is Doctor Livingston." Mantu stepped forward and shook the man's hand.

Anton Livingston wore khaki explorer clothes complete with a pith helmet. He had short white hair and a long mustache, and his skin was tanned from years traveling the world. A small monkey sat on his back and flicked its tail. Livingston smiled and said, "You presume correctly, sir."

"World traveler, explorer, writer and renowned for your study of plants and animals in the Lele Island chain," Mantu continued. "Your books inspired me to become the man I am today."

"Please, sit," Moratrayas told him. "Friends, I left an open invitation to those in our field to join me here, and you four came. Our cause is to save a world burdened by poverty, violence and corruption. You know from personal experience how hard it is to accomplish worthy deeds when so many stand in your way. Many people bar our path because of jealousy, for if we succeed they might lose their stranglehold on power.

"Alone we were unsuccessful. Even my defeat of Stoth Voluk wasn't real progress. I stopped him, but I lacked the strength to replace the evil he perpetrated in Stone Heart with lasting peace and prosperity. Beyond Refuge I was powerless to effect real change. But now there are five of us dedicated to the same cause, and we are surrounded by worthy people ready to help. Together we can do anything."

Moratrayas smiled at his new allies. He reached over and wrapped an arm around Sandra's waist. "Now then, let's save the world."

Made in the USA
Las Vegas, NV
15 January 2022

41445049R00111